THE WRAITHS OF WHISTLESTOP

THE WRAITHS OF WHISTLESTOP

BY

JOHN MCCLELLAN DANIELSKI

www.penmorepress.com

ISBN: 978-1-957851-91-4(EBOOK)
ISBN:978-1-957851-92-1 (Paperback)
BISAC Subject Headings:

FIC014000FICTION / Historical
FIC121010FICTION / World Literature/Scotland/19th Century
FIC002000FICTION / Action

Editors: Julia Lorraine Smith and Chris Wozney
Cover: Emilija Rakić PR Emily's World of Design

Please send all correspondence to:

Penmore Press LLC
920 N Javelina Pl
Tucson AZ 85748

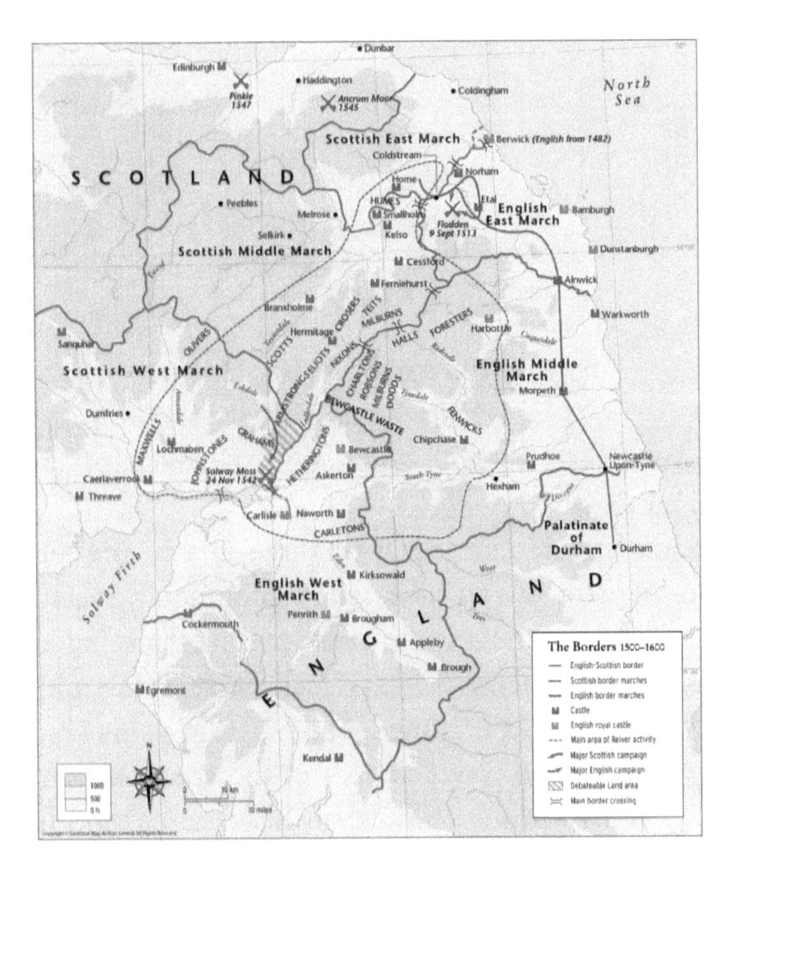
North Sea
Edinburgh
Dunbar
Pinkie 1547
Haddington
Ancrum Moor 1545
Coldingham
SCOTLAND
Scottish East March
Berwick (English from 1482)
Coldstream
Norham
Home
Etal
English East March
Bamburgh
HUMES
Peebles
Melrose
Smailholm
Kelso
Flodden 9 Sept 1513
Dunstanburgh
Selkirk
Scottish Middle March
Cessford
Alnwick
Ferniehurst
Warkworth
Bransholme
TEITS
Hermitage
CROSERS
MILBURNS
FORESTERS
Harbottle
Coquetdale
Sanquhar
SCOTTS
OLIVERS
NIXONS
HALLS
Redesdale
English Middle March
Scottish West March
ARMSTRONGS ELLIOTS
CHARLTONS
ROBSONS
MILBURNS
DODDS
Tynedale
RENWICKS
Morpeth
Dumfries
MAXWELLS
BEWCASTLE WASTE
Chipchase
Lochmaben
GRAHAMS
Bewcastle
FORRESTONES
HETHERINGTONS
Askerton
South Tyne
Prudhoe
Newcastle Upon-Tyne
Caerlaverock
Solway Moss 24 Nov 1542
Threave
Carlisle
Naworth
Hexham
CARLETONS
Palatinate of Durham
Durham
Solway Firth
Kirksowald
West
ENGLAND
English West March
Penrith
Brougham
Cockermouth
Appleby
Brough
Egremont
Kendal
N
The Borders 1500–1600
English-Scottish border
Scottish border marches
English border marches
Castle
English royal castle
Main area of Reiver activity
Major Scottish campaign
Major English campaign
Debateable Land area
Main border crossing
1000
500
0 ft
10 km
10 miles

CHAPTER 1

Pirates and the Big Bang

5th April 1815

"Pickers dead ahead!" shouted the lookout of the twin-masted pirate ship *Fatwa.*

A hammerhead shark leaped three feet in the air as the captain snapped his spyglass shut. Mahmoud Salasi smiled like the human equivalent of a shark, interpreting the rare sight as a good omen. "It is as I had hoped. Our raid is well timed." His cold eyes assumed a hot sparkle as his ship glided silently through the warm waters of the southeastern Indian Ocean." The rice pickers have their backs to us, and our men ashore have eliminated their roving lookouts."

"How many captives do you think we shall bag today?" inquired his scar faced First Mate.

"Perhaps fifty. More than enough to fill Ahmed Ali's orders. Our payment for these fresh slaves will be handsome indeed." Salasi rubbed his hands in anticipation.

"Shall I begin forming the landing party, Captain?"

"Yes. Twenty men with cutlasses and pistols should be sufficient. Field hands will offer no more resistance than beaten dogs."

"And if one or two fight back, do I pursue the usual policy?"

"Yes. Behead one; the rest will grovel and submit."

Two miles away, British Midshipman Nico Ruzzini of *His Majesty's Ship Dispatch*, a two masted brig-sloop, was scared, excited, and pleased. He was scared because his first battle lay just minutes in the future, excited because he was eager to prove himself, and pleased that, as fourteen-year-old, he had been entrusted with the command of two main deck carronades and the twelve men who manned them. At present, the ship's sails were furled, save for her driver and flying jib, which controlled steering; she shifted only slightly in response to the hot, dry wind. Her crew stood ready and silent, and he took pride in their discipline. The only sounds that escaped *HMS Dispatch* were those of a wooden hull creaking in response to the caress of lapping waves.

Dispatch lay hidden in a small cove on the island of Sumbawa; a mountainous mass the size of Connecticut, eight hundred miles east of Java. That cove was enclosed by palm, fig, and mango trees which provided plenty of concealment. Lianas vines wrapped themselves around the trees, which added to the cloaking effect. The dense, variegated green of the grove was punctuated by red orchid blooms. Miscellaneous calls, clicks, and hisses served notice of the presence of numerous birds, insects, and reptiles. Ricc paddies, half a mile inland, were framed by mountains forested by teak and sandalwood, their tops mostly cloaked in clouds. The tallest was the 14,000-foot, twin- peaked Mount Tambora. Its summit was emitting puffs of gray smoke that seemed to presage the gun smoke which would soon engulf the cove. Ship pilots used Tambora as a navigation marker, and Ruzzini guessed that the quarry his ship sought probably had it in view right now.

Commander Clive Lewis, Captain of *Dispatch*, sought to ambush the *Fatwa,* which had a history of raiding the island of Sumbawa for slaves. *Fatwa* was lightly built and armed only with four 3-pound cannons; no match for a King's ship in a standup fight, but more than enough to intimidate villagers, and faster on the open sea. *Fatwa* relied on surprise, speed, and violence; the vessel carried a crew of fifty monotheistic Muslims seeking to enslave polytheistic Hindus and sell them. These turbaned pirates were more ruthless than their Caribbean counterparts; in general, European buccaneers sought loot, not lives. The winter monsoons had put a halt to *Fatwa's* raids, but now that the dry season had returned, young men were working in the fields, harvesting rice. The raiders made a practice of striking swiftly from concealment; the last thing they would be expecting was a British man-of-war protecting the backs of the rice pickers.

Ruzzini knew that most Britons, even with all the talk of abolition, had no idea that the sprawling East Indies Archipelago was home to a slave trade that was only slightly smaller in numbers and scope than the slave trade that plied the Atlantic and had spread the miasma of human trafficking to the Americas. The East Indies produced many commodities that made trade profitable: nutmeg, cloves, ginger, pepper, and cinnamon, to name but a few. Enslaving young men to work the plantations furnished plenty of work for pirates, and the demand was unending because the life of a slave was usually brief; the Chinese overseers were notorious for their cruelty.

Sumbawa and the surrounding islands had been captured by the British from the Dutch in 1811, but British control was tenuous, and the Liverpool Administration in London had not yet decided if it wanted to retain permanent possession, with all the attendant responsibilities and expenses of governance.

Dispatch had been sent to the area by Stamford Raffles, the Lieutenant Governor of Java, to resupply the British Officiating Magistrate at Sumbawa's capital, Bima. Her secondary mission was to round up specimens of the local flora and fauna for Raffles—a famous naturalist, historian, and collector of all manner of exotica. Battling pirates was not explicitly stated in Lewis's orders, but it was understood that if he encountered any, he would be expected to fight them. Two days before, Lewis had received detailed information from a local informant of the Officiating Magistrate, and that news had sent *Dispatch* to her present position.

"Deck there, sail ho," The masthead lookout spoke just loudly enough to be heard by the officers below. "Two points off the larboard bow."

"What do you make of her?" queried Lewis, as he unfurled his spyglass.

"She's a pinisi." A pinisi was an Indonesian ketch, with a bow and stern that curved upwards like the pointed toes of Ottoman slippers and a mizzenmast stepped just forward of the rudder.

"What range?"

"Mile and a half."

"Course?"

"Bearing directly on our position."

While Lewis could see his enemy clearly through his spyglass, the tropical foliage made it unlikely that the reverse was true. Still, Lewis was a prudent man and wanted to take no chances. "Quartermaster, the depth here is four fathoms, so you can move us a little closer to shore. Say thirty yards out from that tall jackfruit tree over yonder, so we shall have a little extra concealment."

"Aye, aye, Captain."

Lewis spent the fifteen minutes of *Fatwa's* approach making one final check of the crew and equipment. *Dispatch's* 120-man complement was confident and steady, made up entirely of prime seamen and officers; the reduction in size of the Royal Navy after Napoleon's fall meant that good sailors were plentiful, and captains were not compelled to rely on personnel of dubious quality. The weaponry of the *Cruizer Class*, 100-foot-long ship was formidable at close range: sixteen stubby 32-pound carronades that could hurl a large weight of lead over a short span, and two long-barreled 12-pound cannons that provided firepower for greater distances. Lewis had instructed his crews to insert two charges in each carronade; each gun would aim a 32-pound ball at *Fatwa's* hull chased by a round of canister — a large tin can of musket balls that turned a cannon into a giant shotgun.

Lewis spoke briefly with Ruzzini, who had become a protégé. "I doubt the action ahead will last long, Mr. Ruzzini. Our justice will be of the best kind: swift and certain."

"Aye, Captain. What about survivors?"

"Our carronades will kill many outright. Survivors will go down with the ship if they cannot swim. If there are any that try to swim toward shore, I will instruct marksmen to shoot them."

"Pardon me, Captain, but that does not seem consonant with the tradition of British magnanimity in victory."

"I applaud your sensibilities, Mr. Ruzzini, but in this instance, they are misplaced. I ask you to remember that pirates have no right to expect quarter, and men who traffic in human flesh, and have done so for years, are the vilest of creatures, undeserving of your finer instincts." He pointed to the rice fields to the west. "Take a good look at those men in the fields. You will be saving them from a life of wretched and cruel servitude by doing away with the approaching blackguards. Children yet to be born will owe their lives to our actions today."

Ruzzini thought the ten minutes that it took *Fatwa* to enter the cove's mouth were the longest of his life. Remembering what his stepfather, Sir Thomas Pennywhistle, had told him about battle, he willed himself to relax and assume an expression of *sang froid*, the better to inspire his men. He had reserved the honor of firing the first round of his number two carronade for himself and gripped its lanyard, awaiting his captain's command.

Fatwa's captain was overconfident; he had his lookouts focused on spotting prime abduction specimens ahead, rather than watching for danger from *Fatwa's* flanks. *Fatwa* slowed as the water shallowed, and armed pirates clustered around the landing launches which would soon be lowered. *Fatwa* was only 200 yards from *Dispatch's* port bow when a lookout frantically shouted "*Safina! Safina!*" The captain followed the lookout's jabbing finger and beheld with terror the sight of eight carronades being run out.

"Fire!" shouted Lewis, as his sword flashed down. *Dispatch's* carronades roared and recoiled on their slides. Choking clouds of grey-white smoke filled the air, causing Ruzzini to cough. *Dispatch's* 32-pound balls blasted through *Fatwa's* thin scantlings so that huge holes appeared just above the waterline. *Fatwa* listed to the right as water poured into the jagged gashes in her hull. The 704 musket-size balls in the charges of canister created a hailstorm of lead that shredded the close-grouped landing party, turning men into gobs of flesh, bones, and red mist. As the survivors crawled towards their ship's guns, one unscathed pirate yanked off his turban, tied it to a stick, and began to wave it frantically. He had seen the British colors flying on *Dispatch* and hoped that their king's reputation for mercy would come into play.

Half a minute later, he got his response as a second broadside roared out. The canister swept the deck clean of all but six men, while the shot enlarged the previous hull holes so much that *Fatwa* began to sink. Ruzzini spotted a man wearing a jeweled turban, purple velvet surcoat, and blue silk pantaloons that were unlike the drab working attire of the rest of the crew. Rather than go down with the ship, the man jumped overboard and swam toward shore.

One marine took aim at the fast-swimming man, but Lewis pushed his musket down. "I'll take that, Marine. A parting shot from one captain to another." Lewis raised the musket, settling it firmly against his shoulder. He gentled his touch and meticulously sighted the Sea Service Brown Bess, steading his breathing and adjusting his stance. A hit from a common musket at a moving target 150 yards away would have been problematic for most shooters, but Lewis was a marksman. He squeezed the trigger with steady pressure; the ball sped straight and true to the back of the swimming pirate's skull. A gout of blood erupted, and the man's head vanished beneath the waves.

Fatwa continued her rapid descent and the men on deck milled about in confusion. *Fatwa*'s boats had been smashed, and after seeing their captain's fate they were not inclined to risk the water. They wailed, cried, and cursed at their approaching end, until one pirate produced what Ruzzini guessed was a flask of whiskey and passed it around to his mates. Their cries trailed off as its contents fended off the terror of their approaching extinction. Ruzzini found it strange that alcohol should be available on a Moslem ship, since it violated a key tenet of the religion, but pirates lived by breaking rules. Ruzzini concluded that, despite their fearsome reputation, pirates were cowards, preying on the weak and living in fear of death. *A man should meet his end with sober dignity,* he thought.

Fatwa sank under the waves, only the tops of her masts marking her grave. Flotsam and bodies stained and darkened the clear turquoise water; the absence of bobbing heads confirmed the annihilation of her crew. Cheering erupted from the workers in the rice fields, and their shouts were answered by three loud huzzahs from *Dispatch's* crew. Lewis smiled his approval, but Ruzzini remained silent, a troubled expression on his face.

"Captain!" shouted Master's Mate Jones, "We missed one. His head just popped up. He's clinging to a chunk of rudder. There," Jones pointed, "thirty yards off the port bow."

Lewis and Ruzzini followed the mate's finger and spotted an exhausted, baby-faced pirate kicking frantically as he tried to propel his improvised life raft toward shore.

"Mr. Ruzzini, would you do the honors?"

"Sir?"

"Shoot the blackguard." Lewis loaded the Sea Service Brown Bess and handed it to Ruzzini.

Ruzzini accepted the weapon as if he had been handed a snake. He hesitated briefly, for the man seemed utterly defenseless. No, not a man; a boy, not more than a year or two older than himself. It was one thing to argue intellectually for the elimination of pirates, quite another to serve as the executioner of one. And that is what he would be: an executioner, not a warrior.

"Mr. Ruzzini, he's getting away," said Lewis impatiently.

"Aye, aye, Captain." Ruzzini hastily brought the musket to his shoulder, aimed quickly, then squeezed the trigger.

Ruzzini's round caught the pirate between the shoulders, but he was already dead. A dorsal fin speeding by and the odd way the corpse bobbed about indicated that the pirate had only half a body. Strangely, the shark relieved him of guilt: there was no shame in executing a corpse.

"Deck there, sail ho!" bellowed the masthead lookout, to everyone's surprise.

"What do you make of her?" replied a startled Captain Lewis.

"A pinisi, Captain. *Fatwa's* twin. "

"Range?"

"Two miles."

"Course?"

"West northwest, towards Makassar. She's just unfurled her t'gallants."

"Blast those fuckers!" snapped Lewis, "She must have come out of the Teluk Cempi Estuary! She's got her cargo and is going to make a run for it! Damn the Virgin Mary's blood!"

Ruzzini and the First Officer blinked at their captain's hot profanity and how it stood in contrast to his usual cool nature and polite speech.

"My informant told me only half the truth, the bastard." Lewis pounded one fist into the other in frustration and began pacing back and forth. "That death's-head-upon-a-mop-stick gave me one fish so that another could get away! These new scoundrels must have some connection to him." His blue eyes blazed with the anger of a banker discovering that he'd been given counterfeit coins, and his voice had the edge of Bloody Mary condemning heretics to the stake. "God's death, I shall smash every last one of them into kindling!"

Ruzzini and the First Mate stared at each other. Lewis was rumored to be a closeted Catholic who had evaded the Test Act with cleverly chosen words. He had just uttered insults that were abhorrent to subscribers of that faith.

Lewis unfurled his spyglass and surveyed the people on the distant deck. Twenty were pirates, and thirty were rice pickers.

"What's happened, Captain?" inquired Ruzzini.

"*Fatwa* was part of a two-ship attack, each ship targeting a different rice paddy."

"How could we have missed this ship, Captain?"

"She must have arrived last night before we did and has been lying doggo until the first rice harvesters reached the field," responded Lewis, thinking out loud. "The same foliage that concealed us from *Fatwa* also prevented us from seeing this intruder."

"We must stop them!"

"Indeed, we shall!" Lewis bellowed. "No Oriental bugger is going to make a fool out of me!" He stopped abruptly, realizing that a captain must never seem subject to the emotions besetting mere humans. He corralled his tantrum, took a deep breath, and relaxed the taut muscles of his neck and shoulders. The instructions that followed sounded urgent rather than angry. "And I shall need your remarkable eyesight, Mr. Ruzzini."

"Aye, aye, Captain, you shall have my best effort."

Lewis gave the commands to pour on every ounce of sail that *Dispatch* could manage, intending to overtake the intruder before she reached the open sea. He also ordered the ship's two 12 pounders repositioned along with their tackles to act as bow chasers.

The intruder had apparently spotted *Dispatch*, for she had cracked on every square inch of canvas in the hope of outrunning a ship which threatened to deliver summary justice. The rising wind off her port quarter came at just the right angle to give the ship her maximum turn of speed.

However, while the intruder was fast, her seamanship was no match for the disciplined professional sailors on *Dispatch*. Lewis conducted a bulldog pursuit, closing the distance to his opponent. His face paled with the excitement of the chase, and he leaned forward as he muttered, "Come on, come *on*, old girl, you can do it!" After four miles, *Dispatch* had shortened the distance to 1,200 yards. Lewis ordered Ruzzini to sight their improvised bow chasers.

"Remember, you are firing to slow them, not sink them, Mr. Ruzzini. We must think of the hostages. Aim for her foremast."

Ruzzini motioned for sailors with handspikes to position the two pieces, then sighted the weapons, knowing the eyes of everyone on deck were tracking his efforts. This was a moment to make a man's reputation, as well as strike a blow for humanity by stopping slavers. He factored in wind speed and direction, as well as distance and relative heights. He looked over the tops of both barrels — they had no actual gunsights — and adjusted the elevating screw beneath each barrel. Finally, he took the lanyard of the first cannon in his hand, said a silent prayer, and jerked it hard. The twelve-pound shot departed with a bang, making whizzing noises as it sped toward its destination.

There was a sharp crack as it hit its target, the base of the foremast. The mast swayed but did not fall.

Ruzzini frowned, then directed two sailors to move the second cannon six inches to the right. He took the lanyard and pulled.

The second ball ricocheted off the capstan but still had enough force to strike the mast and finish the job. The broken mast toppled into the sea, its wreckage acting as a giant anchor, the drag slowed the interloper's progress. Pirates with axes chopped frantically to sever the wood and canvas mess from the ship.

Lewis turned to the ship's first officer. "Mr. Ridley, assemble a boarding party and standby with grappling hooks."

"Aye, aye, Captain."

"Your primary goal is the safety of the hostages. Secure them at the earliest opportunity."

"Acknowledged, Captain."

Dispatch had closed to four hundred yards when the pirates began lowering their 24-foot longboat: abandoning ship, intending to seek sanctuary on one of the small jungle islands in the area. Two pirates remained on deck and began shoving rice pickers overboard at gunpoint in a variant of the Caribbean buccaneer ritual of "walk the plank." The rice pickers screamed and flailed their arms when they hit the water, never having had a reason to learn to swim. When the last hostage had plunged into the water, the two pirates dived overboard and began swimming toward their companions in the longboat.

Large dorsal fins began to circle the flailing rice pickers.

Lewis cursed at the inhumanity of such an action, even as he had to admit that the pirates understood British attitudes. No captain of a man-of-war would abandon the helpless to chase brigands.

"Lower the launches, Mr. Ridley!" barked Lewis. "We'll need plenty of boathooks."

"Aye, aye, sir!"

Dispatch's three boats were soon being rowed toward the shouting, bobbing heads, but already three men had gone under.

"Yaaaaah! Yaaaah! Yaaaaah!" screamed two men being devoured by sharks.

Ridley's boats pulled in fifteen terrified survivors, all babbling in a language that he did not understand. A Malay of perhaps thirty years spoke a few words of broken English to Ridley. "Dank you, Dank you, Engleesh. I got vife and two childs." Ridley, as well as his sailors, were touched by his sincerity, yet were angry that those who had caused his misfortunes had gotten away. Ridley scanned the waters for the pirate launch, but it was nowhere in sight. It had probably been beached and hidden; its passengers were no doubt congratulating themselves on a narrow escape, he thought bitterly, and in another month, they'd be plying their despicable trade again.

The fifteen pirate survivors were in fact loudly cursing the British as they sat around a jungle clearing, dripping sea water and passing botas of wine around. Next, they directed their curses at the man who had sent them on this expedition and then argued over what to do next.

"I say we wait until we have a fair wind and darkness, then make for Komodo," said Utman Farha, their captain. "Such a journey will present many challenges, but it can be done."

"Komodo is an island filled with dragons!" exclaimed his First Mate.

"They are just giant lizards, and they don't breathe fire. But because people fear them, few ships call at the island, making it perfect for a pirate haven. There is a large pirate compound at the north end of the island, and the man who runs it owes me a favor. It will serve as a way station on the journey home."

"But it will be a long voyage, and we don't have any provisions," complained the First Mate.

"The jungle has wild fruit, and the monkeys don't seem afraid of us. It should be easy enough to take down a few," said Farha.

"I fear Ahmed Ali's reaction when we tell him that we not only have no captives, but that we have lost his ship. He has been known to stake down men who have failed him and then let loose crocodiles. Not just any crocodiles, mind you, but Borneo crocodiles, some of which reach 21 feet in length."

Farha shuddered. "We might just have to avoid him entirely and see if we can sell our services to other slavers. But we can't do that until we get off this island."

By the time Ridley's boats returned to *Dispatch*, she had pulled alongside the now empty pirate ship and thrown grappling hooks and extended boarding planks. Ridley climbed through *Dispatch's* entry port, followed by sailors and bedraggled, bewildered rice pickers.

"Well done, Mr. Ridley," said Lewis. "Don't look so downcast, nobody could have done more. You are lucky to have saved as many as you did."

"I realize that, Captain, but some of those lost were little better than boys."

"I sympathize, but for now see that these poor souls get some food and drink."

"Aye, aye, Captain." Ridley saluted and departed. Lewis walked over to Nathan Nairn, the ship's second lieutenant.

"Mr. Nairn, take Mr. Ruzzini and ten sailors, board our prize, and jury rig the mainmast. I recognize the Arabic characters on her stern from my time in the Persian Gulf. Her name is *Shahaba Tuhturaq, Burning Cloud* in English. She'll fetch a good price at auction. Follow *Dispatch* into Bima Harbor; there we'll conduct a thorough inspection and inventory."

"Aye, aye, Captain." Nairn saluted and departed, but Ruzzini lingered, a distressed expression on his face.

Ruzzini had just killed men for the first time, and the triumph he'd expected to experience had not materialized. Instead, he felt empty and uncertain: his hot Italian blood had turned as cold as the winters in his adopted land. He knew the pirates had deserved their fate, but the words of an old priest on his home island of Lissa came back to him: "*Killing is wrong. Sometimes it is unavoidable, but think hard about alternatives before you do it.*" He almost wished that he were not an officer in training but a schoolboy at Harrow like his brother Marco, with no concerns other than battling the mysteries of Greek composition or larking about on the school's spacious grounds.

Lewis noticed Ruzzini's distress, and he put a comforting hand on the lad's shoulder. "I know why you are loath to celebrate. I felt the same way after my first fight. Killing changes a man in unpredictable ways: you are never the same after. It is also shocking for a young man to discover that sometimes bad men get away with the most heinous of crimes while innocents perish through no fault of their own. However, in our profession, being reflective can be a liability. Don't dwell on melancholy things, or your equanimity will disappear into a vortex of despair. Instead, take comfort that you have done your duty and more. If you must consider anything, imagine what would have happened if we had not been present today."

Ruzzini's pondered the captain's words, and his countenance brightened, as visions of broken bodies and drowning rice pickers began to fade. "I thank you for your consideration, Captain. Being over thoughtful has been a failing of mine, one that I shall work to correct."

"Allow me to cheer you up, Mr. Ruzzini. Once you and Mr. Nairn have brought the *Shahaba* into Bima, you shall dine with me tonight at the Officiating Magistrate's home. I need to give him a report of our actions, and I know he would appreciate hearing your observations as well. You will probably get a chance to meet the local suzerain, the Maharajah of Sanggar, who is his frequent dinner companion. I understand that he is a talkative chap who is knowledgeable about many local matters that a lad with your natural curiosity would find interesting."

"I look forward to it, Captain."

"All part of your education, young sir. With Napoleon gone, naval officers are going to have to learn to be diplomats as much as warriors. Especially out here, where the grip of British power is uncertain, and native satraps exercise local control. This is an area capable of great prosperity, but first the lawlessness plaguing it must be stamped out. Today we have taken a small but important step toward that end."

Lewis and Ruzzini went ashore just before five thirty. Accompanying them was Nairn; *Shahaba Tuthturaq* had been placed under the temporary command of Master's Mate Desmond Jones, whose skill with ships was legendary. Lewis's coxswain and general factotum, John Cameron, and four rowers were aboard the captain's gig at Bima's main dock. Ridley, as *Dispatch's* first officer, remained aboard and in command. Ten other ships lay moored alongside *Dispatch*, all small trading schooners.

The waters of the bay had grown deathly still, and the wind had dropped to nothing. The normal bobbing motions common to ships were oddly absent. Ruzzini observed with alarm that the grey puffs of smoke rising from 14,000-foot-high Mount Tambora had grown thicker in the last few hours. For a volcano designated as extinct, it was showing disturbing signs of life. Ruzzini could not shake the feeling that the sleeping giant, a mere forty miles away, was about to wake up.

Bima's harbor was one of the finest in the East Indies, but the village alongside it looked cobbled together, as if the island capital of 1,000 souls was someone's afterthought. Chickens, pigs, and goats roamed freely on its dirt streets, and noisy monkeys lurked everywhere, eager to steal anything exposed to their view. People walking about conversed in a Malayan dialect that was nearly unintelligible to those on the other side of the island. Bima's structures were an odd assortment of hovels, palm thatched cottages, and wooden one-story buildings that looked like warehouses. While it possessed a granary for storing rice and a large stable for the horses that were one of the island's principal exports, the only buildings of any distinction were a small Hindu temple and an even smaller mosque. There were two European style houses: the two-story dwelling place of the Officiating Magistrate, a 28-year-old bachelor named Walter Christie; and its three-story neighbor, the townhouse of the Maharajah of Sanggar, the largest landowner on the island and its most influential resident.

Once they had been ushered inside, Ruzzini gazed about with interest. Christie's home was furnished in the Chinese fashion: lacquered chests of apple-red rosewood, rectangular tables of tan sandalwood, yoke back chairs of russet colored elm, yellow silk wall hangings featuring scenes of Chinese rural life, and peanut-brown bamboo carpets. Rooms were partitioned by five-foot-tall folding screens of teak and silk. Each colorful screen was a work of art with a theme: flowers, mythical beasts, and waterfalls were the most common. The oddly still air was perfumed with the scents of cloves, nutmeg, and cinnamon.

Lewis made his report to Christie in the study, and Ruzzini and Nairn offered their observations when Lewis deemed these would be helpful. Christie took careful notes and pronounced himself well pleased. "*Fatwa* was the most notorious of the slavers. Her elimination will send a warning to lesser pirates."

Drinks were served at 6:15, after the Maharajah of Sanggar arrived. Instead of the usual libations, Christie served an island punch of passion fruit, mangos, papaya, and a powerful local rum. Two servants circulated, carrying trays of hors d' oeuvres that included squares of snakefruit, dragonfruit, coconuts, and sausage made from the local pigs. The smell of Sumbawa chicken and rice filled the small parlor that Christie used as a reception room. Tonight's main course would be a famous local delicacy that featured poached chicken atop a bed of fluffy rice flavored with a mixture of local peppers, ginger, and saffron, the whole crowned with cucumber slices.

Ruzzini was smart enough to know his drink's delicious taste masked an alcohol content that could lay him low, so he nursed his beverage, vowing to stay in the background and learn from the conduct of his superiors. Nairn drank more freely, and his face flushed as the alcohol took effect. He wound up in a conversation with the Magistrate's secretary about the hunting opportunities offered by the island.

Lewis, Christie, and the Maharajah were on their second round of drinks when their talk transitioned to a discussion of Sumbawa's future. Christie led the impromptu forum.

"I see Sumbawa becoming part of an island empire based on the free trade model described in the writings of the esteemed Adam Smith. An empire free of the piracy and slavery that have plagued this archipelago for centuries; one devoted to the betterment of all its inhabitants, with sea lanes protected by the guns of the Royal Navy. It would provide a stable environment where the great potential of these islands could finally be fully realized. I believe Lieutenant Governor Raffles shares my views."

"Fine thoughts and a noble vision," commented Lewis, "but this empire you speak of would be expensive to maintain, and the government in London is feeling parsimonious right now. What you propose is like seeking to build a mansion with a beggar's budget. London wants quick profits, and the future that you wish for might take years to develop."

The Maharajah frowned and burst forth in heavily accented English. "While I would welcome the protection of the British Navy, I should prefer the area to become more of a federation than an empire. I would like to see a host of independent kingdoms bound together under the lightest of British yokes, rather than a collection of provinces ruled directly by either the British Crown or," he wrinkled his nose in distaste, "the former masters of these islands, the Dutch. They were only interested in sucking us dry of wealth."

"I understand that a Congress of the great powers is underway in Vienna," replied Christie. "This pan-European gathering will sort out the results of the late wars, probably redrawing the map of Europe, and will likely decide the final disposition of these islands. I like to think that the British presence in this area will become a powerful and permanent thing."

The Maharajah flushed red. "That is a polite way of saying that Sumbawa and its sister islands are condemned to be mere objects that are bid and bargained for, like rugs at a bazaar. This Congress you speak of is nothing more than a convention of diplomatic horse traders; their actions carried out in a palace rather than a barn," he said indignantly.

Ruzzini thought the characterization of diplomats was as amusing as it was accurate, but the frowns of Lewis and Christie indicated that they found the maharajah's remarks distasteful.

The Maharajah ignored the baleful looks and pressed on. "Don't try to sugarcoat how unimportant we are to you! Europeans simply don't grasp the realities of life here. I understand that your Lieutenant Governor Raffles loves the ideals of your Enlightenment, but they will have a hard time taking root in these parts. Trying to apply European solutions to Asian problems is not a proposition I would bet on if I were a gambling man. I thank Vishu that I have never acquired that evil European habit."

"I see nothing wrong with small wagers made in an occasional game of whist," remarked Christie.

"Take the administration of land," continued the Maharaj. "Mr. Raffles has made a great many unsettling changes to how it is handled on Java. He has, for example, given peasants the right to choose what crops they may cultivate rather than having their landlords decide for them. He has also directed them to pay their taxes directly to the government instead of to the freeholders of their plots. Such practices undermine long held traditions and cause peasants to think with a dangerous independence."

"I assure you, sir, that Lieutenant Governor Raffles is not a revolutionary but a clear- thinking visionary who wants to reap the greatest profit while doing the greatest good for the greatest number. He has no wish to overthrow the established order: he just wants to make it more efficient."

"Bah!" snorted the Maharajah as he dismissively waived his right hand. "I do not wish to disrupt the pleasant concord of this meeting, but, Mr. Christie, you fail to understand the geography of the islands. Our volcanoes erupt from time to time, and they disrupt the best laid plans of the wisest ministers and their most learned clerks. Here volcanoes symbolize political power. I know Christians like you and Commander Lewis look down on our gods, but we Hindus are wise enough to reckon Shiva, who holds lordship over volcanoes, a singularly dangerous God whose caprices must always be factored into our daily prayers. We have enjoyed tranquility for many years, but—"

His words were interrupted by the ground shaking violently, enough to literally set everyone's teeth chattering. Several thunderously loud booms followed. The glass in the parlor window shattered. The walls swayed as if they were made from toffee rather than sandalwood, and drinks flew off trays as servants screamed in terror. "It is Tambora!" exclaimed the Maharajah. "We must flee this house lest the walls collapse on us!"

Exiting the house could not be managed at a run because the floor was undulating, like the ripples caused by shaking a long towel. Once the group had made their way outside, everyone turned their eyes toward Tambora. What they saw was awesome in the truest sense of the word: terrifying, primordial convulsions that showed the inherent superiority of Nature over the bipeds who inhabited her realm.

"Shiva is angry!" cried the Maharajah. "We shall soon see just how great that anger is."

A huge geyser shot high into the sky, as if every fire in Hell had been compressed into a column of flame. The fire pulsed with an energy that was almost palpable; the crimson column seemed like a living creature vowing vengeance against mere mortals. The air grew hot and humid, great clouds of grey-white ash blasted forth, blending with the flames. The combination blotted out the moon and stars entirely. A shower of ash began to fall, a few flakes at first, then denser. The ashes were warm, and Ruzzini and his companions were soon caked with them. Ruzzini spat and rubbed away the ashes that covered his lips. Their taste had a nasty alkaline flavor.

Terrible as the eruption was, Ruzzini relished the extraordinary and epic, and he realized he was being furnished a sight that most men would never see. He remembered that the Chinese character for danger was the same one used to mean opportunity.

"If this continues," exclaimed the Maharajah, "it will destroy the rice crop and poison the wells."

The booms gradually subsided to the sounds of distant cannon blasts.

"Let us move back inside," said Christie. "I believe it is safe for now. We can watch the rest of this catastrophe through the front bow window. I will have the servants bring camp chairs."

For the next two hours, Christie's guests watched the ash storm play out. The dinner had been salvaged; rather than being presented on the formal mahogany table, it was served on wooden trencher plates that had been left by a Royal Navy ship a few months earlier.

As the case clock in the hall struck ten, the rumblings ceased, and the wind dropped. The diners rose to their feet and cautiously moved outdoors, scanning the sky and cautiously sniffing the air, which reeked of the rotten egg scent of sulfur, and was as still and thick as the inside of a tomb. Six inches of ash covered the street, and the town looked fit only for ghosts.

"The worst may be over," remarked Lewis, "but it looks as though the Devil himself has left his mark."

"I have never seen anything like this," said Nairn.

"This would be a fit subject for a report submitted to the Royal Society," observed Christie.

"This is very, very bad for my people," sighed the maharajah. "Come morning, everyone will have to head out to the rice fields and see if they can scrape off this muck and save the rice crop. It will be back-breaking work, but if the rice crop fails, we may be looking at a famine. More immediately, I wonder if the water is safe to drink?"

"There is no time like the present to find out," said Christie. "Let us fill a bucket from the well and take a few sips." Christie summoned his servants and instructed them to bring tin cups.

Once the bucket was hauled up from the well, everyone dipped a cup inside. Cups were brought to lips, but then everyone hesitated.

"Bottoms up," exclaimed Christie and he took a gulp. The group watched expectantly. Christie's face wrinkled in distaste, but then he smiled. "That is the worst tasting water I have ever had, but I think it's drinkable."

Emboldened by Christie's verdict, the rest of the group took cautious sips. Their faces confirmed Christie's assessment, but no one spat the water out.

"This gives me hope," said the Maharajah. "Cleaning the rice stalks will be thirsty work."

Ruzzini spoiled that optimism by giving voice to the dark thought that lurked at the back of everyone's mind. "But what if we have not seen and heard the last of the volcano? What if tonight's eruption was only the opening salvo? What if there is more to follow? What if..."

Lewis cut him off. "Enough, Mr. Ruzzini! Sufficient unto the day is the evil thereof! Our ship will be taking on provisions and making repairs for the next few days, so we will have time to see what happens next."

"I apologize, Captain," said Ruzzini sheepishly. "I sometimes speak too freely."

"True," replied Lewis. "And yet your concerns are not unreasonable."

"And the young man is not wrong," grumbled the Maharajah under his breath. "Consequences can be far reaching, extending far beyond our scope of comprehension. Shiva has danced, and the world has changed."

"I must return to my ship," pronounced Lewis, "and see what damage has befallen her. My men will have a lot of work to do. Clearing the decks and rigging of all this ash will not be easy."

"I too have work," responded the Maharajah. "I must meet with the village elders and discuss how best to remove the coating of ash from the rice stalks. Done incorrectly, it would damage the harvest."

"The lieutenant governor will want the complete details of this remarkable event," added Christie, "so I shall have to roam about during the next few days recording my observations. On that note, gentlemen, is anyone feeling any ill effects from the water?"

"None... so far," offered Nairn. The rest of the group nodded.

"And now gentlemen, my officers and I must take my leave of you," concluded Lewis. He turned to Christie and the Maharajah. "Let us meet back here tomorrow night at seven to share what we have discovered."

"Agreed," responded Christie.

The Maharajah nodded in assent. "Before that, I shall be paying several visits to the temple to pray to Shiva to assuage his wrath."

***

Ruzzini slept fitfully in his hammock aboard *Dispatch* and rose early. The rising sun was visible, but its light was dim, obscured by a haze of ash floating in the atmosphere. Tambora looked quiescent, no puffs of smoke were visible from the twin peaks of her summit. Ruzzini climbed the masthead to get a better view of the island and saw workers moving out to the rice fields.

It took the whole day to cleanse the ship of ashes. It was dirty, nasty work that set the sailors cursing. Once the deck was cleared, it had to be thoroughly swabbed. Purser Tompkins went into town to buy supplies, but found it mostly deserted and returned empty-handed. He was worried about water, since *Dispatch* only had half the supply necessary to make a voyage to Java, her next port of call. Tompkins estimated he had enough food for the journey but also wanted some live pigs and goats to make the meals more enjoyable.

In town, Christie was appalled by what he found. The flimsiest houses had collapsed under the weight of ash, and efforts to sweep the street had not even begun; the rice fields took precedence. Two workers were industriously cleaning the grime of the statues in front of the Hindu Temple, doubtless hoping to propitiate Shiva.

The ash in the fields had turned to slime and had to be scraped off carefully. The workers complained about the drinking water, but none took ill. By the late afternoon, the Maharajah knew that most of the rice crop could be saved, but it would take at least a week of unremitting effort. The entire village made prayers and offerings to the gods at sunrise before going into the fields, and in the evening after they returned, exhausted.

Three days after Tambora's eruption, the heavens opened wide and a soaking shower that lasted for eight hours thoroughly cleansed the fields of ash grime. The streets of Bima turned to mud, but that was better than being covered by ash. Peasants collected rainwater in buckets and cisterns, and Purser Tompkins filled his ship's barrels.

Tompkins was finally able to purchase the livestock that he needed. He got animals at a cheap price because the volcanic eruption reminded the peasants of just how precarious their existence was; a handful of coins firmly in their grasp now was of more use than the possibility of more money later. By ten p.m. on the eighth, *Dispatch* was fully provisioned and ready to depart on the morning tide. The *Shahaba Tuhturaq* would sail under Lieutenant Nairn, with a prize crew of ten.

Ruzzini made one last extended walk through the town, careful to take note of what he saw. He kept a diary and did not want to forget a single detail of the remarkable event that he had witnessed. He brought a sketchbook with him and made ten drawings of the town and volcano. When he returned to England, he planned to discuss this experience with his stepfather, who was interested in all manner of extraordinary events.

Dispatch departed Bima with the red-skied dawn on the ninth, but her progress was slow because the winds were capricious. By nightfall, *Dispatch* was only ten miles from her starting point.

***

By evening of the tenth, the longboat of the pirates who had escaped was within twenty miles of its destination of Komodo.

"I am still worried about the volcano," said the First Mate.

"Quit being an old woman," said Farha. "That mountain has shot its bolt. We have nothing to fear."

6 p.m. on April 10th found Christie and the Maharajah sitting down to an exceedingly pleasant dinner of a spicy coconut soup called *laksa,* and *gorengan*, fritters filled with meat and vegetables. They had just returned from inspecting one of the Maharajah's country estates on the western side of Sumbawa, only ten miles from the foot of Tambora.

Dispatch had logged 12 more miles.

At seven p.m., everything changed. Tambora roared back to life.

The wind disappeared completely, leaving *Dispatch* becalmed on a strangely still sea. Three huge, blazing shafts of lava shot ten miles into the sky. Tambora's summit turned to flame as gigantic gouts of ash, molten rock, superheated gases and water belched forth. The wind returned with a roar, carrying pumice stones the size of walnuts that slammed into *Dispatch*.

Lewis ordered all but the most essential personnel below. Top men swiftly reefed the sails lest they be torn to shreds. Performing that task in darkness while being pummeled by rocks was beyond dangerous, and one top man fell to his death after he was hit in the head by a fist-sized rock.

Ruzzini remained on deck because his curiosity was stronger than fear. He was fascinated by the holocaust, rather than frightened, because he realized that he was being offered a once-in-a-lifetime chance to see Nature's most powerful force unleashed. In the balance, his personal safety seemed irrelevant.

The holocaust raged for a full hour. Massive clouds of debris obscured the twin peaks in a haze of soot and ash. Suddenly, large fissures appeared in the sides of Tambora, lurid orange, gold, and red brightly visible through the darkness of night and ashes, and rivers of lava gushed down her slopes. The lava moved at the speed of a horse's gallop, while the sky above rippled with the heat of poisonous gases vented through the fissures. Ruzzini gasped. Christie had told him at least ten thousand people inhabited the villages on Tambora's slopes, and Ruzzini feared that those suffocated by ashes and fumes would perish when their villages caught fire.

A powerful wind sprang up as the superheated air above the lava flows met the cooler ambient air. Lewis took advantage of that and directed the unfurling of *Dispatch's* courses, mainsails, and topgallants. It was a risky move, because if the wind grew much stronger the sails might be savaged. But he wanted to put as much distance between his hundred-foot brig and the volcano as fast as possible. Given the darkness and the ash that made breathing labored, the task was accomplished far more slowly than usual. But soon *Dispatch* was flying through the waves at what Ruzzini estimated was close to her top speed of 12 knots. She plowed ahead strongly for the next two hours, and Ruzzini began to dare to think that he had seen the worst of the eruption. He was proved wrong. Almost dead wrong.

When the molten rivers flowed into the sea, there was a violent reaction. A huge, sucking vortex sprang up and the winds rose to gale force. The wind ripped *Dispatch's* sails from their yardarms, leaving only her flying jib intact. She bobbed about like a cork as waves grew steeper and steeper. It took every ounce of Lewis's seamanship to keep her bow into the wind and prevent her from broaching: being blown sideways and flooding.

Shahaba Tuhturaq, astern of *Dispatch,* was lighter and not so lucky. A wave that *Dispatch* weathered hit *Shahaba* hard. One second, she was there; an instant later, it was as if she had never existed.

The vortex uprooted whole sections of mountain forest and hurled them in all directions. Large trunks of oak and chestnut plunged into the turbid waters around *Dispatch,* and it was only by the grace of God and Lewis's inspired steering that none crushed her hull. Several strikes from the massive bolts dented it badly, necessitating the frantic working of her bilge pumps.

Corpses of men, animals, and all manner of debris accompanied the flying trees. Ruzzini could barely distinguish the dark forms that coursed through the air, but then the bodies of an old man, a young woman, and two children fell into the water directly next to *Dispatch's* port side— at least, that's what he thought they were; their bodies had been reduced to charcoal husks by the terrible heat. They bobbed against the hull, as if begging sanctuary within.

The vortex also generated a fifteen-foot wall of water five miles offshore which eventually crashed into the island. While it lifted *Dispatch* and caused no damage, the wave crushed any villages and people in its path.

One hundred miles away, the sail on the pirate launch was torn off—along with the mast that held it. The hurricane force winds sounded like the interior of a tornado and generated a mountainous wave that smashed into the longboat's side, drenching its occupants and leaving 6 inches of water in the boat's bottom. "I warned you," bellowed the First Mate over the howl of the wind, "that we should delay departure when that volcano first blew its top! Our violations of Allah's laws have made Him angry, and He has sent this tempest as vengeance!"

"Shut up and bail!" yelled Farha.

The pirates bailed as fast as they could, but a second wave swamped the launch, nearly capsizing her and filling her bottom with a foot of water. One pirate started wailing *"Allahu Akbar, Allahu Akbar, Allahu Akbar!"* and the rest of his mates joined in. They fervently hoped that repeating "God is great" would show Allah that they would return to their faith if only

He would spare them. They were living the truth of the aphorism "There are no atheists in a hurricane."

The tempest abated slightly, and the crew grinned in relief. "Praise Allah!" exclaimed the First Mate. "Our prayers have been—" A wave hit so hard that it flipped the launch upside down, Nature administering the justice that man could not.

On *Dispatch*, Ruzzini saw that the series of explosions were causing Tambora's twin peaks to collapse, for even in the dark their silhouettes were visible. Over the next forty-eight hours, the peak of Tambora would go from 14,000 feet to 9,000: the equivalent of the Matterhorn being reduced to the size of Mount Olympus.

Ruzzini wondered about the fates of Christie and the Maharajah; he knew it would be a miracle if they survived. But that miracle had occurred. When the lava began to flow but before the superheat took effect, the maharajah, his family of six, and Christie fled on horseback toward a gilded shrine that stood atop a rocky outcrop well above the surrounding countryside. The maharajah held that it was special to Shiva, and he dared to believe that the volcano would leave it intact. Their path lay along an elevated road; a hundred feet below on either side, the lava flow was fifteen feet deep, an eerie river of heat, fire, ash and melted rock that hissed and muttered as it consumed the grasses of the mountain side.

The blast furnace heat from the flanking rivers of lava made the air hard to breathe. The horses were agitated and difficult to control. The maharajah's children cried, his wife wept, and Christie almost lost hope, but the maharajah's strong will prevailed and the beleaguered group pressed on. The shrine proved to be the equivalent of the eye of a hurricane: an island protected from the violence that surrounded it. The lava flowed around the hilltop, and strangely enough, none of the debris in the air inflicted severe damage; the shrine was one of the few places on Sumbawa that remained intact on April 11th.

Tambora continued erupting far into the night. The emptying of the magma chambers had begun the formation of a six-mile-wide caldera. The winds dropped from gale force to merely strong. Ash continued to pour from the sky and the prevailing direction of wind would likely blow much of it toward the West and onto the islands of Lombak, Bali, and Java.

Ruzzini stayed on deck until dawn, or when dawn should have occurred. It was still black as midnight by 8 a.m., and even by noon, Ruzzini could barely see the hand in front of his face. The temperature was twenty degrees cooler than the day before, and Ruzzini noticed the complete absence of any sea birds. Clusters of dead ones and fish floated by every few minutes.

"Do you feel that you are dreaming when you look at the sky and sea, Mr. Ruzzini?" inquired Ridley, who had paced over to the side of the ship to join him.

"I do, sir. I feel that I am looking at a nightmare tableau. Life at sea has taught me much about Nature's power, but what is unfolding makes me realize just how little we understand her."

"I feel like a child in a nursery, Mr. Ruzzini, who has just discovered that the playful kittens with whom he is familiar are part of a family that includes man-eating tigers."

The ship's deck was choked with three feet of ash, the weight dangerously affecting the ship's stability. The deck had to be cleared before any repairs could be made. The standing and running rigging were intact but covered by ash grime. Fortunately, the men on the pumps were winning their battle with the sea and *Dispatch* would survive.

It took four days of hard work before the ship was able to begin limping toward Java under the crudest of jury rigs. The ship proceeded at a snail's pace of two knots, but the winds held firm, so at least *Dispatch* was able to maintain a steady speed. Each day was a little less dark than the previous one, and every so often the sun peeked through the glowering overcast of ash-laden clouds. Sometimes lookouts spotted large floating patches of what looked like seaweed. Closer examination revealed them to be large blocks of pumice. The ship had to make a half day detour to avoid a huge expanse of them.

The ship's speed increased daily as more repairs were made, but it took a month and a half to reach Java. It was well that her purser was honest and had stocked her with sound victuals and good water; as it was, supplies were exhausted by the time they reached harbor on May 25th.

Lewis intended to give an eyewitness's report to the lieutenant governor in Batavia. He realized the account would sound fantastic and unbelievable to someone who had not been on Sumbawa, but the lieutenant governor, Raffles, was that rare man, one who would listen closely. Unfortunately, his dreams of a maritime empire under the British aegis would have to be put on hold. It would be years before Sumbawa and the islands within a hundred miles would again be economically viable.

Lewis figured that the rice crop on Sumbawa had been destroyed. It was likely that the life sustaining crops on the neighboring islands of Lombok and Bali also had been obliterated. The water in their wells would be contaminated and undrinkable. Those islands had a combined population of at least 75,000, and mass starvation would be a menace in the months to come. Added to the deaths on Sumbawa, Lewis calculated that the loss of life from the disaster would reach 80,000, three times the number that had died at Pompeii. The only possible good to emerge from this catastrophe would be that the pirates would find no workers fit to kidnap in the coming months. But that was cold comfort. The prospect of children starving to death as parents watched helplessly sickened him.

He and Ruzzini conversed quietly as the carriage sent for them approached Raffles' country residence of Buitenzorg, 25 miles west of Batavia: a Dutch built mansion that he had transformed into a combination salon and museum. "Not exactly the cruise you had in mind when you were posted to *Dispatch*, is it?" remarked Lewis.

"No, Captain, it is not. I must confess, sir, that after the pirate battle and the drowning of the rice pickers, to say nothing of the storm at sea, I have become convinced that a naval career is not right for me. When I return home, I shall resign from the service and seek a more stable and less dangerous career. I hope you will not think less of me for that decision, sir."

"No, Mr. Ruzzini, I shall not. You have demonstrated courage under fire, and the life of a sailor is a lonely one that a gregarious soul might well reject. You are young and have a promising life ahead of you; you have plenty of time to make a career course change and sail into uncharted waters. Have you thought about what your new occupation might be?"

"I should like to explore natural philosophy more deeply, Captain, though I am not sure what calling would make that possible. I suspect that what we saw at Tambora will have lasting effects far beyond the East Indies, but that is only my intuition speaking. I would like to study the effects with men of science."

"Hmm. As a sailor who lives by the weather, I am curious what Tambora's long term effects will be on navigation. Perhaps you will be so good as to keep me informed of any discoveries and conclusions reached by men of science ashore."

"My stepfather, Sir Thomas Pennywhistle, is a Fellow of the Royal Society. He once told me of a paper written by the esteemed Dr. Benjamin Franklin, who traced a connection between the eruption of Laki, a volcano in Iceland, and the very poor European harvest of 1783. It was met with skepticism when it was presented at the Manchester Society, but looking at the glowering skies above, I think Dr. Franklin might have discovered a causality that should be explored."

Lewis smiled. "I always suspected that you were too smart to be a sailor. I feel certain you will prosper in any career you choose, and I shall make the highest representations of your conduct to any who inquire about your character."

"I thank you for that, sir. How long do you think it will be before *Dispatch* is ready to sail for Portsmouth?"

"*Dispatch* is in bad shape and will need a thorough refit. The nearest well-equipped dockyard is in Calcutta, at least five weeks sail and it will take them at least a month for them to make sufficient repairs to get us home. We will be detained here for a minimum of two weeks and added to all that is a five-month voyage to the Solent. Allowing for contingencies, you will be lucky if you arrive in Portsmouth by Christmas. So, you see, Mr. Ruzzini," Lewis smiled, "you will not be rid of the sea anytime soon."

"That I shall not be able to enjoy your company on a continued basis is my chief regret in leaving the service, Captain."

"You flatter me, Mr. Ruzzini. Might I suggest you send off a few letters to your stepfather, since they will reach him faster than you will. You say he is well connected to men of science, and I warrant they will want to know what we have seen."

<h1 style="text-align:center">Chapter 2</h1>

Diplomatic Fishermen

London, England, 20 March 1816

Thomas Pennywhistle spent most of the eight-mile journey from his Portland Street home to the village of Ealing reviewing notes of his recent conversations with Lord Castlereagh, the Foreign Secretary. Those conversations had been lengthy and complicated and so it had taken him a week to distill the main diplomatic concerns into ten pages. He had reviewed the notes so many times that he could recite nearly every word from memory, but he understood intellectually what the best actors of Shakespeare's Globe had known by heart: a smooth, effortless performance was always the result of careful rehearsal.

As his carriage rumbled along, he looked up from time to time and marveled at the fact that London was finally enjoying a sunny day after many weeks of snow, rain, fog, and mist. London's winter weather had never been something to boast of but this year it had been notorious. If he had believed in vengeful ancient Gods, he would have sworn that one of them was taking delight in tormenting London's inhabitants by sending capricious fluctuations of weather down on their heads. Weather was always the random element in even the best laid plans, and he hoped that someday men of intellect and resource could devise ways to understand and predict it. The recent outbreak of strange weather was provoking a great deal of uninformed speculation, much of it reeking of the superstition that he disliked. Today was the first time in a month that he had been able to dispense with a greatcoat and don the lightest weight boat cloak. If Winter had been a lion, the first day of Spring was proving to be a lamb. He hoped the improved weather was a portent for the success of the negotiations that lay ahead.

His mission involved back door diplomacy. Since he occupied no official position in Lord Liverpool's government and enjoyed no formal diplomatic accreditation, his visit could be explained as that of a public-spirited private gentleman interested in promoting Anglo American amity because he had an American wife. If successful, the results of his mission could be translated into official action: if unsuccessful, his efforts could be ignored as those of a citizen too full of himself.

And yet, he understood that when he spoke the words, "His Majesty's Government believes that..." his voice would be interpreted as that of George III himself. He stopped the inner voice of his thoughts abruptly, aware that he would soon have to make a hard choice between his government's instructions and its best interests.

Many of the provisions of the Treaty of Ghent had yet to be fully carried out. That agreement had ended Britain's war with America, but new problems had arisen that were unaddressed by that by the formal stipulations of the treaty. Castlereagh had spoken directly to John Quincy Adams on a handful of occasions: Adams was American Minister and Plenipotentiary to the Court of St. James charged with carrying out his nation's obligations under the treaty. The two men did not, however, get on particularly well. They both were thoughtful, scholarly men of principle who were also willing to make pragmatic compromises as the needs of the moment dictated, but Castlereagh had the temperament of a thoroughgoing aristocrat while Adams had that of a prickly, egalitarian New Englander.

Castlereagh was busy man confronted daily with a host of thorny issues and could not spare as much time dealing with "The American Problem" as he would have wished. He had cast about for a deputy who had the time and patience to deal effectively with the formidable Mr. Adams and had finally settled on Pennywhistle. He had been impressed with Pennywhistle's intellect, tact, and integrity during the Congress of Vienna and decided that he might be able to bring about the results that Castlereagh had only been able to imagine. Sometimes the meeting of equals created tensions due to large, competing egos: sending an underling devoid of his master's hubris could reduce them.

Pennywhistle also realized that sending an underling might send the message to Adams that Castlereagh considered America unimportant. He would just have to hope for the best.

Pennywhistle was glad of the employment. The effects of the Waterloo concussion had lingered longer than he had expected and had kept him from the vigorous, productive life to which he was accustomed. His virtuoso memory and keen intellect had finally returned, and he was back to consuming two books a week. Starting in January, he had begun a grueling physical regimen whose results were just now becoming apparent. That included plenty of walking, riding, fencing, swimming, and frequent sessions with an ex-officer of the Imperial Guard who was an expert of the French art of street-fighting: *Savate.*

He had retained his commission as colonel of The Royal Marines during his recovery and had submitted a written report for their reorganization and reduction the previous month: a necessity occasioned by the end of the Napoleonic Wars. His plans managed to combine cost savings with increased efficiency and were well received. It was hinted that he might be offered a higher rank and an overseas command of importance, but he let it be known that Waterloo would be his last combat outing and that he had no wish to leave Britain. He had seen enough war to last an eternity and was far more interested in the arts of peace. One of those peaceful arts was cleaning up the messy results of the late wars with Bonaparte and so he was well pleased with his present assignment.

"I see our destination just ahead, sir." Shouted his coachman, Ronald McBeavy, from the driving box at the front of the two-door carriage. McBeavy who had fought with the 42nd at Waterloo, also doubled as his manservant.

Pennywhistle looked up from his papers and spotted a very modest, half-timbered Elizabethan manor house ahead. Rumor had it that Adams was underfunded by his government and had chosen this residence to rent because the costs were much cheaper than in central London. He checked his Blancpain watch. "Very good. I am pleased that we have arrived with time to spare. I am glad you knew of that shortcut."

It suddenly hit him that using the carriage with the arms of the Earldom of Leith emblazoned on its side had been a mistake. The vehicle had come with the purchase of his townhouse from his godmother, and he had never got round to having the carriage repainted in plain colors without an escutcheon. The carriage spoke of an aristocratic hauteur to which the home ahead seemed fundamentally opposed.

Adams was a New Englander who stood foursquare against special privilege and just might be as scornful of aristocratic pretense as his father had been. Adams was the son of the second president of the United States and occupied the same position his father had after the end of the Revolutionary War. He had spent much of his life abroad, growing up in the world of international diplomacy. He spoke French, German, Dutch, and Russian fluently and had a working knowledge of Spanish. He read Latin and ancient Greek as well. He was a gifted writer and scholar who had a great love of the theatre, particularly Shakespeare.

He was a devoted family man with three sons and a formidable wife. He was said to be warm and spontaneous to his intimates but reserved and sometimes cold with those with whom he was not acquainted. He was said to prepare for any diplomatic meeting with great zeal, so Pennywhistle suspected that Adams knew as much about him as Pennywhistle knew about Adams.

It was amusing in a way: two men who were supremely well prepared would pretend to have a spontaneous conversation that was anything but. Inspirations that would appear to come as the gifts of magic moments, would really be gambits thought out well in advance. As with much diplomacy, things would not be as they appeared but both men would find it useful to pretend that their artifice was reality.

McBeavy deposited him in front of the home's front entrance. "Now don't overexert yourself, Sir Thomas. Lady Pennywhistle warned me that you sometimes push yourself too hard and we both know that your return to health is recent: it would not be wise to tempt fate."

Pennywhistle sighed in annoyance. Despite being a retired sergeant from a famous regiment, McBeavy had a lot of mother hen in his character and loved to *tut tut* over him.

"I promise I shall be careful," replied Pennywhistle indulgently. "Now I won't be needing you for... He glanced at his pocket watch: it showed 2 pm..." either for an hour or until... well perhaps the late evening. The first, if things do not go well, and the second if things proceed as I hope they will. Why not take the carriage around to the carriage house and make the acquaintance of its master? Take your ease, you have earned it. I shall arrange for a meal to be sent out to you.

"Very good sir, and remember, don't overtax yourself."

"I promise I shall pace myself carefully...mother." Pennywhistle laughed. "Now be off with you."

Pennywhistle's knock was answered by the home's butler, an older man with an unplaceable accent who was so unprepossessing that he almost seemed part of the furniture. Pennywhistle presented his card. "I believe I am expected."

"That you are, Sir Thomas. Please follow me to the study where Mr. Adams is waiting."

Adams looked up from the book he was reading, "The Collected Works of Cicero," and smiled a smile that was courteous but devoid of warmth; the practiced response of a seasoned diplomat. He rose from his desk, advanced a few paces, and shook Pennywhistle's hand. His sharp eyes assessed Pennywhistle as he performed the gesture: the handshake was like his smile: business like but perfunctory. His eyes softened and Pennywhistle guessed that his initial judgment was favorable.

The face opposite Pennywhistle was that of an aesthete. He had a round face that reminded Pennywhistle of an owl: a broad intellectual forehead, inquiring eyes, slightly aquiline nose, and thin, prim lips that Pennywhistle guessed did not smile overmuch. Pennywhistle knew he was both a Harvard graduate and a successful attorney, but Pennywhistle felt his manner would be much more at home in a staid, senior professors' chair than arguing a case before a boisterous Massachusetts jury. Yet his career as a diplomat had been a successful one so his tongue had to have some persuasive ability.

"It is a great pleasure, to meet you, Sir Thomas. Your reputation precedes you."

"As does yours, Mr. Adams. I am honored to make your acquaintance."

"Please sit down, Sir Thomas, and make yourself comfortable." Adams motioned to a red leather wing chair. "My manservant will arrive momentarily with two glasses of sherry."

Adams voice was like a crisp breeze bearing a pleasant scent: it compelled your full attention. His accent was one Pennywhistle had never heard before and he guessed that its sharp, gritty vowels were a perfect reflection of the hard scrabble soil of New England.

Both men sank into their seats and when the sherry arrived, their lips took cautious sips as their eyes probed and assessed. Their faces wore neutral expressions that have been useful in a game of Poque, or Poker as the Americans were starting to call it.

"I could not help noticing that you were reading Cicero. Do you consider yourself a devotee of his works?"

"More than that, Sir Thomas. His works have informed much of my writing and a great deal of my thinking. A world without Cicero would be like the weather of late: a world without sun. What about you?"

"While I consider Cicero valuable, I must confess that some of his thoughts seem... well... dated and occasionally *recherché*. Though I believe that we can learn much from him in a generalized way, the conditions of his Rome and present-day Britain are greatly different. Take the new industry for example: the Coalbrookdale Bridge, built entirely of iron, is something Cicero could never have imagined, and I believe if he were confronted with it, his powerful intellect would be at a loss for words. I far prefer Gibbon who writes as a historian for all mankind while Cicero was an orator whose words were sometimes intended to secure political advantage rather than reflect genuine wisdom. Gibbon's observations about the Roman Empire are sharp, insightful, and of much greater relevance to our modern world."

Adams looked startled for a moment, then his face resumed its neutral demeanor. "Your response surprises me, Sir Thomas. I too have read Gibbon but gave up after his first volume. I found his pen a little too glib for my taste; sometimes more concerned with creating a clever phrase and shocking his audience than with telling the plain truth. What about Shakespeare? I find his works sublime. If I were stranded on a desert island and had no access to books, save one, I should choose a copy of his First Folio."

"I quite agree, Mr. Adams, though I would have thought that being from New England your first choice would have been the Bible."

"My father is a Unitarian, Sir Thomas, who believes that much of the Bible is fanciful. He does not hold with the concept of the Trinity, for example. While my own beliefs are far more traditional, the impact of my father on me has been considerable. Though the Bible is good for moral guidance, the works of the Bard provide far greater insights into the varieties of human behavior."

Both men took sips of their sherry as their minds contemplated a way to transition to the real business they had to discuss.

"I want to apologize for not responding to some of Lord Castlereagh's correspondence, Sir Thomas. I have only recently recovered from an eye infection that became so severe that I feared that I might lose my vision entirely. And if that were not enough, I developed a strange palsy in my writing hand. It is only in the past week that it has abated enough for me to write at all, though the malady has reduced my once fine penmanship to that of a scribbling schoolboy."

"I understand, Mr. Adams, because I suffered a concussion at Waterloo that turned out to be more severe than was first thought. I was plagued with headaches, vertigo, memory loss, and generalized fatigue. So, we are alike: partial invalids just returning to normality."

"Since we have both been cursed with suffering, let us speak of things that bring pleasure. My friends tell me that you like fishing, Sir Thomas, as do I. I have always found it an agreeable way to spend an afternoon, and it is a common way to do so back in Massachusetts. Cod from the Grand Banks built Massachusetts, and our statehouse has a weathervane atop its dome in the shape of that fish. Some wags even went so far as to say that in Massachusetts God was originally spelled C-O-D."

Pennywhistle disliked the taste of cod, but he nonetheless curved his lips into mirthless smile that suggested that he understood Adams perspective perfectly.

"Would you be agreeable to dispensing with the formality of this study and instead continuing our talks while fishing on the banks of the River Brent outside? The river contains some splendid specimens of trout, and my groundskeeper believes conditions are ripe for them to be biting today. I feel we should enjoy the rare beauty of this day since it may be only a temporary respite from the unusual weather of late. I have taken the liberty of having my cook prepare a large picnic hamper and I have selected the best bottle of claret from the stock that I brought from France."

Pennywhistle smiled at this unexpected flexibility, though he wondered if Adams proposal was merely a way to throw him off balance. "I think it is a splendid idea, Mr. Adams. Communing with nature brings out the best in a man and reminds that us however self-important we become, we are still her servants."

A walk of twenty minutes ended with Adams and Pennywhistle sitting in camp chairs as they reviewed the contents of a large tackle box containing Adams' extensive collection of artificial flies. Selecting just the right one was an art form with which Adams appeared well acquainted. Pennywhistle had ideas of his own about the best ones but let Adams guide the conversation.

"I think the soft hackle fly will work better today than the pheasant tail nymph or bead head wooly bugger. I tied it myself," said Adams proudly.

"And a fine job you did too, Mr. Adams. I shall be happy to use it."

Adams beamed and Pennywhistle knew that he was getting to know Adams the man rather than Adams the diplomat.

Neither man said anything for the next twenty minutes as they made expert casts with their rods. Fishing was relaxing and meditative but there was an air of competition between the two men, as each sought to be the first to land a fish. Pennywhistle's rod bent first, and he landed an eight pounder that put up an impressive amount of fight.

"My congratulations, Sir Thomas, this calls for a drink of celebration." Adams was about to pluck a bottle from the picnic hamper when his own rod began to vibrate vigorously.

"You've got a big one, Mr. Adams. Now bring him in, bring him in," exclaimed Pennywhistle with genuine excitement.

Adams tussled with the fish for a good two minutes, allowing the trout to tire itself with fruitless struggles. Adams finally brought in a fish that was an almost exact copy of Pennywhistle's trout. As Adams dropped it in the bucket, both men smiled.

"It seems our unspoken competition has ended in a draw, Mr. Adams: perhaps the best outcome for two diplomats."

"Yes, both sides getting what they want and neither feeling shortchanged. Now is truly the right time to break out the wine and enjoy the sweat meats, sandwiches, and strawberries."

Both men talked pleasantly about their past fishing exploits as they ate and drank claret for the next twenty minutes. The trivial talk and tasty repast proved relaxing, but the subconscious mind of both men was using the time to calculate what it wanted its master to say about far more serious matters.

Pennywhistle was about to take a bite of a sandwich of ham, onions, peppers, and olives when a magpie swooped out of the sky and snatched it from his hand. He blinked in surprise and then laughed, as did Adams. "The best laid plans disrupted by an unexpected actor. Rather like diplomacy, wouldn't you agree Mr. Adams?"

"I would. Victory snatched away just before it is tasted."

"Mr. Adams, since we are greatly enjoying the joys of water recreation perhaps now is a good time to bring up maritime matters. I refer to two issues: the repatriation of US sailors to America and the matter of boarding vessels suspected of carrying slave cargos."

"I agree, Sir Thomas. Let us consider the sailors first. I have seen far too many Americans who have no means to get home wandering the streets and reduced to begging. Just yesterday, a man approached me speaking with the accent of Boston and lurching forth unsteadily. He assured me that he was not in liquor but had suffered a leg injury when his ship was captured. I gave him two shillings but was chagrined that he had been placed in that position by both our governments."

"Both our governments? Pardon me, sir, but aren't American sailors an American problem?"

"Under the strict terms of the Treaty of Ghent you are right, but I think your government has an implied obligation to help get these poor men home."

"I sympathize," sighed Pennywhistle, "but isn't the real problem that your government is so parsimonious that it has allocated insufficient funds for the task?"

"Regrettably true, but it would be greatly in the interest of His Majesty's Government to fix this sad problem once and for all. I know Lord Castlereagh is interested in fully restoring the once lively trade between our two nations and a gesture on his part toward aiding the sailors who would carry out such trade would be greatly appreciated by the entire community of American merchants. Those merchants would be the same ones most interested in importing English goods. You will recall that before the War, the United States was your third largest trading partner."

"Would the gesture you speak of involve the deposit of additional funds into the American account with Baring Brothers; possibly by parties that wish to remain anonymous, so as not to embarrass Mr. Madison's government? Or perhaps, given by our government under the guise of funding something else rather than repatriation?"

"It would."

"His Majesty's government is committed to cost cutting at present, so that might be difficult."

Adams frowned.

"But not impossible. The Prime Minister has certain discretionary funds available for "unassigned projects." In the past, those have been clandestine subsidies to foreign gentlemen and organizations to secure their cooperation against Bonaparte or fund causes and services of future use to the British Crown. Liberating the kingdom from impoverished American sailors could be represented as pension payments to "individuals who have rendered unique service." The general population greatly favors the payment of pensions to men presumed to be veterans."

"That would be irony indeed."

"Those sailors have indeed rendered service: the public need not know the nature of that service. Funds might also be siphoned from the Post Office since they are concerned with the free and easy worldwide delivery of mail and operate a fleet of packet ships to do that. Those could be represented as payments to facilitate cooperation with your Postmaster General and his agents. The Foreign Minister has said publicly that he is committed to the gospel of free trade in all its forms and delivery of the mail certainly qualifies as facilitating that. The combined payments would not be large but likely enough to fill the gap between the money your government has given you and the amount necessary to carry out the remaining repatriation."

"I would be willing to endorse such an arrangement. What would your government want in return?"

"We would like Canadians to be allowed to trade with Indians on American soil. Just trade mind you, no exciting Indians to ever take up arms against your government."

Adams shook his head vigorously. "That would be too politically unpopular. No matter how sincere the promises of this present government, the memory of the role those British traders played in inciting the violence of Indians in the last war is too fresh. We also know that the Northwest and Hudson's Bay Companies operate numerous illegal forts and trading stations on American soil and regularly poach our furs. Our government wishes those posts evacuated and their trappers to never again visit American soil. I would also ask your government to accept members of American tribes who wish to join their brethren already in Canada. In return, we offer a far-reaching proposal which bodes well for future generations."

"What is that?"

"President Madison's Government proposes a border between Canada and the United States that is entirely free of forts, military installations, or reservations of any kind: one that stretches from Maine west to the Great Lakes. The details of the border with the Louisiana Purchase could be decided at a mutually agreeable later date. It would be a demilitarized zone that would reduce tensions between our countries as well as save both your government and ours a great deal of money: perfectly in line with their mutual parsimony. It would also promote the Free Trade Doctrine, of which Lord Castlereagh is so fond. Merchants would be allowed to cross the border at will without any requirement for passports and citizens of both countries would be granted easy access to their relatives. A Commission composed of both British and American diplomats could be formed to formally survey and establish the specifics of that boundary."

Pennywhistle smiled. "That would allow us to reduce the size of our garrisons in Upper and Lower Canada. If we could be certain that they were not likely to fight, we could scale back our forces to those of palace guards. I will have to speak to the Foreign Secretary, of course, but I am confident of his answer. Regarding boundaries, I should like to know the United States intentions regarding the Florida Frontier."

Adams frowned. "It is no secret that many of our citizens covet Florida. It is a haven for runaway slaves and several of our prominent citizens, especially General Andrew Jackson, would be more than willing to use military force to seize it from the Spanish. I would prefer to simply buy it, and I believe that is the course our government will eventually pursue. Spain is plagued with rebellions in Venezuela and Colombia, and Florida is a drain on the Spanish purse that she can no longer afford. Many Americans are sympathetic to the rebels in those two areas and some in our government favor aiding them with men and guns. We Americans would prefer to see the New World rid of all colonial powers. Am I correct in thinking that the British Government would prefer not to have the Spanish reclaim their colonies?"

"You are, but that is a thorny problem since Spain is officially still our ally because of agreements made during the Peninsular Campaigns. His Majesty's Government has every interest in wishing to see South America divided into a host of fully independent states; that will ensure that we British will capture the bulk of her trade. We cannot officially endorse the rebels and yet we are unofficially involved at the most basic levels. The rebel infantry that forms the hard core of Simon Bolivar's armies is composed of ex British soldiers displaced by the reduction of our army after Waterloo. The rebel merchants who furnish them the tools to fight have been covertly buying surplus British Arms and have even grown so bold as to commission the manufacture of thousands of new ones. Many of those merchants have secured covert, low interest loans from our chief banking houses to finance their purchases. We, like you, have no interest in seeing Spain return and you will recall that Lord Castlereagh graciously bought off any Spanish claims on Louisiana for a payment of 400,000 pounds."

"We are much obliged for that although we made a legitimate deal with Napoleon. The Spanish claims that he stole Louisiana from them were ludicrous."

"The Royal Navy controls the seas, Mr. Adams, and has the power to stop Spain from sending reinforcements but publicly declaring the New World a "hands off" zone for Europeans would provoke the wrath not just of Spain, but of some of our other allies who have formed a reactionary Holy Alliance: dedicated to suppressing any rebellions or revolutions which threaten the established order. But if a proclamation declaring the New World out of bounds to the Old was issued by a nation like America, a nation forged in the fire of Enlightenment ideals that are both feared and admired by European princes, it would be seen in a more favorable light and would have the clandestine backing of our Navy. Is that a course you might consider at some future date?"

"Yes, we would but it would require the cooperation of two navies who only recently stopped fighting each other. In essence, our two nations would be forming a secret partnership without the signing of any formal documents. I know the English are interested in suppressing the slave trade and I am sure your research has told you that I regard slavery as a cancer that must someday be cut out of the United States body politic if our nation is to achieve its full potential. Would the British government want this uh...cooperation to extend to the search and seizure of vessels carrying slaves from Africa?"

"We already are stopping slavers on the high seas and confiscating their cargos. We pay a bounty to the crew of each ship based on every African they liberate. The cooperation of the United States Navy would greatly expand our reach in the New World. There has also been a troublesome outbreak of piracy in the Caribbean which your navy, like ours, is working to end. If our two navies could work together and share information that would greatly speed the end of those brigands. "

"I can pledge the cooperation of the United States regarding piracy, Sir Thomas, but I will have to consult with Washington about the slave issue. Though the importation of slaves into the US has been illegal since 1808, a great many Southerners welcome the clandestine visits of slave vessels."

"I realize that the abolitionist movement in the US is in its infancy, Mr. Adams, and has nothing like the great support that ours enjoys in Parliament. Your nation has yet to produce an American Wilberforce but given time, I am sure one will emerge. Our nation would be willing to allow American naval officers to board British flagged merchant ships if they were suspected of carrying slaves. Would your government be willing to allow the same arrangement for British officers and American merchant ships?"

Adams bowed his head in thought, after which he looked up with an expression of sad resignation. "Alas, no. At present, the memory of the last war is still too warm to permit a reciprocal arrangement but given a little time, American attitudes will soften. I am also under pressure from slave owners who seek compensation for the abduction..."

Pennywhistle glowered.

"Let me rephrase that. For the *liberation* of more than 2,000 slaves by the British during the Chesapeake Campaign."

Pennywhistle's voice rippled with barely suppressed anger that was undergirded by a deep passion that he rarely expressed publicly. "Those slaves came to us of their own free will. No one stole them, damn it. We promised them freedom if they reached our lines, our only request being that they answer a few questions about any military forces or installations that they might have seen on their journey. I personally liberated two and I am uncommon proud of what I did; playing a small part in the greatest mass emancipation in your history was a great honor. One of those two became my manservant and he gave his life to save a young white lad." He felt tears forming in the corners of his eyes, then brusquely banished the moisture with two quick strokes of his right sleeve.

Adams recognized the pain of a man in secret mourning. A deep emotion wanted his hand to reach out and touch and clasp Pennywhistle's in sympathy, but his New England granite core snatched it back at the last second.

"Some of the slav...no...refugees, were formed into a Corps of Colonial Marines that fought well at Bladensburg. Their presence on the field incensed many of your soldiers so much that they swore instant death to any captured Colonial Marines. We promised them land at the end of their service and have been as good as our word. They are in the process of being resettled on South American lands captured from the Dutch in the last war."

"I have never been in any doubt about the British honoring their promises, Sir Thomas. A British gentleman's oath is recognized as reliable in even the most obscure of countries. The trick is to persuade an Englishman to give his oath in the first place."

Pennywhistle calmed his indignation and returned his voice to its usual comforting equanimity. "His Majesty's Government is not prepared to pay their former masters one shilling in recompense; in your parlance, that would be one red cent. Unless of course, you propose to fully compensate us for the burning of Niagara on the Lake and the displacement of a thousand of its citizens. I think that is about as likely as fish developing wings."

"Privately, I respect and admire your conduct, Sir Thomas. I would be personally delighted to tell every slave owner with influence in the government to go to the devil but that would be political suicide. I will report back to my government that Lord Castlereagh is...*taking the matter under advisement.* That phrase can mean anything a hearer wants it to. Both governments can then allow the issue to wither on the vine."

"Extended delay is indeed a useful remedy," obser Pennywhistle. "A fine way to prevent small matters from blocking progress on great ones."

"Let me share something with you in confidence, Sir Thomas. Mr. Madison's term will soon be ending, and it is likely that his replacement will be James Monroe. Rumor has it that he will appoint me as the next secretary of state because he is a Virginian and needs a New Englander in his cabinet. As the Secretary, I will have the president's ear and would be perfectly placed to write...let's call it "The Monroe Doctrine": a document based on some of the ideas that we have been discussing."

"James Monroe?" gasped Pennywhistle. "I saw him at the Battle of Bladensburg, just before Washington City fell in 1814. He gave some bad military advice to your president that had a great deal to do with the American defeat. But perhaps I should be grateful. His faulty advice resulted in American troop dispositions that saved my life."

"Indeed, his advice was unfortunate, Sir Thomas, and if he becomes president, he will need advisors with more wisdom than he. I hope to count myself chief among them. There is also the matter of trade with India and the Spice islands that you have recently acquired from the Dutch. American merchants do a brisk trade with China at Canton but have been excluded from those other markets. Allowing Americans easy access would be in line with the Foreign Minister's free trade policy, would it not?"

"The answer is regrettably not as simple as I would wish it to be. India is run by The Honorable East India Company, a private corporation. While the government exercises some oversight regarding its affairs, it is a monopoly that answers chiefly to its stockholders, not the British people. Allowing full penetration of The Subcontinent would not be welcomed, but Lord Castlereagh might be able persuade its board of directors to allow a certain number of American merchantmen to call each year."

"A company running an empire is odd indeed," remarked Adams. "I have also heard disquieting reports that slavery exists in some of the territories controlled by the East India Company."

Pennywhistle frowned. "I will not deny that, and I consider it a blot on British honor. The problem is that in some areas John Company rules indirectly through a series of princes and maharajah's who act as satraps. Those satraps are free to control the domestic concerns of their kingdoms which sometimes include slavery, while The Company controls their foreign affairs. The Company is usually able to persuade them to name a Company appointed regent if they die with very young heirs or no heirs at all. In such cases, that regent usually abolishes slavery at the first opportunity. It is my hope that the East India Company will be eventually disbanded, and the Subcontinent placed under direct government control, but it will probably take a sepoy mutiny to accomplish such a dramatic change."

"So, you believe slavery will eventually end in India?"

"I do, but the highly restrictive caste system will be far harder to eliminate. As for Java and the East Indies, the British signed the Convention of London with the Dutch last year. In theory, we have agreed to return the area to them, but we have not been able to work out the details yet. The Netherlands were devastated by the wars with Bonaparte and they may not yet have regained enough of their former financial standing to stage a return to those islands. Should the Dutch not be able to reestablish their control, it is uncertain whether Liverpool's government would wish to retain them. That is all part of the parsimony that we have been discussing. British control at present is very loose, administered from Java and relying on a string of officiating magistrates in the outlying islands to carry out British wishes. Piracy there is also widespread and though the pirates typically avoid European vessels, American merchantmen might be in some danger."

Adams sighed. "You are right, the problems in the East are complicated. Could we at least agree to begin some informal negotiations, say several of our most prominent traders quietly meeting with representatives of the East India Company's Board? Their recommendations would be non-binding but the men on both sides would be of sufficient stature that they would be taken very seriously by both our governments."

"I think that is an excellent idea, provided that the negotiations are done with the utmost discretion and the American representatives limit their expectations to something short of unimpeded free trade."

"I would be agreeable to that, Sir Thomas. As the esteemed Doctor Franklin put it, "if a cabinet maker wishes to make a strong joint, he must shave a little off both parts to be joined."

At that moment, a trout of at least twenty pounds leaped out of the water and plunged back down with a giant splash. That action broke the mood and caused both men to realize that they had done more than enough for one day: diplomacy was as much a process as an outcome and weighty matters took time to settle.

"What do you say that we finish this claret and then see if we can add to our haul before sundown, Mr. Adams?"

"An excellent suggestion, Sir Thomas. I am so glad that we see eye to eye...on fish.

"I think we have made some excellent catches today... and the fishing has been good too."

"We have gotten our hooks into some fine ideas, Sir Thomas."

"And we have done a good job tipping the scales of justice in the right direction."

"Let us spend another day fishing together in one month, Sir Thomas. That should give your master plenty of time to examine...uh... the fillets from today's outing."

"And return a verdict on how Castlereagh's digestion has handled their taste, Mr. Adams."

"It's such a shame, Sir Thomas, that while many in our governments are as slippery as fish, few have ever learned the lessons that casting for real ones can teach."

Pennywhistle's smile faded and his expression turned thoughtful. "Despite mankind's missteps, I believe there is hope for humanity. Allow me to relate a story that recently came to my attention. Last December, Mr. Ashley Cooper, a philanthropic gentleman with a fondness for horses, asked Lord Bathhurst, The Secretary of State for War, about the fate of cavalry mounts injured at the Battle of Waterloo.

"Told that all were being sold off to private parties and that the worst injured might end up as fertilizer or glue, he purchased a dozen of the most hopeless and brought them to his estate in Berkshire. He employed two of the best veterinary surgeons to nurse them back to health; a difficult process that took months, since many of the horses had weeping wounds and all still carried imbedded musket balls and fragments of canister. Once the horses were fully mobile, a strange thing happened. Each morning when Cooper came out to inspect them in their pasture, the twelve would carefully form themselves into a line of cavalry, employing the precision steps that they had been taught. Once formed, they would first canter, then trot, then charge, stopping directly in front of Ashley Cooper. He was moved to tears and their morning charge became a ritual that soon attracted enough attention to turn them into local celebrities. If these poor beasts can find a decent second life, there is hope that the benighted souls that we have been discussing may yet find happiness if we do our jobs right."

Adam's eyes glistened slightly. "I think the beastliest thing about the late wars was the way they made innocent animals suffer. Men understand what they fight and even die for; most of them engaged willingly, knowing the risks. The beasts, whom God enjoined us to care for, have no such understanding. I have had several soldiers tell me that the cries of wounded comrades gradually fade from memory, but those of injured horses never do. Cooper deserves the highest praise for treating those horses as honorable veterans, not rubbish to be discarded."

By the time Pennywhistle departed at eight, his bucket contained seven fish: the chef at his residence would be making trout-based dishes for the next week. Trout with lemon dill rice was one of Chef Renard's specialties and a vision of it danced in Pennywhistle's head. His wife Sammie Jo loved fishing as well and would likely be envious of today's results. The old family estate of Whistlestop had both excellent trout and salmon fishing and now that he was almost back to his former self, it was time to investigate its rehabilitation.

Before he could do that, a lot of work lay ahead. Two months ago, he would have slept all the way back to Portland

Street but tonight he felt alert and more than willing to write out his report directly, even if he had to work into the wee hours to finish it.

When he opened his townhouse door, he was surprised to find Sammie Jo waiting for him, with a grin on her face that suggested she had a surprise for him. "A package has arrived, Tom, one whose long delay has caused you some worry."

An olive-skinned man of five-foot-ten, clad in a midshipmen's uniform, stepped out from an alcove and smiled a cheerful smile that showcased large, perfectly formed teeth. "Hello, sir."

Pennywhistle blinked in astonishment. "Nico! My God, is it really you? You've grown at least two inches! And your face... it's not a boy's anymore. And your eyes are different too: you've had some seasoning. Two years have done wonders! If only your mother could see you now!"

A wistful look crossed Sammie Jo's face. Nico's mother had been her husband's first love. She wondered how well she would do as a stepmother. She had never met Nico until two hours before. Nico had considerable charm, but she would never permit him to compete with the baby Nicholas for her husband's attention.

Pennywhistle dropped all reserve; he advanced and enfolded Ruzzini in a great bear hug. "I am so glad to see you. I expected you two months ago from what you said in your letters."

"The voyage home took longer than expected. The flow of the monsoons was badly disrupted by... well, I am not sure, but it might have something to do with that volcano. Tambora."

"Your letters made it clear that you saw something extraordinary, and I am eager to discuss that with you. This calls for a drink. This is your home now. Well, at least until your next posting to a ship. Let us open a bottle of champagne and talk until our tongues grow tired and our eyelids turn to lead!"

"You have no idea how long I have waited to hear those words!" said Nico. "All that is missing to make this reunion perfect is my brother, Marko." He did not have the heart to tell Pennywhistle that he had resigned from the Navy that morning. That could wait until tomorrow.

CHAPTER 3

Raiders of the Border Arc

31ˢᵗ August 1816

Marco Ruzzini, Peter Charlton, and Kerr Nixon were Harrow schoolboys celebrating their final days of freedom with a brisk hike designed to let them forget that the start of the autumn term lay only a week away. They had spent most of their holiday roaming the Scottish estate of Charlton's father, seven miles from the English border city of Berwick-on-Tweed. That estate featured an 18-hole golf course that had been completed mere days before their arrival, and the three had become enamored of the Scots sport that incorporated so many features of the terrain: woods, water, hills, vast spaces and sheep-cropped greens.

All three boys were what the British called "enthusiasts", people who tended to get carried away by subjects on which they had fixated, but they could not have been more different physically. Ruzzini was of medium height with the swarthy complexion and coal black hair that spoke of his Mediterranean ancestry. Charlton was lean and lanky with a shock of bright red hair and a face full of freckles that proclaimed his Celtic heritage. Nixon resembled the Vikings

63

who had once raided the area: tall, blonde, strongly built, with pale skin and ice blue eyes.

The last day of August 1816 was proving to be one of the few that featured a bright sun, though a band of clouds moving in from the West threatened the sun's dominance. The temperature flirted with seventy on the Fahrenheit Scale, warm for these climes, and the beneficent atmosphere was a pleasant contrast to the cold, rainy weather which had plagued the area of late. The trio had decided against riding because the late afternoon was a fine time for exercising the strong legs of three lads who had excelled in Harrow's numerous athletic competitions. Charlton was a budding amateur botanist, so the trio stopped from time to time to pick samples of local blooms such as marigolds, dwarf cornels, and bog myrtles.

The trio had stopped at the estate of Whistlestop on the English side of the River Tweed, because they were all entranced by Sir Walter Scott's *Tales of the Border Minstrelsy,* a romantic, stirring collection of poems, ballads, and stories which constituted an extended ode to the Scottish Borders that had already gone through four editions since its publication. Whistlestop estate was open to them because it belonged to Ruzzini's stepfather, Sir Thomas Pennywhistle.

Pennywhistles had not lived on the estate since 1650, when it had been partly blown up by the forces of Oliver Cromwell during his war against the Scottish Covenanters. Most of it was habitable, if you were willing to ignore the unrepaired damage. Ruzzini supposed that his stepfather had been too occupied with the Napoleonic Wars to pay attention to the land; its management had probably been left to an agent hired by his family solicitor.

The estate had been leased to a variety of tenants over the 166 years since Cromwell had called. The current occupants were three yeoman farmers and their relatives who raised sheep and grew oats and barley. Despite its warlike past, it was currently a place of prosperity and beauty; even possessing a large rose garden that contained several varieties only recently imported from Italy.

Whistlestop's main structure sat atop one of the few bluffs in the area. The walled enclosure was surrounded by acres of hardwood forest in front of which lay something uncommon in a region cursed with marginal soil: fields of black, productive earth that were part of the river floodplain. The placid River Tweed, which flowed slowly around the base of the bluff, was famous for the salmon in its waters.

The structure itself was what the locals called a border pele: a poor man's castle. It had been built in 1370 to keep out border raiders from the north, a fortified L- shaped tower house, sixty feet high with nine-foot-thick grey-white sandstone walls. Its western face, the base part of the L, was missing a large crescent shaped chunk of masonry, courtesy of Cromwell's artillery.

The tower had five barrel-vaulted levels divided into 11 rooms, including a great hall, great chamber, quarters for armed retainers, an interior well, and a dungeon beneath the ground floor. It had arrow slits on the lower floors, though four large windows had been added to the upper stories in 1750. There were two fortified pathways on the roof, circular guard turrets called bartizans at the four corners, and a beacon that could be lit to warn neighbors of attacking brigands. A large bell next to the beacon could also be wrung to sound a warning. The roof was reached by a narrow winding stone stairway which ran anti-clockwise, or "widdershins", because left-handedness ran in the Pennywhistle family.

The ground in front of the tower was enclosed by a ruined, rectangular wall, four feet high, called a barmekin, with two long low buildings backed against its left and right sides. The grounds were entered through a single road that passed under a crenelated gatehouse that no longer had a door. Though it was a shadow of its once proud self, the pele was impressive enough that it had recently been depicted by the artist JMW Turner. The blood-red skies in his recent landscapes had reflected the oddly colored sunsets which had appeared in British skies since mid-April.

Marco Ruzzini and his friends had just entered Whistlestop's courtyard when some presentiment of danger caused him to about face. He beheld a group of horsemen rounding the bend on the estate's approach road. They were headed toward the main gate, generating a large cloud of dust as they rode. He blinked and wondered if he was experiencing a strange sort of waking dream, because the riders were heavily armed and resembled something that had not existed for three hundred years. He recognized their old-fashioned attire from the history books of which he was so fond, for it was as distinctive as the livery worn by servants of the Royal Household. But while Royal liveries inspired confidence, their garments inspired dread.

Ruzzini shook his head twice and blinked hard, but the apparitions did not vanish. His two friends were staring in a bewilderment that matched his own.

"Am I dreaming?" murmured Charlton. "Are there wraiths at Whistlestop?"

Ruzzini shook his head. "Not wraiths. Reivers."

His heart skipped a beat and sweat broke out at his hairline, but he shoved his fear into an inner dungeon so it would not forestall him from taking quick action. He himself had encountered military marauders before on the Adriatic Island of his birth, but his two friends stood frozen in stupefaction. They had never experienced anything more threatening than an angry headmaster.

Ruzzini was strong for 16 years. He grabbed his friends by their collars and hurled them into a large haymow, then scrambled in after them, whispering fiercely, "If you value your lives, be still and keep silent." Both boys' eyes widened, but they nodded in assent.

Five minutes later, thirty men on horseback trotted slowly past their hide. Ruzzini gulped as he got a good look at their faces; these were hard men, hungry for loot, completely unlike the dashing, romantic border buccaneers that Walter Scott had made the heroes of his tales.

The border people called them Reivers, from the old English word for raiders: a combination of cattle rustlers, sheep thieves, gangsters, pirates, and extortionists. Reivers had invented the term "blackmail: "mail" being the old English word for rent, it was originally protection money paid to ensure that these fast-moving marauders spared your property from a late- night visit. Those who failed to pay suffered "bereavement."

Three hundred years ago, Reivers had operated as bandit armies of up to 2,000, although the typical raiding party was only 20 to 50 men going after small, soft targets of small holdings. They knew every nook, cranny, hiding place, and ambush site in the Cheviot Hills and possessed an intimate knowledge of the deep, gnarled valleys that formed the warp and weft of the Border Country. They usually struck by night and without warning, but these riders had broken tradition and were riding openly by day; Ruzzini deduced that, for some reason, they wanted to be seen.

Ruzzini kept his eyes firmly fixed on the all too solid apparitions that paraded past him, reminding himself of something his stepfather had repeated often. "Before you take any action, conduct a thorough reconnoiter of your enemy." He wished that he had some way to warn the three shepherds on an adjacent low hill of the approaching danger, but to do so would expose himself and his three friends.

Ruzzini redirected his attention from the shepherds to the leader of the Reivers: a red-bearded, granite-faced man who looked as if his favorite pastime was skinning cats. He was dressed in the classic Reiver fashion of three centuries before, wearing a steel helmet called a combed murrion that featured a curved brim and a crescent-shaped plate that surmounted the crown to deflect sword cuts. His neck was protected by a curved steel plate called an allymagne, while his chest was shielded by a long sleeveless coat called a jack: three layers of heavy brown cloth with steel plates and bone fragments sewn in between and faced with heavy brown leather. A jack was much cheaper than chainmail yet afforded nearly as much protection while allowing more mobility. The long, stout leather boots which completed the outfit were naturally called jackboots.

The leader's weaponry consisted of a basket-hilted broadsword, a long dagger called a ballock, and a nine-foot lance whose bottom fitted into a leather aperture attached to his right stirrup. The butts of two long pistols were visible in short holsters on either side of the saddle. Ruzzini noticed that the pistols were not of the same era as their attire; they were modern flintlocks, not matchlocks. While their antique outfits and edged weapons were meant to evoke fearful memories, their modern firearms were meant to increase the efficiency of their depredations.

"Time to show these folks what happens when you don't pay up!" barked their leader. "Let's demonstrate just how good Scott's Bairns are at spoiling!" Spoiling was the word for wanton destruction.

"Damn right, Captain Elliot," bellowed one of his men, whose cruel yet supine voice marked him as the classic evil sycophant. "All the other farms have yielded to us after a simple show of force, and I, for one, am damned disappointed that we have never had a chance to show what our weapons could do! I have a sword that is thirsting for blood! People may begin to think we are just mounted actors unless we do some wholesale slaughtering. These folks have defied us three times. High time we made an example of them!"

"Aye!" yelled a third man with a face ravaged by smallpox. "A bloody first example that no one will forget! No quarter and no mercy!"

"Dear God," gasped Nixon.

"Shut up," hissed Ruzzini.

Elliot and his raiders rode shaggy black horses called hobblers, each equipped with a heavy war saddle which kept a rider firmly in his seat while allowing him the free use of both hands. Hobblers were only about three feet eight inches in height at the shoulder; Elliot atop his mount looked as if he had borrowed a child's pony. But these animals were anything but children's pets. Sometimes called Galloway Nags, these horses were famous for their agreeable temperaments, easy trainability, and incredible endurance. A hobbler had a far greater range than the average cavalry horse and could manage up to 120 miles before stopping for hay and water.

Thus equipped, Reivers had an extensive raiding range and had once been considered the finest light cavalry on the planet.

"We should make a run for it," whispered Nixon.

"Too dangerous," responded Ruzzini. "Be patient."

Reivers had traditionally come from both sides of the borders, Scots only slightly outnumbering the English, and were loyal to surnames rather than crowns: a criminal mutation of the clan system. They were opportunists who sometimes switched sides at the height of battles. Reivers had played the crowns off against each other, resulting in a lawless zone of warlords and crime bosses that had extended thirty miles on either side of the boundary that separated Scotland from England. Reivers intermarried, ensuring that there were both Scots and English representatives of powerful families like the Armstrongs, Grahams, and Kerrs.

Their dominance had ended in 1603 when James VI of Scotland became James I of England and united the two crowns. James had ruthlessly suppressed the Reivers, and by 1615 their power had been broken. Until now. Ruzzini wondered if he was witnessing a Renaissance of lawlessness. Why had an institution deservedly long dead sprung back to life?

"Remember, any jewelry or valuables you find must be turned over to a common pool once we are done and its value shared with us all," bellowed the red bearded leader. "I will personally punish any man who tries to keep such goods for himself. I don't care how badly your families are suffering, the good of our brotherhood comes first. Understood?"

His men nodded grimly in assent, knowing that their leader enforced a discipline that made the Draconian practices of Frederick the Great's Prussian Army seem like mollycoddling. "Running the gauntlet" was the favored method. A culprit, with his hands bound and his head down, walked slowly through a tunnel of his associates. He was poked with sharp sticks, beaten and kicked as he passed, and if his comrades chose to wear their jackboots, this resulted in severe injuries, or even death. The punishment increased the identity of Reivers as a group because it made disloyalty to the group seem the gravest of crimes.

The locals were under severe economic distress, and desperate times caused good souls to become dark. Ruzzini realized that men might return to the ways of the Reivers because the force of tradition suggested a way out of present difficulties to hungry men faced with shriveled crops, gaunt wives, starving children, and uncaring tax collectors.

Since April, England had endured unseasonably cold temperatures; snow had only melted in mid-May. That snow had sometimes been odd hues of orange, brown, and flesh colors that no one had ever seen. The sunsets had frequently been red, sometimes purple, and occasionally orange, colors that lingered in the clouds for up to thirty minutes after the sun had set. The painter JMW Turner had remarked that the sky often seemed to be on fire. Country folk said it was some kind of curse, while the science mandarins at the Royal Society posited that it might have something to do with an increase in sunspots. An almost continuous barrage of cold rains since late May had made 1816 a year without a summer.

The lack of sunlight and the brutally heavy rains had reduced the harvest by 75%. Most of the lost crops were grains, which were generally made into some form of bread or porridge which constituted as much as 60% of the diet in many families. A 30% reduction in the grain harvest doubled the cost of bread, while a 50% reduction quadrupled it. People could compensate by cutting down on what they and their families ate, but the effects were inevitable. A man who lost 20% of his body mass typically lost half his energy. If enough families became destitute, villages ceased to be viable, resulting in forced migrations.

A Scottish physician named Dr. Robert Ribald had published a paper on the human costs of famine that Ruzzini's stepfather had once read to him. Ruzzini had not understood much of what he had heard, but he'd caught his stepfather's indignation as he read aloud what famine looked like: "Some women stumble through the streets, their poor nursing babies sucking at teats empty of milk, then wailing until they have no breath left. The mask of approaching death is seen everywhere on the wandering poor: their thin, pinched faces, their hollow cheeks and sunken eyes, their scarecrow figures, their feeble walks, their flus and fluxes, give them a ghostly look that is constant reminder that life for the many is often short and sad. Diarrhea, dehydration, and dysentery follow closely like wolves trailing a wounded animal. As falling snow covers their bodies, their organs freeze, and their bodies stiffen like wood. First, they groan, then they cough up phlegm, and then they die."

Added to the distress caused by the weather was an upsurge in unemployment brought about by a contraction of the economy after the end of the Napoleonic Wars. Evictions had become common, and wandering bands of displaced families roamed the countryside. Beggars became as thick as flies in many cities of the realm. Hundreds of thousands of children went to bed hungry. Lord Sidmouth, the Home Secretary, had no idea what to do and brutally repressed any demonstrations of workers and laborers who protested in public about their sad lot.

In addition, thousands of veterans had returned home to find there was no work for them. Ruzzini wondered if some of the bandits in front of him were former soldiers who had helped bring down Napoleon. Veterans with skills acquired in combat were far more dangerous than desperate peasants.

"Troop one," yelled Elliot, "you take those shepherds in that near pasture. Amuse yourself with them as you see fit. Remember we are dispensers of Border Justice! We want word of our visit to get around, and for everyone to know will happen to those who do not pay up."

"And any children we find? Skewer and roast a few perhaps?" Said one rider.

Ruzzini gasped as he realized the man was not speaking figuratively.

"There must be a score around here, and women, too," interjected a rider whose eyes glowed with a malicious look that suggested he was not in today's raid for the money.

"Make their deaths quick," responded Elliot matter-of-factly. "But for God's sake be careful with the sheep. Merino wool is fetching a high price these days and we don't want to lose a single head. Spare the most terrified person, because we need a shocked survivor to spread the word of our actions."

He pivoted his horse and addressed the other half of his men. "Troop two, take the tower. Search it thoroughly for cash and coin. There will probably be silverware and jewelry. These yeomen are thrifty types who conceal their wealth, so don't forget to rap the walls and listen for hollow spaces. Troop Three and I will conduct a general reconnoiter of the far pastures. My informants tell me the people here raise only sheep and not cattle, but they could be wrong."

"And the women, Captain Elliot?" said a man whose lust rippled through his voice.

"Ravish any wenches you find before you dispatch them. We can't take them with us lest they slow our pace. Their screams will be the memory the sole survivor will take with him. The oats have already been harvested and sold, but the barley is ripe for burning. And don't forget the hayricks."

"But, but, but," stammered one Reiver, "if we burn their crops, how will these people eat and how will they have money to pay us in the future?"

Elliot glared at him. "Angus Heatherington, we need a stout heart, not a faint heart. We have come to set an example that will not be forgotten. Scorched earth may lose us a few pounds here, but it will ensure that neighboring estates pay up, promptly and in full."

The expression on Heatherington's face told Ruzzini that the man thought Elliot's decision stupid, cruel and short-sighted. He nevertheless replied obediently, "Understood, Captain."

"Sick! Monstrous!" whispered Charlton, angry at the appalling implications of the leader's words. He sprang up from his hide, poised to deliver a warning. Moving with the speed and energy of a greyhound, he made a dash for the heavy oak front door of the tower. Though the distance from the haymow to the door was only a hundred yards, he was spotted immediately.

"We have our first target of the day, gentlemen!" roared Elliot.

"I've got him," shouted a man wearing a green hat called a tam o'shanter, a cross between a felt beret and a bonnet that had a steel skullcap underneath. Shooting the man would be a waste of a bullet; besides, it required none of the skill with edged weapons that Reivers of old had prided themselves upon. Wanting to impress his comrades, he lowered his lance and put the spurs to his mount. "Go, Leander!" he yelled in his horse's ear. His shaggy mount broke into a gallop and quickly closed the distance.

Charlton was five yards from the wide-open tower door when the spear pierced the lad's left shoulder. By sheer luck, he had stumbled on a rock just before the lance struck home, and so it missed his heart. Tam o'shanter snarled as he withdrew the lance, preparatory to delivering a second stroke.

Charlton hit the ground hard; badly hurt but very much alive. He rolled on his back and saw the raised lance poised to end his life. With the catlike reflexes of youth, he threw his body to the right and the lance missed him by an inch. He scrambled to his feet and backpedaled toward the door so that he could keep his attacker in sight. He shouted as loudly as he could, "Fire, fire, fire!" as that exclamation was the likeliest to attract attention.

His opponent thrust at him again, but Charlton dodged at the last second. The rider then swung the heavy shaft of his lance at Charlton's head, but the boy reared backward out the reach.

"I'll no' be bested by a wee bairn!" The rider's frustration was so great that it caused him to do something stupid. He stowed his lance, dismounted, and drew his heavy broadsword. He wanted to look the lad directly in the eye as shoved his blade through the whelp's beating heart. He advanced swiftly, but the interval of transition from a mounted warrior to a footed one had bought his quarry sufficient time to reach the doorway.

A tall, gaunt woman, her iron-grey hair bound in a tight bun, appeared in the doorway, drawn by the urgency of Charlton's shouts. She was perhaps fifty years of age, with a lined face that showed the sternness of a Spanish hidalgo. Since most of the people in the tower were engaged in candle-making today, the danger of fire was a real one.

She saw no fire but did spy the raiders, the wounded boy, and Tam o'shanter's right arm cocked to deliver the death stroke. She reacted with Border instincts. In blur of motion, she grabbed Charlton by the back of his coat and yanked him inside the doorway. When Tam o'shanter's blade arrived at the point where it should have cleft Charlton's chest, it met empty air.

Before he could manage a second blow, the woman swung an iron grate called a yett sideways on its hinges and drove the locking bolt home. Yett's were variants of portcullises and were common backup defenses to the stout doors of border peles. Their metal latticework was nearly impenetrable once the grate was locked.

"You bitch!" roared Tam o'shanter. "You think you've won? You've only bought a mite o' time. You and everyone inside are dead once me and my mates have done a little scumfishing." Scumfishing was the practice of starting a large fire on a doorstep and using the clouds of smoke to choke out the inhabitants of a fortified tower.

"We'll see about that, you mangy old dobber!" With that insult, the matron disappeared, dragging Charlton behind her.

Tam o'shanter bellowed curses, then mounted up and galloped toward his mates, vowing to return with fire and destruction. The old hag and the boy would pay for their impudence!

The woman hauled Charlton into a bedroom that had once been the tower's armory. She laid him gently on the mattress and assessed the boy's wound as life threatening but not fatal if he got good care. "My name is Maude Dacre. Tell me who you are and what is happening. Be quick about it, those brigands will be back in short order." She summoned her two daughters May and Minnie, both close to Charlton's age, and set them to cleaning and dressing the wound as he talked.

Charlton's pain was evident in the way he choked out his words, but he gave her a concise precis of the situation, just as he had learned in school. Harrow educated boys to be officers, and the swift communication of pertinent, tactical information was an essential skill.

"We must act immediately!" she exclaimed when he had finished. "The only way to warn the men in the fields is to light the warning beacon and ring the bell. I thank God that we have followed tradition and always kept them ready." She turned to May. "Round up everyone in the house and assemble them on the fourth floor. We've ten people, five muskets, plenty of shot powder, and lead bars. We have tubs of hot wax and a furnace. We will damn well make those jobbies pay for trespassing. No Reiver is setting foot inside this house while I still draw breath!" With that, Maude ran out of the room and began speeding up the narrow, twisting stone staircase that five floors later would bring her to the roof.

Charlton thought she moved astonishingly fast, age apparently no barrier to the quickening of survival instincts that were inbred from a heritage of Border violence. Madam

Dacre seemed a tough old bird, and Charlton rejoiced that the raiders were in for a nasty surprise. His wound was painful, but he could still move. Rather than being a bedridden observer, he wanted to be an active participant in the home's defense. He raised himself on his good elbow and inquired of May, "Can you find me a spare musket?"

The men of the three households that lived within the castle were tending the sheep on a hillside pasture and did not apprehend any danger, nor did their three sons who were assisting their fathers. The animals were more perceptive than their shepherds. Several sheep suddenly started *baa baa*-ing in agitation. One of the boys turned around and saw what his flock saw. He cried out in alarm, just as his father Matthew, Maude Dacre's husband, shouted and pointed skyward. "Look, the beacon!"

After she fired up the beacon, Maude began frantically ringing the large bell next to it. Its peals sounded loud and clear and alerted the two boys roaming the barley fields, making some final checks before the grain was harvested. From sixty feet up, Maude had an encompassing view and stayed where she was to observe the effect of her warning.

Alerted by the bell, Brewmaster Allen Maitland stepped outside of the brewhouse. He was appalled to see a line of charging horsemen headed toward the men and boys in the pasture, and two riders armed with torches who had aimed their mounts toward the barley fields. He had no idea who the men were, but their actions made it clear they were hellbent on murder and rapine.

Maitland had been hired two years ago to turn some of the estate's barley into single malt whiskey. The tenants had erected a limestone brewhouse for him, and he was proud that it had been built to last, reflecting their confidence in his efforts over the long term. Maitland's distillations were ready for the market, and he had already arranged with shippers for transport to key cities and towns of the area.

It occurred to him that if there was anything that a Scotsman liked more than coin or a roll in the hay, it was a wee dram of whiskey. The word itself had originally meant "elixir of life." The thrifty, or stingy, Scot became something else when proffered whiskey. Maitland had a hundred barrels of the stuff stored in a cellar twenty yards from the brewhouse. Its entrance would be easy to miss unless you knew where to look.

He trundled toward the test barrel that he had brought up for inspection and sampling, turned it on its side, and began rolling it out of the brewhouse with all his strength. As he pushed the barrel outside, a rider galloped toward him with lance extended. "Wait, wait," Maitland shouted frantically as he waved his arms. "I have whiskey! Lots and lots of whiskey! Enough to keep you happy for a dozen lifetimes. Kill me, and all you will get is this one barrel!" He turned the lever atop a bunghole and let the rider see some of the golden liquid draining out. The rider stopped abruptly and so did four of his friends.

The rest of his companions kept about their deadly business.

Matthew Dacre shouted to all within earshot," Run! Run! Make for the forest!" Four men and boys burst into a fast run, closely pursued by brigands eager to test their skills with lances and inclined to play with their targets as cats did with mice, toying with them before killing them. Dacre's son, John, did not run but stood closely by his side.

"What about Ma?" urged John. "Shouldn't we see to her?"

"She can handle herself! Now run!"

A second later, Dacre died as a lance penetrated his heart from the back. His son cried out, but his exclamation was cut short as a lance protruded through his mouth.

The other riders concentrated on the running men and left the boys alone for the time being. Three horsemen took turns jabbing and cutting at Alan Brown, the oldest of the trio of yeoman who leased the estate. They lanced him in the shoulders, chest, and groin, and enjoyed watching him bleed, stumble, and scream. They inflicted a dozen wounds before he went down.

Alan's fellow yeoman, Daniel Johnstone, suffered six painful gouges from three other Reivers, but their strikes dealt no fatal blow, though they caused plenty of bleeding. The Reivers were not being merciful; they had deliberately chosen Johnstone as the designated survivor.

The boys, William and Steven, saw the horror but knew they could do nothing to help. Both sped for the forest, several hundred yards' distant. One rider who had yet to hurt anyone pursued them and soon caught up with William. But just as the Reiver was about to plant his lance in William's back, Steven picked up a rock. Blessed with a strong arm and a keen eye, he hurled the stone and caught the rider squarely on the nose, breaking it and stunning him. The two boys gained the safety of the forest and threw themselves beneath a rock outcrop that made them well-nigh invisible.

Once the shepherds were gone, the Reivers turned loose the pack of Rough Collies they had brought with them, to round up the sheep.

The two teenagers in the hilly field of barley, Harvey Ross and Ronald Peters, flattened themselves as two horsemen with torches approached, and prayed that the four-foot-high stalks of grain would hide them. A slowly rising wind caused the grain to ripple, giving them hope that their movements might be concealed as they inched towards a hidden depression several yards away. That depression was five feet across and boggy, there was a chance it might act as a firebreak. The brigands made no attempt to search the field; anyone sheltering within would be incinerated once they ignited the barley.

The two horsemen lowered their torches, and the fields began to burn.

The boys wiggled the last yard into the declivity and began covering themselves with the thick mud that they hoped would serve as armor against the flames. The depression did indeed act as a firebreak, but as the fire spread and its heat and power increased, they would be surrounded by deadly, choking flames.

"All that labour for nothing, ha, ha, ha!" chortled one Reiver.

"No point in being a farmer, what with all this bad weather, ha, ha, ha!" laughed his mate. "It's dull watching a field burn. Let's see if we can find some wenches!" With that, the two riders departed.

The boys had no way of knowing the Reivers had gone and so endured a full five minutes of fire crackling around them before they grew desperate enough to rise and run. They raced down the hill toward the forest, surprised that there was no pursuit. Once they had found cover, they cried as they watched the crop that they had nursed carefully go up in smoke.

Hungry times lay ahead. Even so, they knew they had been lucky that their Guardian Angels had been willing to pull extra duty today.

Tam o'shanter and his reinforcements approached the tower house slowly, each carrying bundles of wood and slabs of peat with which to build a smoking fire. The fourteen men were fifty yards in front of the house when Maude fired from a fourth-floor window. The ball penetrated the forehead of Tam o'shanter, an eighth of an inch below the protection of his steel cap. He grunted in painful surprise before sliding off his horse. A second shot rang out a moment later, fired by Maude's daughter Minnie. She had her mother's fire and her father's determination; the ball from her musket tore a large gap in the shoulder of a scarecrow-like Reiver, who toppled backward then began rolling about as he mewled in pain.

"God damn it," shouted one of Tam o'shanter's mates. "Those bampots in the tower will pay for that!"

The remaining dozen quickened their pace toward the tower's entrance. Two more shots rang out; one missed entirely, but the second inflicted a painful flesh wound.

Undeterred and angry, the Reivers laid their bundles on the doorstep, covering the entrance with five layers of trouble. Peat strips formed the bottom layer, topped by bundles of new wood, green and damp. The third layer was peat strips, topped with older, dryer wood plundered from a small storehouse. A band of the oldest wood formed the fourth layer; it would burn hot and set all the pile a-smoldering. The whole was crowned with peat strips that would generate thick smoke in short order. This was a formula perfected in Medieval times, and it would work just as well today. As an additional accelerant, Reivers thrust bricks of charcoal into the various layers, then applied their torches. A thick smell arose, and tendrils of smoke grew to billowing smoke.

"It's just a matter of time," snickered one Reiver. "We just stand back and wait. We can skewer them one at a time when they come out of the door and—" His mouth stopped as an old rapier shot through the latticework of the yett, propelled by the arms of a ten-year-old boy and his twelve-year-old sister who stood behind him, all four hands guiding the point. Unlike the rest of his mates, this Reiver wore no allymagne, and his neck was bare. By pure luck, the blade pierced his jugular vein, and blood began spurting. The man clapped frantically at the wound in a vain effort to stop the bleeding.

One of his mates drew his pistol and fired at the children, but the ball glanced off the heavy metal grate and rebounded. Rather than being frightened, the children taunted the men. "Come and get us if you can! You're only cowards dressed up in costumes. Go back to whatever rubbish heap you came from!"

The taunts had an effect. Two more men drew their pistols but before they could pull the triggers the children were gone. The men cursed and vowed vengeance.

Maude saw their disorganization and decided the moment was ripe for her first secret weapon, even as she had two women readied her second. She and another woman dragged a large tub of molten wax to the edge of the window, then dumped it on the Reivers below.

Three Reivers howled in pain and surprise as the waxy rain poured down upon their heads and shoulders. They tried to scrape off the globs of hot wax, but the wax was sticky and resisted their efforts. They began rolling in the gravel in front of the doorstep, hoping that the small stones would scrape off the burning blots. Their efforts instead resulted in gravel becoming enmeshed in the wax, which increased their pain. For the next few minutes, they became targets, not combatants.

Maude and two girls began sniping at the rolling men, although the steep angle from which they fired made their musketry more of a nuisance than a threat. Beside them, Charlton steeled himself to fire a shot, but he was so weak that he passed out after his weapon had discharged. More effective than bullets were rocks. The ruined west face had piles of rubble left over from Cromwell's visit and the stone slabs were both small enough for women and children to lift and big enough to cause real damage when dropped from a height. The rain of rocks broke bones, and two Reivers suffered injuries bad enough that they could no longer rise without assistance from their companions.

By the time the injured Reivers had gained their feet, Maude's third weapon was ready. Because of the tower's height it also doubled as a shot tower. Lead bars were heated in a furnace, then poured through a copper sieve in their molten state. Tension and gravity passed the lead into molds that formed balls. The balls cooled as they dropped from the tower and landed in a pool of water. Maude bypassed most of the process and simply turned the ten pounds of lead bars into enough grey lava to fill five buckets. She and her assistants dumped the contents with angry vigor.

The contents of the buckets burned off the faces of three Reivers and set their clothes ablaze. The mad jerking, jinking, and flailing of their death throes made them resemble fiery scarecrows bewitched by some pagan cult.

"Let's get out of here," screamed one Reiver.

"Damn right," shouted the only other Reiver still on his feet.

"We will come back when the fire has done its work."

The men rose slowly and stumbled out of range of the rocks. As they did so, their backs presented an inviting target for musketry. Maude and two women fired at the same time, and while two bullets missed, Maudes' shot penetrated one Reiver's back between the shoulder blades. He collapsed and lay unmoving.

The lone Reiver quickened his pace, jumped aboard his waiting horse, and moved to a safe distance, which he judged to be one hundred and fifty yards. He needed help and they would soon have it. The revenge he conceived was horrific and reeked of sadism.

The two Reivers who had torched the barley field had spotted a target. Not a woman, but a girl, her youthful face marked her as barely of child-bearing age, but she was already full-figured. Joan Johnstone was fifteen years old, a cheerful, freckled redhead who had been salmon fishing in the Tweed. She was running up the hill toward the tower, having heard the alarm bell. Her ten-year-old brother, James, trundled behind her, refusing to leave behind his bucket filled with a pair of salmon.

The two Reivers galloped down on the pair so fast, and inflicted a shock so great, that the girl and boy saw them as wraiths from a dream rather than men. Neither the boy nor girl grasped what was about to happen.

A swift stroke of the first Reiver's broadsword sent the boy's head tumbling from his shoulders. Before his sister's consciousness had a chance to embrace the horror, the second Reiver had halted his horse, leaped from the saddle, and thrown his fourteen stone weight down upon her. The impact knocked the wind out of her, so she was not able to scream. He slapped her hard several times, nearly reducing her to unconsciousness because he liked a helpless victim. He ripped the clothes from her body, briefly ran his hands over her mounds and curves, and then inserted himself with no thought of foreplay or finesse. The act was over in under five minutes. The girl moaned in confusion and pain.

"Don't hog all the fun for yourself, Carter, let me have my turn," laughed the second Reiver.

"She's all yours, friend."

The second Reiver dismounted and dropped his trousers while the first one smiled as he checked the boy's bucket. He and his friend would have a very fine fish dinner tonight.

The second Reiver's assault was over even faster than the first ones. By its end, the girl had mercifully passed out. He was about to run his broadsword through her throat, when the first Reiver grabbed his arm. "Wait: this one reminds me just a bit of my sister." Thinking of the salmon in his bucket, he continued, "the little fish we can throw back."

A second woman, Marion Simmons, who was Maude's cousin, was just returning from walking the tower's pet Irish Wolfhound, Seamus. The Reiver rapists spotted her after mounting up and decided they were game for a second bout. They galloped toward her with lust and madness in their eyes. She turned and fled.

Seamus charged. He was a massive grey beast of 120 pounds who moved with preternatural speed. He jumped up and clamped his teeth into Reiver one's boot and yanked. The force of his bite jerked the Reiver from his saddle and pulled him to the ground. Seamus clamped his jaws on the gap between the base of the Reiver's jack and the top of his boots and shook the man with the force of an angry tornado. The Reiver howled in pain. He tugged frantically at the canine's jaws, but the dog's vice-grip proved unbreakable. Seamus's teeth clawed into the femoral artery and the Reiver began to bleed out.

His mate stabbed down with his lance, and three strokes ended the dog's life, but it was too late. He dismounted and held his friend's hand as he passed. "May all dogs fry in hell," he muttered.

Two hundred yards behind Marion, a veteran beggar took shelter, wondering what unexpected hell he had just wandered into. For a few moments, he thought that he had stumbled back in time to Salamanca, but the buggers on horseback did not look anything like Napoleon's cuirassiers. Toby Scoggins was tired and hungry from hours of trudging along back country roads. He needed a place to shelter for the night and had heard that Whistlestop was kind to beggars if they were veterans. His ragged green jacket proclaimed him a former member in the 95th Rifles, and a white stripe on his right sleeve showed he had once been a Chosen Man, a designation of merit and honor. He was ashamed of how far unemployment and drink had caused him to fall, but he still had enough self-respect to have kept his Baker Rifle in good working order.

Though he had no idea of what all the fighting was about, he saw Marion's distress and Seamus's death. The old instincts to protect sprang to life. It was an easy shot for an old hand like Scoggins and his ball neatly clipped off the top of the rapist's head.

He rushed toward the fleeing girl. When he caught up with her, she recoiled in fear. "Don't be afraid, Miss. I will protect you," he said in a soothing voice. "I'm Toby, Toby Scoggins. On my honor, I will not let any harm come to you. I wish I could have saved your dog. I love dogs."

Marion saw the kindness in his face and the gentleness in his manner. She needed a protector and instinctively decided to trust him. "I'm Marion, Marion Simmons. You look like you could use some food. Protect me and I will make sure you get all you can eat. Is that a fair bargain?"

"Done!" said Scoggins, noting that the girl was now speaking with confidence and composure. She was a levelheaded survivor, just like himself. He wished to know her better, not in a biblical sense, but through a formal courtship, as crazily unlikely as that seemed possible. He wished she could have met him in his prime. In a flash of insight, he realized a woman like this just might be the one thing to help him recover the best version of himself.

Marion nodded her head. "Follow me. I know a place where we can shelter."

"My fate is in your hands," he responded with ironic gallantry.

Maitland at the same time was handing a third cup of whiskey to the Reiver who had been so keen on killing him a few minutes before. Maitland noticed the whiskey appeared to dull the man's violent inclinations. He was smiling as he drank, and Maitland thought a little conversation might cause him to see Maitland as human rather than just as a walking clod of flesh waiting to receive the business end of a lance. "What's your name? Mine is Alan Maitland."

"Heatherington, Angus Heatherington."

"Where from?"

"The Debatable Land." That area was a strip of turf 5 by 12 miles just north of Carlisle that for centuries had been a sort of "no man's land" between England and Scotland.

"How did you come to be part of this lot? You don't look like a man given to brutality," said Maitland with a sincerity that was both cunning and persuasive.

The Reiver's expression reflected surprise that a potential victim wanted to hear his story, then transitioned to a thoughtful cast, as he considered how best to tell a tale that no one else had wanted to hear.

"I was a farmer years ago, but my wife and child died from the bloody flux, and my farm was foreclosed after a bad harvest, seized by a bastard. The man who owns this estate is no doubt one of the same: a conceited London swell who cares only for profits. An Army recruiting party found me, and I fought for England in Spain for five years. When I returned, I lurched from job to job, each one worse than the last and for less pay. I was considering self-slaughter when I was approached to join Scott's Bairns. At the time it seemed a heaven-sent chance at a new life. But now..." he hesitated and his voice roughened, "I am not so sure." The light in his eyes hardened. "I do this because every man I kill wears the face of the landlord who stole my farm."

Heatherington stared into the distance as he gulped his whiskey. "I think of my wife every day. In my dreams she weeps."

His drunken musings were interrupted by eight of his mates who came trotting up, prodding two hostages with their lance tips. They had been informed of the problems at the main house and thought that the torture of hostages might compel the inhabitants to surrender. Two more Reivers had remained in the main pasture, following the expedition's Rough Collies as they herded fleeing sheep.

"You always did have a keen nose for sniffing out the good stuff, Angus," jeered the leader of this group. "Don't think of drinking it all yourself. All this killing has made us thirsty!" Two of his mates held up lances bearing severed heads. They had belonged to workmen who were part of a crew that had been building a canal on the estate designed to shorten the distance from Whistlestop to Berwick.

"Happy to share, Hamish," replied Heatherington in a slurred voice. The sight of severed heads sickened him, but he could not let his mates know of his revulsion.

Maitland saw an opportunity and addressed their leader, a stout man whose jack was a curious shade of blue. "Hamish, if that's your name, man, there is more whiskey where this barrel came from. But it's hidden! I can show you the stash, but I demand your solemn pledge to spare my life if I provide that information." A man's promise was considered sacred on the Scots Borders. Being labeled an oath breaker was worse than cheating at cards or discharging your pistol in a duel before the signal to fire had been given.

The man in blue regarded Maitland closely and eyed the brewmaster's apron. Having one fewer corpse seemed a small price to pay for free-flowing whiskey. "Consider that pledge given. Now lead us to the whiskey."

Maitland did as he was ordered, leading the men to a large cellar whose twin doors were concealed by a large turf-colored tarpaulin. Maitland lit the two torches at the entrance to the cellar, then led the way down the stairs to the rows and rows of barrels. A single Reiver remained above to mind the horses and guard the hostages.

"I have died and gone to Heaven," marveled the man in blue. His mates nodded in assent.

"Now sir," said Maitland. "I have kept my part of the bargain and trust you will keep yours by allowing me to depart."

"We honor our word. Go."

When Maitland reached the top of the stairs his first thought was to get off the estate as fast as possible. Then he realized riding was a much faster way to do so than walking. He looked at the forlorn faces of the two hostages and felt a great wave of sadness because he knew them well. Giles Thornton and his son were everything that was good in English yeomanry. Maitland was no hero, but an insane thought suddenly possessed his mind, and for the next few moments he became a version of himself that he never imagined could exist.

The single Reiver standing guard had his back to the entrance. Maitland had a blackthorn stirring stick attached to a hook on his apron, a standard part of a brewmaster's equipment. It was nearly as long and thick as an Irish shillelagh. He quietly stepped toward the unsuspecting Reiver and struck him hard on the back of the neck. The Reiver went down without a sound.

Maitland untied the two hostages. "Mount up and follow me. You know the path through the forest that leads to Berwick? Let's take it and be gone. We must get word to the authorities!"

The Thorntons heeded his words and quickly mounted up. Maitland thought about trying to stampede the other horses but doubted he could succeed, since their agreeable natures probably rendered them immune to blind panic.

The three men kicked their horses to the gallop and were about to disappear into the forest when the alarm was raised.

"Damn it!" shouted Elliot, spying the three fugitives. He and his group were trotting back from finishing off the remainder of the canal workmen and smashing up the partly built canal with axes. "What bloody fool let those men get away?" He railed to the five men on horseback next to him. His five men looked ready to put the spurs to their mounts, but he barked, "No, let them go! We need to focus on the keep. That is where the money is!"

As if to mirror Elliot's dark mood, ominous thunderheads came rolling in, blotting out the sun and turning the sky a murky grey. The wind turned strong.

Ruzzini and Nixon peeked cautiously out of the haymow and retched at the sight of severed heads that several Reivers paraded on lances. They feared for the safety of Charlton, but realized they could do nothing to change his fate. The Reivers all seemed occupied and Ruzzini whispered to Nixon, "I think that we can make a run for it. We must find Charlton's father so he can mount a rescue effort. When my stepfather hears of this outrage, I guarantee you he will make sure these outlaws are brought to justice." Ruzzini clasped his friend's hand hard in reassurance, then together the two crawled toward the main gate, then crouched behind an old cart. When the coast was clear, they sprinted to the summit of the hill behind Whistlestop, charting a course for the Charlton estate that was eight miles away. They broke into a downhill run and ran faster than either of them had ever run before. Danger was a sharp spur.

Maude Dacre and her friends had tried to put out the wood and peat fire but had only partly succeeded. Water from the small well within the tower had to be brought up bucket by bucket; each discharge of water retarded the fire only a little because such fires require a torrent of water to be extinguished. The clouds of smoke were making breathing within the tower difficult.

Elliot and his companions angrily galloped up to the whiskey drinking Reivers. He gave them a tongue lashing that drove off the haze that had begun to engulf them and restored them to their senses. He singled out Tristram Douglas, the most abstemious of his men who only drank to excess once a month. "Douglas, go down into that cellar, smash open a few barrels, and set the liquid ablaze. Since we have no way to get those barrels to market, we will make sure the folks here never do."

"Aye, aye, Captain," Douglas responded.

Elliot's men groaned at the sacrilege of destroying perfectly good whiskey.

At that moment another Reiver trotted up, pushing a teenaged boy in front of him. "I think this lad may be just what is needed right now in the way of a demonstration," the man said confidently.

"Just the thing!" responded Elliot. He turned to his riders. "Time to reclaim your honor. Take those piles of firewood over yonder and add them to the blaze at the tower door. Johnson and I will ply our skill with lances on the boy. I doubt it will be long before those in the tower beg us to stop."

The Reivers did as they were ordered. Maude and her friends fired at them as they advanced toward the tower, but the Reivers were wise to her game and zigzagged as they went about their business, and none of the shots went home.

Flames poured forth from the whiskey cellar as the alcohol inside ignited, eliciting a collective sigh from the Reivers that almost sounded like a chant of mourning.

As the clouds of smoke swelled, Elliot and his companion brought the captive boy into the castle courtyard and bound him to a tall birch shaft that they drove into the ground. He looked to be about 14, with the beanpole figure of a fast-growing adolescent. Elliot called up to the women that he could see anxiously peering from the fourth-floor window. "I make no promises, but I might be persuaded to spare your lives and that of the boy's, if you come out and give me a full account of all money and valuables that reside within. Resist and I give you my promise that you will die slowly — and badly."

Elliot rode slowly past the boy, jabbing his shoulder with the point of his lance and inflicting a bloody wound designed to cause pain, not kill. The lad screamed. Elliot's companion followed and pricked the boy in his chest, careful to make the wound shallow enough so as not to touch the heart. The boy flinched and screamed again, choking as he tried not to.

"Please, Maude, please," pleaded Mary Loxley, the boy's mother. "We must save Josh! The smoke is getting worse, and we have no chance anyway. Let's give that Reiver what he wants!" She burst into tears.

"Not on your life!" Maude's voice was edged with grief, but firm as a general's in the thick of battle. "Once out in the open that blackguard will rape us all, then murder us and never lose a second of sleep. We must hold on. If it is a choice between your son and all of us in the tower, he is the sacrifice, just like our lord and saviour. Think, Mary. Josh is a loving son who has a good and brave heart. Would he ask you to endanger your life, the lives of all of us, to save his own?"

"No," quivered Mary with anguish in her voice." No, he would not."

Hearing no response from the tower, Elliot and his companion again made runs at the helpless boy. Elliot wounded him in the right leg whilst his companion inflicted an identical injury to the left leg. Josh no longer screamed but moaned, "Mama, mama, mama."

The piteous pleas excited the worst elements of Elliot's sadistic nature, and so he made a third charge at Josh, striking at his groin. This time the pain was so great the boy did not scream but passed out, sagging against the ropes that bound him.

A pair of Reivers had used the torture time to make a game out of skewering the goats and chickens which roamed freely in the courtyard. It was a poor parody of a medieval hunt but provided momentary amusement to men who had not yet had their fill of killing. They left the bodies of the goats to rot but gathered up the chickens for a late-night supper because poultry was preferred over everything except beef. Then they set fire to a shed containing plows and farm implements. They completed their spree by torching the rose and kitchen gardens. The smell of scorched roses made the scent of an obscene act oddly pleasant.

The clouds of smoke grew thicker inside the tower, becoming bad enough so that vision was limited to only a few feet. Several women began to cough, one child retched, and a newborn began to cry in her cradle. Maude was not a religious woman, but she prayed for a miracle.

A bolt of sheet lightning blasted out of the sky, looking like a giant artery of light with five veins of electricity radiating from its sides. The first vein struck Elliot's companion in the chest and turned his jack into smoking ruin. He flew from his saddle as his horse raced off. Two other veins caused the usually docile hobblers to rear and whinny, while a fourth created a spectacular light show, illuminating the fear and confusion on the Reiver's faces. The fifth homed in on the steel in a Reiver's sword and electrocuted the man who had raised it.

The thunderheads that had quietly moved in turned suddenly from threatening messengers to executioners of Nature's wrath. Torrents of rain descended from the cumulonimbus clouds, accompanied by gale force winds. The rain came in heavy sheets, like horse blankets of moisture, soaking everyone and everything in their path. Visibility became limited to arm's length. But most importantly, the pounding rain drowned the blaze at the tower door, while the cold winds that gusted through the castle's windows dispersed the smoke within. Storms such as this had been striking since late May, causing flash flooding and disrupting the lives of ordinary folk. But today the menace saved them.

The fire in the whiskey cellar was also extinguished by a veritable river of rainwater that cascaded musically down the cellar steps, leaving a quarter of the barrels intact. The deep soaking rain put out the fire in the barley field as well, saving some of the crop.

Queen Nature and Dame Fortune are sisters who delight in countermanding the orders of men, thought Heatherington. The ancient truth that he had heard from a story-telling bard in his youth made him realize that what he had been doing today ran counter to the order of The Great Chain of Being. He fancied for a moment he heard his wife weeping and calling to him in the sound of the falling rain.

Two chickens who had escaped the slaughter in the courtyard cackled madly. The three barn cats mewled loudly beneath a small hayrick that the raiders had neglected to torch. Sheep by the hundreds stampeded, and even the Rough Collies who herded them sought shelter. But the dogs would recover quickly, and the sheep would not get far.

The Reivers' hobblers desperately wanted to run as well, and this forced their riders to abandon their present position and take shelter in the dilapidated low stone structure that had been the castle's stables before Cromwell's depredations. The slate roof leaked badly but was resistant to lightning and protected them from the worst of the storm.

Elliot knew he could prevail against men, but not the weather. He waited until the lightning strikes ceased and the storm transitioned to a deep soaking rain, then gathered his bedraggled and dispirited men. "Time to go home, boyos. It's not the result we wanted, but we spread more than a little terror and can still take home the sheep as a prize." His men muttered in assent but the slump of their shoulders and the lack of fire in their eyes let Elliot know that they did not reckon that the gain was worth the losses.

Claire Johnstone, Joan's older sister, was reckoned a tomboy. She was blunt and direct in her manner, and more comfortable with a musket than a sewing needle. She had seen her sister's rape but had too far away to intervened, and she knew that if she had tried she would have been used just as hard. She had taken refuge in a small barn that contained a dozen bales of hay and lay just beyond the barmekin, a structure too unimportant to warrant the raider's attention. She felt a great rage rising at what had happened to her sister and her eyes filled with hate. Those blazing coals caught sight of two items in a corner that should not have been there. One was a hunter's kit, probably thrown there in anger by the teenage Robert Bobkin, who was being trained as a hunter but was doing poorly. The other was a partly rusted, highly unusual weapon. Her grandfather had brought it home from his naval service, along with the partial loss of his sanity, and had boasted of his exploits with it against the French. Owing to his mental troubles, he could never remember what he had done with it. She had even wondered if the weapon was a figment of his imagination. Until now.

She picked up the heavy weapon and examined it carefully, reading the name "Nock" engraved on the lock plate. It was a seven-barreled volley gun, one of only six hundred made. It had been designed to repel borders; one charge ignited all seven barrels at once. This was a fine idea, but the terrible recoil had a nasty habit of dislocating shoulders. She fully expected it to be rusted and useless; to her surprise, it had been maintained. Had Robert planned to use it, or had one of the hunters decided to keep it ready in case of dire need? She blessed the forethought of whoever had found the gun, oiled and cleaned it.

In an instant, her mind made a connection between the gun and the hunter's kit, and then she thought of the hay bales. She moved to the barn door and peered through a crack. The raiders were leaving. The driving rain made them look like ghosts. Their path was taking them across her line of sight, and soon they would only be a mere twenty yards away. She knew she should do nothing. Then she saw Seamus's face in her mind's eye and the thought of revenge overpowered common sense.

She found plenty of balls and shot in the hunter's kit, which was designed to keep damp out and away from the precious contents, as well as several spare flints. The balls were small enough to fit the strange weapon's barrels, but she had no idea how much powder each chamber required. She made a guess and hoped she was right. The flintlock action seemed functional. She inserted a flint, then put the weapon down and lugged two bales of hay toward the barn door. Once she had them in position, she balanced the barrel of the weapon on one and lined the second up behind its butt, to absorb the recoil. She took a deep breath, said a silent prayer, and slowly opened the barn door.

The dispirited riders had their heads bowed to the pelting rain.

She threw herself on her belly, far enough away from the gun to be safe from the recoil. The barrels of the gun were at an angle to catch the intersection between saddles and riders' rumps. She waited until all but the rearmost Reivers had passed, then reached out with her arm and pulled the trigger.

The weapon boomed, but its report was drowned out by a burst of thunder from a laggard bolt of lightning striking the forest nearby. The discharge killed two riders and badly wounded a third. All the riders had been looking ahead, not sideways; none of them had seen the muzzles flash. They had no idea what had struck down their comrades. They milled about in confusion and fear as Claire quietly shut the door and said a second prayer.

Elliot brought his horse around, cursing. His attention had been elsewhere. Now he had a mystery on his hands, and if he did not calm things quickly, he might be facing either a mutiny or a full-blown desertion.

A few seconds later, Scoggins added to the confusion. The Reivers were disorganized, and he had time for a shot of his own. He aligned the Baker's sights and squeezed the trigger.

His round wounded a Reiver in the shoulder. He swayed in his saddle and dropped his lance that held a severed head. He shook his head as if trying to recover from a boxer's punch, then touched his wound. Apparently, the verdict of his fingers was damning. He slowly tumbled from the saddle.

"Good shooting, Toby."

"You inspired me, Marion." Scoggins was pleased that danger, plus a shared cache of cherries and small apples gleaned from the thin harvest, had brought them closer than months of formal courtship. Being on a first name basis was something reserved for couples who were formally engaged. Scoggins was not a superstitious man, but he was starting to think that something more than mere coincidence had brought this woman into his life. For the first time in a year, the onset of evening brought no craving for a stiff shot of rotgut whiskey.

Elliot yelled and stormed, threatened and bullied. He rode up to individual riders, looking them in the eyes as he flourished a pistol and warned of the dire penalties for disobedience. He threatened violence against the families of those who did not respond. Such was his fearsome reputation that he finally succeeded in restoring order, but the process took time.

Elliot got his reluctantly reformed men to round up his Collies and the sheep they herded. As his band departed slowly in the pouring rain, he worried about what he would tell his overlord, who was a harsh and unforgiving taskmaster. He had not been able to despoil the tower of cash and coin, and the unexpected resistance had cost the lives of men, some of them veterans with skills who could not easily be replaced. Elliot would have a lot of explaining to do and he hoped his glib tongue would be equal to the task.

He motioned Daniel Johnstone, the designated survivor, to mount up behind the rider in front of him and delivered a stern lecture. "We will release you at a doctor's home a few miles from here. He is a man who is aligned with our cause, and he will see to your wounds. Once that is done, he will convey you to Berwick and give you a few coins. Your job will be to visit every inn, tavern, and public house in the city and spread the tales of our depredations. Your bound up wounds will furnish proof of the truth of your tale. Be warned that we have spies in many places, so if you fail to do your duty, word will get back to us. Drawing and quartering will be too good for you if you betray us."

Johnstone shivered and nodded. He hoped the doctor was a good one, then realized these raiders could not operate successfully unless they had an underground network of secret collaborators, including doctors.

Elliot summoned a second rider. "Jellicoe, I want you and Withers to return tomorrow night with a bag of quicklime. I want the faces of all our dead removed, so that the authorities will have no clue as to their identities."

"It will be as if they never existed," replied Jellicoe.

As Heatherington despondently rode along, he thought of how different he felt from when he had been a soldier. The conclusion of even a modestly successful army campaign had generally left him with a feeling of inner satisfaction, while today's action left him feeling empty and hollow. He had become something he had formerly despised: a mercenary, a man who fought for cash instead of country. He also realized how resentful he had become of Elliot's brutal and dictatorial leadership. He thought of what real leadership looked like, and a face came into his mind of an officer under whose command he had served when he had been part of the Connaught Rangers. Thomas Pennywhistle had briefly commanded his company at Salamanca and had been everything that a good officer should be. He wondered if the man was still alive; quality officers often died young.

Heatherington noted that there was a lot of muttering, cursing, and quiet complaining as the riders plodded on through the wet, starless night, indicating he was not alone in his dissatisfaction. Elliot was so annoyed that he thrice had to stop the caravan and threaten the men into silence. The men obeyed with a surliness they had never displayed before.

Just then a man screamed in terror as a hawk attacked his head. He swatted at it vigorously, but it inflicted two deep gouges before he drove it off. Hawks did not normally attack people so Heatherington guessed that the man must have had the bad fortune to have passed very near to its nest, one that likely contained chicks.

Bad luck has been the curse of this entire raid, thought Heatherington. He remembered Elliot's words at the start of the raid and his mouth curled in angry contempt. "*Men, I am so lucky that I once broke a mirror and had seven years of good luck!*"

The streams and rivers they had yet to cross would be running high tonight and would present some problems getting three hundred sheep across. He cursed the day that he had met Elliot, as a picture of his weeping wife flooded his mind's eye.

Maude watched the Reivers depart, and as soon as she was sure they would not return, she and Mary descended to the courtyard to rescue Josh, who had been left bound to his pole. He appeared comatose, but he was breathing, and while his wounds were bad, they might be managed if tended with skill and loving care. After seeing Josh to a bed and binding up his wounds, Maude left a child to watch the injured boy, then and her companions set about cleaning up the mess of the castle's defenses.

Two hours later, Josh began spitting blood, gasping for breath, and shuddering intermittently. The watching child called out. Maude and Mary rushed to his bedside and held his hands. He regained consciousness, but his look of painful confusion suggested that he was not in his right mind. They whispered prayers, hopeful words about the future, and assured him of their love. They took turns wiping the sweat from his body as he passed in and out of consciousness. At two minutes past midnight, his breath slowed, became the rattle of death, and then stopped. Maude and Josh's mother held the corpse's hands for a full hour, sobbing as they did so.

Maude's head drooped as she wondered whether her husband and son had survived: deep down she feared she was clinging to a fool's hope. They had all worked so hard to bring the estate back to working order and now it looked like that it had been all for naught. She had heard that the owner of the estate, Sir Thomas Pennywhistle was a war hero, and she thought that such a man might be willing to help set things right. But he could only do so if he knew the full particulars of the horrors that had befallen the estate and the people on it. As soon as she restored some semblance of order, she would write a letter. And it would be a corker.

Later that same night, Ruzzini and Nixon related their terrible tale to Charlton's father, Sir Peregrine Charlton, that contained some of the details that Maude Dacre was penning. "Monstrous in this day and age!" gasped Sir Peregrine." I will round up my retainers and depart for Whistlestop within the hour!"

Maitland told a similar story to the Sheriff of Berwick. His response echoed exactly the words Sir Peregrine had used.

William and Steven, the two boys who had sheltered in the forest, slunk back to the castle in the wee hours of September 1st, waiting until the soaking rain had subsided to a light drizzle. Both were badly shaken and chilled to the bone, but their wits were intact. They stumbled into Harvey and Ronald, the lads from the barley field, and breathlessly compared experiences. All four had lost their innocence: brutal reality had shoved them a few steps closer to becoming men in a very harsh way.

Maude welcomed them back with open arms and fierce hugs of relief, then with a meal of spruce beer, mutton, and bread while listening attentively to their stories. It was Steven who told her the news that she dreaded. "I am sorry to tell you this, madame, but I saw your husband and son die. It was your husband's warning that saved William and me. I am powerfully sad that he is gone, but he died doing a noble thing."

Maude said nothing and stared into the kitchen hearth fire. She was a widow and would have to make the best of it. Right now, she had no idea how, but she believed in herself strongly enough to know that she would eventually figure it out: the entire estate would be depending on her, and she would not let its people down. She felt a hand on her shoulder.

"I hope to God that we have seen the last of those outlaws, Maude," said Mary.

"No, Mary," Maude replied, looking up with eyes bright with unshed tears, but the edge of steel in her voice. "They'll be back, but next time, we'll be ready."

CHAPTER 4

A New Home and a New Job

8th September 1816

Pennywhistle entered his pine-paneled study with a spring in his step and a smile on his lips, carrying the blueprints for the rebuilding of Whistlestop in a map case under his left arm. His destination was a 75 by 45-inch knee-hole partners' desk of chocolate-brown mahogany, the designation coming from the idea that partners should trust each other sufficiently that they would be willing to share an unusually large desk. He sighed in satisfaction as he unfurled the blueprints on the desk's wide surface, then seated himself in a green leather tub chair and began to examine the plans in detail.

He had spent many hours consulting with John Nash, the Prince Regent's personal architect, and these plans represented his amateur ideas refined by a professional. Nash was in high demand, but the Prince Regent had made him available because Pennywhistle's secret diplomacy at the Congress of Vienna had saved the Royal Family from the scandal of the Clarke Letters.

Pennywhistle had shown Nash examples of architecture that he liked from several authoritative books and had given a general idea of the funds he was prepared to spend. The home would be a three-story Palladian cube of whitewashed sandstone that would feature bow windows, scalloped shell and neoclassical friezes, triangular pediments over doors and windows, and a two-story crescent shaped entrance framed by four Corinthian columns. Landscaping would come later; he would need to inspect the grounds to make sure that its natural features were enhanced, not obliterated.

He had kept his consultations secret from Sammie Jo because he intended a grand surprise. They had often spoken of creating a residence in the country where she could hunt and fish to her heart's content. She had grown to like London, but her backwoods roots meant that the city would always be a residence rather than a home. His slower than expected rehabilitation had caused her to place her country dream on indefinite hold; today, he would let her know the dream was taking shape.

He expected her to return in an hour or so. She was currently sharing afternoon tea with Deborah Dale at the Glass Slipper, a fashionable new tearoom recommended by his godmother, the Countess of Westminster. Deborah was the widow of his most trusted subordinate, and she had blamed Pennywhistle for her husband's death. She had not spoken with either him or Sammie Jo since Waterloo, until today's tiffin.

Sammie Jo had been pleasantly surprised when Deborah had accepted today's invitation, after pointedly ignoring five previous ones. Tea today was not a mere social outing, but an exercise in bridge building. Both women were direct and plain spoken. He hoped the initial sparks would give way to a remembrance of the regard that each had for the other in times past.

Deborah printed a radical newspaper called *The Laborer's Clarion*. It championed the causes of men working in industries like textiles, steel, and the manufacture of the new gas streetlights. The paper was unpopular with the government, but Liverpool could not shut it down without angering the powerful patrons for whom she supplied a written voice: wealthy Midland's industrialists who resented their underrepresentation in Parliament. Her egalitarian outlook had much in common with that of John Quincy Adams, and it occurred to Pennywhistle that if fate ever brought the two freethinkers together, they would get along well.

He had grown to like Adams, and he felt Adams had also come to enjoy his company. Once Adams had become comfortable with his visits, he revealed a side of himself that showcased his wit, humanity, and his passion: three things that casual acquaintances could easily miss. Their wide and varied interests led them to talk of many topics besides diplomacy, touching on such obscure subjects as vulcanism, whether Linnaeus's classifications of plants needed further refinement, and the effects steam power would have on the future of sailing ships. Pennywhistle always felt his intellect invigorated after a visit. Diplomacy was so much easier when it was conducted between men who respected each other, even if they represented different flags.

Several months of fishing with Adams had not only improved his diet but had put in place all the tools necessary to solve the prisoner-of-war repatriation problem once and for all. The issues associated with slavery were thornier, but progress was being made. The East India Company was receptive to the idea of a limited number of American merchantmen calling each year, though the allowed number had yet to be worked out. Recent news from America also confirmed Adam's speculation that James Monroe would probably be the next President and Adams appointed his Secretary of State. As Pennywhistle had been looking at plans for his own house, he wondered if Monroe had any plans for rebuilding the President's Palace. Pennywhistle had been present at its burning in 1814 and thought its deliberate destruction had been a great mistake.

Pennywhistle worried that his plans for Whistlestop bordered on the visionary, for they not only included transforming a rough old border pele into an elegant Regency mansion of thirty rooms, but building a solid, respectable cottage for every family on the estate. He wanted Whistlestop to be less the center of an estate dedicated to one family than the center of a community committed to the betterment of many families.

His concussion had taught him much about suffering, and he was determined that the workers on his estate should live free of want and fear. He wanted his workers to be paid fairly, treated well, and given long leases rather than yearly ones. He wanted a school built and a Scots school master hired, because he considered knowledge a gift of God and ignorance the curse of the devil. Repairing the run-down church near the estate and providing a living for a parson would happen only if the workers on the estate desired him to do so. Too many country parsons were aristocratic no-accounts, third and fourth sons who were placed into livings because they were too incompetent to do anything else.

He wanted a modern canal built to connect Whistlestop to the deeper parts of the Tweed. One was underway, but he was dissatisfied with the reports he had received on its progress. He laid the blame on the inexperience of the chief engineer and wondered where he could find a more competent replacement.

He planned to hire as many displaced veterans as possible for the construction work. He wanted an overseer for the estate who was familiar with the most advanced ideas on scientific farming and animal husbandry. He admired the crop sowing methods of Jethro Tull and the land management techniques of Thomas Coke. He was fascinated by the idea of using newly developed fertilizers, of mixing soils, planting hybrids, and draining swamplands preparatory to sculpting them into productive fields. He wanted to introduce new breeds of animals such as Hereford cows and Holkham pigs. The overseer would be a teacher as much as a supervisor, for he would be tasked with communicating his advanced ideas to his workers. And he would let Sammie Jo choose a ghillie from among the many worthy ones who had been displaced by enclosure acts.

His plans would be expensive and take a minimum of two years to carry out. He enjoyed a comfortable income but not an extravagant one, so his new home would also be comfortable but not extravagant. Unlike many of the gentry engaged in such projects, he would give the builder no blank check but would keep a careful accounting of every farthing spent.

He leaned back in his chair and poured himself a cup of Malaccan coffee, which had recently displaced Brazilian as his favorite. He had just taken his first sips when there was a knock on the door.

It was McBeavy. "Mails just come in, sir. I know you like to read letters immediately upon their arrival. There are four today, and one is on some mighty fancy stationery." He handed the silver tray to Pennywhistle.

"Thank you, McBeavy."

McBeavy closed the door quietly as he departed.

Pennywhistle opened the "fancy" letter first. It was from Sir Peregrine Charlton, a man he had never met but who had a strong Tory following in Parliament. In the second sentence, Charlton mentioned Pennywhistle's stepson Marco Ruzzini, which got his complete attention. The tale the letter told was as shocking as it was frightening. Whistlestop had been attacked by raiders: crops burned; herds plundered; all the resident families had suffered losses, for the men, women and children caught in the fields had been tortured or slain. Charlton, as the local Justice-of-the Peace, had begun to make inquiries about the attackers, but had turned up no firm evidence as to their identity because the locals were too frightened to be forthcoming. The one detail all the witnesses confirmed was that the raiders had resembled the reivers of old, so much so that they were described as "ghosts", "wraiths", and "apparitions with bloody blades." Marco was safe, but Charlton's son had been injured and was under the care of a physician. Charlton said he could not come to London because of the ongoing investigation, but he invited Pennywhistle to visit him at his estate so they could discuss matters in person. Charlton had also submitted a full report to the Home Secretary.

Pennywhistle put down the letter slowly, realizing the truth of Robert Burns' wisdom. "The best laid plans of mice and men gang aft agley." He wondered if the other three letters on the tray might relate to the same matter. He tore one open and read quickly.

It was from the Sheriff of Berwick and contained the lengthy story of a man who had been spared by the raiders. It was a graphic account of the ruthlessness and cruelty of the raiders.

The third letter was from Marco Ruzzini. Marco first assured him that he was fine and then went on to confirm every detail in Charlton's letter from the perspectives of himself and his two friends. A school holiday had turned into a life and death struggle.

The final letter was written in an unsteady hand, and there were blots on it that Pennywhistle guessed were dried tears. It was from Maude Dacre, who had lost her husband and her son. She described the defense of the tower in restrained prose, but Pennywhistle had seen enough battle to know that she had put up a fight that would have done credit to Zenobia of Palmyra. She described in detail the people who had died and suffered; her words were so vivid that Pennywhistle could almost see their faces in his mind's eye. She felt it likely that Whistlestop would be attacked again if future protection payments were not paid in full and on time. It was clear that the people of the estate needed relief, and they needed it immediately.

He checked the dates of the letters; all had been penned less than a week ago.

He carefully placed the letters in a folder, having a feeling that he would refer to them frequently in the weeks ahead. His grand plans would have to wait. It was time to open his purse and conceive a plan for the relief of Whistlestop.

McBeavy knocked on the study's door. "Sorry to interrupt, sir, but a messenger has arrived from the Home Secretary. He says his message requires a verbal RSVP."

"Right, show him in."

The messenger was a well-turned-out man in his early twenties, likely someone's confidential secretary at the Home Office. "Thank you for seeing me, Sir Thomas." He handed Pennywhistle a letter. "I am instructed to remain and convey your response directly to the Home Secretary."

The letter was short and direct.

A matter of considerable urgency has arisen which concerns your estate in Northumberland and could affect the safety of the realm. Castlereagh has the utmost trust and confidence in you and believes that a consultation would be to our mutual benefit. Could we meet this evening at eight at The Travelers' Club to discuss this matter?

—Sidmouth.

Pennywhistle guessed what Lord Sidmouth wanted to discuss and was surprised that the depredations at Whistlestop had already reached the ear of a cabinet minister. For them to be part of "a threat to the realm" meant that the raid on Whistlestop was no anomaly but part of a dangerous and more widespread design.

The Traveler's was a club founded by Castlereagh and favored by diplomats both domestic and foreign. It was a comfortable place where important matters could be discussed completely off the record. A great many official issues had been settled over drinks served in a lounge atmosphere rather than in formal government offices.

"You may tell Lord Sidmouth that I shall join him at eight," he said to the messenger.

"Thank you, Sir Thomas. I shall convey that message to him at once."

McBeavy escorted the young man to the door. Pennywhistle sank down into his chair and poured a second cup of coffee. He sipped slowly as he composed his thoughts.

The study door opened again, and Sammie Jo sauntered in, a smile of triumph on her face. "I am right glad of this day. Over tea and scones, I fixed things with Deborah. She finally realized that her husband was proud to die in your service, and her blaming you for Dale's death was her grief keening in her ear. It will take a while to put things back the way they were, but I made a good start today."

Her smile faded as she noticed that her husband was only listening with half an ear. "I thought you'd be delighted. Let me guess, is that agitated look on your face related to that young man who shot past me when I was coming up the walk?"

"It is. He informed me that the Home Secretary desires a meeting this evening." Pennywhistle rose, walked over to Sammie Jo, and kissed her.

"I know that kiss, Tom. It means 'Something big is coming.' Now I expect that you want me to listen real careful like while you tell me what it is."

"I never realized I was that predictable. Let me give you the good news first." Pennywhistle completely forgot the Foreign Secretary for the next hour, as he showed her the blueprints and explained his two-year plan for the estate. She smiled with delight, but her expression changed to an angry glower when he read excerpts from the four letters. "Who were those damn people and where did they come from? They must be stopped!"

"I expect my meeting with the Home Secretary will supply some answers. And to think all I wanted to do when I awoke this morning was show you a safe and prosperous future!"

"Safe and prosperous is fine for ordinary gentry," responded Sammie Jo with fire in her eye, "but you and I ain't exactly ordinary. We like peace... to a point. This reminds me of a story told me by one of the Welsh friends of your godmother, Tom. Long ago, there was a prince whose kingdom had been taken over by dangerous men. This young prince learned the three skills that he'd need to rescue his kingdom and the people who were suffering. One was 'the Art of Peace in the midst of War.' Well, I've seen you keep your calm and give good orders when most folk were losing their heads, figuratively and literally! I know that calm place. When I'm taking a shot, everything around me slows down and everything inside me fires up, and no matter how much noise and killing is goin' on around me, I am alignin' my sights and waitin' to pull the trigger when I feel it come right."

She looked thoughtful, and said, "The worst mistakes I ever made were when I lost my temper in a fight so that all I wanted to do was hurt someone bad, and I forgot what I was there for." She shook her head slowly, then continued.

"Now, the second skill the prince learned was 'the Art of War in the midst of Peace.' And that's what you've done since Waterloo. You've taken up arms against complacency and ignorance and poverty." Pennywhistle looked embarrassed and opened his mouth to say something, but Sammie Jo raised her hand.

"Wait, hear me out, Tom. You and I know the darkness in ourselves, so when the world turns dark, instead of getting scared, we know what to do. I think the universe understands that, and so now and again it likes to throw a hammer at us. But the universe was polite this time. It waited until you were fully recovered before tossing you this challenge."

"Like Thor hurling his hammer at me but expecting me to intercept it?"

"Yup! You always said the most important things in life are gained through struggle, not handed to you on a silver platter. If we want the new Whistlestop, we are going to have to fight for it. And we won't just be fighting for ourselves, but for the folk who will make this new Whistlestop a living concern. You are the kind of man who needs the responsibility for others to be at his best, and I think that you have missed that since Waterloo."

Pennywhistle stroked his chin in thought. "Maybe our need for adventure is like an opium eater's addiction and we need a dose from time to time."

"Maybe, but addicts only look out for themselves. Every time you have been called upon to fix things, you leave the world just a little better than you found it. You once said, 'God does not give gifts to people that he does not intend for them to use.' That's why he gave you might, because he knew you would use it to do right."

"'Might for Right' was something drummed into me by my first tutor. Deep down, I still wish to be King Arthur."

"And I am right pleased to be your Guinevere, though no Lancelot could ever come between us. Admit it, Tom. Much as you have enjoyed parts of the year since Waterloo, with your meetings with the Royal Society, evenings spent with up-and-coming musicians, the balls, your books, and your vegetable garden, haven't there been some moments when you felt too comfortable? Life tastes sweetest when you realize it can be snatched away at any moment and only shows its brightest luster when you hazard your life."

Pennywhistle smiled. "For 'a little ol' country girl', you have a sense of drama that would do credit to The Bard himself. I cannot but wonder if we are not at this very moment at the exact spot that our destinies intended for us to be."

"That sounds just like what Bonaparte would say! You also like puzzles, Tom, and get bored when you don't have any to solve. You like stuff that stretches your mind."

"Sometimes I think you know me better than I know myself." He rose, advanced toward Sammie Jo, took her in his arms, and kissed her long and hard. She ran her strong fingers through his hair, then began to undress him as they continued kissing.

"Our dark sides are not all negative. Right now, I want to do bad things with you. I promise I won't make you late for your meeting," she murmured between kisses. "Your desk looks mighty inviting."

"We are about to give new meaning to the term, "I will clear my desk."

Their love making was a hurricane that left the floor strewn with blueprints and papers but left the two lovers with broad smiles.

Pennywhistle sighed with a mixture of exhaustion and pleasure. "I feel like I have just ridden a comet! Funny how talking about death and destruction brings about an act designed to give life."

"That's kind of rush to judgment I love to make. And that judgment is *mighty fine!*

"That whirlwind blew away every ounce of tension."

"The world would be a much saner place if more people acted like we just did before trying to face down a problem."

***

Pennywhistle arrived at his appointment with a few minutes to spare. The Traveler's Club in Pall Mall was a white Palladian block of three stories. The interior was notable for its yellow walls, carpets, and curtains, as well as its sweeping mahogany staircases. His sexual flush was gone but a few perceptive souls noticed a faint afterglow. Discreet smiles followed him as he walked the steps to the majordomo's booth and presented himself.

A footman, summoned by the majordomo, conveyed Pennywhistle to the Home Secretary's domain: a small, walnut-paneled room was furnished in the most *au courant* Regency style, though the elaborate carving on the mahogany fireplace mantel was reminiscent of Grinling Gibbons' 17th century work at Hampton Court Palace.

Henry Addington, 1st Viscount Sidmouth, was a distinguished looking man who radiated the snobbish *gravitas* suitable to a prime minister. He had in fact been the Prime Minister from 1801 to 1804 and had been the Home Secretary since 1812. During both tenures, he had shown himself to be firmly opposed to democratic reforms. Yet despite his aristocratic hauteur, he had come from middle class origins and his title was a recent bestowal. His father had been the personal physician of William Pitt the Elder.

He rose from his tub chair and advanced to meet Pennywhistle. His handshake reminded Pennywhistle of John Quincy Adams': firm but devoid of warmth. "Thank you for coming on such short notice. We have much to discuss. I have taken the liberty of ordering for you the same drink that I favor, Bushmill's neat."

"An excellent choice, my lord." Pennywhistle accepted the drink and sat down in a very comfortable red leather library chair.

Sidmouth folded himself into a tub chair opposite Pennywhistle and slowly sipped his whiskey before speaking. "Castlereagh tells me that you are a well-informed man, so I will hazard that you have some idea of why I have arranged this meeting."

"I do, my lord. Four letters arrived with today's post, and each furnished an account of a strange and destructive raid on my estate of Whistlestop. The raiders were dressed in the garb of Reivers, brigands from three hundred years ago." Over the next few minutes, he summarized the contents of the letters.

"Your correspondents reports are no doubt accurate, but they could not have known that two other estates also suffered attacks, in the days following the Whistlestop raid; the brigands apparently emboldened by their first venture and wishing to inaugurate a reign of terror. An epidemic of sheep and cattle stealing has suddenly exploded, with thousands of beasts involved. Banks have been robbed, and shopkeepers and tavern owners in several towns have been forced to pay protection money to unknown parties. Even small cottagers have been brutalized. Whoever is behind this has put deep fear into people who normally would cooperate with the local constables and justices of the peace. The problem is changing from a local one to one that threatens our national security. This country is going through an economic upheaval, and the last thing it needs is an outbreak of organized brigandage, with the Scots clamouring that Liverpool's justice is only for the English." Addington positively scowled.

"How might I help, my lord?"

"An extraordinary situation requires an extraordinary solution. To that end, I want to revive an old office to solve a new problem. For more than three hundred years, the Border region was policed by 6 Wardens: three English and three Scots. They were part policemen, part soldiers, and part marcher lords. They were granted nearly unlimited powers to enforce the law in a lawless region: in essence, military plenipotentiaries. Occasionally they had to stand above and beyond existing law to do their jobs. Sometimes, they even had to make preventative raids on people who had not yet broken the law but were about to."

"Power is a dangerous thing, my lord. The temptation to abuse it for personal gain would be great in such an office."

"Quite correct, Sir Thomas. Some wardens became drunk with power and behaved little better than the brigands that they were supposed to keep in check. Your ancestor, Sir John Pennywhistle, served as Warden of the English East March based in Berwick from 1570 to 1585 and earned Queen Elizabeth's personal thanks for his even-handed approach. I intend to resurrect that post and appoint you to it. The salary will be modest, but you will be provided with funds to hire a fair number of assistants."

"My Lord, won't the revival of such a powerful office spark an uproar among the liberals and radicals in Parliament? Will there not be cries of 'tyrannical power'?"

"Quite right, Sir Thomas, but I can hold them off for four months or so. Thus, you would have no more than four months to clean up this mess."

"Why appoint me, my lord? Surely there are many distinguished general officers who would jump at the chance to occupy such a post, whilst I have only just recovered from my injuries at Waterloo."

"That's just it. You are a hero of Waterloo and your commission as Colonel of Marines is still active. You also fought at Trafalgar; only a handful of men have fought in two of Britain's most decisive battles. Wellington speaks well of you, and Castlereagh said you did a splendid job in your negotiations with John Quincy Adams. You have a personal stake in the area, and I see no Cromwell in your character. You strike me as a Cincinnatus, a man able to accept power, use it responsibly, and then return to his ordinary life once his task is done."

"The only man in recent times who resembles Cincinnatus is George Washington, and I certainly do not possess his remarkable character."

"Perhaps not, but I think you are equal to the task. I can give you three days to consider the offer, but I would prefer that you give me your answer now, as every minute this problem goes unsolved invites further disasters. "

"I would need a cadre of reliable men to assist me in such a difficult enterprise. Say the equivalent of a Roman century: eighty men. Could you find sufficient funds to manage such a number?"

Sidmouth frowned. "If you were certain that you needed that large a number, I suppose something could be managed. I should also point out that local justices-of-the-peace, sheriffs, and constables will be expected to give you their full cooperation."

Pennywhistle took a long swallow of his whiskey then sighed in resignation. "I have never been able to say no when my country calls, so I accept... reluctantly."

Sidmouth gave a frosty smile. "If you had accepted the job too eagerly, I would have been worried. The appointment will take effect at the stroke of midnight and your funds will be available tomorrow morning by ten. They will be in a special account at Coutt's Bank, accessible only by yourself. Give me a final tally of the total of men that you will need, and I can have additional funds ready two days after that. I will have all the current background reports delivered to your home by noon tomorrow. How soon do you think you could proceed north?"

"I don't like to go into battle with half a scissors. Finding good men to pull this assignment off can't be done overnight. I will also need to familiarize myself with a thousand and one details, because lack of preparation usually results in disaster. The best I could manage would be to depart for the north in ten days. Is that acceptable?"

"It is, Sir Thomas. Keep me informed if you need time beyond that. Just bear in mind it is critical that this matter be resolved as fast as possible."

Pennywhistle finished the last of his drink in one unseemly gulp. His mind had already begun working on the problem and so he hardly noticed the splendid taste. He rose and extended his hand. "Let us shake on our arrangement, and then I must depart. I won't be getting much sleep tonight."

Sidmouth shook his hand with real warmth this time. "Thank you, Sir Thomas. You have just relieved me of one very large headache."

Pennywhistle's own head started to throb, and he wondered if the handshake had just transmitted Sidmouth's malady.

Sammie Jo knew Pennywhistle's moods and facial expressions well. When he returned to Portland Street, he was lost in thought and barely acknowledged the kiss that she gave him. Something big was up.

"Is this something we ought to discuss?"

"Tomorrow, perhaps. For now, I need a large pot of coffee and a quiet place to think."

"So, you're back in harness again?"

"Yes, but I am not sure how this particular harness fits."

CHAPTER 5

The Man in the Shadows

9th September 1816

Hermitage Castle was a brooding medieval structure that crowned a lonely, windswept hill, ten miles from the English border and forty miles from Whistlestop. It had once been known as "the guardhouse of the bloodiest valley in Britain."

Most thought of it as merely a decrepit ruin and had no idea that it was home to a man who ran a vast criminal empire.

Walter Scott hated being confused with his third cousin and namesake, the author Walter Scott. His cousin was a romantic dreamer, while he was a realist. His cousin wrote fanciful books that brought him fame and rendered him a celebrity; he ran an underground empire and kept in the shadows. It irritated him that men newly taken on, meeting him for the first time, invariably asked, "Are you the man who wrote *Waverly*, then?"

"Mr. Scott, are you sure about using Toby in this demonstration? There's a fair chance he will no' survive." Steven Pullum was Scott's general factotum, a man who rarely raised questions about his master's orders.

"Yes, quite. Toby has had a good run, but he has outlived his usefulness. His exit will make my point exactly."

"I thought maybe a dog would suffice."

"Even the most ferocious dog would be inadequate. No, it must be Toby."

"Very well, Mr. Scott."

Scott was frustrated with the results of the raid on Whistlestop, and he had called a general meeting of his hirelings to make his displeasure known. Some of his men had begun to lose heart; worse, they had begun to think for themselves— a dangerous development.

No, he thought, the raid *did not fail; the captured sheep brought a handsome profit. And the tenants of Whistlestop will finally pay, rather than endure a second visitation.*

"The stage is ready for you, Mr. Scott. I have given the trumpeter the music you want him to play," said a man who was so self-effacing that Scott could not even remember his name.

"I shall be there in a few minutes."

Scott was a self-made man who despised his humble origins and was determined to rise above them, no matter what it took. Born the fourth son of a poor country parson, he had reached his 18th birthday as a well-educated man cursed with slim job prospects. He was distantly related to the Duke of Buccleuch, but far too distantly to expect favour or be invited to ducal events. With a more prudent father, he might have been sent to Oxford to study for a divinity degree, such as his father possessed, or perhaps married off to the daughter of a prosperous farmer willing to overlook his genteel poverty in return for his grandchildren bearing a name with a solid pedigree. But while his kindly father was well-beloved by his parishioners, he was privately addicted to gambling and had squandered what little money the family possessed betting on horses.

A week after his eighteenth birthday, Scott departed for the docks of Bristol, fifteen miles away. Because of his reading prowess, penmanship, and skill with numbers, he was hired as the captain's clerk on a ship named appropriately, *Destiny;* bound for the port of Philadelphia. He was not just setting sail for the New World, he was journeying to a new life.

Scott found he liked the sea, and over the next fifteen years roamed the world, rising steadily in rank because of his intelligence and determination. On his last voyage, he had served as the first mate of the Royal Mail Ship *Diana*, carrying the mail from Portsmouth to British Guyana. The ship had sailed into a gale on its return journey, foundering on hidden rocks only miles from Land's End. He had the presence of mind to seize two small canvas pouches before he jumped overboard. Royal Mail ships often carried jewels under private arrangements; the pouches he had snatched contained ten large green Colombian emeralds, enough to set a prudent man on the path to real wealth.

He had swum for a full hour against high seas and hurricane winds, passing out just before he reached shore, the tide taking him the final few yards. When he'd awoken, he'd discovered that an item of cargo had washed ashore with him; a hemp and rattan container filled with water and containing a dozen live eels, intended for a gentleman ichthyologist in Bristol. At the time, Scott considered his own deliverance and theirs remarkable, deciding that Providence had set a grueling test of character that he had passed... swimmingly. From that moment on, he looked upon himself as a man marked for a special destiny. He had a fortune of two kinds on his hands, one mineral and one animal. He could get a high price for the jewels, and if he sold them on the black market no one would inquire about their origin.

Once he entered the world of criminals, he never looked back. He was much smarter than most crime lords, and it proved easy to use the money from the emeralds to begin building his own criminal empire, first in Bristol and later in London.

A year ago, one of his clients had mentioned the unrest along the Scottish border. A depressed economy opened windows of opportunity and supplied recruits who, in better times, would never have thought of breaking the law. He immersed himself in a study of the area's history and customs and decided it was the ideal region to build a new empire, one free of the fierce competition that was destroying his London operation.

His own family had come from that area three generations before, so in a way, he would be returning to his roots. He would pose as a savior of the poor and downtrodden, but he would really be doing the same thing he had done in London: plundering the people he pretended to protect.

Scott had acquired a silent partner in London, an aristocrat from one of the oldest and most influential families, whom Scott disliked and who would be eliminated when he had outlived his usefulness. But for now, the partner was a necessary evil; his financial backing enabled Scott to expand his networks very quickly and gave him access to lucrative international markets.

Pullum tapped Scott on the shoulder and brought him back to reality.

"The last of your guests have arrived," said Pullum.

"Good. They are about to receive an education." Scott smiled coldly.

Pullum stepped back, nearly recoiling, and stammered, "I... I am ready to release J... Jack and Jill into the water. As per your instructions, they have not been fed for two days."

Scott's final goal was to demand a blanket pardon and a title in return for disbanding his organization and returning Border affairs to normality. That would give him the one thing that nearly all criminal overlords desired: respectability. His research had showed him there were several precedents for such outcomes, chief among them the case of John Forester in the late 16th century. Forester had engaged in many criminal activities, but because Queen Elizabeth desperately needed his services, he had been given deeds to some of the land he had stolen, granted a knighthood, and been appointed a Border Warden. He had been called upon to keep in check the very Reivers he had once been part of. Scott felt that if he inflicted enough pain and suffering, and stretched it out long enough, the government would find the pain unbearable. Liverpool's government was a prisoner of its own frugality and was more interested in stability than justice.

Scott had made a deliberate decision to rule by fear, because fear commanded obedience faster and more efficiently than reason. The trouble was that fear had to be fanned. Sometimes deliberate cruelty was necessary. Ten men, or spears as he called them, had deserted in the past week, and there were other signs of disaffection. The best way to ensure the loyalty of all was to make a fatal example of one who had betrayed his trust in a particularly egregious way.

***

"I cannot do this. I just cannot!" Bill Clemons complained to his friend, James Jackson. Both were standing outside the open doors that marked the entrance to a long ramp; a ramp which led to the heart of a large cavern beneath Hermitage. The pouring rain dampened their already gloomy moods. "I don't want to listen to yet another lecture about why our destinies and Scott's are inseparable, and why leaving his side would be some kind of treason!"

"But you must admit, Bill, that we have more money jingling in our pockets now than before he came along. And our families eat meat almost every night. Is that not worth a little dark dealing?"

"I don't like what I have become, Jaimie. My mother did not raise a thief, or a thug. "

"Neither did mine, but neither did they raise beggars, and that's what we would be if Mr. Scott had not come along. Paying work has been as scarce as pearls since Waterloo."

"Work? I guess you could call it that, but I am sick of seeing people hurt by what we do. Stealing is one thing, but raping and killing makes us no better than animals."

"But that don't happen often."

"Do you hear yourself? 'That don't happen all that often' ignores the fact that they should never happen at all. Have you never thought that some of the girls getting raped are the same age as your own daughter?"

"I try hard not to think about that." Jim scowled and fingered the coins in his pocket for reassurance.

"That's just it. Mr. Scott does not want us to think. Because thinking also causes us to feel, and that reminds us that we should feel bad when we do bad things. Most of the time I just feel numb when we go on our rides. But I am having trouble sleeping, and the only dreams I can remember upon waking are nightmares." Bill's face paled with the recollection.

"I have nightmares too sometimes. In my dreams, a big and terrible creature is chasing me. I can't see its eyes, but its mouth is full of huge teeth and flames are coming out of its nostrils. It reminds me of a gargoyle I once saw on Durham Cathedral, just a lot larger."

"Dreams aren't the worst of it. I have been having trouble with my wife."

"I thought you and Carol were happy."

"We have been. But lately, it is when we get into bed that sometimes... well... things... uh, don't go as planned. Let's just say the fireworks don't get lit."

"You mean old Private Parts won't come to parade ground attention?"

"Nothing like this has ever happened to me before. In the past, a stiff breeze could make my soldier stand tall. Now he is not responding to any kind of reveille. Carol says it's my body's way of punishing me for riding with Scott. She wants me to quit. She says that once I am done with Scott, frolics in the bedroom will restore themselves to normal."

"I don't know what normal means anymore," said Jackson.

"I see just how abnormal my life has become since Scott entered the picture. It's odd: when I first met Scott, I admired him. I thought, here is a man who can fix things and do for us what the government does not. Now when I look at him, I don't see his face, I see his soul, which is disfigured with warts and tumors and crawling with bugs. "Clemons shuddered and scowled. "When I hear his voice, I no longer hear a man but a Lorelei singing a song to lure me to my death. Here's what I think, Jaimie, lad. I think we have been lucky so far. Most people have paid up, and the local constables seem afraid to pursue us. But Whistlestop changed things. "

He wrapped his arms tightly around himself, as if to squeeze out the memory of that awful day; the first time that anyone fought back in a big way. "I think it's just a matter of time before the government gets involved and sends troops. They won't be scared like the locals because they know how to fight. The saddest thing is we might just know some of them; Waterloo veterans like us. I am fed up. He lifted his right boot and stomped it hard on the ground. "I'm not staying for his harangue. I am heading home and never coming back."

Jackson replied quietly, barely above a whisper. "It seems to me that signing on with Scott was like when we joined the army. You aren't allowed to leave just because you don't like things and want to go home. Don't forget that desertion in time of war carries a death sentence. I'm no' so sure it's any different with Scott. Who is to say that he will not send a few of his nastiest thugs to remind you of your obligation?"

Bill glanced furtively around to make sure they were alone. "I thought of that. My family and I will stay with Carol's family in Berwick until this whole mess blows over. I've a gut feeling that a day of reckoning is coming, and Mr. Scott will have much more important things than myself to be worrying about."

"You may be right about Scott, but I think you are making a mistake.'"

Clemons clapped his friend on the shoulder and smiled. "Don't look so glum. I will be fine. Now take care, Jaimie. I won't be seeing you for a while." Clemons turned and walked toward his horse.

"I will say a prayer for you," said Jackson under his breath.

Jackson entered an underground cavern illuminated by torches and took a seat on the cold ground, alongside 1,200 other followers of Walter Scott. The air was damp, laced with wisps of mist, and a slight breeze caused the torches to flicker and cast odd shadows. Bats hung from the ceiling, centipedes and millipedes prowled the cavern's edges.

The castle above had a unique feature that was in keeping with the atmosphere of the cavern: twin portcullises. Visitors thought they were safe when the first portcullis was raised, but having advanced a few paces, the second portcullis slammed down while the first dropped to its former position, creating a kill box. Five rivals had accepted dinner invitations as a prelude to peace talks with Scott but left Hermitage in pine boxes.

Several of his men manned a booth at Hermitage's entrance, offering guided tours to any holiday makers touring the area. The men were well spoken and personable, trained to charm all manner of tourists. They were in fact sentries placed to deflect unwanted curiosity. Visitors departed pleased by the results of their guided tours, never suspecting the criminal network that operated from beneath it.

The cavern's pond that lay to the right front of the assembled men was deep and cold; it had originally served as an emergency water supply. A small wooden stage had been erected to the left of the pond. A burly man mounted the stage, flourished a trumpet, then blew a stirring series of notes that silenced any conversations among the men. The notes acted as a sort of fanfare, announcing that a magnate was about to make an appearance and that all should give him their fullest attention.

Scott emerged from a passage behind the stage and walked slowly and deliberately toward it. He wanted to impress the men that he was sufficiently self-possessed that even matters of great importance did not need to be rushed. He was dressed in a close-fitting black jacket and a kilt featuring the red, green, and purple tartan of Clan Buccleuch.

"Look at his face," whispered one follower to Jackson. "He's a got a twitch by his left eye. That means he's angry, and that always trouble for us."

"I see it," replied Jackson. "I wonder whose head will roll." *I wish I had left with Clemons,* he thought.

Scott paced back and forth several times once he mounted the stage. He looked carefully at the men in his audience, gauging their mood. Most faces reflected expressions of obedience and loyalty, but he noticed that a few visages reflected skepticism, frustration, and worst of all, boredom.

"Guardians of the Borders!" he thundered. He liked to reinforce the idea that they upheld a splendid tradition. "During the Whistlestop raid things went wrong and some of your friends died. I remind you that we are fighting a war against poverty and the neglect of the English government that takes our taxes and gives us nothing! A battle might not work out the way we planned, but we do not abandon the path that leads to victory! Sacrifice and loss are part of every war, but I am determined to make sure that your comrades did not die in vain. The events at Whistlestop have caused some of your comrades to desert our cause; others begin to doubt our prospects for success. Even now, I see uncertainty, fear, and confusion in some faces. So, a demonstration is necessary to remind you that our brotherhood is an unbreakable bond, based on obedience, shared goals, shared rewards, and above all, loyalty!"

His words boomed off the cavern walls, the echoes adding to the impact of his words.

Pullum had been listening and motioned to two assistants. A large rattan basket, lined with oiled canvas and filled with water, was brought forward. It contained two marine creatures, each the length of a broomstick. Resembling eels, they were actually tropical fish of the genus *Electrophorus*. One assistant removed the cover, the container was tilted forward, and its inhabitants slid sinuously into the dark water. The men were not sure what they had seen, but the animals looked sinister.

"Those creatures," Scott's voice resumed its booming cadence, "are carnivores who kill their prey with electricity."

Pullum's assistants brought forward a long, low cage containing a ten-foot Colombian crocodile. The audience gasped when the cage door was opened and the creature lumbered into the water.

"All three of these monsters are predators," thundered Scott. "All three are hungry! You may think you can guess the outcome, but banish speculation, and observe. Things are not always what they seem."

The crocodile swam slowly through the water and circled the pond three times before his sense of smell detected the presence of the eels. If Toby had not been old, he would have detected the eels sooner. Hungrily, he advanced, jaws widening. The eels, rather than retreating, attacked. Scott, who knew the difference in their markings, could easily tell apart the two creatures he had, in a moment of whimsy, dubbed Jack and Jill.

Toby's jaws clamped down on Jill's tail. Jack drew alongside and thrust his own tail into Toby's side. Toby's body began to jerk violently, and a sharp smell of electricity filled the air. Toby convulsed for a full minute, then lay still. His corpse began to drift. The eels repositioned themselves and began feeding, tearing into the soft belly with razor sharp teeth that flashed in the flickering red light of the torches.

The crowd murmured with shock and amazement.

"We Guardians are like these eels," announced Scott. "Small and underestimated. Toby stood for the English government: big, ferocious, ever hungry! But beatable. Now it is time to administer rough justice. Mr. Pullum, please bring the prisoner forward."

A bound and gagged Jock Elliot was pushed forward from the shadows. The man who had led the raid on Whistlestop looked terrified, bereft of his usual bravado and bluster.

"You see before you the man who failed us all," said Scott in the dread tones of a judge handing down the sentence for a capital crime. "What went amiss at Whistlestop was his fault, not yours! But understand, the fate about to overtake Captain Elliot will be the same for any one of you who fails to give me his complete loyalty."

Whispers of fear rippled through the audience. Then something happened which was exactly what Scott had hoped for. His men were looking for a scapegoat, someone who could absolve them from blame over the Whistlestop affair. The eyes of the audience became lances, flaming arrows, hot pokers. Jaws stiffened and nostrils flared. Angry smiles blossomed on some faces, and teeth flashed in snarls. One man shouted, "Send Elliot to Hell!"

"Aye, yes!" The cries swelled to a chorus.

The crowd began chanting, "Elliot, Elliot, Elliot," sounding like the death tolls of bells in some barbarous basilica. Fists were raised, men rose to their feet and began stomping their boots. Some picked up rocks and hurled them at Elliot.

This was mass hysteria under his personal control, and Scott loved it. Public executions were popular spectacles that regularly attracted thousands. Once the restraints of civilization were gone, men could be conditioned to believe almost anything, if it was presented to them with confidence and conviction.

Elliot shuddered with fear. Several rocks hit his forehead.

Scott signaled for his trumpeter to blow a short fanfare, then he motioned to Pullum, who prodded the prisoner forward at the point of a sword. Elliot tried to turn round when he reached the pond's edge, but a hard shove from Pullum's boot propelled him into the pond.

Elliot thrashed and kicked violently, trying to free his hands but succeeded only in roiling the water. The vibrations attracted the attention of the eels, and although they were not man eaters by nature, they were hungry, and the soft flesh of a person was more palatable than the hard carcass of a crocodile.

The creatures glided through the waters as the crowd pointed and shouted. One eel's jaws clamped onto Elliot's bound hands, and he began jerking convulsively. His teeth rattled and his eyes bulged. When the body ceased jerking, the crowd erupted into cheers. Scott let the cheers die down before he spoke. "The dogs will have a good meal tonight, once the eels have finished with Captain Elliot."

Most laughed, but a few frowned in disapproval. They were Presbyterians and Church of England men who felt that while it was fair to execute a man, it was not fair that he should be denied a Christian burial. Vengeance in life was one thing, but in death it lay beyond the pale.

Scott, unseeing, continued, raising one arm on high. "Remember the lesson! Now I will introduce you to Captain Elliot's replacement. He will explain the target I have set for today."

Scott had the trumpeter blow another blast. A man stepped forth out of the shadows, one who was familiar and popular with the crowd. Three loud huzzahs greeted him as he mounted the steps to the stage. His name was William Hexham, an ex-sergeant in the Coldstream Guards who had fought at Waterloo. He was tall and well-built but walked with the pronounced limp that had caused him to be invalided out of the service. Nevertheless, his erect carriage and the energy he radiated suggested that he had plenty of fight left in him.

Unlike the blustering Elliot, Hexham was soft spoken and commanded with persuasion rather than threats. The sheer force of his personality awed men into obedience and made harsh words or physical blows unnecessary. He had joined Scott's gang reluctantly, and only because the government had lost his paperwork and had failed to pay the pension due him for twenty-one years of sterling service.

"Good day, gentlemen," Hexham said quietly. "The pele we shall raid today is small but strategic. I have prepared a detailed plan which I can explain better to a small group than this large assemblage. I will need fifty voluntee—"

Before he finished, hands shot skyward and nearly every man began shouting, "Take me! Choose me!"

Scott rocked on his feet and smiled inwardly.

The dark spell of Whistlestop had been broken.

Chapter 6

Plans and Plots

11th September 1816

Pennywhistle closed his copy of Caesar's *The Gallic Wars,* then climbed the library ladder to put it back on its shelf. As he descended, he realized that the wide-ranging powers conferred upon him could enable him to act as a modern-day Caesar. He had never considered himself as a potential dictator but given his reputation as a man of efficient action, he understood that others might see his appointment in a sinister light. While he had no wish to rule by fear, a small dose of it might help to open doors that local authorities, jealous of their prerogatives, strove to keep shut.

Chief among his powers was the ability to "raise the hue and cry and engage in the hot trod." In the event of a raid, he had the right to call upon every able-bodied man that he could find and compel him to join in the immediate pursuit of any fleeing raiders. This gave him access to a considerable pool of manpower, but the sad truth was farmers and villagers would be of little use in a fight against well organized, blooded raiders. Of far more use would be the services of local veterans who knew their way around a musket.

He would also have at his disposal an understrength regiment of mounted yeomanry, roughly 200 sabers. The trouble with them was they were glorified militia, not regulars; nearly all would be aristocrat sprigs who had never seen battle but liked to dress up in splendid uniforms to impress the local ladies with military airs. Given intensive training a few might measure up, but that would entail finding a good cavalry instructor.

He had decided to rely on a system developed by his ancestor, Sir John Pennywhistle. He would appoint people who would act as an early warning system and intelligence network. The whole amounted to a government within a government, and he would have to create it in a matter of weeks. Those helpers would include 1 assistant warden, 4 deputy wardens, 8 castle keepers, 10 land sergeants, 10 land bailiffs, 10 water sergeants, 10 water bailiffs, 5 roving constables, 5 setters, 5 searchers, and 2 clerks.

In Elizabethan days, such men carried messages and organized watches at key fords, supervised roving patrols, and maintained a string of fortresses to keep out disreputable elements. Each fortress maintained a beacon that, when ignited, signaled the alarm to the next fortress. Each fortress was a link in a chain of beacons situated at high points in the Cheviot Hills. Beacons were a method of sending signals that went back millennia; there was a famous example in the first play of Sophocles' *Oresteia* trilogy that fired his imagination when he'd read about it as a boy.

Land Sergeants arrested any lawbreakers who crossed their paths in the countryside, while Land Bailiffs conducted them to trial. Water Sergeants and Water Bailiffs performed the same function if the miscreants were apprehended when fording a river or a stream. Roving constables filled in any gaps left by Land and Water Sergeants. Setters set steel traps for any Reivers who poached game during their raids, while searchers were engaged when a man was kidnapped and was expected to be held for ransom.

Wardens had maintained their own courts and had been allowed to dispense swift and summary justice. Oftentimes, only a few hours elapsed between a man being apprehended, indicted, tried, and executed.

Pennywhistle knew that family name and family ties counted for a great deal in the Borders, and he would be seen as an outsider. Therefore, he had decided to hire a few key people in London, but the rest of his officials would be selected from amongst the people who knew the lay of the land and the characters of their neighbors. He needed a man with ties to the area who could help him with his hires.

The man he had chosen was Maximillian Maxwell, whom he expected to arrive within the hour. Maxwell had been the worst of aristocratic reprobates when they had first met, and he had once written in a journal entry that he wanted to kill Pennywhistle. Pennywhistle had pushed him long and hard and had turned him from a roisterous, insubordinate hell-raiser into a good soldier. He had shed his drunken, violent ways to become a good husband and father, and since Waterloo had begun a successful career as a banker with Baring Brothers; beneath his combative nature, he had a good head for figures. Maximillian had not sold his commission but had voluntarily placed himself on the inactive army list. The Maxwell's were an old and influential border family in a region where kinship counted for more than laws or kings.

There was a knock on the library door. McBeavy opened it and poked his head in. "Mr. Maxwell is here, sir. Shall I show him in?"

"Please do."

Maxwell did not so much enter the room as thunder into it. He was a big man of six feet five inches who weighed 240 pounds. He had shed a great deal of fat, and the weight that remained was sinewy muscle. He navigated the welter of books, reports, and large maps that littered the library floor to extend a right hand with hearty good cheer. "It is wonderful to see you, Sir Thomas."

"It is good to see you, Mr. Maxwell. I apologize for the mess, but I have spent the last two days and nights trying to gather every scrap of information that I could about my new command. It is a daunting task."

"Could you explain what that task is? All you said in your note was that there was some trouble along the Scottish border and that you would welcome my assistance in dealing with it. I am most curious as to the nature of that trouble."

"Take a seat and I shall explain."

Maxwell did so as Pennywhistle went round to a side table and poured two glasses of orange juice. He handed one to Maxwell, then took a seat behind a spindle-legged Sheraton writing desk. "I know that you no longer drink wine or spirits, so I prepared a healthier beverage. This juice was freshly squeezed this morning and comes from the orangery that is a recent project of mine."

Maxwell took a healthy gulp and smiled. "It's very good."

The library case clock struck three. Pennywhistle glanced out the window at the grey, lowering day. "What I am about to tell you must remain in the strictest confidence. The trouble that I mentioned is a crisis of dangerous proportions."

Maxwell started. "You usually understate things. For you to utter the word 'crisis' must mean the situation is dire indeed."

Pennywhistle spent the next ninety minutes explaining the situation. Maxwell listened closely, first with surprise and then with concern. The orange juice in the pitcher had vanished entirely by the time Pennywhistle concluded.

"And you have been given four months to clean up this mess?" said Maxwell. "This seems a problem that might take years to set right."

"Agreed, but as with all campaigns, a less-than-ideal set of circumstances is a given. We must make do with what we have, not what we would wish for. The funds that I have been given will be stretched to the limit. Your experience as a banker will be helpful, but it is chiefly your military expertise that I will call upon. I am allowed one assistant Border Warden to roam the countryside and speak in my name. I would like to offer you that post. It would not pay very much and would necessitate you taking a leave of absence from Baring Brothers. I could speak to them on your behalf. The board knows me because of my dealings with Mr. John Quincy Adams, who uses the bank as the official depository for American funds in Britain."

Maxwell considered Pennywhistle's words, then said, "You stood by me when everyone else wanted me thrown to the hounds. I did no small share of harm when I was a drunkard, and I would like to make up for it by doing some real good. So, I shall accept the appointment as Assistant Warden of the East English March, and I shall do everything in my power over the next four months to bring justice to that troubled area." He rubbed his chin slowly in thought. "It seems to me that once we stop these reconstituted Reivers, we might also be able to bring some economic justice to the region. If we succeed, I might even consider relocating my family to Berwick, where Baring Brothers has a branch."

"Excellent, but we have a lot of ground to cover first. We will need the Board of Ordnance survey maps that you see in that untidy pile in the corner. The only way to see the big picture is to spread them out and spend time on our hands and knees for the next few hours. I have assembled a registry of places that have been attacked and homesteads that have lodged official complaints. I want to see if there is any sort of pattern."

The maps that Pennywhistle and Maxwell examined covered all six of the old Border Marches, an area of roughly 1,800 square miles that encompassed high hills, deep valleys, elevated moorlands, agricultural plains, and a rocky coast. Pennywhistle read aloud reports of raids, thieving, extortions, murders, and robberies, while Maxwell marked their locations with colored pins on the various maps. Pennywhistle cautioned that what had made it into the reports was only a fraction of the Reivers' depredations, because many locals were too frightened to report an incident.

A pattern began to emerge: 90% of the pins were in just two Marches, the English East March and the Scots East March. And of that 90%, 60% of the pins were in the English East March. That meant that Pennywhistle could focus on policing 600 square miles rather than the entire Border area. And he could further tighten that focus to just the 300 square miles of the English East March. It was still a large territory to cover, but it could be done.

"I have been making some banker's calculations of the financial damage caused by these raids," said Maxwell. "I would say, factoring in stolen goods, we are looking at a sum greater than 250,000 pounds. And that does not include the discouragement of new businesses caused by the fears generated by these raids."

"And there will be the costs of rebuilding," responded Pennywhistle. "Not just restoring buildings and livestock but restoring people's confidence in a safe future. Dread and uncertainty can poison men's minds long after the original cause of the fear is gone."

"I have had the experience of rebuilding myself. I like to think that redemption can be an option, no matter what has gone before."

Pennywhistle was of two minds on that point. Once, he had once nearly died — according to Sergeant Dale, he had been dead for several minutes before mysteriously reviving — and his vivid memories of those few minutes had changed his life profoundly. He knew redemption was possible in the most unlikely of souls, but he had also known men who rejected every option of decency, who took dark delight in the indulgence of their worst appetites, who relished the harm they caused to others. If any of the Reivers were of that cast, it was his chosen duty to curtail their cruelties.

"I have chartered a packet ship, *The Star of the North,* which sails in one week. I have spoken to the Earl of Westminster, who runs a charity for Waterloo veterans; he has been preparing a list of veterans who have the character and training to withstand the rigors of a short but hard campaign. I asked for details of their service and for the Earl to give his general impression of each man. That list and those evaluations should be arriving this evening. I anticipate hiring fifteen men in London. I need a quartermaster, armorer, gunsmith, blacksmith, farrier, cavalry instructor, drillmaster, fencing master, five riflemen, a mechanic who can repair anything and..." he paused, "a bodyguard. I shall need an extra set of eyes to watch the shadows at my back. I want men who have no connections to the Borders, of whose loyalty I can be sure. The remainder of the personnel will be hired once we arrive in the East March. You will assist me because yours is an old Border surname, which will give me added credibility."

"How do you foresee this enterprise unfolding?"

"We first need to know who we are up against. The leader of the Reivers has concealed his identity, and I think he is playing a long game. But the tighter his grip on his followers, the more likely some will slip through his fingers. There are always disaffected people in any criminal organization ruled by a strong leader, men who are willing to cooperate with authorities in return for a bribe or a pardon. We will need to investigate the sites of raids and interview a great many people. But most of all we will need to establish a network of informants."

"You mean spies?"

"Yes, but not the kind of spy who makes a profession out of espionage. These will be ordinary people who simply keep their eyes and ears open and report any encounter with the Reivers or their helpers. My guess is that the Reivers periodically seek new recruits or people who can assist them, both by inducement and coercion. We will need to establish headquarters at a central point. Berwick would be best because it is a walled city with modern defenses and a small garrison. Being walled, we can observe any comings and goings through its gates. Berwick also has a personal connection: my widowed sister-in-law lives there with my two nieces in the city's grandest mansion. Nicholas Pennywhistle erected it in the early 18th century, relying on a fortune built on gun running in India."

"So, you have a bounder in your background?" Maxwell chuckled.

"I do, but I make no attempt to pretend otherwise. I trust that people will see the strength of my character. Show me any pedigree of more than ten generations and I guarantee there is a bastard or a blackguard in the lineage."

"I know there are more than a few reprobates occupying the branches of my family tree," responded Maxwell. "Chief among them is my father. I know you said that I should try to reconcile with him, but I cannot shake a suspicion that when my mother fell down the stairs to her death, he might have given her the fatal push."

"That would be an unpardonable sin, but you would have to be certain before confronted him with such an accusation. And judging from the expression on your face, you are not quite certain. Am I right?"

Maxwell nodded.

"Perhaps that is just as well. Your father owns considerable estates in the Borders, and we may have to interview him. I need to know that you can face him without losing control. Can you do that?"

"It will be hard, but yes."

"The scars of childhood run deep and can take years to heal," murmured Pennywhistle. "Speaking of relatives, I have not seen Sarah, my brother's widow, since my return from America in 1814; a visit is long overdue. She wields considerable influence in the social circles of the city, and her home is a magnet for exactly the kind of people who might be pressured by the Reivers. Unlike the shadowy prime mover of these depredations, we wish to make our presence very public, to represent stability and trustworthiness, in order to encourage fearful persons to talk to us."

He tapped the map beside which he was kneeling. "Berwick's location on the North Sea will facilitate the arrival of supplies from London. It is but eight miles from Whistlestop, and many of the raids have occurred within a 20-mile radius of the home of my forebears. For the quick pursuit of raiders, we will need a mobile strike force of at least fifty riders, who would be ready to move at a moment's notice. Ideally, they would be able to apprehend any band of raiders before they got far."

"What will we do with the Reivers we capture?"

"We shall evaluate them on a case-by-case basis; the most egregious might receive summary justice from field versions of the Court of Star Chamber, but I should prefer that most be tried according to the present legal system. I want to return the Borders to a state of civility, and that is best done by staying within the bounds of existing law. I should add that we will also have to go after the men who fenced the stolen livestock and valuables."

There was a knock on the library door.

"Come," said Pennywhistle.

Marco Ruzzini entered the room. "You asked me to call, sir, when Mr. Maxwell arrived, and here I am."

"Yes, Marco. I want you to tell Mr. Maxwell exactly what happened during the raid on Whistlestop. It is one thing to read the words of an after-action report, quite another to hear an account from an eyewitness."

Marco advanced toward Maxwell and extended his hand, which Maxwell shook firmly.

"I understand that you were present at Whistlestop during the raid and that you are lucky to be alive. I welcome the opportunity to hear the full particulars."

Marco spent the next hour recounting his experience in the most vivid detail. He concluded with, "I am sure that the red-haired man with the nasty features was behind it all. Everyone was afraid of him."

Pennywhistle disagreed. "No, Marco, I think the man who led the raid is not the same one who planned it. I think the man we seek would never allow himself to be seen by people who could identify him to the authorities. He would get others to take the risks while he played the puppet master pulling their strings. He has assembled a formidable organization, and I do not think bringing him to justice will be easy."

"I want to help," said Marco stoutly.

"I am reluctant to expose you to danger, but I must admit that your eyewitness testimony would be useful in the trials of any Reivers we capture. And at 16 you are old enough to hold the King's Commission. But is this what you really want? You had spoken of desiring to matriculate at Oxford, perhaps to study history."

"I would still like that, sir, but I want to see with my own eyes justice done to those who injured my friend Peter. Please let me come, sir. I ride well enough that I could be one of your messengers."

Pennywhistle frowned. "I will consider your request, Marco, but this will be work for men, not boys."

"I promise that I will not fail you, sir."

"Be careful of making promises that you might not be able to keep."

"Nico wants to come as well. He says his experience fighting pirates in the East Indies will make him useful. These Reivers are pirates of a kind."

Pennywhistle sighed. "I have grown tired of watching him mope about trying to decide what to do with his life. The campaign ahead might be just the medicine to cure him of his indecision."

"Neither he nor I will let you down. We're not afraid!"

Pennywhistle looked Marco hard in the eye. "Fear can save your life. Fear is like the falling mercury in a ship's barometer: it's designed to warn you when a storm is coming."

CHAPTER 7

A Little Fright Music

15th September 1816

James Jackson was scared. The execution of Jock Elliot had silenced all murmurs of complaint or conscience. Being a member of Scott's gang had gotten much worse. Not content with terrifying his followers, Scott had begun to test their loyalty by making them participate in the commission of multiple felonies. Jackson and two others were tasked with hijacking a small shipment of silver bound for the silversmiths in Berwick.

Two previous shipments had been seized easily; when confronted by three heavily armed men, the merchants had preferred to keep their skin intact than risk their lives. But the silversmiths had taken precautions with this one, and the wagon was accompanied by two heavily armed guards who were rumored to be former hussars from the 16th Light Dragoons.

The main road into Berwick from the south lay atop a flat, treeless plateau with little in the way of ravines, folds of ground, or stands of trees which could furnish a hiding place for highwaymen. There was only one spot from which to stage an ambush: a low hill with a grove of trees known as Becket's Knob. Jackson and his companions waited there on horseback.

Jackson scanned the road with his spyglass, and it was not long before the small convoy hove in view. The two mounted guards had drawn their pistols and were looking in his direction. They were clearly familiar with Becket's Knob and were anticipating an attack. Jackson closed his spyglass and spoke to his companions. "I think we should call the whole thing off. It's too dangerous. I am no great shot with a pistol and have only used my sword against unarmed men. Those guards have probably seen real battle."

"Are you insane?" replied Rex Tillerson. "Do you think Scott will accept failure and just say, 'Better luck next time'?"

"Scott will kill one of us as an example to the others," responded Noah Fenwick. "At least with those guards we have a fighting chance. I say we wait until they ride past us. Maybe they will believe they are safe and will relax their vigilance, and we can attack from behind. We will draw our swords, ride like devils, and pitch straight into them."

The convoy was now 200 yards away, and the guards were scanning the top of Becket's Knob, but the three Reivers made sure they were below the crown of the low hill. They waited, tense with apprehension, lest the guard decide to ride over and investigate the high ground, until the sounds of hooves and harness plodded past. Then they rode forward under the shelter of the trees.

"It's now or never," said Tillerson. "Are you with us, Jackson?"

Jackson shuddered but knew he had no choice. He drew his sword and pasted a fierce look on his face that he suspected was less than convincing." God help us! Let's go!" He put the spurs to his hobbler and raced out of the grove onto open ground. Milburn and Fenwick followed close behind.

But one guard had moved to the rear of the wagon and was on full alert. Seeing the raiders, he shouted a warning to mate, who wheeled his horse smartly to assess the threat. The guards retained the aggressive nature of hussars and did not wait to receive an attack; they put the spurs to their own mounts and raced uphill, closing the distance to the raiders so quickly that in mere seconds they were in pistol range.

At thirty yards, the first guard fired his pistol, and Tillerson tumbled from the saddle.

The second guard fired but missed. He drew his saber and charged straight at Fenwick. He and Fenwick slashed at each other, but the difference between a fierce amateur and a seasoned professional was like the difference between hot embers and roaring flames. Fenwick took a slash to the throat and fell sideways off his horse.

Jackson in a panic fired his pistol at Fenwick's killer, wounding him in the stomach. The guard doubled over, moaned, and used his thighs to guide his horse away from his opponent, knowing he could fight no more that day.

Jackson faced the second guard from twenty yards, and their gazes locked. Jackson's eyes were wide and pale; he knew had no chance in a saber fight against the man he opposed. The second guard's eyes were hard, but his expression seemed to say, "Do you really want to do this?" The guard knew he would prevail, but considering what had just happened to his friend, he had no wish to take an unnecessary risk. He was, after all, fighting for money, not king and country.

The two stared at each other for another few seconds, then Jackson surrendered to his fear, about- faced, and put the spurs to his horse. He galloped off, thinking of nothing except that he had escaped certain death.

The second guard turned his horse away from Jackson and trotted over to his wounded friend. He had done his job of protecting the silver, and now it was time to see if he could save his friend's life.

Once Jackson was safely away, the consequences of what he had done began to eat at him. He could not go back to Scott, and returning home might bring danger to his family. Then Bill Clemon's face appeared in his mind's eye, and his nerves started to steady. Clemons had a plan for a self-imposed exile, and Jackson thought that perhaps he could join him. He cursed himself for not having joined Clemons during his exit in the first place, but he had at least a day before Scott learned of his failure and he would make good use of it.

Angus Heatherington was a large, strong man, and so he had been saddled with a role that he had never performed and which he found highly disagreeable. He was to be used as muscle, an enforcer for the loan sharking operation that Scott conducted in the city of Berwick. Short term loans with interest rates approaching 40% were made to selectively targeted businesses: tailor shops, bakeries, and jewelers whose owners teetered on the edge of bankruptcy and who had been denied loans by conventional banks. Most of those who took loans were hard working, but victims of economic hard times. Repayments on the loans were required monthly, and a missed payment incurred a stiff penalty. Enough missed payments would make it nearly impossible to reduce the original principle, resulting in men having to repay 900 pounds on a 500-pound loan. When it was clear that a borrower was about to default, Scott would send a persuader to explain the situation and an enforcer to break some bones.

Heatherington thoroughly disliked the persuader with whom he had been paired. Oliver Mason was a short, weasel-faced man with greasy skin and a heart of stone. He talked fast and aggressively, a born bully, and he brooked no compromise. He liked to see people quake in fear and particularly enjoyed watching men of good character reduced to tears.

Currently, Heatherington and Mason faced a tailor named John Wilburn, whose wife and daughter huddled behind him, terror on their faces. Wilburn's shop employed four assistants and was a mainstay of Berwick, but the son of a local lord had refused to pay his extensive bills, and Wilburn didn't even have the money to resupply his stock.

"I just need a few more days. My cousin says he will get me the money. I can have it by sundown tomorrow."

"You have missed three payments," said Mason with icy menace. "We have been more than generous, and you have presumed on our generous nature. You need a physical reminder of what happens to those who do not pay. I realize that you need your hands for your business, but your legs are another matter."

"No please," pleaded Wilburn. "I swear on my mother's grave that I will get you the money."

Mason scoffed. "Then you must hold your mother in low regard to make such a promise." Mason turned to Heatherington. "Mr. Heatherington, break Wilburn's left kneecap."

Heatherington hesitated. Kneecapping was a particularly painful and debilitating injury.

Wilburn turned to flee, but Mason seized him by the arm. Mason glared at Heatherington, making plain his irritation that his enforcer had failed to act instantly.

Heatherington sighed, raised his cricket bat and lined it up with Wilburn's patella. He cocked his arm and swung it — but not with all his might. Even so, there was an audible crack as it connected with Wilburn's kneecap, followed by a shriek of pain as he collapsed on the floor. He rolled about in agony, whimpering, "Oh god, oh god."

His wife and daughter burst into tears.

Mason smiled.

"We shall return in two days. If you do not have the money, your other kneecap will be forfeited." He bent down, stopped Wilburn's rolling, and jerked Wilburn's head level with his own. "Do we understand each other?"

"Yes, yes, yes," moaned Wilburn. "You will get your money."

"I had better! And if you say a word to the authorities, I will hear of it and increase your pain tenfold."

"I will say nothing to anyone," moaned Wilburn.

Mason rose, contemptuously turned on his heel, and walked toward the door. Heatherington followed, cries of pain and sorrow echoing in his ear.

Once outside, Heatherington confronted Mason. "Why did we injure that man? We should have gone after that lordling who failed to pay his bill."

"That would bring down too much attention from his fellow aristocrats, who would be outraged and might have the power to cause real trouble for us. Wilburn has no influence beyond his family and employees."

"It still seems like shooting the messenger instead of the man who caused the message to be sent. How many more of these errands do we have today?"

"Three. Just like the rhyme. "A butcher, a baker, and a candlestick maker. Don't look so glum, Heatherington. Once I let them know what you did to Wilburn, I am certain they will pay up. By this time tomorrow, I will have everything that is due."

Heatherington feared what he was becoming and wanted out of Scott's organization. He realized Scott was harming the very people that he had vowed their organization would help. He thought about talking to the authorities, but he knew some were on Scott's payroll. He had never felt so impotent in his life.

While Heatherington was thinking of ways to escape Scott's Bairn's, a young man named Tristen Barnes was being initiated into its ranks. The initiation took place in the ruins of an old monastery ten miles north of Heatherington's location. A monastery was appropriate since the ceremony had quasi-religious overtones; this was a deliberate effort to make the criminal organization seem like a brotherhood with sacred ties.

Barnes had been taken to the spot blindfolded with his hands tied. He was a short, squat twenty-year-old who had acquired a reputation as a brawler, and he looked forward to having more scope for his favorite activities of drinking, fighting, and intimidating men, especially ones older and taller, but weaker than himself.

A tall, burly man with a large head and uneven teeth removed his bonds and blindfold and spoke menacingly. "Do you know where you are?"

"No," said Barnes.

"Good."

"You are about to become part of the family known as Scott's Bairns. Do you have any objections to that?"

"None at all," replied Barnes. His eyes took in the four companions standing behind his interrogator. They looked just like the tough, ruthless customers who were the stuff of his dreams.

One man advanced with a knife. A second paced forward, holding up a picture of a saint with a halo. A third advanced with a candle.

The man with a knife pricked Barnes's index finger. The man with the picture thrust it forward and allowed Barnes's blood to fall on it. The third man ignited the picture.

His interrogator spoke. "Now, repeat after me. 'May I burn, may my soul burn like this paper, if I ever betray anyone of my new family, Scott's Bairns.'"

Barnes repeated the words with the appropriate solemnity.

His interrogator acquainted him with the terms of his bargain. "Your new family takes precedence over all others and all former allegiances. You are not to discuss your new family with anyone. You are to maintain yourself at readiness at all times, and when your captain calls, be it day or night, you must come instantly. You must comport yourself with respect to all others in your new family. If any disputes arise between you and other members that you cannot resolve, you must look to your captain for a resolution. You must never lay your hands on family members, and you must never bother their wives and children. Remember, I am talking about OUR FAMILY, not the families of outsiders. You must never engage in activities unsanctioned by your captain. You must never kill a government official without approval from Mr. Scott himself. You must never wear red, for Mr. Scott believes that is a color favored by informers. Failure to meet any of these conditions will result in your execution. Do you understand and accept these terms?"

"I do," replied Barnes, cockily.

"Good." His interrogator clapped him on the back. "Welcome to the family. You are now what we call a made man, a full-fledged member of a grand brotherhood."

As Barnes was being inducted into one brotherhood, Thomas Selby, another made man, was bedeviling a brotherhood of an entirely different kind. The organization was The Working Man's Benevolent Society, a group of men who had formed themselves into a loose organization that was ostensibly dedicated to establishing schools for the children of their members but was in fact the forerunner of a trade union. They were poorly paid mill workers, and their numbers had swelled to the point where they would soon be able to stage a strike for better wages. For now, they kept their true purpose secret, since if their real intentions were discovered before they were ready to act, their employers would fire the lot of them.

But one member had been careless and shot his mouth off when drunk. That information had swiftly traveled back to Walter Scott. And now Scott's man, Selby, was threatening to reveal their existence to every mill owner in the area unless they paid him a hundred pounds a month. That was a stiff fee, and it came out of the fund that they had established for the widows and orphans of their members.

Selby met their president, Henry Potts, in the darkest corner of a seedy tavern that no respectable working man would ever frequent.

"Do you have my money?"

Potts handed him a small canvas pouch. "I do, but that is the last payment we can make for the next three months. We need to husband our resources for other purposes."

"You mean a strike?"

"I did not say that."

"You don't have to. Your face says it for you. It would be bad for your group, maybe fatal, if word of that strike leaked."

"You'd be stupid to do that. If we were dissolved, your principal would never get another penny."

"We have enough other sources of money that we could afford to make an example of you."

"You would harm a great many families."

"And just how does that concern me?"

"Have you no humanity, sir?"

"I do, and because of that I shall grant your organization a week's reprieve. You have that long to reconsider suspending payments to us."

"I will have to take it up with our board, Mr. Selby."

"I am sure you can be very persuasive, Mr. Potts. Meet me here in one week with your answer. If it is not the right one, you are going to be a very unpopular man, and not just with your fellow workers."

"Meaning my home might get unwanted visitors?"

Selby looked Potts hard in the eye and hissed, "You know exactly what I mean. Now I must be off. I have bigger fish to fry than you. Remember, one week."

Selby exited the tavern, and Potts stumbled to the bar, where the bartender was serving drinks. "I'll have a whiskey shot. No, make that a double." He fumbled in his pocket for the coins, wondering if he would even be alive 8 days hence.

Selby's next call was to the head man of a group of rubbish collectors who disposed of the trash in Berwick. Despite the literal bad smell associated with its collection, there was a small fortune to be made in rubbish disposal. William Harbinger had been able to threaten all but two of Berwick's trash collectors into looking for other work and had replaced them with people loyal to himself and Walter Scott's chain-of-command. He had formed them into a new company called, "Clean Berwick." As soon as the last two independent holdouts were gone, Harbinger would have a monopoly and would immediately double collection fees.

"They are proving more stubborn than expected," Harbinger informed Selby. "But if I continue to apply pressure, they will quit in a few weeks."

"That timetable is too long for The Big Man."

"What do you propose?"

"Give me the location of the tenements in which they live, and I will burn them down."

"A lot of other people live in those tenements besides the rubbish men."

"That will just be their bad luck. I can have a group of my bully boys ready with torches by tomorrow night. Those tenements are firetraps anyway, and who is to say that the cause of a fire was not just sheer carelessness on the part of one of its inhabitants?"

"Very well then, Mr. Selby, have your boys meet me at this location tomorrow night. I don't want any trouble from The Big Man."

"Right oh. My lads will meet you here at the stroke of midnight."

Selby's final call was to a gambling den called The Magic Lantern, which also sold opium. All the dice were loaded, every game was rigged, and the gamblers who were also users were rendered stupid and oblivious by their addiction. Scott was not an opium dealer per se but received shipments from time to time from a sea captain who ran guns to outlaw Indian rajahs; cash poor princes sometimes offered opium in lieu of hard coin.

"How is business?" said Selby to the den's proprietor, Archibald Simpson.

"Never better. The worse the economy gets the more people come to visit me. I look at these misguided souls and thank God that I never acquired a taste for opium. Most of them are in a perpetual fog."

"A distributor should never use his own product. What's the take this month?"

"Ten thousand pounds."

"That is better than expected. The Big Man will be pleased."

"The high amount is due to two aristocratic sprigs who have become frequent visitors. They are burning through money like it was going out of style."

"Would you not agree, Mr. Simpson, that nobody ever went broke underestimating the foolishness of the British people?"

Simpson laughed. "Thank God for foolishness!"

When Selby exited The Magic Lantern, carrying his sack of coins, he was being watched and his path shadowed, not by a ruffian or a rival of Walter Scott, but by a woman of quality.

Her name was Sarah Pennywhistle. She was a prim woman that some called a busybody. She found it disgraceful that an opium den existed in a city that she had done so much to make respectable. She had no idea how to shut the den down, but she knew someone who might.

She had just received a letter from her brother-in-law, Thomas Pennywhistle, informing her that he was coming to visit, preparatory to proceeding to the old family estate of Whistlestop. He would probably arrive within a week. He mentioned "getting agreeably reacquainted," but his letter hinted that his visit was something more than a personal journey.

He was a man of courage and action, and right now she needed someone for herself and her two daughters to lean on. He had taken excellent care of them since the death of her husband Peter, Tom's older brother; he had hired good managers to run her husband's mines and mills. As a widow, she was entitled to one third of her husband's estate and properties, but Thomas had deeded the mansion in which she lived entirely over to her and had set up a 50/50 split of the profits from the Pennywhistle mines and mills. He had also told her that she should feel free to remarry any man she chose, regardless of his lineage or estate, that made her happy.

She had plenty of would-be suitors. Rich widows attracted them in importunate droves, but she was too canny to remarry. As a widow with property, she had far more control of her affairs than if she remarried. She lived lavishly but also donated to numerous charitable causes and involved herself with four societies dedicated to good works. Chief among them was the Society for The Betterment of Berwick.

As its president, she had identified the Magic Lantern as the chief source of the city's misfortune and an affront to every notion of good taste and respectability but try as she might, she could never identify who owned it. The mayor of the city and the Sheriff of Berwick proved no help and always made excuses as to why the Magic Lantern could not be shut down. Privately, she guessed they had either been threatened or bribed. However, since she had no proof, there was little she could do. And being a woman, even one of quality and influence, her opinions were taken far less seriously than would those of a man of the same social standing. She did not even have the leverage of the vote to express her displeasure with their... underperformance.

For now, it was time for her to return home, because her French tutor did not like to be kept waiting. What she did not know was that her French tutor also tutored another wealthy client, one who lived deep in the country and was closely guarded 24 hours a day. A man named Walter Scott.

CHAPTER 8

Reading in

23rd September 1816

Two weeks after Pennywhistle's talk with Sidmouth, the masthead lookout on the merchant schooner *Star of the North* spotted the breakwater that marked the entrance to Berwick Harbor and called out, "Land ho!"

Pennywhistle unfurled his Ramsden and panned it over the town ramparts, erected during the reign of Queen Elizabeth I. Berwick had changed hands six times during the border conflicts with Scotland, and these walls were designed to make sure that it stayed permanently an English possession. Such was their strength that they had never been attacked once they had been completed.

He had last visited in 1812, and little seemed to have changed since then. It was still a grim garrison city with 10,000 people and little in the way of charm. Most of the homes were small undistinguished edifices of sandstone, limestone, or brick, but there was a street known as "Mansion Row" which featured some very impressive Palladian Residences, one of which had been built by his ancestor

Nicholas Pennywhistle in the early 18th century. It was now occupied by his brother's widow, Sarah.

As a boy, he had lived there only for short periods and so had a limited attachment to the place. He had spent most of his childhood at his mother's Edinburgh townhouse, his Scots grandfather's estates, and his father's hunting lodge.

His last visit had been the final time that he had seen his brother Peter. Unpleasant memories sprang to mind. The two brothers had spent most of the visit arguing about matters that now seemed utterly inconsequential, and it saddened him that he had never been able to make amends. It was only after his brother's murder that Pennywhistle had discovered that the avaricious, acquisitive Peter had led a secret life as a government operative that was greatly to his credit.

Sammie Jo joined him on deck. She peered at the forbidding gray ramparts of Berwick under the brooding skies. "Don't look like a real friendly place."

"It's not. It's strictly an acquired taste. The people are clannish and suspicious of outsiders, the legacy of hundreds of years of conflict between England and Scotland. I am hoping that the time I spent there as a boy will count with the locals."

Pennywhistle explained to Sammie Jo that the 1.2 miles of wall would resemble a maple leaf if viewed from the gondola of a hot air balloon. Berwick's gray walls were low, thick, covered with turf, and fronted by wide ditches which would expose any men entering them to a withering fire before they got close to a wall. They had been laid out according to the principles of geometry that would later be popularized by the French Marshal Vauban: the walls zigzagged, creating overlapping fields of fire, and five bastions bristled with artillery. A barracks had been added in 1717 and now housed a peacetime garrison of two dozen men under the command of a senior corporal, the successor to a roundly disliked sergeant who had died unexpectedly, to the great relief of the townspeople.

"So, you see, we will be safe from attacks from across the border. These newly minted Border Reivers would be insane to attack the town."

"The expression on your face says you are lying," replied a confused Sammie Jo, "but you never lie."

"Ah, here we come to the crux of the problem. The real danger to us will come not from outside the walls but from inside. I am convinced that the Reivers have eyes and ears everywhere, so we will have to constantly watch our backs. While the authorities have been notified of my coming, no one else has. It will be interesting to see if we have an uninvited reception committee lurking in the shadows."

"If we do, does that mean that there is a spy among the authorities?"

"Not necessarily. When we boarded, you and I may have been recognized. That is one of the drawbacks of being a war hero with a beautiful wife. The fact that we were accompanied by some very fit young men, likely from a military background, could provoke speculation about why they would be traveling to Berwick."

"You think the mastermind's reach extends all the way to London?"

"I would be surprised if it did not. Since London is the chief port in the United Kingdom, it would make sense for him to keep tabs on its shipping. The operation my opponent is running is a large one, and I should not be surprised if certain members of Parliament have been bribed to keep him informed of what Liverpool's government is doing. Sidmouth trusts his staff, but all it takes for a secret to leak is one wayward clerk."

"But maybe a leak ain't a bad thing. You said you want everyone to know who you are and what you intend. If people have advance word of your coming, it just might give them hope, even as your opponent starts to realize that you are someone he should fear."

Maxwell joined them. "I hope I am not interrupting."

"Not at all. Sammie Jo and I were just speculating about whether word of my coming proceeds us."

"As far as I am concerned, you should have commissioned a large banner to be hung over the city hall announcing your arrival, and maybe some pennants as well. My guess is that most folks here are tired of living in fear, tired of paying protection, tired of hijackings and murders, and sick to death of never knowing what misfortune each new day will bring. They just want their normal lives back. They have probably lost faith in the city officials. They should know they now have a champion who can't be intimidated, can't be bribed, and can't be killed."

Pennywhistle smiled. "I most certainly can be killed."

"I know you don't like people referring to you as Bombproofed, but the story of how you got that nickname got around."

Pennywhistle sighed. "I assure you that the incident has been exaggerated."

"Maybe it has, but I think rather than denying the story, you should let us spread it about town. "

"I agree," Sammie Jo said firmly. "Maybe you think the story is horse sh... uh... manure, Tom, but spreading manure around grows a lot of things: like the conversations that will set people thinking that there is a new sheriff in town."

"It elevates you to legendary status," said Maxwell, "and legends cast a glamour, a spell on the minds of men. Many people here believe in supernatural interventions, and if your enemies think that you may have hidden allies from Above, it will make them think twice before taking a whack at you. Think of your nickname as an insurance policy."

Sammie Jo nodded. "Yes. Some people claim to have God on their side, but you can make the case that you can prove it! From what you told me, some of these Reivers are devils, so it would make sense if you cast yourself as a warrior angel."

"This is getting ridiculous," huffed Pennywhistle. "I don't like the idea that people might think that I possess some sort of divine mandate. I have always been an opponent of superstition and don't plan on changing my position any time soon."

"I declare, Thomas Pennywhistle," Sammie Jo put her fists on her hips, "you are being a fool. You have a lifeline, and you are throwing it away. I want you around for a long time, and I am not going to stand for you courting extra danger just because it does not fit in with your view of the universe."

"She's right, you know," said Maxwell gently.

Pennywhistle glared but then began to chuckle ruefully. "I don't want to fight both of you; you may very well be correct. But when we get back home, I never want to hear 'Bombproofed' again. Agreed?"

"Agreed," chorused Sammie Jo and Maxwell.

The ship docked an hour later. A representative of the mayor greeted Pennywhistle as they stepped off the gangplank.

"Welcome, Sir Thomas, Lady Pennywhistle. I am William Armstrong, and I shall be your guide to this fair city. I trust your voyage was a pleasant one. I have a carriage ready to take you to the mayor's office, where he has laid out a welcoming feast. He apologizes for not coming himself, but there has been an incident which I will explain on the way."

He is scared, thought Pennywhistle, but all he said was, "A pleasure to meet you, Mr. Armstrong." Pennywhistle nodded but did not extend his hand. It was a gesture of dominance, making it clear that Armstrong was not his social equal. It was also a way to express his displeasure at being met by an underling. While he wanted to appear approachable, he did not want to seem too approachable. People expected a little arrogance from a man who had been appointed a local suzerain, and he wanted to play his part.

Maxwell was disembarking, one foot on the gangplank. He looked over the stevedores who seemed to be making no move to unload the ship. There was a lot of furtive whispering among them. He heard "Bombproofed" muttered several times. Someone had tipped these dockworkers off. Maxwell gripped the pommel of his sword and shot baleful glances in their direction. He scanned the dock and noticed a man on a widow's walk above the harbormaster's office. He did not look like he worked for the harbormaster, and something about the man's movements was off. He walked quickly and lightly, not with the rolling gait of a sailor. As Maxwell watched, the man bent down, opened a long canvas sack, and extracted a rifle.

"Shooter! Take cover!" yelled Maxwell at the top of his lungs.

Pennywhistle instantly obeyed, grabbing Sammie Jo's arm and pulling her down with him. Armstrong froze.

"Crack!" The bullet intended for Pennywhistle struck Armstrong in the back.

Before Armstrong hit the ground, Maxwell had jumped the gangplank and begun a pursuit.

Pennywhistle and Sammie Jo rose, then knelt beside Armstrong. Bubbles of blood foamed at his lips and his complexion was an ashen grey. Pennywhistle recognized the signs of imminent death. "This is not how it was supposed to be," Armstrong mumbled.

Not how it was supposed to be. Did that mean Armstrong was appalled that the formal reception had come under attack, or did it mean something more sinister? Had Armstrong known about the ambush?

Maxwell moved fast, closing the distance quickly as his quarry descended from the rooftop was a short-legged man who was not a particularly swift runner.

The assassin glanced behind him several times, a terrified look on his face, natural enough, considering he was being pursued by an angry giant. When Maxwell judged the distance right, he took a flying leap and his 240 pounds crashed down on the man's back, squashing him as if he were a fly and Maxwell the fly swatter. Maxwell rolled off and drew his dagger. The old instincts were strong; he wanted to slit the man's throat and be done with him. But the need for information trumped retribution.

"Who hired you? Speak, if you value your life!" Maxwell jerked the man to his feet, then stomped hard on one booted foot while gripping his prisoner's arms.

The man gasped and struggled. "I don't know his name!" he whimpered. "He approached me last night in a tavern. He said he had heard I was a good shot from my years as a gamekeeper. He seemed to know my whole life."

"What else did he say?" Maxwell shook the man as if he were a terrier worrying a rat.

"He said he'd heard I was down on my luck and asked if I wanted to earn 100 shillings. I told him I did! He explained what he wanted and gave me a description of the target. I didn't want to kill anyone, but he offered me a five-pound note and said there would be another one when the job was done. Ten pounds would pay my food and board for a year. Besides that, he did not look like a man who would take no for an answer. I was not sure I would live out the day if I refused! I'm thinking he works for the same man who has taken control of so many of the dockworkers of the city."

"Did he give you a place to meet when the job was done?"

"At the Old Tabard Inn on Pudding Lane. He said—" The man's body jerked, and his eyes widened into a blank stare. Maxwell started in shock as the man slumped lifelessly in his grip. A swift examination discovered the entry hole of a bullet in the keeper's back. Maxwell looked up at the half-timbered buildings whose upper stories made the alley seem like a rabbit warren, trying to determine where the shot had come from. He wondered then if he might be next and drew the pocket pistol that he kept handy. Seeing no movement at any window or casement, he backed away, then turned and ran for the docks. He was frustrated, but he had learned something. Pennywhistle was right about a leak. His shadowy enemy had a long reach and was bold enough to risk a preemptive strike. And he was ruthless about silencing anyone who was willing to talk to the authorities. Pennywhistle had his work cut out for him.

While Maxwell dealt with the assassin, the fifteen men who Pennywhistle had hired had exited the ship and formed a protective cordon around him and Sammie Jo. They had their weapons at the ready, and the fierce expressions on their faces dared anyone to trifle with them. Bill Masters, the drillmaster, left the cordon and paced over to one of the watching stevedores, reclining against a bale of wool. His posture was arrogant, and Masters judged him to be the leader of the dockyard workers.

Masters bellowed in his best drillmaster voice. "You, there! Wot's your name?"

"Travers," replied the man whose posture suddenly became a lot less arrogant.

"Travers! I want you and your mates to unload this ship immediately. Snap to it, now!" He waggled a large bag in his hand, then drew forth a cat-o-nine tails. "I am holding you personally responsible, Travers, for the actions of all the stevedores on the docks. If you do not unload this vessel swiftly and carefully, so that nothing goes missing or broken, I promise you I shall apply this whip to your back until it is a bloody mess." His hard eyes and the menace in his voice were not lost on the dockworkers. Twenty of them jumped off the crates they had been sitting on and began walking briskly toward *The Star of the North*.

Masters watched them closely and added, "Handle everything with care. If anything gets damaged or broken, the man responsible will get from me a thorough flogging that he will not soon forget. I want the crates, trunks, and luggage loaded onto wagons and the lot delivered to the Berwick Barracks. Some of my comrades will provide you with an escort. There have been several hijackings in and about the city of late. Woe to anyone who attempts to steal from Sir Thomas Pennywhistle!" Masters saw alarm and recognition on the faces of the stevedores, confirming his employer's suspicions that the expedition's arrival had been anticipated.

Pennywhistle observed the whole thing and knew he had chosen wisely. The men he'd hired were being paid well, but Masters' conduct and the willingness of his mates to protect Pennywhistle indicated that had won something that no amount of money could buy: their loyalty. He had taken the trouble when he hired them to thoroughly explain his purpose, telling them that they were going to bring to justice exactly the kind of men who exploited out of work veterans like themselves. They might be strangers to the North Country, but there was a bond among veterans that transcended regional suspicions and prejudices.

A grand carriage came rolling up to the docks, its sides emblazoned with the arms of the City of Berwick. A footman stepped down from the driver's box and opened the door. A man of medium height stepped out, wearing the ceremonial attire of the Mayor of Berwick replete with ermine and jewels. He walked toward a startled Pennywhistle and Sammie Jo, and the protective cordon around the two parted reluctantly to admit him.

Despite his pomp, he looked flustered as he announced, "I am Mayor Charles Flanders. I am sorry I was delayed, Sir Thomas, I do beg your forgiveness. I have prepared a dinner in your honor at the Guildhall, with the city's worthies in attendance, but you look to have met with some... ah... misfortune."

"That's putting it mildly," said Pennywhistle with acid in his voice. He pointed to Armstrong's corpse. "Do you know this man? He said he was your representative."

The mayor looked at the corpse with an expression of distaste that changed to shock. "I do know him, but I assure you he does not work for me. He has often been the "respectable" front man and spokesman for one of the loan sharks plaguing our city."

"He was part of an assassination plot that came within a breath of succeeding. My arrival was supposed to have been kept secret, but I get the impression that someone has been selling tickets."

"I apologize, but the city is riddled with informers." The mayor looked harassed and frustrated. "I only told the city's best people this morning when your ship was first sighted."

"That will have to change in short order, Mayor Flanders. I have some ideas on the subject, but you and your administration will have to follow my orders exactly. Are you prepared to do so?"

"I would welcome your ideas, Sir Thomas! This city and the country around it are in a crisis that is beyond our power to solve."

"Solve it we shall," said Pennywhistle confidently. "Lawlessness must become a thing of the past.

Maxwell returned at that moment, a downcast look on his face. Pennywhistle stepped forward to talk with him privately. "I see you are empty-handed," he said quietly.

"I caught him, but he died before he could say much."

Pennywhistle frowned.

"No, I did not kill him. He was murdered."

"My opponent is a thorough man. Useful to know."

Masters joined them and addressed Pennywhistle. "The wagons are loaded, Sir Thomas, awaiting your command to move."

"Those stevedores work uncommon fast."

Masters smiled. "They just needed some motivation."

Pennywhistle pondered his course of action. He wanted to move quickly to get his assets in place, but undue haste would suggest fear and possibly panic.

"Mr. Maxwell, I am putting you in charge of the wagons. I want you to use my loyal fifteen as an escort and convey the wagons to the barracks. Unload the military supplies and see to their storage. My personal belongings I will sort out later. Find quarters for my men and inform the corporal in charge that he is now under your command."

"But, Sir Thomas, in light of what has just happened, shouldn't a few men remain with you and Lady Pennywhistle to act as bodyguards?"

"No. It is admittedly a risk, but it will take time for my opponent to organize another shot at me. I will attend the dinner at the Guildhall and behave as though nothing untoward has happened. Arriving with an armed escort would send the wrong message to people whose cooperation I very much need."

"I don't like it," sighed Maxwell," but I will do as you say."

Pennywhistle turned to the mayor, displaying his patented diplomat's smile. "You have heard what I have said, Mayor Flanders, and know my intentions. Now I should welcome dinner and conversation. Lead on and let us see if we can salvage the remainder of the day."

The startled mayor responded, "Yes, yes of course. I thought perhaps to take you to my own house to allow you and

Lady Pennywhistle sometime to recover from this unpleasantness, but we can certainly proceed directly to the guildhall."

"I assure you that we are fine." Pennywhistle decided to do something he detested: invoke his standing as a war hero. With the audience at hand, word would travel swiftly. "When you have fought against Napoleon's Imperial Guard, the actions of a dockyard miscreant seem insignificant." That was a deliberate insult aimed at his opponent, and his slight emphasis on the words "Napoleon's Imperial Guard" underscored the message: *I have fought against a tyrant and his best warriors. I survived them; I am not intimidated by the likes of you.*

"Waterloo was a great and a terrible day," said the mayor solemnly. "Would that I could have been present to see the triumph of our brave men in red."

Spoken like a true civilian, thought Pennywhistle. War was only glorious when you were at a safe distance from its bloody reality.

The mayor opened the door of his carriage himself instead of having his footman do it. That pleased Pennywhistle, for it meant that the mayor acknowledged his authority. The mayor shouted orders to the driver, and the carriage began to move.

"And now, Mayor Flanders, could you please tell me something about the guests you have invited to this banquet. I do not like to go into bat— ah, attend events devoid of such information as can make conversations pleasant and productive. I should welcome any information, no matter how trifling."

"I am happy to oblige, "said the mayor importantly. "I have invited thirty guests; chief amongst them is your sister-in-law,

Sarah Pennywhistle. She is regarded in the city as an angel of charity."

Doesn't sound like the prissy snob I knew, thought Pennywhistle. *But perhaps Peter's death has changed her perspective.*

The carriage rattled along as Pennywhistle acquired a treasure trove of information. The mayor was a born gossip, as well as a keen observer of human frailty, other than his own.

Sammie Jo was a keeper of secrets, and she held tattlers in low regard. Pennywhistle could see she was having a hard time restraining herself from delivering a barbed commentary on the mayor's gossip. Her disapproval did not prevent her from listening closely, however.

He wondered how many of the people he was about to meet could be turned into useful allies, and how many were there simply for recognition, wanting to have their reputations enhanced by being seen with the man of the hour; and whether any might be in the pay of his opponent.

As the carriage stopped in front of the Guildhall, Pennywhistle realized that the grandest thing about the structure was its name. It was of a piece with the city: functional, not beautiful; a square, red brick Tudor building that looked like a budget-minded copy of the front section of St. James' Palace, quite unlike the magnificent Gothic guildhalls found in the Low Countries.

A pair of trumpeters clad in the red and blue livery of the city blew a summons as he, Sammie Jo, and the mayor alighted from the carriage. A crowd of several hundred had gathered, yet more proof that his coming was less than secret. The crowd looked to be a mixed lot of tradesmen, street vendors, apprentices, and coal delivery men. Pennywhistle smiled and waved to them, playing the part of the gracious grandee rather than the aloof lordling. The crowd seemed pleased, and many waved in return. Sammie Jo waved as well, and her wave was met with a chorus of cheers.

A receiving line had been arranged in the Guildhall's Great Hall, a joyless Jacobean construction with small windows and black oak paneling that sucked up light. The people in the line were mostly men, although four had brought their wives. Their attire was appropriately grand, at least for Berwick, though much of it would have been considered unfashionable in London. At the head of the line stood Sarah Pennywhistle with an uncertain smile on her face. She and her brother-in-law had not parted on the best of terms.

All eyes were on him as he advanced, Sammie Jo following close behind. Instead of greeting Sarah with a formal bow followed by the expected stale words of a polite reintroduction, he did something uncharacteristic of his reserved nature: he embraced her, then gave her a quick light kiss on each cheek, in the French manner of greeting.

"Hello, Sarah, it is so good to see you. I hope you and your daughters are well."

Sarah was startled by the unexpected warmth but recovered quickly. "We are quite well, Thomas. My daughters and I have followed your progress in newspapers brought from London and were distressed to hear that you had been injured at Waterloo. I hope that you are fully recovered."

Pennywhistle was surprised to hear sincerity in her voice rather than the pretended concern that he was accustomed to from her. "Yes, I am, but it took longer than expected, which is the chief reason I have been unable to visit before now. We have much catching up to do."

"You must stay with me. There is plenty of room in the house, as you know. I can accommodate your aides as well."

This caught Pennywhistle by surprise, but the mansion was a powerful symbol of respectability, and it would be a bad look if he appeared estranged from a close relative. It was time to stow his pride and engage in a little fence mending.

"I accept your gracious offer and look forward to seeing the girls again. I am a father now, myself."

"Your son's name is Nicholas, is it not?"

Pennywhistle started in surprise.

Sarah smiled. "Berwick is not quite the backwater that you think. I follow the baptismal announcements in *The Times of London* closely."

"Where are my manners?" exclaimed Pennywhistle as he motioned for Sammie Jo to come forward. "Allow me to present Nicholas's mother, my wife, Samantha Josephine."

Sammie Jo curtsied. "Pleased to meet you, I have heard a lot about you." Sammie Jo's voice was diplomatic rather than friendly.

Pennywhistle noticed that she did not say her usual, "I'm just plain old Sammie Jo."

Sarah curtsied in return. "I am pleased to meet you as well. You are a lucky woman to have met a man like Thomas. Is Nicholas still in London?"

"No, he remains on board the ship that brought us with his nanny and an armed guard. I wanted to be sure that he would be safe before bringing him into the city."

Sarah nodded in understanding. "That is sensible. I assure you that he will be both safe and welcome at my home. My daughters will enjoy fussing over him."

Sammie Jo's expression softened at this. "He is already walking, and the assistance of your daughters in guiding his forays will be most welcome."

"I have a collection of children's toys from my daughters' earliest days that he will enjoy. I think it's a fine thing that he will get to know his cousins."

"I do as well." Sammie Jo smiled genuinely. "We should also get to know each other better, so just call me Sammie Jo."

Sarah looked puzzled. "That's so... informal, but," she hastened to add, "delightful."

"I'm from America, and we ain't much for formality. I apologize in advance for the social mistakes I am bound to make. I have been learning English ways, but there is still a heap I don't know. Maybe you can help me with my education."

Pennywhistle realized that Sammie Jo was trying to make Sarah an ally rather than a critic, but Sammie Jo's experience at the Congress of Vienna, as well as the guidance of the formidable Countess of Westminster, meant that she probably knew more about etiquette and protocol than did Sarah; she was not at all the backwoods rustic who had arrived in England two years ago. Still, Sammie Jo had often found it useful to let people underestimate her, since it gave her freedom of action.

"I should be glad to help in any way I can." Lady Sarah glanced behind her. "But I must not monopolize you and Thomas. Allow me to make introductions."

It took an hour for the receiving line to pass Pennywhistle and Sammie Jo. Pennywhistle bowed and Sammie Jo curtsied. Sarah proved to be a great help, since she seemed to know all the guests well. Before each introduction, she whispered in Pennywhistle's ear a single word like "iron", "cotton", or "coal" to give him an idea of their chief business. He matched this to the gossip furnished by the mayor. Her obvious confidence in her brother-in-law encouraged the worthies to exchange more than the usual pleasantries with the Pennywhistles. Six people became bold enough to ask for Pennywhistle's help directly, their concerns urgent enough that they were unwilling to wait for a private audience.

Thomas Soames, a distinguished looking man of fifty with an almost incomprehensible Glasgow burr told him, "I need yuir help badly. Six prize horses were stolen from my stables in the past week, and there's noo help to be had from the constables."

William Welles, a beady-eyed man who was the owner of the city's largest bank, told him," We had a robbery yesterday at one of our branches, and the thieves got clean away."

Stephen Chalmers, a scholarly man who ran the city's most important apothecary shop stated, "My shop was broken into last night and my entire stock of laudanum was stolen, along with many valuable herbs and supplies."

Peter Townshend, with the weathered face of a sailor who had seen many voyages, was Berwick's Harbormaster. "I have had my life threatened more than once. Some nights, I have been told to stay away from the docks entirely. I suspect that on those nights stolen goods are shipped to parts unknown."

Reginald Hinchcliff had the friendly face, pleasant manner, and rotund belly of an experienced publican. He ran the best gaming house in the city, one that offered games of whist, baccarat, and faro to a genteel clientele. His house had a reputation for honesty, and he made sure that his patrons enjoyed the finest food and drink. "I am losing business to the Magic Lantern. That place is an opium den disguised as a gaming establishment, and I know the games are rigged. Some of my customers are patronizing it because opium is given free to new gentlemen clients. Once they get hooked, the owners resupply them only if they agree to engage in ludicrous bets, which of course they lose. Several of my best customers have lost fortunes there and have been reduced from gentlemen of consequence to men with no futures. I should also point out that the owner runs an illegal lottery, one that is cutting into the revenue that our government so badly needs in these difficult times. I wish I could tell you who the owner of the Magic Lantern is, but my best efforts to discover his identity have proven fruitless."

Remington Yates, a dandified man for whom the word snob seemed to have been invented, told his tale. "Two days ago, my wife and daughter were accosted on the street by three ruffians and relieved of all their jewelry. This happened in broad daylight! In broad daylight! And on a busy street! Such is the fear rampant in this city that not one man came to their aid! This is monstrous and must stop!"

The dinner of local fish, fowl, and beef that followed proved tasty and featured good local wines. But the tension among the guests was so palpable that Pennywhistle had the impression that most were not registering the aromas and flavors. Pennywhistle himself focused more on the faces and voices of his companions than he did the food. He chatted with the people beside and across from him, as did Sammie Jo. Both concentrated on the emotions of the speakers as much as the topics of conversation.

A speech was called for at the dinner's end. The folded parchment in his pocket contained Pennywhistle's formal appointment as Warden of the East March. "Reading in," was the time-honored ritual by which the new captain of a ship read aloud his orders to proclaim his formal assumption of command. Pennywhistle had intended to read himself in the following day at a formal ceremony at city hall, but he realized that the people at the long table were the same ones who would be attending that ceremony. He might as well start directly.

Pennywhistle rapped a spoon three times against the table. He rose and took the parchment from his pocket. "Ladies and gentlemen, I have a formal announcement to make. I was going to save this for tomorrow, but there seems no time like the present. The title of Warden of the East March has not been granted for three centuries; it has been revived in answer to the present peril. Some of you may be unacquainted with the post's duties or may have formed incorrect assumptions. Let me dispel any ignorance, as well as state my purpose."

He cleared his throat and began to read in his most imposing command voice. "Know all men by these presents that his gracious Majesty King George III, reposing especial trust and confidence in his well-beloved and trusty servant, Thomas Pennywhistle, appoints him Warden of the East English March: with all the honors, duties, and obligations attending to that office." He continued for several minutes, spelling out exactly what the sovereign expected of him as well as what the new Warden had a right to expect from those under his protection. As he read aloud, he glanced around the table. He saw expressions that ranged from cautious, reserved, and sardonic to hopeful and relieved. When he finished, there was a brief pause followed by polite, and in a few instances, obviously heartfelt applause.

Two men listening in the hall outside took careful note of his every word. They worked for Walter Scott, and by the end of the day he would know what they did.

When Pennywhistle sat down, Sammie Jo whispered to him. "Good speech, Tom, but if wishes were horses, beggars would ride."

CHAPTER 9

Hidden Assets

Walter Scott made meals an occasion, rather than a nod to necessity. He liked them relaxed and quiet, featuring the best food and wine. He liked to ponder matters over a meal; some of his best ideas had come to him while he ate.

He favored French cooking; two favorite dishes were *Salmon Almondine* served with a creamy chardonnay and *Poulet Chasseur* served with a fruity Pinot Noir. Unlike Napoleon, who rarely spent more than fifteen minutes at a meal, he never spent less than an hour. He admired the Corsican and sought to emulate him in many ways, but it made far more sense to savor every mouthful of food and every sip of wine rather than treating them as mere fuel for the furnace.

A solitary man compelled by his occupation to deal with a great many throughout his long day, he generally dined alone, save for a violinist who serenaded him while he ate. He sometimes wished he that had a woman with whom he could share his meals, but he had never been popular with them and so had to rely on a string of ladies of the evening to satisfy his lusts. One woman had told him that he reminded her of a plate of fruits and vegetables: head shaped like a melon, hair like corn tufts, complexion like a beet, eyes like two peas, and a body that resembled a cucumber. He counted himself lucky that nature had blessed him with a deep resonant voice which always commanded attention and respect. Today's meal of coq au vin had been a good one and he savored the memory of its taste as he slowly mounted the steps to the roof of Hermitage Castle. An under-butler greeted him, poured him a large cup of after- dinner coffee, then retreated into the background awaiting the orders that would inevitably follow.

Scott seated himself in a comfortable chaise lounge and contemplated the Liddesdale Valley below as he slowly sipped his coffee. It gratified him that everything as far as he could see belonged to him. Not officially of course, there were tiresome things like deeds, contracts, and the King's Law that stood in the way: unofficially through his network of agents, enforcers, and men-at-arms, he exercised complete control. He wished that control had been based on voluntary compliance rather than fear and terror but reminded himself that Napoleon had been known to deal harshly with newly conquered areas if they had substantial elements who refused to submit themselves to his control.

He endeavored to soften the harshness of his rule by portraying himself as an anonymous Robin Hood. He kept for himself 50% of the proceeds taken on raids and through his network of criminal activities and distributed 30% to his followers, according to rank and achievement. He used the remaining 20% for charitable purposes. He had established 15 soup kitchens and second-hand clothing centers, funded a hospital that catered to veterans, widows, and orphans, and contributed monies for the betterment of the workhouses established by the Poor Law.

Workhouses were only one step better than homelessness and starvation and the inhabitants were often compelled to work at a variety of degrading jobs that no one else wanted. A particularly troubling development was the introduction of treadmills. A person for whom no work could be found was forced to walk in place for hours, his mindless footsteps turning a large iron wheel that encircled the platform that that he walked on. Scott's deputies saw to it that the wheels were banished and that workhouses were brought up to a level where their residents could live tolerably well, though far from anything approaching comfort.

His deputies made a great show of paying veteran's pensions to ten men whose paperwork had been lost by the government. Word of that spread quickly and added greatly to his reputation.

Once he finished his coffee, he summoned the under-butler and gave him the usual instructions. The man nodded in understanding then disappeared. What was to come was part of a weekly ritual that always took place at 3 pm every Sunday. Sunday to Scott was not The Lord's Day, but a day to review the events of the previous week. It was a time to decide what plans had succeeded and which ones had failed, a time to give praise and fix blame, and a time to make new plans for the week ahead.

Scott's chief assistant, Samuel Perry, walked up to him, one hand holding a small portmanteau which contained the weekly reports of Scott's principal assistants. Perry nodded to Scott and then took a seat in a camp chair opposite him. Perry had the mind, skills, and temperament of a born bureaucrat. A fussy, fastidious man who always appeared meticulously groomed, he had a great eye for spotting the key details in every report and had the ability to sum up its chief conclusions in a few well-chosen words. He had read every report in the portmanteau several times and had prioritized their contents. Scott was a busy man and only read a report in full if something Perry had said about it piqued his interest and demanded more detailed information.

"Well, Perry, I think we both know what my chief concern is."

"Of course, Mr. Scott. Pennywhistle is being closely watched."

"I was distressed to hear of the failure of our assassination attempt but upon closer reflection that may have been misguided and premature. It occurs to me Pennywhistle's efforts against me will help us ferret out the weaknesses and vulnerabilities in our organization. If we can get an idea of who is helping him and what he perceives as our weak points, we can take corrective measures." The grim glee in his eyes suggested those measures would be violent ones.

"He has been very active, Mr. Scott. In the past five weeks, he has established himself in the city and takes long daily walks, stopping frequently to talk to all manner of people, asking them what they wish to see changed in the city. He holds a two-hour audience at his headquarters every day, welcoming petitioners, supplicants, and crime victims. He has a secretary take notes and requests some of his visitors to remain to speak at greater length.

Pennywhistle has built a network of spies, confidants, and informers. An effective one too, I am sad to say. Receipts are down 20% from last week in all the rackets and industries that we control in the city. Some of our best men tell me that they are no longer sure who they can trust as they suspect some of their friends may now be informers for Pennywhistle."

"That is very bad."

"It gets worse. The men controlling the docks, the lottery, and the garment trade have been arrested and will be tried in two days. Our usual efforts to intimidate jurors and justices of the peace will not work because Pennywhistle himself is keeping a close eye on them.

Our man in charge of horse acquisitions is being closely watched and says he must lie low for the next two weeks.

Pennywhistle pays a cash bounty to men who provide tips that lead to the arrest of those controlling the rackets in the city. He is something of an artist and has himself drawn pictures of some of the city's main troublemakers based on the descriptions of informants. He has had those drawings made into wanted posters that are now posted all over the city. Each poster is headed in large bold letters:" Have you seen this man?" A reward is promised to anyone providing even a scrap of useful information on the men in the posters. Some of our men who previously enjoyed anonymity are now easily recognized and can now only go about their business at night."

He has worked with the Sheriff to reorganize the local constabulary and has supplemented them with some very tough veterans that he hired in London. These veterans lead four-man constable patrols that sweep the city three times daily. They are catching a lot of our little fish and the fear that we relied upon to keep the locals in line is beginning to dissipate. These patrols are gaining the trust of the people and street children follow them eagerly, children who see and know a lot. Men and women who kept silent in the past are now approaching constables when they see something untoward."

"Damn!" barked Scott. "When an empire falls apart it comes gradually. Before large chunks fall, there is a process akin to erosion. What you are describing is like a new breeze slowly sweeping away grains of sand that have long been dormant and stable. Given time, that breeze will swell into a gale that will wipe a landscape clean of any sand at all. Pennywhistle is currently just a breeze. He cannot be allowed to become a gale."

"How do we do that, Mr. Scott?"

"I have a few ideas, but before I can refine them, I need more information. Please proceed with the rest of your report."

"I warn you, Mr. Scott, it will cause you distress."

"Then I shall have to pass that distress onto Pennywhistle when I know the full particulars of his actions."

"He has formed the chief merchants of the city into an advisory council and meets with them twice a week. These are men of real influence. We had several thoroughly intimidated but now they are refusing to pay protection money any longer. Worse yet, they are daring us to do anything about it. We tried to make an example of one by setting fire to his business, but our men were spotted and chased off by one of these new patrols. While the old constables were content to look the other way or only use harsh language, Pennywhistle's hirelings have turned them into aggressive beasts who are not afraid to break heads."

"It is as I feared. Pennywhistle is not just a man using a piece of government parchment to give him authority, he is a moral leader bent on transforming the character of an entire city. Such men quickly acquire influence far beyond the bounds of any official appointment and that worries me greatly. We need to discredit him, entangle him in a scandal that will reduce him to human dimensions. He must have some vices. They may be the usual ones, gambling, women, greed, drink, or selling secrets to a foreign government. Perhaps his flaw is something more exotic and less easily detected. Maybe he likes boys. Maybe he likes beasts. Maybe he worships Satan."

"Alas, Mr. Scott, he seems to be a man of sterling character spoken well of by all who know him. If he has any vices, it is that he is far too modest and shuns the honors thrust upon him. "

"Bah!" protested Scott. "Every man has an Achille's Heal. We just have to look hard enough to find his."

Perry sighed inwardly. That was the problem with Scott: he believed every man as privately polluted as himself. "I shall make every effort to discover those flaws, but it may take time."

"Then begin immediately. I get the impression that so far Pennywhistle has confined his efforts against us to the City of Berwick. Has he made any efforts against us in the countryside?"

"I hear rumors that he is about to put into operation an early warning network in the countryside, but I have as yet no proof. Still, certain developments in the city cause me to think those rumors might well be true."

"What would those be?"

"There is a lot of activity at Berwick Barracks, a great deal of heaving drilling being carried out under a very demanding and experienced drill master. The garrison has always been quiet before, more like background scenery than soldiers getting ready for a campaign. New men have been observed, local citizens who have enlisted as auxiliaries for short term service. They have been given uniforms and are training alongside the regulars. I have seen no recruiting posters so I would assume they have been funneled to Pennywhistle by the Council of Merchants that he has formed.

He also has a core of specialists that he brought with him from London. These are the sort of people you would engage if you were planning on doing some active campaigning."

"I don't like the sound of that."

"He also has cavalry from the local yeomanry regiment drilling outside of town under the watchful eye of an experienced instructor."

"Families always make men vulnerable" observed Scott. "It makes me glad that I have no living relatives. If Pennywhistle is not open to attack, what about his wife and son? He also has a widowed sister-in-law with two daughters, does he not? Perhaps they have some skeletons in their closets that could be useful."

"His wife is formidable, and she and his child are always well protected. He has two stepsons, but both are often by his side. Both are physically strong, and one has served with the Royal Navy in the East Indies, fighting pirates. His sister-in-law, Sarah wields significant influence in the social circles of the city, but I do not know too much about her background. I will make inquiries. I do know however that her two adolescent daughters, Sybil and Sally, are both guarded, like their mother, but the girls have been known to deliberately run from their guards on occasion: challenging the guards to find them like some girlish game of hide and seek. I am not sure in what regard Pennywhistle holds for them, but he seems very keen on family."

"Do you think kidnapping them would give us leverage?"

"I think it likely but do not know for sure."

"Then find out as fast as you can. Pennywhistle is a bleeding ulcer that must be stanched."

****

Three four-man teams left the Berwick Barracks just after dawn. Acting on hot tips from reliable informants, the teams intended to put a severe dent in three criminal enterprises that were putting a lot of money into the pockets of Pennywhistle's hidden antagonist. Team one was headed by Bill Masters the drillmaster and its target was the counterfeiters who had been flooding the city with fake five-pound Bank of England notes. Robert Meadows, the blacksmith, led the second team and his objective was to shut down the extortionists who had been plaguing the city's fish markets and threatening the fishermen who brought their catch to it. Mark Mason, the armorer, led the final group. His objective might have provoked laughter from those who gave them little thought, but no city could function without them: the city's new rubbish haulers who had strong-armed out the old ones, then immediately doubled the fees charged their clients.

The counterfeiters occupied a nondescript wooden building that had once been a print shop. "Haverford and Sons" was the name emblazoned on the sign outside with a picture of a printing press beneath. A banner had been plastered across its padlocked front door that read, "closed for renovation." The windows had been blacked out.

Masters watched the place for half an hour to make sure that no one left or entered and that there were no hidden sentries. His observations confirmed the particulars supplied by his informant. His men quietly approached the front door. Two of his men, Jack Stevens and Desmond Reese, readied a two foot long, two handled iron battering ram. Masters and his number 2, Peter Sims, drew their pistols. Masters made a quick hand motion. Stevens and Reese retreated ten feet, then ran at the door with their battering ram extended. The ram smashed through the padlock with ease and the door flew open.

Master stepped quickly across the threshold, followed by Sims. Masters panned his pistol menacingly and bellowed, "Hands up! You are all under arrest."

Four frightened men immediately complied. One was stirring sheets of paper in a long tray filled with unpleasant smelling chemicals, one was using a scalpel to put the final touches on an engraving plate, one was running a printing press, and one was applying an iron to the sheets of notes that had just come off the press. Several four foot high stacks of notes had been placed on a small side table. The notes had been neatly bundled into packets each valued at one hundred pounds.

Masters searched the eyes and expressions of the men to decide who was their leader. He finally settled on the engraver, the man whose task required the greatest amount of skill and exactitude. He was a bespeckled man of early middle age who seemed the least panicked of the men.

"What's your name?" Masters barked at him.

"Miller, Steven Miller."

"You are in a lot of trouble Miller."

Miller's eyes turned pleading. "Look, I was forced into this. It's the same story with my friends. We were respectable printers until a few months ago, but when our families were threatened by thugs in the middle of the night, we had no choice but to change over to counterfeiting."

"I have yet to meet a felon who does not proclaim his innocence," said Masters cynically. He pointed to the stacks of notes. "You have been busy, and those notes will be damning evidence at your trial. Counterfeiting is a capital crime. You will all hang."

One of the men began to sob.

"Please, have mercy," pleaded Miller.

Masters believed Miller since other men he had arrested had told similar tales of being coerced. Masters said nothing for a minute, allowing fear to work its magic. He was interested in catching the big fish and was prepared to use the small fry to do it. "I might be prepared to look the other way, but my ignorance would have a price. I would need the names of those who give you orders, I would need to witness the destruction of all your equipment, and I would require all of you to assist me in identifying the products of your trade. I would ask merchants to bring with them any cash remaining from their receipts of the past month to city hall. In secret, under my supervision, I would have you examine each note to determine if it is real or fake. Could you meet those conditions?"

"Yes, yes, yes," said Miller breathlessly as he looked at his mates. "I think I speak for everyone."

"Good, let's start with the names of your superiors."

Miller frowned. "They have never given us names, but I can give you descriptions. As a matter of fact, both will be arriving be arriving here two hours from now. They come once a week to harvest the results of our efforts."

"Describe them exactly."

"One is tall, thin, and has a face with skin like a cadaver. He is missing a front tooth, and has a long scar on his neck, just below his earlobe. He has a tattoo on his right forearm of a mermaid and anchor."

"He goes by Otto Skull in the underworld here," replied Masters." I have been eager to make his acquaintance for some time. And the other?"

"He is short, has the face of a goat, and is missing two fingers on his left hand."

"That's Carl Deathridge. He is wanted for multiple crimes. Where you find Skull, you usually find Deathridge. I should be pleased to bag them both. Under interrogation they will help me to solve many crimes and removing them from circulation will be a great boon to the city. While we wait for their arrival, Miller, I want you to explain to me how the counterfeiting process works from start to finish. Tell me everything, no matter how trivial. The more I know about the process the better I will know the warning signs to look for. I also want you to show me tell-tale signs of a fake bill."

Miller was pleased to have his expertise recognized. "Certainly Mr..."

"Masters. You may call me sergeant major."

"Let me start with the paper, sergeant major. It is important to mix the chemicals for its treatment just right. Oh, I think I forgot to mention that Skull and Deathridge are always punctual and always appear at the stroke of ten."

The next two hours passed quickly. Miller proved a gifted instructor and Masters acquired a peerless education in knowledge that never found its way into any books. At ten minutes before ten, Masters ended the tutorial and instructed Miller and his mates to go back to doing what they usually did. He wanted nothing out of the ordinary to greet the arrival of Skull and Deathridge. Masters replaced the padlock and banner on the front door. The padlock no longer worked but could at least be shut. He hoped Skull and Deathridge would be careless enough not to notice that their key would no longer be necessary. Masters and his assistants drew their pistols, hid themselves in the back room, and waited.

Skull and Deathridge were on time and strolled into the room with cocksure arrogance. Both carried pistols in sashes round their waists but had done this pickup often enough that they knew their flunkeys and felt no need to draw their weapons. "Do you have our money, Miller?"

"I do, its stacked on the table over there. I know you will want to count it as usual.

"Yes," laughed Skull. "We can't have you using your own product."

Masters and Sims stepped from the backroom at that moment. "Hands up you two," barked Masters, "you are under ..."

Masters never finished the sentence. Skull fired his pistol without removing it from its sash. The shot just missed Master's temple, but his replying shot struck Skull square in the chest. Deathridge's hand was struggling to free his pistol from his sash but when he saw Skull fall, his hands shot into the air.

Sims leveled his pistol at Deathridge while Master's demanded he stand still. Masters searched him thoroughly. He found nothing. Deathridge smiled at his frustration.

Sims whispered something in Masters ear and this time Masters smiled. " I had not thought of that! Deathridge take off your boots, now!"

Deathridge's smug expression vanished.

Masters examined his right boot, but it proved ordinary. His left was another matter. Masters found a tiny button on the heel and pressing it caused the heel to slide back, revealing a small compartment. Inside was a miniature book that looked like a ledger. Masters leafed through it quickly and realized he had just been handed The Encyclopedia Brittanica of Berwick counterfeiting. The book contained names of recipients and distributors, past and future delivery dates and locations, and a careful accounting of monies received and paid out. He had enough information to shut down the entire ring of counterfeiters by sundown if he acted quickly. He would need more men. Most of the constables were out on patrols at present but he had been given permission to press any of the garrison soldiers into service in an emergency.

"Sims, bind and gag our prisoner and take him back to the barracks immediately. I will join you there shortly."

"Got it sarn't m'jr." Sims obeyed quickly and a minute later had begun frog marching his captive to the barracks.

"Stevens and Reese, I want you to knock on every door in this block and tell people that there will be a bonfire commencing in twenty minutes. People love spectacles. Tell them that we have broken the counterfeiters oppressing the city and that their equipment and product will be burnt publicly. Tell them it will be a chance for them to literally see money go up in smoke."

Stevens and Reese nodded and dashed off down the street.

Masters turned to the counterfeiters. "I want you to take those axes in the corner and smash up all your equipment. You may spare your printing press, as I am a generous man, and you will need it if you return to your former life. I then want you to smash demolish the desks, chairs, and tables so they can be used as kindling. Take the lot outside. I will supervise them being assembled into a pyre. We will coat the whole with the dyes and inks you use. From what you told me, Miller, they will burn much faster and hotter than even grease or oil."

"That is so, Sergeant Major, but some of the other equipment could be repurposed for the time when we again open our printer's shop."

"I am granting you your lives and granting you that chief tool of your trade, so don't whine to me about the destruction of your property. Now step to it and look like you mean it!"

The four men reluctantly complied. By the time they finished, a small crowd had gathered around the soon to be bonfire. Masters doused it liberally with chemicals then flourished a torch. "Citizens and friends, you see before you the end of the counterfeiting operation that has been the enemy of us all. You see beside it four counterfeiters that I have apprehended. I examined them and discovered that they participated only because of threats against their families. They have identified the people behind all this, and they will hang. These men have promised me their good behavior and their assistance in identifying fake bills. I now release them. He turned to the four. "Go to your homes and be well." The four smiled gratefully then walked briskly away.

The crowd cheered as Master's lit the fire. It burned high and hot. It finished in fifteen minutes, but the crowd left satisfied at the show as well as happy that real justice had been done: the little people would go free while the big ones would be punished. Masters and his two men waited until the last embers flamed out. "And now, my lads, follow me back to the barracks. We have a long day ahead, but it will be a very profitable and satisfying one."

Meadow's men lay hidden behind boxes and barrels at the end to Angler's Alley. They awaited the courier bearing the cashbox containing monies exhorted from vendors at the Berwick fish market. They had followed him before but would arrest him today since it was time for his monthly drop. Meadows had learned that his visit would be followed by that of three other extortionists bearing funds that were the product of threatening the fishermen of three nearby villages with the destruction of their boats. At the monthly meeting an accountant and his assistants compiled a complete tally of all ill-gotten gains from these two very profitable rackets. The underlings were paid well, but the majority went to a man whose identity remained a well-guarded secret.

The fish market courier walked confidently down the alley, whistling a merry tune, having no idea that things were about to be bent completely out of joint. Half an hour after he disappeared the rest of the couriers appeared, walking together and laughing, acting like brothers who had just come from their favorite tavern. Each man carried a large cashbox with a handle, swinging it happily in rhythm to his stride. They smiled broadly as they entered the warehouse, likely anticipating a healthy payoff.

Meadows let twenty minutes lapse before he acted, wanting those inside to be well about their business when he entered, so that everything would literally be on the table. Meadows gave the signal to his men who rose quietly and followed him single file. The door had been left unlatched. Meadows glanced back at his men, put a finger to his lips, and tiptoed through. His men followed and positioned themselves on either side.

They faced the backs of six men at a long table. Four were couriers, one was a counter, and one was a bookkeeper. Each man had a tankard of beer beside him and the mood of the low buzz of conversation was celebratory. A large pile of coins and banknotes lay in the middle of the table: the counter examining each one and calling out its amounts, and the bookkeeper recording it in his ledger.

Meadow crept up behind the accountant and bellowed, "Surprise! You are all under arrest!"

The men turned in shock and horror to see four muskets pointed at them.

Meadows saw men who were thoroughly cowed, not likely to offer any resistance.

Meadows walked over and snatched the ledger from the bookkeeper's hand. He leafed through it quickly." Gentlemen, I gather you have a good idea of the contents of this ledger. This book, the pile of money on the table, and the eyewitness testimony of me, my men, and others who have witnessed your crimes mean that you are all dead men. Except for one. I shall see that one among you is transported to Australia rather than hanged. I am informed that it is not nearly such a bad place as rumors would have us believe. That lucky man will give me information and contacts not contained in this ledger, that will enable me to proceed quickly against the top tiers of your group. I shall interview each one of you separately. You will have ten minutes to tell me the names of others who will be helpful in my investigations. Don't try to protect anyone; worry about protecting yourself. Don't think of lying because your testimony will be checked against that of your mates to ferret out contradictions. I shall write key names and facts down in a notebook. I will track down the men you name. At the end of a week, I shall decide which man helped me the most. He will be tried separately from the rest of you and his life will be spared."

Meadows smiled maliciously, grabbed the bookkeepers tankard of beer and finished it in a single long gulp. "Better than I expected. Tracking you is a thirsty business and I deserve a reward. And now let us begin the interviews."

Meadows set up two chairs in the adjoining room and summoned his first interviewee. Two of his constables guarded the rest and enjoined strict silence to prevent them from coordinating their stories. A third constable bound the hands and gagged each man who left the interview room, guarding him with his musket. The process took one hour and yielded more actionable information than six weeks of careful investigation would have. Their extortion money was confiscated, and the prisoners were frog- marched off to the Berwick Jail, anxious expressions on their faces as they wondered which among them would live.

Once the prisoners were placed in cells, Meadows sat down and began to compare the information in his notes with that of the ledger. At the same time, the quartermaster tallied the money, finding it amounted to 5,000 pounds; extortion was indeed profitable. Meadows began planning a series of raids, which would take a week to complete. At their end, he would have shut down every extortion racket in the city. Only when he judged the results of those raids would he determine which among today's prisoners would live. He was perfectly happy to let them all sweat out that week.

Mark Mason and his men encountered armed resistance, and it came from people that many barely noticed: rubbish collectors. Rubbish collectors were looked down upon, but their services were essential to the welfare of a city. They made good money though their superiors reaped 80% of the profits from their fees. The previous rubbish collectors had worked for five separate companies, but those companies had been bought out by one much larger one. Bought out was a polite term; their owners had been threatened into selling. Any rubbish haulers who did not like the new arrangement were none too gently enticed to quit. As soon as the takeover was complete, rubbish collection fees immediately doubled.

Mason had discovered that the chief thugs behind the garbage racket met once a month with their superiors in a large stone house near the city's water gate. He wanted to arrest the lot of them. He currently lacked the evidence to bring charges that would stick, but after he got done with some intense interrogations, he would have more than enough evidence to send all of them either to the gallows or Australia.

He waited until ten garbage men and two unknowns had entered the house before his men left the cover of the barrels and boxes that constituted their hides. His soldiers proceeded carefully but his advance man had missed the presence of a hidden sentry who spotted them. That sentry fired off his musket and loudly shouted the alarm. Mason was about to rush the building when the inhabitants came to him. The ten were all armed with muskets; garbage men often carried muskets to ward off the stray dogs and beggars who followed their large wagons. The trashmen took positions of cover behind barrels near the entrance and opened fire.

Mason had his men take cover and return fire. The spit spat of musketry continued for two hours. The garbage men's fire was not skillful, and its net result was to graze one of Mason's men in the left shoulder. The better musketry of Mason's men began to tell, as five garbagemen succumbed to their fire. Both sides grew increasingly tired as the fight turned into a war of attrition. Mason sensed that the battle hung in the balance. His men had bayonets, his enemy did not. The introduction of cold steel with its potential to inflict deep and often unrepairable wounds had decided many a battle.

Mason gave the signal to fix bayonets and told every man to choose a target and run at him with all possible speed. His opponents' rate of fire had slackened to almost nothing, indicating fatigue had greatly dulled their reflexes.

"Charge!" yelled Mason. His men did just that. His opponents got off just one shot which went wild. Three garbage men were swiftly bayoneted and the rest broke and ran. They quickly disappeared into an adjoining alley. Mason decided pursuit was pointless and told his men to stand down. He guessed that their superiors had fled out the back door when the musket battle began. He was deeply disappointed that he would not be able to discover the identity of those men but at least he had been spared the necessity of ten trials. More investigative work would be needed to discover the identities of the garbage overlords who had escaped but he doubted they would be hiring replacements for the lost ten anytime soon. He would put out word among the displaced rubbish haulers that he could personally match them with homes and businesses that needed their services. It would mean a lot of extra work, but the Warden had stressed that his job was not just to stop damage but to repair its effects and make things better than he had found them.

***

Sammie Jo sat down to breakfast tea with Sarah Pennywhistle just as Mason's musket battle was ending. The two rattan chairs that they occupied were in a gazebo in the center of a lovely garden filled with white and red roses. That garden lay directly behind the Pennywhistle mansion and Sarah was proud of it. A plate of scones, tea cakes, and straw berries sat invitingly on the wicker table between them. Each sipped her cup of tea daintily and then both chose a scone.

The setting was tranquil but the air of tension between the two women was so thick as to almost be visible. They were like two female cats contending for dominance. It was clear that neither trusted the other and that lack of trust could easily turn into a strong dislike. Both were women of strength but neither knew exactly what to say to the other.

Sammie Jo had requested the tea not because she thought she could make Sarah a friend but because she needed her help. It was up to her to break the ice. She summoned her best fake society smile and spoke cheerfully. "Thank you for opening your home to me, Sarah. You have treated me, Tom, and Nicholas like royalty. Allowing Tom to use your home as his headquarters has helped him a lot. He has plenty of space to receive visitors and your husband's old office has every tool he needs. I know that office brings back memories for him and he is very sad that he and your husband parted on... well... uncertain terms. He wants to make that up to you by helping you in any way he can. That goes for your daughters Sybil and Sally. They love playing with Nicholas and he has grown very fond of them. They have been very kind to me, and I think if I ever have daughters, I want them to be just like your two girls."

"I think Nicholas is a fine boy. He is the mirror image of his father, and I am sure he will grow up to do great deeds and bring honor to the Pennywhistle name."

Both women had no idea what to say next and sipped their tea in silence. Sammie Jo finished her scone then stiffened her resolve. She took a deep breath. "I guess its no-good pretending to be something I ain't. I've never been much of a diplomat, because I like to get right to the point instead of dancing around it. I have a plan to help my husband and I need your help. I want to set up an intelligence network of my own, a copy of that which my husband has established. You know most of the ladies of influence in the city and they have access to all kinds of information. They not only run their households and hear all manner of servant gossip, many control or at least strongly influence their husbands. Husbands tell them things that they would say to no others, whether in casual conversation or as part of pillow talk. The women in this town know a lot of secrets. I would like to gain access to them."

"You would ask wives to inform on their husbands? Betray confidences? I don't like the sound of that."

"You misunderstand. I ain't interested in all of their secrets, just a few particular ones. I don't care about their private lives, the details of their marriages, or any scandals abrewing. I just want to know what their husbands are thinking about matters that are of concern to Tom. Sometimes men also pick up pieces of information that they think trivial but would be of great value to someone who could see them as elements in a much larger picture. What Tom faces is like a jigsaw puzzle with lots of missing pieces. Some of your friends could supply those pieces."

"And just how would this all be accomplished?" said Sarah with skepticism in her voice and face.

"Through teas like this one, parties, soirees, and maybe even a ball or two; completely social, entirely unofficial. The same places women where women like to gossip and share secrets. Get them relaxed, add in plenty of wine, then ask a few questions casually. Those questions would seem spontaneous, but you and I would work them out well in advance. We could not ask all of them on our own, we could use the help of two or three friends that you completely trust. I am just asking you to do something that you are already good at, playing the gracious hostess. "

"There is a difference between being a hostess and being a spy."

"Maybe, but both acquire all manner of secrets and confidences. I think the only difference is in how they use them. I don't want no one hurt. Quite the reverse, I want to use secrets to help people."

"I suppose something could be managed, "said Sarah dubiously. "But espionage seems so sordid and so... Ungenteel."

"Sometimes, to preserve the things that we love, we must act in ways that we might once have considered unthinkable."

"A man in his time plays many parts?"

"That sounds like Shakespeare."

Sarah nodded.

"Well, that's just right then because I am thinking that what we need to do is stage a theatrical production with us as the playwrights, set builders, and prop masters."

"What would be our first step?"

"You and I will have to start planning a party and it will have to be a barn burner!"

***

Pennywhistle and Maxwell had stationed themselves at the edge of a large field just outside the city walls. They were accompanied by five proud fathers, eager to see if their roistering sons had acquired some professional skills. Sergeant Major Luke Pyestalker, his cavalry instructor, had told him that his pupils had made sufficient progress that they were ready to stage a demonstration. It would be a day long exercise, but Pennywhistle planned to stay only for the first hour, to get a representative sampling. Those pupils were dressed in scarlet jackets and grey breeches with a red stripe. Their heads were crowned with helmets of leather and brass, that resembled something that might have been worn by a Roman gladiator.

At Pyestalker's signal, the two hundred men of the Northumberland Yeomanry formed their horses into four single file columns of fifty men. The field in front of them contained two hundred six-foot poles, each designed to represent a man on foot. Each pole had a large number on its top, painted in green: they also had three wide strips, painted in blue: those strips represented the knees, chest, and head of a man. The number on each pole corresponded to a mounted trooper and was intended to be the target for his saber. The poles had been planted purely at random; the opposite of neat, measured rows and their numbers were completely out of sequence. Each trooper not only had to spot his post but would have to do a considerable amount of zigzagging to reach it.

On the return journey, each trooper would have to identify and target a second post, these with numbers painted in black. The top of these poles contained a paper bullseye target. The trooper would have to discharge his pistol at the trot, then gallop back to his starting point.

One of Pyestalker's assistants held a stopwatch to clock their times, while a second would write them down. Once the exercise was finished, Pyestalker and his assistants would walk the field, examine the poles, and give every trooper a score based on their skill with saber and pistol as well as their time. A trophy would be awarded the following day.

Pennywhistle judged from the eagerness of the troopers faces that that trophy would be a coveted prize. From what Pyestalker had told him, he had convinced these amateurs that with a lot of practice and even more determination they could become the equals of the cavalry that fought at Waterloo. Pennywhistle knew that was impossible in a short space of time, but setting a high bar would bring out the men's best efforts. Belief was important; if these men believed they were as good as professionals and acted as if they were, the heat and tumult of battle might transform fantasy into reality.

All seven observers had their spyglasses unfurled so they could observe the action more closely. Pennywhistle also had his Blancpain watch at the ready so he could roughly estimate the time of each man.

The first trooper rode skillfully and zigzagged well. His saber struck the center of his pole at the middle line. His pistol shot, however, was a clean miss, since the bullseye showed no puff of impact. He was back to his starting point in what Pennywhistle guessed was two minutes.

The second trooper rode less skillfully, and his zigzagging was ragged. His saber cut missed the top of the pole. His pistol shot was more successful: his bullet penetrated the outer ring of the bull's eye. Pennywhistle estimated his time at three minutes.

The third rider's horse stumbled on an unexpected divot and nearly through his rider. The trooper recovered but was disoriented. His saber entirely missed the pole, and his pistol shot went wild. Pennywhistle estimated his time at four minutes.

The fourth trooper performed superbly, he and his horse moving as one. His saber struck his pole square in the center line and his pistol shot was only a few inches from the center of the bullseye. Pennywhistle estimated his time at an astonishing minute and a half.

The fifth man leaned too far over when he cut at his pole and fell off his horse. Red-faced, he remounted and rode toward the second pole, but he had injured his hand in the fall and his shot came nowhere near the target. He took five minutes.

The sixth man rode the slowest, but his saber cut, and pistol shot both struck the center of their targets. His time was just under three minutes.

The seventh man's horsemanship was amateurish, barely managing to stay on his horse. His swordsmanship and pistol skills were worse. His time was six minutes. Pennywhistle recognized the man's face and knew he was well connected. Under other circumstances, he would have been washed out of training.

The eighth man was a showoff, but he was good. He rode with great flair, wanting everyone to notice. He flourished his saber theatrically before striking the post dead center. His pistol shot was the first to strike the bullseye dead center. When he finished, he removed his helmet and waved it madly in the air in triumph. His time was three minutes.

The ninth man was sure and steady. He rode slowly and deliberately as if reciting in his head the ABCs of good horsemanship. He waited a moment before slashing at the pole, as if reviewing in his mind the ABCs of swordsmanship. He struck it where a man's head would have been. He took the same care before firing his pistol. His shot hit the outer ring of the bullseye. His time was four minutes.

The tenth man rode far too fast and shot past the pole before he even had his saber fully drawn. He slowed down to a slow walk before he reached the second pole and his shot hit the middle ring of the bullseye. His time was three minutes.

Pennywhistle watched ten more troopers and noticed a pattern was emerging. Some of the men were expert, some were good, some were fair, and some were marginal. With one exception, none of the men was bad. He had a mixed bag of troopers at his disposal but a month before he would have had a mounted rabble in fancy uniforms. He thought that they had made excellent progress, but they had a long way to go. He also realized that the slashing the hell out of poles and shooting the daylights out of paper targets was a very poor imitation of actual combat.

What pleased him most was that these men wanted to get better. While some would be disappointed when they received their final scores, he knew that those on the low end would redouble their efforts to improve their scores during the next exercise. He sensed the beginning of a real esprit d' corps among a group of men who had not long before been a mere collection of independent operators. These well- off men served without pay and had no need to seek plunder. That would set them apart from the men they would face for whom booty taking was a central concern.

Pennywhistle had seen enough. He furled his telescope and told Maxwell to remain and observe the rest of the demonstration. He offered his felicitations to the five expectant fathers, saying that based upon what he had seen, their sons would do them proud. He knew he had just made five very well-connected friends. He mounted up and rode off reassured that the mobile pursuit force that he had envisioned was well on its way to becoming reality.

Michael Savage, one of The Big Man's men, had once served with Ponsonby's cavalry and was a good judge of troopers and horses. He had observed Pennywhistle riding away and took note of the confidence of his posture and the satisfied look on his face. He had seen the same demonstration Pennywhistle had and knew it meant trouble for The Big Man. He had told The Big Man that he did not think that these mounted yeomen would be good for anything other than simple tasks for at least three months. He now knew that he had been badly mistaken. He would continue to observe the rest of the demonstration, hoping he would be wrong, but he feared that he would have to eat his earlier words. He did not look forward to The Big Man's reaction.

Pennywhistle's next port of call was Berwick Barracks. He was pleased to see a company of men drilling, and rode slowly along their front, trying to gauge both their skill and their mood. They were not regulars but recently recruited auxiliaries to whom he had given the name "The Warden's Independent Company." Their brick red uniforms were from surplus stocks and did not fit well, yet they seemed proud of them. The men were older than the usual recruits, most in their late thirties or early forties. The majority were tradesmen who had been crime victims and wanted a way to strike back. The remainder were mill workers; let go when the largest mill in the area had reduced its workforce because they no longer made the cloth for army uniforms. Each man had given a five-pound bounty for enlisting. The term of service was for three months. A few skeptical townspeople had referred to them as "ninety-day wonders" but Pennywhistle felt that they were learning faster than youthful recruits. More importantly, they would be defending their homes and families rather than a remote king in London.

Pennywhistle rode up to the aged corporal in charge. The corporal barked "Ten Sion!" and the men froze in place. Pennywhistle was pleased at their instant obedience.

Pennywhistle faced the corporal who saluted him and returned the salute. A warden he did not merit that honor, but all knew he was a Royal Marine Colonel as well. "Jonas Grant, isn't it?

"Yes, Sir Thomas."

"Where is Masters? I expected to find him conducting the drill."

"He is out on a big raid right now. He turned the drill over to me because he thought I was ready to assume more responsibility. He said he needed a good number 1 to assume command in case he fell in battle."

Sensible, thought Pennywhistle. "I do not wish to put you on the spot, but I should welcome an extended demonstration of what your men have learned." Pennywhistle felt an impromptu demonstration would give a more realistic verdict than one which had been prepared with advance warning.

"My pleasure, Sir Thomas. You will find my men more than willing. Would you give me five minutes to organize a few things?"

"Of course."

Grant motioned for two regulars who had been cleaning a stand of muskets to attend him. "Heston, I want you to set up our four bayonet dummies. Andrews, I want you to ready the firing range." The two acknowledged the order then dashed off eagerly.

"And now Sir Thomas, let us start with the manual of arms."

"Very good, corporal."

"Shoulder Arms." The men brought their muskets to their left shoulders.

"Change arms." the men brought their weapons to the opposite shoulder.

"Present arms." The men placed their muskets vertically in front of them, the butts of their weapons just below their waists.

"Order arms." The men brought the butts of their weapons to the ground and held them close.

"Port arms." Weapons were brought to the front of each soldier, with right hands on the butt and left ones on the forestocks.

"High port arms. "The weapons were raised a foot.

"Trail arms." The men gripped their muskets in their right hands, their barrels inclined at a forty-five-degree angle with their butts just above the ground.

"Support arms." Weapons were brought close to the left side, with arms crossed across chests, each musket supported by the crook of the left arm above the elbow.

"Slope arms." Muskets were brought to the left shoulders, with their barrels tilted at a forty-five-degree angle.

"Fix bayonets." The men drew them from their scabbards and attached them to the muzzles of their muskets."

"Unfix bayonets." The men returned them to their scabbards.

"Shoulder arms."

"Load." The men swung their muskets to their fronts at a horizontal angle of forty five degrees, then brought their hammers to the half cock position.

"Handle cartridge. "The men reached behind and opened the top flap of their leather cartridge boxes, which hung from white straps over their left shoulders. Each drew a paper cartridge with a ball at the top and powder underneath. Each bit open the top of the cartridge with his teeth.

"Prime," Musket pans were opened and a small amount of powder was poured in.

"Shut pan." The frizzen above the fan was pushed down to seal it shut.

"Cast 'bout." Muskets were swung away from the men and down, with the butt of the musket close to the men's left feet and the trigger guard facing outwards. The men poured the remainder of the cartridge's contents down the barrels.

"Draw ramrods." The men drew them then wrapped the cartridge paper around the ball and inserted it into the barrel.

"Ram." The men rammed the ball down the barrel so that it sat directly atop the powder.

"Return ramrods." Ramrods were returned to their channels beneath the musket barrels.

"Shoulder Arms."

"Attention."

Grant stopped at this point. Rather than continue and have them discharge their weapons into the air, Pennywhistle guessed that he wanted to show them the effect of a volley. One of the regulars that Grant had sent off earlier returned. "The big target is in place. The firing and bayonet dummies are ready to go."

Grant turned to Pennywhistle. "Now Sir, Thomas, I am going to march my men to the range and training area that lies on the other side of that arch over yonder. If you will follow us, I think you will be pleased at the results of our musketry."

"I look forward to it corporal. Your people executed your commands with crispness and exactitude."

"That means a lot coming from you, Sir Thomas." Grant faced his men. "Company, left face. Forward, march."

The company did as they were ordered and marched at the standard rate of 75 paces per minute. Pennywhistle dismounted and followed on foot, noting that a few were completely out of cadence with the rest. That was to be expected but the general movement of the file was efficient.

The courtyard they emerged into had a long dirt berm at its far end. The berm was the size of a standard Cricket pitch: 25 yards long and four yards wide. Pennywhistle estimated its height at eight feet and guessed it was four feet thick, more than enough to absorb musket balls. A line of stiff linen stretched in front of the berm. It was five feet high and bodies of men, representing a line of enemy musketeers, had been drawn upon it.

"Company halt."

Grant stopped the marchers fifty yards from the berm; a good distance at which to deliver a volley.

"Company, form line and dress ranks."

Shifting from a column to a line was hard for new men to do. Grants men did it very slowly, but their execution was good.

"Eyes front."

"Poise firelocks and make ready." Muskets were brought to a 90 angle in front of each man.

"Cock firelocks." Muskets were full cocked.

"Present." Muskets were leveled at the target. Pennywhistle noted the men were actually aiming at individual figures on the cardboard. That pleased him. Many British soldiers just pointed their musket in the general direction of the enemy and waited for the command to fire. Some men even fired with both eyes shut.

"Fire." A volley crashed out and clouds of gritty grey, white smoke rose skyward. To Pennywhistle's surprise, numerous holes appeared in the cardboard indicating that very few shots missed the cardboard entirely. Shooting high was a common failing of new recruits.

Grant did not wait for Pennywhistle's approval. "Reload, in quick time."

This time no commands were issued. The men reloaded as fast as they could and when finished brought their weapons to the poise firelock position. Since muskets were single shot weapons, speed in reloading was just as important as accuracy. Pennywhistle estimated that the company was ready to fire in just over thirty seconds. Not perfect, but good.

"Fire!"

This volley put fewer holes in the target, but it was still a good one.

"Reload."

The men complied and fired a third time.

The results were marginal this time but that was to be expected with new recruits.

"Recover firelocks. Shoulder Arms." Those commands signaled that the musketry demonstration was over.

Pennywhistle walked over to Grant. "Impressive."

"Thank you, Sir Thomas. My men have worked hard. We drill two hours each morning, two hours every afternoon, and an hour in the evening."

"That is a punishing schedule that would demand much of even regulars."

"These men know what they are fighting for. And now Sir Thomas, I have selected five of my best shots to give you a demonstration of individual marksmanship."

Pennywhistle noted that two regulars were furling up the long cardboard target while two others were setting up five individual targets. These were not cardboard silhouettes, but full-sized dummies wearing castoff uniforms and stuffed with rags. The uniforms were blue and French, scavenged from God knows where. Wooden shafts attached to their backs held them upright. Whoever crafted the dummies had a sense of humor. Each dummy had had a painted face with a handlebar mustache and a fierce snarl.

After a two-minute interval, one of the regulars signaled to Grant that things were ready. Grant turned to Pennywhistle, "I should like to add that the heads and chests contain a layer of fresh paint. That will enable impacts to be more easily seen."

"Amusing, but practical. Anything that adds to realism is most welcome."

"Bailey, front and center."

Bailey stepped out of line, stepped quickly, stopped in front of Pennywhistle and Grant and snapped to attention.

"Relax Bailey," said Grant. "Load your musket, select a dummy, and do your worst."

"I will take the one on the far left, corporal." Bailey loaded carefully and took his time aiming. His shot hit his dummy square in the left pectoral, judging by the spurt of red paint that erupted.

"Good shooting, Bailey," said Grant. "Now return to the ranks. Booth, front and center."

Booth chose the dummy to the right of Bailey's. His round hit his target in the stomach.

The next man, Cooke hit his target in the right shoulder.

The fourth man, Burton, hit his target in the right hip.

The final man, Dixon, stepped up with a cocky smile on his face. Though it violated protocol, he spoke directly to Pennywhistle with smooth confidence in his voice. "Let me show you some real shooting Sir Thomas. Take a good look at the last dummy. Focus on the area right between its eyes. That's where I aim to put my ball."

Pennywhistle was amused rather than offended by the man's confident arrogance. If he was as good as his word, he was indeed a fine marksman. Such a man would be an inspiration to the rest of the company.

"I find that hard to believe private, but I will put a guinea in your purse if you can do it."

The rest of the company murmured in surprised approval.

Dixon took a full minute to line up his shot. Pennywhistle recognized a craftsman at work. Dixon breathed in and out several times, just as Pennywhistle himself would have done. He squeezed the trigger gently as he let out his breath.

The round struck exactly where Dixon intended it and the top half of the dummy's head exploded in a shower of red paint.

The men cheered and Grant and Pennywhistle smiled.

Pennywhistle made a great show of depositing the guinea in Dixon's hand. The men cheered again.

"I have one last demonstration prepared," said Grant. "A bayonet drill. There targets will be those dummies." Grant pointed to a line of five dummies similar to those used in target practice. "They are not filled with any paint since you will clearly see the blade go in. To make the demonstration more interesting, I will time the demonstration for you. I have selected five different men for this drill. Each man will bayonet all five dummies as quickly and thoroughly as he can then return as fast as possible."

"I like that idea," said Pennywhistle. You could not buy skill, but you could reward it. Napoleon had understood that well. Pleased by the reaction of the bestowal one guinea he decided to bestow a second. "A guinea to the man with the best time!"

The men cheered.

At Grant's command five men lined up with their bayonets fixed. Pennywhistle took out his pocket watch while Grant took out a stopwatch.

Grant pointed to the men. "Sir Thomas, these are privates Harvey, Henderson, King, Lee, and Morgan."

All the men saluted Pennywhistle correctly but the grins they wore were distinctly unmilitary.

"I wish you all luck," said Pennywhistle. Their eagerness was a good sign.

Grant pointed to Harvey and readied his stopwatch. "On your mark, get set, go!" Grant started his stopwatch as Harvey brought his musket to the charge bayonet position and dashed forward. He charged thirty yards to the dummies but stopped abruptly when he reached the first one. He bayoneted the dummy in the stomach. It was no quick thrust that might wound, but a killing blow.

Pennywhistle watched the man's lips mouth the necessary steps as he executed them. "Thrust, develop, gore, recover."

Harvey raced to the second dummy five yards away and repeated the process.

The next three dummies were dispatched within a minute. Once finished, Harvey dashed back to his starting point.

"Two minutes," Grant called out.

Pennywhistle was impressed by Harvey's thoroughness. If the dummies had been real, none would have survived.

Henderson was as thorough as Harvey but slightly faster. His time was one- and three-quarter minutes.

King was slower and less thorough, but his time was a respectable two and a quarter minutes.

Lee took extra care with his thrusts and was not as fast a runner as the previous three, so his time came in at two and a half minutes.

Morgan, a stubby little Welshman proved to be the best. He was fast and efficient, turning in a time of a remarkable one and a half minutes.

The men gave three loud "huzzahs" when his time was announced.

Pennywhistle walked over to him and deposited the guinea in his hand. "Well done. I would have liked to have had you at my side at Waterloo."

The man beamed at the compliment from a man that he considered a great hero.

Pennywhistle took Grant aside. "Form the men up. I have a few words I want to say to them."

Grant gave the appropriate commands, and the long straight line came to attention.

"Stand at...ease." Pennywhistle used his command voice but this time it had friendly undertones.

"I am very impressed by your conduct today. You have come a long way in a short time. Much work remains to be done but I have confidence you will complete that quickly and with the same excellence that you displayed today. It will not be long before you will meet our mutual enemies in battle. I have no doubt that they will receive a sound thrashing. As a reward I will request that Corporal Grant suspend the evening drill and instead issue every man an extra pint of beer."

"Three cheers for Sir Thomas. Hip, hip, huzzah. Hip, hip, huzzah. Hip, hip, huzzah."

Pennywhistle doffed his hat and made a quick bow in acknowledgement.

"Corporal Grant, dismiss the men."

"Very good, Sir Thomas."

"And Corporal Grant."

"Sir?"

"You are now Sergeant Grant. It is unseemly that such excellent men should be commanded by a mere corporal."

"Thank you so much, Sir," Granted sputtered in surprise.

"Don't thank me. You earned it."

Grant dismissed the men as Pennywhistle returned to his horse and trotted away from the barracks.

I have cavalry and infantry, now all I need is artillery, thought Pennywhistle. *Mountain howitzers would be just thing, light, easily dismantled, and could be carried on the backs of mules. I wonder where I can find some.*

Private Martinson watched Pennywhistle ride off. He was impressed with the Warden despite himself. He had been planted in the unit by The Big Man to spy on his mates and report their progress. But a change had been taking place in him over the past weeks of training, a chance that had reached its final stage in the moments just past. He liked the man that he was becoming, and he was acquiring a deep pride in his unit. He worked for The Big Man out of fear, but today that spell had been broken. To hell with his weekly report to The Big Man, he was done with that scoundrel for good. From now on, he was Pennywhistle's man.

Pennywhistle continued his ride back to his headquarters, pleased by what he was seeing. The city was calming down and the mood on the streets was far more tranquil than when he had arrived. The city was gradually coming round to his vision. Most of the limestone and sandstone houses and businesses were either a dull grey, a muted brown, or a dingy white; of a piece with a rocky, rainy, and fog bound landscape. But he had noticed that some of the wooden structures in the city had recently been repainted in pleasing colors of blue, yellow, and even red. Some residents had added flower boxes beneath their front windows, replacing the flowers each morning with fresh cut specimens. Purple hydrangeas, yellow sunflowers, red tulips, and white peonies were especially popular. A recently arrived Dutch resident had started a custom that was spreading: sweeping the front doorstep with a broom three times a day. It not only cleared off coal dust more efficiently but made doorsteps much more welcoming. They were all small steps, but evidence of the revival of civic pride.

On impulse, Pennywhistle stopped his horse and purchased an orange carnation from a corner flower girl. The girl smiled and curtseyed, pleased that she had such an august customer. He pinned the flower to the lapel of his coat. Orange carnations were traditional symbols of celebration and expressed confidence in the good outcomes of future events. One of his old enemies had favored a red carnation as a personal hallmark and it been a very effective calling card. It amused him to think that an orange carnation might do the same for him, though it would send a hopeful rather than sinister message.

It was almost time to turn his attention to the countryside. Those efforts would stretch his resources to their limits but the increasing local support for his efforts was infectious: many city folk had relatives in the countryside. No amount of money could purchase what he was steadily acquiring.

Two old women ragpickers, both missing half their teeth, watched from an alley as Pennywhistle rode by. "There goes our new lord and master, the exalted and mighty big noise from London," said Jean Hepburn cynically. "What do you think of our new Warden, Marge?"

"I ain't sure," said Marge Traynor." I think he is trying to do the right thing. I think things are a little better than when he got here. My old man has kept all his money this week. The two toughs who usually show up to demand half of his tips for street sweeping, seem to have vanished. I was able to buy some mutton for dinner, the first time in two months."

"But you and I must still use the soup kitchen every so often, and that ain't run by him. Whoever pays for the soup kitchen has my loyalty. I wish I knew his name."

"I heard a rumor that Pennywhistle's sister-in-law is going to be opening a big soup kitchen on Cricket Lane next week. And a secondhand clothing store to go with it."

"Who told you?"

"Mary Meecham."

"She is so sozzled with gin half the time that you can't trust anything she says."

"Maybe, but I am willing to give our Warden's relative the benefit of the doubt. You should too."

"Bah! Sarah Pennywhistle is a born snob whose nose is so far in the air that it scrapes the clouds. She don't even see our kind when she passes in her fancy carriage. I am going to reserve my loyalty to the man whose kitchen fed me today."

"Times change, Jean. You should be willing to change too."

Two wounded veterans conversed while drinking beer at the Royal Oak Inn: an establishment frequented by ex-soldiers and sailors. Paul Ford sported a peg leg while Jack Preacher was missing his right arm. Both were looking out the window, idly observing traffic, when Pennywhistle passed.

"There goes our new Warden. What do you think of him, Paul?"

"I like him a lot. I never served under him, but I saw him at a distance when the Imperial Guard made its charge. That was just a minute before canister took this off and I passed out." He inclined his head toward the stump of his arm. "The streets are safer now. Before he arrived, I would see people robbed on the streets with impunity. I have seen none of that in the past week."

"I like him too," said Ford. "And I think that he is sympathetic to veterans like ourselves. But he did not arrange for my pension to be paid when the government denied my claim because some damn pencil jockey had misplaced my paperwork. I shall be forever grateful to my unknown benefactor who is paying it out of his own pocket."

"You don't even know who that man is, so how can you be loyal to him? You have only met one of his deputies. I have a feeling that man is connected to some of the worst criminal activities in this city. I think that is why he wishes to remain hidden."

"So, what if he is? I just know I would not be having this beer with you, nor would I have a roof over my head if not for my unknown friend. You can say what you want but it is never a good idea to bite the hand that feeds you."

"I understand, Paul, but that benefactor may not be around for long. Pennywhistle is a new broom with a lot of zeal, and just might sweep your friend into the nearest dustbin. You should think ahead. From what I saw of his character at Waterloo, Pennywhistle might be just the man to fix things for you, the right way this time."

Pennywhistle had nearly reached his headquarters when he passed a married couple strolling with their two young sons. He tipped his hat to the man, who was clearly a gentleman by his attire. The man nodded in acknowledgment.

"I am so glad that he is here, Mary," said Edward Norton to his wife. "We needed an outsider to turn things around. The revenues of the three dress shops that we own is up 30% in the last two weeks. People are much more willing to spend money when they feel safe."

"I agree with you, Edward. When I walk about with my servant whilst you are attending to our shops, I no longer feel compelled to have him carry a pistol. The women in my sewing circle tell me that their husbands are worrying much less about their safety."

"I understand that he is training soldiers from among our townspeople to spread his good works to the countryside. I wish I were not so old, Mary, or I too might have joined his volunteers. I'd have shown the blackguards hurting this city a thing or two."

"You will always be my hero, Edward. You don't have to take up arms to prove it."

One of the children tugged at Edward's coat. "Was that man who passed the crusader that you told me about last night before bed, pappa?"

"Yes, he was, George."

"Is he like one of the heroes who rescues the damsel in distress in those fairy tales that you tell us before bed?"

"Yes, he is, Thomas, but instead of rescuing one woman he is rescuing an entire city. From what I have heard he is a modest man who rejects the label of hero. But to me he is proof that sometimes legends do indeed come to life."

CHAPTER 10

Tomb Time

10th November 1816

Walter Scott scratched his chin in worry as he read a report. It was based on two eyewitness accounts, but contained no information from his usual informant, Paul Martinson. He seemed to have dropped off the face of the earth. Scott wondered why, since Martinson was well paid and had been up for a promotion to a made man.

The report described his opponent's progress in training auxiliaries. The cavalry and infantry were growing proficient, and it did not take a crystal ball to predict that Pennywhistle would soon be ready to take forces into the field against the reivers. Scott had estimated that he'd have three months to prepare countermeasures; now he realized he had been dangerously wrong.

His musings were interrupted by Richard Stansted, a dutiful man with a broad chest, strong arms, and muscled legs who ran his warehouse.

"Mr. Scott, the shipments have arrived. I thought you would want to personally inspect their contents."

"Thank you, I do. You can't be too careful dealing with gun runners. They are always tempted to deliver less than promised; skimming five or even ten percent off the top to sell to other parties is quite common or substituting old guns for new."

Scott followed Stanstead to the cavern below Hermitage Castle. Ten wagons laden with five-foot long rectangular wooden crates lay before them. "I want to inspect the individual contents in each box and test their mechanisms as well. Fetch one down for me."

Stanstead hefted one of the boxes down, then pried off the top with a crowbar. Each box contained ten new Brown Bess muskets. They were contract muskets manufactured by the firm of Barnett and Son and had been originally intended for rebel forces fighting the Spanish in Venezuela. Scott had arranged to have them redirected. Stanstead handed one specimen down to Scott, who checked the quality of the stock to make sure it was of a good grade of walnut and that there were no cracks or slivers. Next, he examined the interior of the barrel to make sure that it was completely smooth and had never been fired. He inserted a flint into the jaws of the hammer and pulled the hammer to half cock. The action was smooth and easy. He then full-cocked the piece and pulled the trigger. A shower of sparks erupted. The weapon was sound.

He spent the next five hours inspecting muskets at random from the 1,200 in the shipment. It was time-consuming, repetitive work, but he did not trust anyone else to do this. Also, it was important for a leader to concern himself with details, both to set an example to his men and act from knowledge that was not second hand.

"Well, Mr. Scott?" inquired Stanstead, when Scott had finished.

"The quality is excellent, and two pounds per musket is not a bad price."

"That's double what the government pays."

"True but buying this number of muskets directly from their manufacturer would leave a paper trail and might lead a government pencil pusher with too much time on his hands to ask questions that we do not want asked. What about the shipments of bayonets to go with these muskets?"

"They will arrive at the end of next week."

"I don't like that at all. Muskets and bayonets are like a pair of boots; you need both. Men must train with both at the same time so that they handle the weights properly. What about the drill master I requested?"

"Lefebvre? He arrives tomorrow. One of my associates is an Irishman who served in the French army and was trained by him. McGeady told me that Lefebvre took a raw crop of recruits and turned them into a respectable fighting force considerably faster than most drill sergeants."

"Tell me more."

"His name is Jacques Lefebvre. He is forty years old and is a veteran of the Russian and German Campaigns. After Waterloo, he could find no work in France, so he came to England to tutor children of the wealthy in the French language, swordsmanship and dancing. He positively jumped at the chance to return to training fighting men. He was so eager that I almost expected him to pay us a bounty for this opportunity."

"He must be very tough to have survived Russia."

"That he is. But I have to ask, sir, why the change to modern weaponry?"

"Because my opponent has changed from a galling nuisance to a dangerous threat. He is training auxiliaries in modern tactics, using modern weapons. Our men need to be able to meet his on equal terms. The Reiver imposture has been effective against country folk, but it has outlived its usefulness. It is time to dispense with the Reiver mantle and adopt that of an army."

The sound of boots echoed off the cavern walls and Scott and Stanstead turned to see a tall, thin man with a beaky nose and pointed chin walking purposefully toward them.

"Bon jour, mes amis!" boomed a cheerful voice, as he walked. When the tall figure had reached hand-shake distance, he said, "Which one of you is the man paying my salary?"

"I am," said Scott. "My name is Walter Scott, and I presume that you are Lefebvre."

"I am indeed. My ship had fair winds the whole way and so I have arrived a day early." Lefebvre bowed.

"We have much to discuss, Lefebvre. I am expecting a great deal from you, and I warn you that your task will not be easy.

"I welcome challenges."

"What have you been told?"

"Only that 1,200 men need training. I was told that they were used to light discipline and that most had some experience of fighting. I was not informed of the cause they support, so I assume they are mercenaries. Have these men signed contracts to fight with South American rebels?"

"No, they will be used only in the border area between England and Scotland. Do you have an idea how long it will take to get them ready?"

"I cannot say until I inspect them. Six months is the standard time to forge a man into a soldier and *estrangees* into a fighting unit, but I can do it in three."

Scott frowned. "I need them ready in a month."

"You are asking the impossible. It is like tasking me to spin straw into gold."

"And if I doubled your salary, would that make things less impossible?"

"If you also double their practice time, but I cannot promise miracles. "

"I might be able to extend that month to six weeks, but no longer."

"That will help, but much would depend on how motivated these men are."

"They are very motivated."

"How soon can I meet with them?"

"If I put out the word today, all of them can be here tomorrow afternoon."

"Very well, Mr. Scott, bring them in and let me see if I have any miracles in my pocket."

***

Pennywhistle knew he was being a damn fool, but he had an obligation to carry out that should have been performed two years before. No, not an obligation, a sacred duty. For too long he had allowed war, injuries, and appointments to divert him from a promise he had made to a dying man.

And so, he had ridden out of Berwick just after 5 am, alone, with no armed escorts of any kind. A heavy fog concealed him, and he wore nondescript civilian clothing so as not to attract attention or mark him as the Warden of the English Eastern March. If the fog held, he could go and return without being seen by a single soul, except perhaps the church parson. But Parson Edwards was said to be a man who liked the bottle rather too well, and morning matins might well not happen at the scheduled time of 8:15.

Neither Sammie Jo nor Maxwell would have permitted his solo journey if they had known. He had thought of inviting them both but had decided against it. This was a solemn and private matter, one that required silence and solitude. They would probably have demanded that he take an armed escort of at least ten men. When they eventually found out what he had done they would have words with him, words that would likely include such epithets as "idiotic", "blockhead" and "irresponsible". He was not a complete idiot, however; he had armed himself with pistols, rifle, and sword, just in case he did meet with any trouble on the way back.

His destination lay five miles ahead. The Church of St. Cuthbert dated from the 13th century, and its sepulcher contained the remains of five members of his family. He was determined to add the remains of a sixth.

He carried in his saddlebag a small reliquary chest of black and gold. It contained a heart that had belonged to a half-brother, born in America on the wrong side of the blanket. Burying the heart of a relative in the family church was a tradition that had started with the Crusaders, when transporting a body home was impractical because of the distance.

Three years ago, he'd had no idea that John Tracy even existed, and they never would have met except for the caprices of war. Tracy was the son of his father's loving coupling with a Virginia woman, Elizabeth Harrison, during the American War of Independence. Tracy had been a 32-year-old United States Marine Corps Captain that Pennywhistle had taken prisoner after the Battle of Bladensburg. Antagonists on the field, they had later become friends. Tracy had died in his arms, and his final wish had been for Pennywhistle to grant him in death what had been denied to him in life: recognition by his father's family.

Pennywhistle had only been to St. Cuthbert's twice as a boy, but he remembered the layout of the crypt. He knew exactly the place to put the reliquary chest where it would remain undisturbed; he would hide it in plain sight. One tabletop tomb featured the full-length sculpture of a medieval knight, Penrose Pennywhistle. That Pennywhistle held a small box in his hands that could have been a reliquary chest, and his idea was to substitute one box for another.

He encountered no travelers during his ninety-minute journey, arriving at St. Cuthbert's just after 6:30. His errand would not take long. If he maintained the same pace on the return trip, there was a faint chance that no one would ever know that he had been away.

When he spied the Norman style church, he stopped his horse, took out his spyglass, and panned it in a wide arc. The fog had thinned enough so that he could see no one was in sight. He rode up to the door, dismounted, and was pleased to find that Parson Edwards had neglected to lock it; perhaps he was of the old school and believed that a church should always be a place of sanctuary. He walked his horse over to a grove of trees and tied the reins around a tree branch in the center of the grove. This provided concealment for the horse. No passing stranger would suspect that the church had a visitor.

He withdrew the chest from his saddle bag and entered the church.

A winding, narrow stone staircase descended from the main floor to the crypt. The air underground was stale and heavy, but rather than depressing him, the air reminded him of the solemnity of his purpose: he was bringing his brother home.

He had memorized a traditional prayer that Crusaders used when carrying out his current task, planning to recite it aloud. He found the knight's tomb, the box was loose in the carved stone hands, easy to prise loose.

He placed the reliquary holding his brother's heart in its new home, then knelt, bowed his head, and began to recite the prayer. "Heavenly Father, Lord Eternal, and Almighty Forgiver of Sins, I humbly beseech The Great Decider of Battles to grant this warrior's heart eternal rest. I—" He stopped abruptly, for he heard the church door open, the thudding of boots, and loud, boorish voices, completely at odds with the hushed tones proper to church. Though he could not distinguish their words, he heard four different voices. What were four unholy men doing in a church on a Thursday morning?

The answer hit him like a mule's kick. The men were Reivers, and the Church was a place where the authorities would never think to look for their loot, especially if it were concealed in the crypt! Pennywhistle cursed himself for having left his weapons with his horse, but a House of God was supposed to be a place where no one carried weapons. But Reivers were notorious for flouting rules. St. Cuthbert's was one of the few churches in the area that had not been burnt by Reivers in the centuries past; now Pennywhistle understood why! It had been one of their hiding places, perhaps with the collusion of former parsons.

The four Reivers would have daggers at the very least, possibly pistols on their persons. He would only have his hands, feet, and guile. But he possessed the most important advantage of all: the element of surprise. The last thing the Reivers would be expecting in a house of the dead would be a live man with fast reflexes. He took cover behind the knight's tomb and waited.

The four Reivers came thumping down the stone steps. Two of them were carrying a case that looked to be full of whiskey.

"We must have taken two hundred pounds worth of valuables today," said a Reiver with deep set eyes and a pointed chin. "That diamond necklace is a rare prize."

"I say closer to three hundred pounds. But this case of Glen Livet whiskey is the real prize! Once we stash the loot, we can break open a bottle," said the fattest of the Reivers.

"Why not two bottles!" chortled a third, whose face looked like a cross between a toad and a snake.

"Let's make it three!" said the fourth, who looked like a prim school master hot to apply the birch rod to the bare buttocks of his pupils. "I have not been stinking drunk for a month. High time to remedy that! There is stream bed out back where we can sleep it off. I wouldn't want to wake up in a place like this."

The Reivers laughed raucously, and their merriment echoed off the close confines of the crypt.

Pennywhistle felt a rising anger. How dare these poltroons debase the place where his brother's heart was to rest! While he was not conventionally religious, he believed in a proper respect for the dead, and felt that decorum should always be practiced in a place considered sacred.

The Reivers carried only daggers. In a way, they were like him: not expecting violence in a crypt. Each carried a large pack over his shoulder, presumably containing the treasure from a dawn raid.

Schoolmaster walked over to the tomb of Baldric Pennywhistle, who had died in 1410. He shoved hard on its right side, and the marble slab rotated and swung away. The Reivers began emptying their packs. From the clinking sounds, Pennywhistle realized the tomb of his ancestor was full of contraband. He glimpsed the hands of the Reivers depositing bags of coins, rings, necklaces, watches on chains, and silverware. He wondered what had been done with his ancestor's body, then guessed that these scoundrels had probably just thrown Baldric's bones on a rubbish heap somewhere. He took that as a serious affront to his family's legacy and it increased his anger.

His moment of opportunity came when the Reivers were closing Baldric's Tomb. Surging forward, he snatched the dagger from Pointed Chin's scabbard and jammed it into the base of his skull, then gave it a twist. Pointed Chin fully erect but did not cry out. Pennywhistle yanked out the dagger, and Pointed Chin dropped soundlessly to the ground.

As the fat one was turning toward the disturbance on his right, Pennywhistle buried the dagger in his left pectoral, jamming the blade in so that only the pommel of the weapon was showing. The man blinked in shock and his eyes rolled upward. Pennywhistle jerked the knife out and confronted the other two Reivers. Both had retreated several feet from the tomb and had adopted fighting stances, daggers at the ready.

In one quick, fluid motion, Pennywhistle sidestepped Schoolmaster's dagger, then gripped his wrist and forced the dagger into the man's thigh. The man squealed, but that was cut off when Pennywhistle slashed his throat. Schoolmaster clutched his bloody throat and dropped to his knees.

Toad Face had moved behind Pennywhistle and had raised his blade. Pennywhistle felt the disturbance in the heavy air and sensed the position of his attacker. His right boot shot backwards, its heel connecting with Toad Face's right knee. The man lurched backwards, howling in pain, and fell to the ground when his right leg buckled.

Pennywhistle spun round and saw that Toad Face was on his back. Pennywhistle advanced, but the man saw the threat and surprised Pennywhistle by springing to his feet. Pennywhistle's boot had not shattered the patella. *I must have lost my edge during recovery*, he thought. Toad Face lunged at Pennywhistle, who sidestepped to the left, but he was a split second too slow, and the man's blade tore a shallow trench on his right arm. Pennywhistle continued moving left as his opponent moved right. Both men circled slowly, each looking for an opening. Toad Face slashed twice at his waist, but Pennywhistle jumped back. Toad Face rushed forward, intending to tackle Pennywhistle, but he sidestepped and shot out his fully extended right arm, which acted like the iron of a turnstile when his opponent's neck hit it, Toad Face's feet flew out from under him.

He lay unmoving on his back, his wide eyes reminding Pennywhistle of a fish that suddenly found itself in a boat. He smashed his boot down on the man's Adam's apple. Pennywhistle saw the horror on the man's face as the realization hit him that he was dying.

Pennywhistle examined his own wound; it would need to be cleaned and bandaged; in the meanwhile, he stopped the bleeding by turning a pocket handkerchief into a pressure dressing, then walked over to Baldric's Tomb and fully opened it. The contents were impressive. His first thought was to wonder how to return items to their rightful owners. It would be difficult to assemble all those who had been robbed in one place and have them reclaim what was theirs. There was also the possibility that some Reivers might infiltrate their ranks and make false claims. He finally decided that he would send men to confiscate the lot and arrange for the loot to be sold at auction. The resulting profits would be placed in a charitable fund that would be used to improve the city. The city needed more soup kitchens, and a new orphanage. The quality of its workhouses demanded improvement, and he was getting reports that several veterans had not been receiving the pensions owned them by the government. All those activities would put money back into circulation: just the right medicine for a depressed economy.

He looked at the bodies and decided he would task Parson Edwards with the cleanup. They deserved the same fate that they had given Baldric's body, but if the parson wanted to give them Christian burials, he was welcome to do so.

He returned to Penrose Pennywhistle's tomb and touched the chest that the marble effigy held. He thought of his brother's face, and tears came to his eyes. He spoke in an unsteady voice, just above a whisper. "I hardly knew you, but I miss you badly. There were so many things I wanted to do with you, so many things that I wanted to show you. You are in a better place, and I hope you will find the peace that eluded you in life. When I cross over, I promise that I shall seek you out."

Pennywhistle knew from his own near-death experience that the Other Side was indeed a better place.

He knelt and spoke the last lines of the prayer. He was not sure of Jesus's divinity, but he respected the thoughts behind the words. "O Lord, give us, we beseech Thee, in the name of Jesus Christ Thy Son our God, that love which can never cease, that will kindle our lamps but not extinguish them, that they may burn in us and enlighten others. Do Thou, O Christ, our dearest Saviour, thyself kindle our lamps, that they may evermore shine in Thy temple, that they may receive unquenchable light from Thee that will enlighten our darkness and lessen the darkness of the world. Lord Jesus, we pray Thee give Thy light to our lamps, that in its light the most holy place may be revealed to us in which Thou dwellest as the Eternal Priest, that we may always behold Thee, desire Thee, look upon Thee in love, and long after Thee, for Thy sake. Amen."

As he rose, he realized that reciting the prayer had calmed him. He gently touched the reliquary chest a last time. "Goodbye, brother."

He hefted up the case of whiskey, mounted the steps, concealed the whiskey in the grove, retrieved his horse, then rode over to the vicarage. He pounded loudly on the door for a full minute before anyone answered. A sleepy looking Parson Edwards slowly opened the door. "Can I help you, sir?"

"I am Sir Thomas Pennywhistle. I have need of your services, Parson Edwards."

"Our new warden!" Edwards suddenly seemed fully awake.

"It is not a pleasant task, but a necessary one." Pennywhistle explained that he had been paying his respects to his ancestors and had been set upon by four brigands intent on taking his life. "By the grace of God, I survived. They did not, and I must task you with seeing to the disposal of their bodies. Here are two guineas, and when the work is done, I will see to it that you and the grave diggers are rewarded with a case of Glen Livet to share amongst you."

Once he was satisfied that Edwards would carry out his wishes, Pennywhistle mounted up and began trotting back toward Berwick. After half a mile, he reached a crossroads that he had barely noticed before in the fog. One road led back to Berwick; the other led to Whistlestop, four miles distant. He halted, realizing in an instant of insight that for all this careful planning, he had gotten one important thing wrong.

He had not visited Whistlestop since his arrival. He had intended to show up at Whistlestop with a large military escort ready to take the field against his enemies, thinking that would be the best way to protect the estate's inhabitants. But he had allowed too much time to lapse. The inhabitants would have heard of his arrival and some of his actions in Berwick, but they probably thought by now he had forgotten about them or deemed them unimportant.

The people of Whistlestop knew him only by reputation and had never seen his face. Now, since his nondescript clothing furnished no clues as to his identity or the office he held, he could pose as a wounded gentleman traveler, weary from a brush with brigands, seeking the hospitality of locals. They might speak more freely to an interested stranger engaging them in casual conversation, than they would to a warden in a formal interview. Henry V had visited the campfires of his men in disguise the night before Agincourt and had heard much that he never would have if he had been speaking to them as their king.

***

Even as Pennywhistle redirected his course for Whistlestop, scouting parties departed from the gates of Berwick. There were six groups of four men. Three men of each group were from the Northumberland Yeomanry on their first real mission, while their leader was one of Pennywhistle's Favored Fifteen and had actual combat experience. Each group was to scout a specific area to see if it was safe for Pennywhistle to commence establishing his Border early warning system. All had been told that it was likely they might run into patrols of Reivers.

Their objectives were varied locations in the countryside surrounding the towns of Norham, Coldstream, Wark-on-Tweed, Kelso, Jedburgh, and Greenlaw. Some were fords and river crossings, some strategic high points and signaling stations, and some were old castles and fortified strongholds in varied stages of repair.

Masters' men reached their objective first. This was Norham Castle, just five miles from Berwick, perched on a mound above the River Tweed. It had been attacked several times in the distant past, and badly damaged during the Flodden Campaign of 1513. Even in its ruined state, it was impressive. The walls of its square keep were 84 feet high and 28 feet thick. A legend came with the castle, one that had caused fortune hunters to dig in its grounds.

King James IV of Scotland had brought a quarter of Scotland's treasury with him during the Flodden campaign, carried in four large chests, a source of ready money to pay the many men under his command. Rumor had it that the defeated James had buried part of the treasure on the castle grounds, lest it fall into the hands of the victorious English.

Masters carried out a thorough inspection of the castle, looking for signs of any recent visitors. Finding none, he decided this would be a safe post for a castle keeper. He and his men then mounted up and made a four-hour circuit ride of the lands to the north. They encountered only farmers in their fields and a few merchants and travelers, all of whom looked to be respectable people.

They were on the homeward leg of their journey, with the ramparts of Norham visible in the far distance, when Masters' two slew dogs began to bark. The bloodhounds' keen noses made them superb trackers. He followed their lead until he spotted a scruffy looking group of ten armed men. They were dressed in the traditional garb of Reivers, and they had large sacks tied to their saddles, probably filled with loot from a raid. Masters' men were near the summit of a high hill and a fold of ground concealed them from the brigands in the valley below. He debated whether to attack or follow them back to their starting point. The summit road paralleled that in the valley for the next five miles, so shadowing them would not be difficult.

His men had plenty of dash and spirit, but they were outnumbered, and their training was incomplete. He feared that each might seek individual glory rather than fight in a coordinated fashion. He looked at their faces and all were eager, perhaps too eager.

"We will follow them back to their hide," he ordered his troopers, "and see if they meet with any accomplices to dispose of their stolen goods. Or there may be a central assembly point. The numbers are against us, so we gather information and return to Berwick."

His men nodded in approval, and he was glad to see that they were able to keep their zeal in check. He formed them up single file and they began their pursuit.

The Reivers below seemed in no hurry. They were anything but stealthy, talking loudly and boastfully among themselves. Master's own men maintained a commendable silence.

After four miles, the Reivers emerged into a clearing filled with wagons. These were the kind of wagons favored by gypsies, covered with curved wooden tops and intended for living as well as transportation. The women, children and older men that Masters saw roving about were clearly not gypsies, though they seemed to be living an itinerant existence. He wondered if they were people who had lost their homes because of the rash of foreclosures over the last years. They looked poor and sad, not threatening.

Two men had set up tables in the north corner of the encampment. Masters unfurled his glass for a better look. The two had the studious faces of accountants, and Masters guessed they had been sent by parties unknown to purchase stolen goods. The people milling about looked poor enough that they would probably settle for being paid a fraction of their true value. The residents needed coins that could be spent without raising an alarm; one could hardly pay for food with a necklace or a brooch which might be recognized by a former owner.

Masters debated what to do. Pennywhistle had given his team leaders considerable flexibility, telling them the judgment of the man directly on the scene was worth more than those in Berwick. He had stressed that he wanted information, and that his goal was to catch sharks, not minnows.

Masters quietly gave his orders. His men followed him down a narrow winding trail and took up an observation position in a stand of tall trees behind the encampment.

The Reivers rode up and dismounted. Many were met with smiles, hugs, and kisses from people Masters surmised were wives and children. Each Reiver shouldered his sack of loot and lined up in front of the tables. Masters whispered his orders to his men, and they drew their Eliot Carbines. "There are women and children about, so be careful. Shoot any Reiver who resists, but I am counting on shock and intimidation to carry the day rather than guns and swords. Listen closely to what I say and follow my lead."

Masters drew his own carbine, made a hand motion to his men, and spurred his horse gently forward. Masters and his men did not charge, but rode calmly out into the open, weapons at the ready. The people in the encampment froze in shock as the redcoats that many viewed as their worst enemy appeared as if by magic. Since some believed in sorcery, that was no idle phrase.

Master's trotted over to the first Reiver in the line and aimed his carbine at the man's head. Master employed in his most intimidating command voice, one which some likened to what a volcano would sound like if it could speak. "In the name of Warden Pennywhistle, you are all under arrest. Come with me peaceably and you will live. Resist and you will die."

The Reivers in line made no moves, since they had left all their weapons in their saddles; daggers were no match for carbines and pistols. One Reiver who had apparently not gone on today's raid, emerged from behind a wagon and leveled his musket at Masters. He was adjusting his aim, when Trooper Jenkins fired, hitting the man squarely in the chest.

"Do any more of you wish to test my patience?" barked Masters.

The crowd looked sullen but cowed. One older man finally spoke up. "What do you propose to do with us?"

"I will escort the lot of you to Berwick, where your cases will be adjudicated. I promise you that you will suffer no harm from us if you behave, and when we reach Berwick, I will see that all of you are fed. I know that you all realize that the penalty for theft and murder is a hangman's noose, but Warden Pennywhistle is prepared to consider less severe penalties if mitigating circumstances can be proved. However," he paused portentously, "any man who provides actionable information that enables Warden Pennywhistle to bring down those above you will have his sentence commuted to transportation, perhaps even something less severe. I would also add that if any woman or child who brings me good information, his family will receive the full extent of the Warden's mercy." He raised his voice and pointed at the fences," and you two, who regularly cheat these people, can escape the hangmen's noose, if you will be forthcoming with the Warden about your accounts and to whom you intended to forward the goods you were to receive today."

The two fences looked at each other in shock, then nodded vigorously in Master's direction.

Murmurs and whispers rippled through the crowd. The line of Reivers said nothing, seeming to wait for the verdict of their families and friends.

One old woman stepped forward. The crowd looked at her with great respect.

"I speak for all here. We are tired of living hand to mouth, getting by on what we can scrounge and steal, and from the occasional donations of "The Benefactor." We are weary of running from the law and hate being outcasts. We are reduced to these circumstances because our menfolk lost their jobs. The yeomen and gentle folk above us can stay within the law because these dark economic times have not hit them nearly as hard as they have hit us. A man's word means everything in these parts. Will you swear on a Bible and on your mother's grave that you will keep your promise to us?"

"I do so swear, madam," replied Masters. "I have never broken an oath, and I have no intention of starting now."

The crowd caught the conviction in Masters' voice and nodded in approval.

"We accept your offer, Mr...."

"Masters, Sergeant Major Masters late of the Coldstream Guards."

"What would you like us to do, Sergeant Major?"

The patrol led by Sergeant Major Pyestalker had a very different outcome. Pyestalker harbored a secret that he had neglected to tell Pennywhistle when he had been hired. His sister had married a Border farmer, and both of them had been murdered in their bed six months ago. The authorities had failed to find the murderer and Pyestalker was convinced that he was being sheltered by people who had lately become Reivers. His sister, who was 15 years his senior, had raised him when their parents died. Pyestalker cared nothing for justice, nothing for information, and nothing for the laws that had failed to safeguard his family. He lived for vengeance and was determined to have it. He had no idea which Reiver had murdered his sister, so he was determined to kill every Reiver that crossed his path and let God make the final judgment. His men knew nothing of his private vendetta and saw only an experienced leader they would trust with their lives.

Pyestalker was an excellent tracker and was accompanied by the two slew dogs with the most sensitive noses of their pack. They picked up a trail of the heavy hoof prints of four horses around ten a.m. Bits of food and bric-a-brac littered the trail at intervals. The Reivers had evidently been sorting out their haul and tossing away items they thought of no value. It was like following a trail of breadcrumbs left by Hansel and Gretel.

Pyestalker was an avid map reader and though he had never visited the area that he was traversing, he had a good idea of its highways and byways. Three miles ahead there was a small valley where four roads crossed. Since the terrain consisted of high hills, undulating plateaus, and gnarled gullies, that crossroads might be the perfect place to stage an ambush. From the depth and freshness of the horse prints, he surmised that the Reivers were only twenty minutes ahead. There was a parallel track close to the present one that would allow him to arrive ahead of the Reivers if he pushed his horses to the gallop.

The four red horsemen covered the distance to the crossroads quickly and tethered their horses in a grove where they would not be visible from the crossroad. He and his men drew their carbines and took up positions in a dry stream bed. "Hold your fire until you can see the warts on their noses," he whispered to his men, "But wait for my command."

Four Reivers emerged from a fold in the road ten minutes later. They were sad specimens of humanity. They rode in plodding silence, their expressions a combination of fatigue and boredom.

Pyestalker's men looked disappointed. These were not the vicious savages they had been expecting, but ordinary men you might meet at a street market on a Saturday morning.

"I think they would surrender if you challenged them," whispered Trooper Marks. "We can take them prisoner, and I don't think it will take much to make them talk."

Pyestalker glared at him. "Shut up. I am in command. Those men are thieves and murderers and deserve no mercy. The only justice that they merit will come from the barrels of our carbines."

The other two troopers heard Pyestalker and looked at each other in confusion. They were gentlemen, not murderers, and had been raised on traditions of fair play, good sportsmanship, and the rule of law.

Pyestalker saw the doubt on their faces. "I remind you gentlemen that mutiny is a capital crime. I expect your instant obedience and your best marksmanship."

All three men gulped, then nodded.

Pyestalker waited until the four Reivers were forty yards away before he bellowed, "Fire!" At this distance and with their marksmanship practice, their carbines tumbled all four from their saddles. The redcoats rose from their hides to inspect the damage. One man was dead, one was grievously wounded, and two had wounds on their upper shoulders.

"Please don't kill me, sirs, I beg of you," one wounded man gasped. "I have a wife and three children to provide for."

Pyestalker eyed him with cold contempt then spat upon him. He drew his pistol and shot him between the eyes. "One less rat to bother us." He turned to his troopers. "Rayford and Fairfield, finish off the other two with your pistols.

Rayford did as he was asked, though a look of revulsion crossed his face as he fired his round.

"No, sir," objected Fairfield, "I won't. You have issued an illegal order, Sergeant Major, and it is my duty to disobey it. It is a clear violation of the laws of w—"

Fairfield stopped as Pyestalker thrust his reloaded pistol against his temple. "I am giving you a choice, Mr. Fairfield," Pyestalker snarled. "Either you blow out that man's brains or I blow out yours. Decide quickly; I have no use for mollycoddlers."

Fairfield executed his man, then retched.

"You need to grow a pair of balls, Mr. Fairfield," Pyestalker said coldly.

Rayford wondered what he had gotten himself into. He could see little difference between himself and the man he had just killed. Sir Thomas Pennywhistle was a good man, a moral man; one whom Rayford admired and wished to emulate. How had Pennywhistle come to employ such a bloodthirsty rogue?

***

Meadow's patrol, ten miles away, was spotted and ambushed as it rounded a corner on the main road to Kelso Abbey. His six opponents were bad shots, however, and their first volley merely served to alert Meadows and his men to danger. They quickly dismounted and took cover in a ditch that was the first stage in the construction of a canal. They opened a brisk fire on their opponents. Their opponents had no stomach for an extended fight and after five minutes of exchanging gunshots, they mounted their horses and fled. Meadows and company galloped in pursuit, wounding and capturing two. One died on the return trip to Berwick but one proved talkative, once Meadows had mentioned transportation as a reward for providing sound information.

Hamish Hopson told Meadows the name of his immediate superiors, then gave Meadows a name that stunned him. "I have heard rumors that Baron Maxwell of Paxton is using his connections with traders to sell many of our goods overseas."

Meadows knew that Maxwell owned 30,000 acres in the Border Lands and was said to have an income of fifty thousand pounds a year. He wondered why such a wealthy man would choose to involve himself in criminal activities. But then, aristocrats were odd people, and Avarice was one of the seven deadly sins. For some, no matter how large their fortune, it was never enough; they were consumed by their insatiable hunger for more. Some had the hoarder's mentality, and rather than enjoying what they had, they were compelled to ceaselessly add to their wealth. Cocksure arrogance sometimes led the obscenely rich to take chances that no sane man would risk. Occasionally it led them into criminal activities. Meadows wondered if Maximillian Maxwell, Pennywhistle's right-hand man, was any relation. He seemed to know and be related to a great many important people in the Border area.

***

Sergeant Gardner's Patrol had the strangest experience of all. They spotted no signs of Reivers on the journey out from Berwick, but on their return, a rider came trotting up to them. He wore Reiver attire but carried no weapons on his person or his saddle. "My name is Angus Heatherington, and I want to turn myself in. I have information that may prove useful to Warden Pennywhistle, and I would like you to escort me to him."

Gardner eyed him suspiciously. "How do I know that this is not a trick? Reivers do not turn themselves in. I am thinking that you want us to bring you to Warden Pennywhistle so that you have a chance to kill him."

Heatherington shook his head vigorously. "It's no trick. The Reivers have put a price on my head. I need protection."

"Why are they after you?"

"Because I killed the vile man I worked with. He committed one atrocity too many and I had enough."

"And you think your information is valuable?"

"Are you prepared to take the chance that it's not? Substitute your judgment for the Warden's?"

"No, I am not," admitted Gardiner.

"I have the name of the man who hired the assassin who tried to kill Warden when he first arrived. He will surely want to know that." Heatherington reached into his pocket and drew forth a small ledger.

"I took this before I fled. Inside are the details of every racket, protection scheme, and dodge being run in the City of Berwick. It contains names, dates, and locations. I have another reason for turning myself in: I trust Warden Pennywhistle and I know he is trying to do the right thing for the Borders. You see, I served under him at Salamanca. I was once Corporal Heatherington of the Connaught Rangers. He was the finest officer that I had ever met, but I had always assumed that his gallantry had brought him an early death. When I heard of his appointment as Warden of The East March, I was very pleased to hear he was alive. After Salamanca, he patted me on the back and said, "Well done." I have never forgotten those words and recalling them made me realize how wrong I had been to have thrown in my lot with the Reivers. When I fought alongside Pennywhistle, I became the best version of myself. I want that man back."

"The Warden believes in second chances, especially for old comrades-in-arms."

"That's just it. I don't just want to be an old comrade in arms, I want to fight for him right now. I want to ask him if there is any way that I can join you gallant fellows."

"You'd fight against the Reivers?"

"Yes, I want to help undo the damage that I have done."

***

Pennywhistle rode up the low hill behind Whistlestop and unfurled his Ramsden once he reached its summit. He panned it slowly over the estate and was depressed by what he saw. The tower looked intact, but some of the outbuildings had been damaged or destroyed. Several new sheds were under construction but looked only half finished. Crops had been harvested, but there were no sheep grazing, and there were wide swaths where fire had done its devastating work. He observed people going about their work, yet there was something off about their postures. They walked warily, casting glances over their shoulders every so often. He had seen the same behavior in men who had been in battle and never quite recovered. The children especially appeared wary and watchful.

A lie was a bad way to start a relationship, but he needed an honest assessment of what had happened during and after the raid, and he feared that his rank might intimidate some people. He was also curious to know what the estate inhabitants thought of their new Warden's efforts so far.

He rode slowly down the hill. As the sound of approaching horse hoofbeats, some looked up with curiosity, some with suspicion, and a few with hostility.

He spotted a girl with an expressive, intelligent face and rode over to her. She looked up at him with a friendly expression and he knew he had chosen correctly. "Greetings, Miss. My name is Thomas Murray, and I am a reporter for the *Times of London*." Pennywhistle was using his first and middle names. "I was set upon by brigands on my way here and was lucky to escape with my life." He pointed to the bloody makeshift bandage on his arm. "I have need of someone with healing skills to tend to my wound, and I can pay. Who on this estate could assist me?"

"You'll be wanting Maude Dacre. You can find her in the tower over yonder."

"Thank you for your kindness, Miss..."

"Mary Simmons. You said you are a reporter. What have you come to report upon, Mr. Murray?"

"I was informed by Sir Thomas Pennywhistle that there was an incident here and I have come to record its details. People in London have no idea of the disruptions that have been happening in the Borders, and it is time that they should know."

"That is welcome news, Mr. Murray. We've been abandoned and forgotten. And don't get me started on *Sir* Thomas Pennywhistle!" Mary said indignantly. "He has never so much as visited. Just another absentee landlord who cares not at all what happens to his tenants, so long as his rents are paid!"

This stung, and Pennywhistle found himself wanting to exonerate himself at least a little in the mind of this forthright girl.

"As Warden he has many estates and many lives to consider, Miss Mary. He might have thought that prioritizing the problems on his own lands would seem as though he regarded only his own losses as important and was using the position for a private vendetta. He may have reasoned that putting his personal concerns last would let people know that he is a public-spirited gentleman who serves king and country before himself."

Mary considered his words. "Maybe he doesn't know how bad things are here. Your reporting could help with that. Do you have the ear of Warden Pennywhistle?"

"I do, and I would like to help."

"Good. I shall introduce you to Maude, and then I will speak to people on the estate who wish to tell their stories. It wasn't only crops and livestock we lost to the raiders, but family and friends. Maude herself lost her husband and son; and poor Joan Johnstone was raped."

Mary ran ahead of the horse all the way to the tower and made introductions, then ran off to spread the news of a reporter's arrival.

"Let's take a look at that wound, Mr. Murray. Sit down over here," Maude said. After Pennywhistle had removed his jacket and shirt, she inspected the slash. "The wound is not deep, and I can clean it without much trouble. Four stitches will close it tight. Who did this to you?"

"Highwaymen looking for easy prey. They ambushed me, but fortunately my horse was faster than theirs. I am lucky to have found you, madam. Of course, I will pay any fee you care to name."

"I do this in the name of hospitality, Mr. Murray, but I want your promise that you will tell the world what happened here."

"You have my word. If you are willing, let us start with your story. Tell me what happened during the raid as you stitch me up; it will distract my mind from the needle's prick and tug."

Maude smiled at that. "Would you like a dram of whiskey?"

"No, I need my head clear. Leave nothing out. Sometimes the smallest detail is the key to understanding the whole event."

Maude told the terrible tale, but her manner seemed detached, as if she could be most accurate when she stood outside of her personal involvement in the events she related. It was of a piece with the clear perspective of the letter she had sent him. It confirmed his impression that she was a formidable woman who would make a very useful ally.

She tended to the wound with the same efficiency that undergirded her tale. As she tied off a fresh dressing, she said, "I have more to say, but why don't we talk over a meal? It's good to get some nourishment into a man recovering from an injury. I can't promise anything elaborate; just eggs, toast, and some sausages made here on the estate."

"I am hungry, madam, and right now, what you promise sounds like a feast."

"I also have lemonade. You said you wanted your head clear."

"Lemonade would be very refreshing."

Pennywhistle listened carefully as he ate in the informality of the tower's kitchen. The meal turned into an extended conversation that gave him a very clear picture of what had happened at Whistlestop. When he had finished eating, he took out a small notebook and pencil.

Maude was pleased that he paid close attention and asked questions frequently, seeking clarification of certain details. She could see why he had become a reporter: he had a good nose for detail, almost like a bloodhound. He asked many questions about the management of the estate, and what had changed since the attack. He even asked whether a memorial service had been performed for the dead and wrote down the names of everyone who had been killed or hurt. There was something about him, Maude concluded, that inspired a feeling of trust — and Maude was not usually a trusting person.

Mary appeared just as the conversation was ending. Her eyes sent a message to Maude's, "Do you trust him?"

Maude nodded in the affirmative.

"Mr. Murray, everyone here wants to talk to you. They are waiting in the courtyard. I hope you can stay all day."

"I have all the time in the world, Miss Simmons. I am in the business of collecting stories and welcome the chance to hear as many as possible." He realized he was being given a priceless opportunity to see the human reality behind the cold statistics.

Maude set up a small table and chair for him in the courtyard and organized the eyewitnesses into a line. She addressed them in firm tones. "Let's not waste Mr. Murray's time. Get to the point, tell your story, and keep the tears to a minimum. Understand?"

It took three hours for Pennywhistle to hear the accounts, and by the end he had filled a second notebook. Even after speaking, people lingered, listening to the other testimonies and interjecting an occasional clarification. To the surprise of parents, he encouraged children to testify. While their language was simple, they often saw things their parents had missed. He acquired not only an education in those hours, but a real understanding of the people who were his tenants. They were no longer anonymous names on leases, but flesh and blood human beings with a panoply of hopes and desires for the future.

He had gained their trust. Now it was time to betray it, and hope that he could repair the damage.

He rose from his chair, paused to be sure all eyes were on him, and summoned his best command voice. "Residents of Whistlestop, you have been completely honest with me, but I have not been completely honest with you."

Looks of confusion appeared on many faces, others waited stoically. A few children hid behind a nearby adult.

"My full name is Thomas Murray... Pennywhistle."

The looks on the adult faces transformed to expressions of shock and anger.

"I am Sir Thomas Pennywhistle, Warden of the East English March. I concealed my identity because I feared revealing it might stop you from speaking freely. I should have known better. And I realize you needed me here much sooner. I deeply apologize for my actions. But I am here now, and if you will grant me a few minutes, I will tell you my plans for the estate."

Murmurs of anger and scorn rippled through the crowd. Things were on the verge of turning grim when Maude stepped forward. "Stop!" she commanded, and called out by name the ones who looked the most upset. "I trust this man, and now I understand why he did what he did. I am willing to give him the benefit of the doubt, and so should you. Do not judge him until you hear him out."

Some of the angry or sullen expressions cleared, but not all, and everyone looked toward Pennywhistle.

"Speak your piece," whispered Maude to Pennywhistle, "but it had better be good."

Facing the Imperial Guard was far less intimidating than speaking to good people whom he had let down. If he chose his words poorly, an unsettled crowd could quickly become an angry mob. But if he could convince his neglected, disappointed tenants of his good intentions, convincing the rest of the Border people might also be possible.

***

Forty miles away, Walter Scott entered the ghillie's cottage on the Paxton Estate, about to make a speech of a kind. Unlike Pennywhistle's, it was carefully rehearsed and aimed at an audience of one. That audience was Lord John Maxwell, Baron Maxwell of Paxton. Maxwell was Scott's silent partner, but he had been making ugly noises of late.

"I responded to your request for a meeting as soon as I could," said Scott. "I think it wise that we are meeting in this remote location, and I am glad that you consented to meet me alone. I have answers to the questions you posed, and the fewer people who hear them the better."

Scott was telling only half the truth. He had come alone, but he had five men hidden in a gully close by. He did not entirely trust his partner; those men would come to his aid if this meeting ended badly.

"I feel safest on my home ground," replied Maxwell. "Now, please favor me with some answers to matters which have caused me to rest uneasy this past week."

Like Scott, Maxwell also had hidden assets waiting nearby: his chief ghille and three of his best assistant ghillies.

"First, my lord, I will not sugarcoat the harm that Warden Pennywhistle has caused. He has damaged my organization and my pride. He has been interfering with the rackets and protections that we control, and people are becoming much more difficult to intimidate. Some of my men's loyalty has wavered. Overall, revenues from our enterprises are down by 30%."

"That is indeed alarming," Maxwell commented. He steepled his fingers and began tapping them together. It was time to consider what it would cost him to cut his losses. The recent worry had been hard on his heart, and he had been finding himself frequently short of breath.

"But fear not, my lord," Scott went on smoothly. "Pennywhistle can be stopped, his actions reversed. I am putting countermeasures into place to take him down. I have an informer placed with his sister-in-law. She is a talkative sort and provides a lot of useful information. I am also giving my men military training, provided by a distinguished French veteran, and am arming them all with modern muskets. I even have purchased a stock of surplus British uniforms from a mill near Durham: with a few modifications, they will give us a thoroughly military look."

"Won't that be confusing? How will the people we control be able to tell our men from Pennywhistle's?"

"That is exactly what I intend, my lord, to sow confusion. It will be a way to discredit Pennywhistle's efforts, and the locals will become more cautious if they are unable to tell if they are speaking to the Warden's men or our own."

"I understand that my son is attendant on Pennywhistle. Have you any news of him?"

"He has become Pennywhistle's right-hand man and chief executive officer. Reports say he is a changed man from the time that you sent him to the army. He seems to be sober, serious, and single-minded, displaying industry and zeal. It is a pity that he is not on our side."

"It surprises me to hear that, Mr. Scott. It surprises me very much. I concluded the boy was a lost cause and sent him to the army so he would die in distant lands and leave my good name unsullied."

"Do you think there is any chance of a reconciliation? If he could be made to see things our way, he would be a valuable asset."

"None at all. Our mutual dislike and disgust is profound."

"A pity, I have no children but hope one day to have a family when this business is over."

"I warn you, Mr. Scott, the bard had it right. 'How sharper than a serpent's tooth it is to have an ungrateful child.'"

Scott heard the anger in Maxwell's snarled response.

"I have a fully developed plan of campaign ready against Pennywhistle's forces, but I can explain it better on a map." He held up a map case.

"Please proceed."

Scott spent the next hour detailing his campaign. Maxwell was impressed with his thoroughness, attention to detail, and ability to anticipate contingencies.

"It is a good plan, Mr. Scott, and I am pleased that you have established a network of early warning outposts. However, I foresee two problems. First, you are betting on Pennywhistle doing what we expect him to do. From what we have seen, that is unwise. He seems to have an unending series of tricks up his sleeve. Second, you are gambling that your men can be brought up to British Army standards in a very short time."

"I may have a way to exert some control over Pennywhistle's behavior. At the very least, I may be able to stay his hand against taking actions against us for some short period. It involves striking at his family. I cannot say more, but I have already set a plan in motion."

"Good. Now I have a further question to ask. How secure is your control of the Berwick docks? I have a large shipment intended for merchants in Buenos Aires that I wish to move in the next week. It represents the cream of the booty we have taken in the past month. I will not move the goods unless I have your word that we can have at least one night when the docks remain unwatched and that the stevedores are fully compliant. The seizure of that cargo would cost us at least fifty thousand pounds."

Scott frowned. "I cannot make that promise. Our control of the Berwick docks is slipping. I have been working on alternate arrangements with the longshoremen in the Port of Dunbar. They are proving very amenable to my demands."

"Damn it!" roared Maxwell. "Is that the best you can do? Dunbar is a very small port, and I have heard reports that its harbor is beginning to silt up. It will be impossible to get word to the ships already at sea of a new destination. We shall just have to wait until they dock in Berwick to inform them of their new destination. That rerouting will cause confusion among ship captains and may also stir up rumors among the townspeople as to why large ships are being directed to a tiny port. Exactly the kind of attention we do not want! I will also have to completely rework my land transportation arrangements, since Dunbar is triple the distance from Berwick. I will have to throw out all my existing timetables and plan on at least doubling my transportation costs. If you had come to me earlier, I could have minimized the disruption. If I had not requested this meeting, you might not have told me at all! Being a silent partner does not mean being an uninformed partner!"

"Perhaps if you had told me that you were planning on moving such an important cargo, I could have done so. But you are very secretive about your operations, and I usually only receive notice just before a cargo is to depart. I run an efficient operation, but I am not a mind reader." Scott took a deep breath to calm his rising anger. "Arguing with each other helps no one but Pennywhistle. Let us agree that we have both made mistakes and that communications between the two of us need to be improved. We need to put blame and recriminations aside and make better plans for the future."

"I agree, but I do not like these bumps in the road, Mr. Scott. When I joined forces with you, you assured me that the risk to me and my good name would be minimal. I warned you that I would cash out if things got dicey."

"I understand, my lord, but sometimes getting into an operation such as mine is easier than getting out of it. When you put your foot down in deep mud, things change. When you try to raise that foot, the mud sucks the boot back down."

"Is that a threat, Mr. Scott? I do not respond well to threats."

"Not a threat, but a statement of the physics of criminality. Perhaps you deceive yourself about what we do, but I do not. I run a criminal organization, and I am therefore a criminal. You are too, my lord. Your title and lineage do not change that."

"Do not ever call me a criminal! Ever! Ever! My people were noblemen while yours were rooting for berries and nuts."

"I am sorry if the truth is too hard for you, but I advise you to readjust your perspective."

"This meeting is over!" hissed Maxwell in a voice as frigid as an arctic wind. "I warn you; our partnership teeters on a knife's edge. Do not distress me further."

"No need to be hasty, Lord Maxwell. Our partnership has been mutually profitable, and it would be absurd to let a setback deprive us of all the future profits that lie in store. You must take the long-term view, my lord. Let us meet here in a week to see how developments unfold. I feel certain that we will again be seeing things eye to eye."

"Very well, Mr. Scott, but nothing further had better go wrong! I bid you good day, sir!" Maxwell donned his hat and stormed out.

Scott followed him out and watched him gallop away. *The man is becoming dangerously unstable,* thought Scott. *If he does not pull himself together something will have to be done about him.* He thought about the five men he had hidden and debated whether to have them pursue. No, killing Maxwell on his own estate would be foolish; he was willing to grant his partner one final chance.

Maxwell was having the same thoughts about Scott as he raced home.

What neither man knew was that the entirety of their conversation had been overheard by James Heatherington, Angus's Heatherington's brother. He was an assistant ghillie on the Paxton estate, part of the group that Maxwell had placed as a hidden asset. He had slipped away from his three mates on a pretext of providing another angle of cover and crept close enough to spy on the meeting. Now he wondered how he could get word to his brother of what he had just heard.

CHAPTER 11

Love and Shifting Loyalties

11th November 1816

Pennywhistle was tired but pleased as he rode out of the fog and up to the main gate of Berwick just past midnight. The twenty feet tall, curved gate had a crenelated firing platform atop it and a large iron yett that could be swung on its hinges to either allow or bar entrance. The two sentries recognized him and pushed the yett open. Both were alert, snapped to attention promptly, and saluted him crisply as he passed by. Daily drill was paying dividends: there was none of the slackness that inexperienced men often demonstrated on night duty. His first instinct was to seek the arms of Sammie Jo, but he put business before pleasure and decided to visit his office first, curious what developments had happened in his absence.

He found an angry Sammie Jo and a worried Maxwell waiting for him.

Sammie Jo hugged and kissed him, then pulled back and let fly a tirade. "What the hell were you thinking, Thomas Pennywhistle, just disappearing like that? We were all worried sick. We thought that you might have been kidnapped or worse! Maxwell and I have spent the whole day trying to discover your whereabouts!"

Pennywhistle sighed. "Perhaps not my best decision."

"You didn't even tell your military secretary. Usually, he knows where to reach you. It was as if you took the day off from your sworn duty, and that ain't like you either." She looked at his coat closely. "Is that a rip I see? Wait, that's a slash mark! Have you been wounded?"

"It's nothing, Sammie Jo."

"Nothing? Nothing? You've been in a fight! You were off on some damn fool enterprise!"

"I was puzzled too, Sir Thomas," said Maxwell. "It is no secret that quite a few people want you dead and I have warned you repeatedly that you should never be without at least one bodyguard."

"You are both right. I did act on impulse, and I should have taken you into my confidence. I simply needed to be alone with my brother one last time."

"Your brother?" Sammie Jo's expression softened, but she nonetheless said, "You should have brought me with you. After all, I was there too when he died."

"You are right, of course."

"Who is this brother you are talking about?" inquired Maxwell.

Pennywhistle explained his promise made to a dying brother.

Maxwell listened carefully. "While I applaud you for carrying out a sacred duty, you still should have taken an escort. And I should add that in your absence I had to run everything for the day, and I had to scramble to do it."

"My unintended absence served a test, Mr. Maxwell. Allow me to say that I would never have left if I had not been confident that you could supervise all the doings of the barracks. You acted as the first lieutenant would have on a warship: assuming command when the captain was absent. Since I know you would immediately have informed me of any crises or emergencies upon my return, I assume any problems have been dealt with."

Maxwell smiled in surprise. "I had not thought of my lieutenancy in that light. And yes, a few problems arose today, but we dealt with them. Your organization almost runs itself since you have taught your men to think independently and employ initiative. The patrols have all reported in and have filed written reports. There is one matter I wish to discuss with you, Sir Thomas. A man named Heatherington was brought in by one of our patrols. He had a notebook that you will want to see. I have him waiting downstairs."

"Hold on, just a damn minute, Tom," said Sammie Jo firmly. "Before you disappear on me again, I want to know just what happened today, and I bet Mr. Maxwell does too."

Pennywhistle sighed in resignation. "Very well, Sammie Jo. Why don't you ring for tea? I would suggest a whiskey nightcap, but this may take a little time, and if I am also to speak with Mr. Heatherington, we need to be fully alert." Pennywhistle spent the next half hour describing his arrival at the chapel, the tomb attack, his decision to visit Whistlestop, and what had transpired. "They told me of matters that needed to be handled immediately. They especially liked the fact that I intend to build new cottages for every family on the estate. I will put Maude Dacre in charge of dispensing funds. It is my intention to dispatch those funds tomorrow."

"So, you think the estate can be restored? Can it be a real home for our family?"

"I do. As the esteemed Mr. Brown would say, "the estate has great capability." And I made more than a few friends on my visit, so we shall have tenants who wish us well. But I am getting ahead of myself. I do not yet think Whistlestop is out of danger. The raiders succeeded in causing a great deal of harm and damage, and they made off with the very valuable flock of merino wool sheep; from reports we have collected, what happened at Whistlestop so terrified the other denizens of the borders that they became much more compliant with demands made by Reivers. Even so, the residents of Whistlestop fought back; they showed defiance. I feel in my bones that our adversary will decide to once again make an example of Whistlestop. He has been losing ground to our recent efforts, and striking hard at Whistlestop will be a way of striking back at me. I am relieved but also surprised he hasn't done so already. Perhaps he has too many irons in his fire. Perhaps he has over-reached himself by taking on too many criminal enterprises that require his direct attention."

Pennywhistle stopped short, paced back and forth across the space of his office, and suddenly said, "It occurs to me that Fate has given me an opportunity in disguise. If I could be certain when my opponent intended to strike Whistlestop, I could prepare a devastating reception. The estate has sound defensive possibilities, if a few earth works were erected. Do you recall that eccentric canal builder that I hired on Nico's recommendation, the chap he met at the Royal Society? I have been holding him in reserve until I thought the people of Whistlestop would be ready to receive him, but now I think I can make solid use of his talents for something besides canal construction."

"William Smith, wasn't it?" Said Sammie Jo. "You were very impressed when you saw his geologic map of England. It was enormous, six by eight feet, and it showed the rock strata of the entire kingdom."

"Yes, I bought a copy of his map because it was a magnificent achievement, something no one else had ever thought of doing. I hired him because he has extensive experience as a canal builder, and Whistlestop needs its canal finished. Considering what the raiders did to the one under construction, he will have to start from scratch. Since he is a skilled engineer, it occurred to me that he could just as well design and supervise the building of earthen fortifications as well. I will send him and a banker with the 500 guineas under armed escort tomorrow."

"He is an odd duck, Tom. He seems to live in another world."

"Men of vision often behave in ways that the rest of us find strange. I think his map will revolutionize the study of geology. The layers of strata on his map are consistent with theories that I have heard advanced by the best thinkers at the Royal Society. They think the stuff that Bishop Usher said about the world being created in 4004 BC is absolute claptrap. It is far more likely that the earth is many millions of years old."

"He's been a busy man, Tom, thanks to Nico and Marco. The three go out to Flodden Field nearly every day and dig for hours."

"Whatever for?"

"Your stepsons are convinced that the tale of the buried treasure of Flodden is true, and they think that having an experienced geologist at their side will help them discover it.

Sally and Sybil go with them sometimes, caught up in the spirit of adventure."

Pennywhistle smiled. "Nico has fought pirates, so it should not surprise anyone that he now seeks treasure and romance. I am concerned, however, if they have left the city without some kind of armed escort."

"You mean like you just did?"

Pennywhistle sighed in embarrassment. "No man is without hypocrisy."

"Two of the Yeomanry accompany them, but I have heard Nico and Marco like to play a game that involves ditching their escorts."

"I will have to speak to them tomorrow. They subscribe to the youthful foolishness that they are somehow immortal."

"I know it is late and we all need our rest, but might I suggest you speak to Heatherington before you retire?" queried Maxwell. "I neglected to mention that he surrendered himself voluntarily. He was most insistent that he talk to you and you alone."

"It is a good sign that he came voluntarily since he must know the penalty for brigandage. I gather that he wants a pardon and understands that one will not be granted unless his information is very valuable. Of course, there is another possibility."

"What is that?"

"That he is a plant: a man sent by my foe to deceive me with false information."

"He seems sincere. He says he wants to fight for you."

"That is unusual. Most defectors just want to vanish. If he went into battle against his former friends, he would make himself a tempting target. But if he is acting out of some newly acquired conviction, that makes him more reliable than someone who is changing his stripes for money or some other kind of reward. You mentioned that he brought a book."

"Yes. I leafed through it and saw it contains details of many more rackets than we have identified, some of them far-reaching. The trouble is many of the people in it are referred to only by their initials."

"And you think he could turn those initials into names?"

"I do."

Pennywhistle thought for a minute. "Sammie Jo, why don't you head off to bed? This is going to be a long night. I was tired, but an idea just occurred to me that I need to test."

Sammie Jo frowned, then sighed. "I know that gleam in your eye. An idea has got hold of you and won't let go. Promise me that you will try to get at least a couple of hours of sleep before dawn."

"I shall commit to two hours but no more."

"I will hold you to that." She kissed him hard. "I will ring for a pot of coffee to be sent to your office." Sammie Jo embraced Pennywhistle, then departed.

"Now, Mr. Maxwell, let's meet this person of interest."

Angus Heatherington was sound asleep in a chair and snoring when Pennywhistle and Maxwell entered the storage room where he was being sequestered. Pennywhistle shook him until he came fully awake, then started in surprise when he saw the man's face clearly. "God's death! I believe we have met before!" He rubbed his chin and dug deep into his memory. "Salamanca, wasn't it? You saved the life of Sergeant James, if I recall. Blocked a bayonet thrust and finished his French attacker with one of your own."

Heatherington smiled in wonderment. "I never thought you would remember me, but I never forgot you, although I thought you must have been killed in Spain. When I heard you were alive, it gave me the strength to do something that I was too afraid to do before."

"I am pleased, Heatherington, but you know that I am the law in these parts, and that you must answer for any crimes you committed."

"I understand that, Sir Thomas, but I also know that you believe in redemption. You rescued Private Crumb from the clutches of Wellington's provost marshal when he stole a chicken. He surely would have been executed for looting if you had not intervened. And now you are intervening on behalf of the people of the border lands. So I brought something that I think will help you in your work."

Maxwell handed Pennywhistle a small book, which he began to read. He was instantly riveted by the material. Maxwell and Heatherington vanished, and his only companions became the figures, initials, and terse lines of commentary in the book.

He read each of its hundred pages over the next two hours. Maxwell handed him cups of coffee from time to time, which Pennywhistle absentmindedly sipped as he read. At the end of his third cup, he quietly closed the book as the hint of a smile blossomed on his face.

"You were not exaggerating, Heatherington. This is indeed a treasure trove of information that I can put to good use. You have earned a pardon and a second chance. However, the service I have in mind for you will involve great risk."

"You have but to ask, Sir Thomas."

"First I need to know who else has seen the book."

"Just my immediate superior who compiled it. He sends it to his superior once a month with the latest entries. I do not know who that is. We just call him "The Big Man.""

"Does your superior know it is missing?"

"No, for he has been away for a few days and won't likely return for another week. There have been problems lately in the more distant parts under his command. He decided that his personal intervention was necessary. He usually keeps the book on his person, but this time he departed hurriedly and left it behind."

"So, your superior has no idea that it is gone."

"None, sir. I was able to slip away unnoticed because discipline becomes slack when he is not around."

"So, no one knows that you have defected, and no one knows the book has vanished?"

"Correct, Sir Thomas."

"Excellent! And it looks like we will have a few days grace to put my plan into operation."

"Could you give us an idea of that plan, Sir Thomas?" queried Maxwell.

"My intention is to send Heatherington back with his book."

Heatherington's eyebrows shot skyward.

Pennywhistle turned to Heatherington. "My plan is to create a duplicate of the book with some significant but hard to detect alterations. I want you to plant it and then go back to your former life, only this time acting as my spy. I know it is not the soldiering you are used to, but it would be the most useful path to take. We could work out a dead drop system where you could leave messages at regular intervals."

"I am not sure how good a spy I would make, Sir Thomas. I am not very good at deception."

"You don't have to act. Just do what you usually do." He turned to Maxwell. "I trust you can find an expert forger among the many criminals that we have arrested."

"I have no doubt of that, Sir Thomas."

"I would need to work closely with him, so that the new information is suited to the plan of campaign that I have in mind. That would take many hours, and our window of opportunity will be small. I need a fast worker."

"I will look into that immediately after we finish here. I assume we can promise the forger a pardon?"

"As long as his work meets my expectations, and he understands I will not hesitate to look for a replacement if his first efforts are not convincing copies of the original penmanship."

"Understood. If I am not needed here, I shall proceed to the holding cells and begin my search," replied Maxwell.

"Yes. Heatherington and I have several hours of work ahead of us, while he tells me the names of the people behind the initials and answers questions about several transactions that I do not yet understand."

Maxwell gave a quick nod to Pennywhistle and departed.

Pennywhistle pulled a chair up next to Heatherington. "This will be a long and tiring process, but I promise you that when it is done, you will have a good meal and a comfortable bed. When we have finally taken down these brigands, I believe I can secure your reinstatement in the army with the rank of sergeant. I am not sure if you want to return to your former life, but you were always an exceptional soldier."

"I would like that very much. I miss the comradeship."

Pennywhistle spent the next two hours learning the names behind the initials in the book. Most were unknown to him, though that would change shortly. The few that were known to him surprised him, as they were respectable people on the surface. He could not act against many of the men without alerting others that he had access to secret information. There were, however, three targets that he could get away with striking without setting off any warning bells. One of those raids could be ready to go by nightfall, and his sister-in-law would be very pleased at its outcome.

"This name Maxwell occurs frequently in the ledger, Heatherington, but unlike the others, there is no first initial. Have you any idea who this man might be? The problem is that Maxwell is a common surname in the Borders."

"I do not know who he is, but when my superior speaks of him there is fear in his voice — and my chief fears few men."

Pennywhistle wondered if this man Maxwell was his chief foe, his foe's underling, or his foe's partner. Whoever he was, he was a formidable obstacle to Pennywhistle's plans and would have to be removed. A thought hit Pennywhistle, and it made him scowl. He did not like what he was thinking, though he could be wrong.

"Something troubling you, Sir Thomas?"

"It's only a hunch, but I need to run it down. I wish to do that in private. I need to detain you no further tonight, so I will ring for a servant to escort you to your meal and your bed."

"Thank you, Sir Thomas."

The under-butler escorted Heatherington to the servant's hall, and Pennywhistle resumed his detective work.

He checked the ledger for entries with the name Maxwell, and he noticed that all involved locations close to the edges of the massive Paxton estate. Paxton House was the home of Maximillian Maxwell's father. A lord being a criminal was strange, yet a powerful man who did not fear to murder his wife might step outside the law if he could gain additional wealth and influence. Power was the most addictive drug of all, and Baron Maxwell seemed a likely candidate to abuse it in the most outrageous ways.

He tried several permutations of his limited information, but Occam's Razor always brought him back to the same conclusion. Lord John Maxwell, Baron Maxwell of Paxton, was a partner in crime with the man who had created all the Border misery that he had been called upon to fix. However, he needed additional proof to be certain. He debated whether to tell the son about the father; the shock might send Maxwell back into nasty old habits. But Pennywhistle valued honesty, and as his chief assistant, Maximillian Maxwell had a right to know his suspicions.

The first rays of dawn were flooding the room when Maxwell opened the door, and he realized that he had broken his promise to Sammie Jo.

"I found your forger, Sir Thomas, and I thought that you would like to meet him directly."

"I would, but there is a matter I need to discuss with you. It's about your father."

Maxwell's face turned red with hatred. "He's in the book, isn't he?"

"I'm afraid so."

***

Just after nine a.m. the day after Pennywhistle had spoken with his brother Angus, James Heatherington and four other Reivers watched their target approach through their spyglasses. They were mounted but concealed behind a stand of tall trees, a hundred yards from the River Tweed's English riverbank, overlooking an undulating field that had been part of the Battlefield of Flodden. The Reivers had shadowed her for three days but had not yet had a good opportunity to do what they had been sent to do. They wanted to minimize the risk to themselves, but Heatherington also had a certain regard for his youthful quarry. Two mounted Yeomanry privates accompanied her, looking surprisingly formidable considering they had probably been privileged swells until recently. The girl was the primary target, but since her young escort was never far from her side her unknown young swain, he would probably have to be abducted as well. Heatherington had volunteered for the job; he wanted to get a message to his brother, Angus, whom he hoped was in contact with Warden Pennywhistle.

Marco Ruzzini and Sally Pennywhistle visited the same spot nearly every day around noon. The happy couple would spread out a blanket, consume the contents of a picnic basket, and talk for an hour. They would laugh and occasionally cuddle, but never take it further; their escorts functioned as diligent chaperones as well as guardians. Then they would take spades from their saddlebags and dig for two hours, searching, as many others had before them, for the treasure chests of King James IV.

Josiah Clark furled his glass in frustration then gestured for the others to gather round. "Three days of this and still no chance for a fast snatch and grab. I say we charge in and take our chances."

"This was supposed to be a simple abduction of a hostage," responded Charles Evers, "but those guards are well armed, and mounted on fast horses."

"I agree," said John Parker, "Those yeomen look like tough customers. Let's wait for a better opportunity." Armed and vigilant guards were a much more daunting prospect than empty-handed, frightened farmers.

"We can't keep waiting," retorted Walter Wincott. "Our orders are to not return home empty-handed."

"Let's charge now and get it over with," said Peter Johnston. "What say you, Heatherington?"

All eyes focused on James Heatherington, and he shuddered inwardly. His mates were relying on him and he felt the pull of that, even though he did not like them since all four were killers. If he was to accomplish his goal, he would have to make a nasty moral choice, one that would change him forever. He glanced toward the two yeoman three hundred yards away and saw that they had dismounted. The two sat down in the grassy field and opened their own picnic hamper: even sentinels had to eat.

"Look there," said Heatherington. "We have the chance we have waited for and must attack immediately!" Heatherington saw uncertainty in the eyes of Evers and Parker, and knew the matter hung in the balance. He drew his sword and shouted," follow me!" He put the spurs to his horse but not too hard. He purposely avoided a gallop because he wanted plenty of time for his next action.

He burst from the trees shouting, "Scotland forever!" in the manner of a battle cry. His mates caught his enthusiasm and kicked their own horses to a thundering gallop. His shouts alerted the two yeomen, as James had intended. They jumped to their feet and raced toward their mounts.

Heatherington let his mates dash ahead of him. They closed quickly on the yeomen, who had just mounted up. The yeomen drew their swords and swiveled their horses, preparing to charge.

Marco grabbed Sally's hand and they both dashed toward their own horses. "I swear to protect you!" Marco shouted to her. He had no idea how to do so because he had come unarmed, but desperation had a way of awakening inspiration. Then it hit him that his spade could be a weapon.

Heatherington's mates were nearly upon the yeomen when he came up behind them, drew the pistol from his left saddle holster, and shot Evers in the back. Next, he drew his right pistol and shot Wincott.

The remaining two were so focused on the Yeomen that they remained unaware of the fall of their mates. Heatherington drew his sword and slashed at the back of Parker's neck. He screamed, then tumbled from the saddle.

The yeomen reined in their horses, baffled by an enemy doing their job.

Heatherington's sword slashed Clark in the face as he was turning to see what happened to Parker. Clark reared back in pain, shivered for a second, then slumped forward unconscious, as blood poured from a massive diagonal wound that ran from his hairline to his chin. His horse turned and galloped back toward the trees, sensing his master was in distress and wanting to save him, but by the time the horse reached the tree line, Clark was dead and dangling from his saddle.

Heatherington stopped abruptly. He drew a large white handkerchief from his pocket and waved it vigorously at the two yeomen, who were drawing their own pistols.

"Hold your fire! Hold your fire! We must talk! Hear me out! I have news for Warden Pennywhistle."

The two yeomen looked at each other with expressions that clearly said, *What the hell is this man playing at?*

Heatherington took out his pistols and threw them on the ground. He did the same thing with his sword and held up his hands. "You can't shoot an unarmed man!"

His appeal to the Englishmen's sense of fair play worked. The yeomen approached him cautiously, keeping their pistols trained on Heatherington's chest.

"Speak your peace and be quick about it!" barked the taller of the two yeomen. "No tricks now, or we will shoot."

Heatherington spoke with an urgency that was unfeigned. "My name is James Heatherington. My associates and I were supposed to kidnap Miss Sally Pennywhistle. It should be obvious whose side I am on. It is vital that I talk to Warden Pennywhistle. I have news that he will want to hear." He saw the doubt in their faces. "What have you to lose? You can keep me under close guard all the way to Berwick. All I ask is that you tell the Warden of my arrival. If he suspects I am playing him false I shall be cast into jail, and you will be commended for taking me prisoner."

The two yeomen turned to each other and the taller one spoke. "The man has a point. Besides, our only alternative would be shooting him, and I am not ready to kill a man in cold blood."

"I agree." The shorter one waved his pistol at Heatherington. "Very well, but we will ride behind you all the way. If you attempt to escape, you will be shot. Is that clear?"

"Perfectly."

Marco and Sally rode slowly up to the group. Sally had never seen violent death before and shivered in her saddle. Marco had and was far less shaken, but he was puzzled; he could only guess at why this Reiver had behaved so strangely.

The taller yeoman turned to them. "This man says he was part of a group sent to kidnap you, Miss Pennywhistle. He says he wants to speak to your uncle, and I am going to give him the chance. We must return to Berwick immediately." The little caravan covered the distance back to Berwick quickly. Heatherington rode silently, but Marco and Sally talked all the way back.

"It's terribly romantic, in a way," said Sally.

"I don't understand," replied Marco.

"A man I don't know risked his life and honor to save me from a kidnapping. I feel like a princess with an errant knight fighting on her behalf!"

"I would have fought for you if I had been given the chance, Sally. I would have even used my bare hands!"

"I know you would have, Marco, and I am glad you did not need to. I do not know what I would do if anything happened to you."

Marco blushed. "And I would be devastated if anything happened to you."

"I feel as though I have just lived through a pirate adventure!"

"But we did not get the treasure. Let's try again tomorrow."

The tall yeoman overheard the conversation and rolled his eyes. It surprised him how quickly his charges had recovered from their earlier discomfiture. He put it down to the opium-like effects of romance. He thought of the girl that he had been considering courting. He had been afraid to approach her, but after hearing Miss Pennywhistle's esteem for heroics, he felt emboldened. He would make his first overture to her tonight.

The taller yeoman delivered Sally to her mother, who was horrified when she heard what had happened and bundled her daughter off to her room while Marco took it upon himself to alert all the staff to the danger and to patrol the doors as a self-appointed guardian.

The shorter yeoman escorted Heatherington to Pennywhistle's office. He requested an interview, and the sentry disappeared to convey the message. Soon after, the sentry returned, followed by Maxwell, who said, "Warden Pennywhistle is not available, but I am. What is your name, Trooper, and how did you come to take this man into custody?"

"Trooper Perkins, sir." He quickly explained what had happened and finished with, "And I believe him, Mr. Maxwell." The prisoner remained silent and watchful as Perkins spoke.

"That's an extraordinary tale, Trooper Perkins." Maxwell glared at the prisoner. "You say your name is James Heatherington, and that the information you bear is vital?" *I've already had this conversation*, Maxwell was thinking. *What is it about Heatheringtons?* The sense of *deja vu* was oddly amusing.

"I swear on my mother's grave that it is all true, Mr. Maxwell."

"I have my doubts about any man who would murder his mates. I do not trust you."

Maxwell turned to the sentry. "Fetch the other prisoner."

"Yes, sir."

Maxwell was curious to see how close the brothers were to each other. Planting one informer in the camp of Pennywhistle's enemy would be helpful, but planting two would be even better. Being family, they could each watch the other's back.

Maxwell's question was answered when Angus was brought in. He smiled broadly and rushed to embrace his brother.

"I was worried sick about you, little brother," said Angus.

"I felt the same about you. You've no idea what I had to do to get here."

*****

Nico Ruzzini, William" Strata" Smith, and two Yeoman escorts arrived at Whistlestop two days after Pennywhistle's visit. Nico was there to deliver the 500 guineas Pennywhistle had promised to Maude Dacre. He was also there to assure the inhabitants that Pennywhistle was a man of his word. Smith's task was to devise a plan of earthen fortifications for Whistlestop, as well as deciding how best to repair the damage to the uncompleted canal or determine whether the canal should be dug in a different location. Smith was an experienced canal builder, and his engineering prowess was held in high esteem by the Duke of Bedford and the Earl of Leicester. Smith had become fascinated by the rocks and strata he uncovered in the process of his labours, and the ancient fossils he found embedded in many of them. He'd noticed that rock layers were arranged in patterns, and that he could date the age of a given rock strata by the types of fossils that were fixed in them: the older the rock, the more primitive that fossils in it. This led him to the conclusion that the Earth was much, much older than most believed: not thousands of years old but millions. He had portrayed his conclusions in the first geological map of England, a hand colored, six- by eight-foot illustration with the colors indicating rock strata, their thickness and elevations. Seven hundred much smaller copies of the map had been printed and were available for sale at fifteen pounds each. Sales had been disappointing, and his debts were growing dangerously high, so he had been relieved when Pennywhistle had asked him to see what could be done with Whistlestop's half ruined canal.

He had been surprised by the request to design fortifications but looked upon it as a challenge. His knowledge of rock layers and soils gave him a perspective that could enable him to see possibilities that a conventional military engineer might miss. He had borrowed and read *A Treatise on Fortifications*, by John Miller, which contained numerous illustrations of fieldworks, showcasing the best designs of Vauban and his predecessors. Smith liked what Vauban had said about fortifications: "More powder, less blood"; meaning that defenders sheltered behind fortifications were able to fire more rounds than in the field and were less likely to be killed.

While Smith went about his preliminary explorations, Nico spoke with Maude Dacre, who was both disappointed and suspicious.

"I was expecting Sir Thomas himself," said Maude.

"I assure you, Madam, that he will come," replied Nico, "but he has many matters in hand, for the Reivers and their accomplices are active across the length of the border. He has asked me to serve as his deputy here and act as his eyes and ears."

"But you are so young and so..."

"I was until recently a midshipman in the Navy with two years of experience in the East. I have fought pirates and assorted brigands, so I am not untested. The people who have bedeviled this estate are land-based versions of the blackguards that I dealt with before."

"But if you were so successful, why did you leave the service? It seems to me that if you are what you claim you threw away a promising career."

Nico frowned. "That is complicated, madam, and it sprang from many concerns that are best kept private. I can tell you that I saw something extraordinary in the East Indies that made me realize that my life might be profitably spent unraveling the mysteries of Nature. I witnessed the eruption of a volcano, whose terrible violence made the explosions of Vesuvius seem mere burps. It is my belief that those elements may be related to the very unusual weather that we are having."

"You sound like a young man of serious mien, so I will give you the benefit of the doubt. Sir Thomas gave us a general idea of his plans for the estate; I wonder if you could spare some specifics?" There was a tart edge to Maude's voice.

"I know that he has some grand design in mind but I do not know the details; that work will be in the hands of Mr. Smith, who is walking the land now. My assignment is to help you intelligently distribute 500 guineas towards the restoration of the estate. Sir Thomas will also be sending ten auxiliary infantrymen tomorrow to help in its defense. I trust that you will be able to provide them food and show them a place to pitch their tents."

"Some real soldiers would be welcome. I feel in my bones that the Reivers will return, and I want to send them running like a pack of whipped curs. In the meanwhile, I will introduce you to the people of the estate. I hope you are a patient man, because they all have tales to tell. I will make a written account of who receives what, and the stated purpose for the payment. Is that satisfactory to you?"

"Yes, it is, madam. I trust you will make it clear that I enjoy the full confidence of Sir Thomas."

"I will do that, Mr. Ruzzini. They heard his promises but remain more than a little skeptical. Your presence, and the guineas, may prove persuasive."

All around the perimeter of the estate, Smith continued his explorations and began to visualize fortifications. He decided that a pair of lunettes would work better than a continuous line of trenches, built on both sides of the single road leading into Whistlestop, so that intruders would be funneled into a crossfire. Four more hours of walking the estate, with the fortification book in one hand and a sketchbook and pencil in the other, convinced Smith that a layered defense was best. Two earthen lunettes built on the top of the hill in front of Whistlestop would be the first line of defense. The crescent shape was better adapted to the terrain than the square shape of a redoubt. Each would have a perimeter of 30 yards, with 12 foot high 4-foot-thick walls earth, designed to hold forty men, though the walls would afford enough protection for half that number to provide an adequate defense. Their walls would be studded with sharpened sticks called fraises, their points facing outward.

Further down the slope and a hundred yards in front of the main gate would be two redoubts, square fortifications also designed to house forty men each. The low stone walls surrounding the tower could be raised two feet with the addition of more stones. Taken together, the works would multiply the defensive capabilities of the defenders by a factor of ten. The people of the estate would have to provide the labor, but since they would be defending their lives and homes, he trusted they would be willing workers.

Smith noticed that the summit of the highest hill in the area, two miles distant, was bare; a good site for a watch post, since the summit commanded clear views in every direction. A sentinel equipped with Congreve rockets could give the defenders of Whistlestop plenty of advance warning.

***

Maude rang the tower bell to summon all the tenants, then introduced Nico to the assembly and told them of Pennywhistle's largess. They were visibly pleased by the presence of two stalwart young men from the Northumberland Yeomanry, whom they saw as portents of future military aid.

Toby Scoggins was the first to step up to Maude's table. "I am grateful to everyone here for letting me stay and helping me start to turn my fortunes around. It's no secret that Mary Simmons has made me a new man, and I am hoping this place can be made safe for good. Since I am the only military man among you," Ruzzini glared at him, "pardon me, the only one here who has fought Napoleon, I speak from experience when I request that a substantial proportion of Sir Thomas's generosity be allocated to the purchase of modern weapons. This estate lacks firearms. I propose we arm every person on the estate, including women and any girls and boys strong enough to shoulder a musket. We will all need training, but I can help with that."

Ruzzini interjected, "And Sir Thomas can send an experienced drillmaster to assist you."

"Good." Scoggins continued. "There is a merchant I know in Coldingham who has a stock of fifty unissued Brown Besses. He is intending to sell them to rebels in South America, but we are old comrades in arms, and I think he could be persuaded to part with the lot if we offered him a price above the standard one pound per musket. He might be able to furnish us with some horse pistols as well."

"The idea of an estate militia is in keeping with Sir Thomas's plans. Would 150 guineas suffice for the weapons that you propose?

"With that, we could probably purchase jacks for everyone as well, a touch of extra protection. If you approve, I can leave for Coldingham as soon as I have the funds."

The next supplicant was Daniel Johnstone, who told how he had been forced to spread the news of the raid to Berwick.

Maude added, "The men who wounded him were the ones who killed my husband and son."

"I speak today as a harvester and husbandman," said Daniel. "We can get the burned fields back into production, but we need funds for buying new plows and other farm implements, since the Raiders stole or destroyed all of ours. I would need money for new seeds as well. And then there is the matter of lost livestock."

"Daniel knows more about crops than even Thomas Coke of Holkham. You may rely upon everything he says," said Maude to Ruzzini.

"Would a hundred and fifty pounds cover the costs?"

Johnstone shook his head. "One hundred will more than suffice. Don't go throwing away guineas, young man. There's no call to be lavish."

Alan Maitland, the brewmaster stepped up. "The brigands damaged my brewery, and I need to make repairs. They also wrecked the wagons that were to take my product to customers. I know that what I do is not vital to the estate, but the sales of whiskey will bring in cash."

"And who says whiskey is nae vital to the estate?" chimed in a voice. There was some laughter and agreement to that.

"Our whiskey is gaining a reputation for fair quality at a fair price," remarked Maude to Ruzzini. "Sir Thomas expressed concern for the future of the estate, and whiskey production might be part of that."

"Yes, we must look to the future" agreed Ruzzini. "How much do you require, Mr. Maitland?"

"Might I presume upon you for the same amount you granted Mr. Johnstone?"

"Consider it done."

"The tower itself needs repairs, and I want to get the shot furnace working again," remarked Maude to Ruzzini. "Fifty pounds I'm thinking it will take."

"You shall have it."

The remaining hundred pounds were dispensed in small lots as the rest of the inhabitants stated their needs. Every family received something. Ruzzini was gratified to see how much hope the money brought to so many. Most need the money for food, home repairs, and the replacements of basic items such as linens and clothing that had been destroyed during the raid.

Once the meeting broke up, Maude found quarters for the two yeomen and told them they should consider themselves members of her family. Fordham Peel and Remington Wainright were surprised and pleased by the welcome since as aristocrats they had never had much contact with the day-to-day lives of the lesser orders. It also buoyed their spirits that they felt truly needed. Their hearts had opened hearing the inhabitant's tales of woe and they were determined to prevent a repeat of the first raid.

Ruzzini and Smith spent the last two hours of their visit inspecting the ruined canal. Smith kept up a constant stream of comments as they walked. "The brigands did us a favor, here. This canal was sited all wrong. It needs to be two hundred yards to the west. That will lengthen the distance but promote better drainage. Construction will also go faster because the rock there will be easier to cut through. Have you any idea when Sir Thomas will want plans for the canal?"

"It won't be until he has settled the depredations on the Border, and that could take many months."

"I had hoped to begin as soon as possible."

"Of course, but there would be no point in building a new canal only to suffer the fate of the old one. And since the workers were all murdered, it would be difficult to bring on new workers unless they had some assurance that they would be safe."

"It is a shame that men devote so much effort to destroying things instead of making them. If the same energy went into studying the natural world, mankind would be much better off. Science before soldiers, I say!"

"I agree, and we have the chance to do some real good here. I think we are lucky to be granted the opportunity."

***

Pennywhistle spent two days analyzing the reports of his scouts and patrols before he deployed his early warning network. He took one final look at the large map of the Borders that he had affixed to the wall of his map room and pondered whether he should make any last-minute changes. It was just after sunrise, and his men would depart within the hour. He sipped his second cup of coffee as he contemplated the array of colored pins on the map, each color representing different categories of his men.

10 water sergeants would guard the main fords over the Tweed between Berwick and Kelso. 10 water bailiffs would patrol the lesser fords on the tributaries of the Tweed. 10 land sergeants would take up posts 12 miles in front of the water sergeants, and 10 land bailiffs would man lookouts in the area between Kelso and Jedburgh. 8 castle keepers would take up posts at castles, bastles, fortified manor houses and abbeys at Norham, Wark-on-Tweed, Greenlaw, Kelso, Melrose, Jedburgh, Morebattle, and Whistlestop. 5 roving constables would patrol the area between Wark-on-Tweed and Waller. 5 setters would be stationed at Norham, and 5 searchers at Jedburgh. One clerk would remain at headquarters to assist him in tracking movements, while a second clerk would take the field and shuttle between Greenlaw, Melrose, and Morebattle.

His network was divided into four zones, representing east, north, south, and west, each commanded by a deputy warden who would act as his proxy in emergencies. The deputy wardens were tasked with recruiting trusted locals to man hilltop outposts equipped with fire beacons. These locals, unlike his own men, were not expected to fight but merely to observe and report. He would keep his mounted yeomanry at Berwick as a mobile defense force, to be dispatched as the needs of the moment dictated. A pack of slew dogs, bloodhounds, would accompany the yeomanry. He would send half of his infantry to Melrose and keep the rest at Berwick.

The shape of his network, which resembled a giant horseshoe turned sideways, did not come close to covering the full area under his command. He was taking a calculated risk about where the Reivers would strike, but he trusted his instincts and analysis and did not want to spread his small resources too thinly. Maxwell would have command of the forces at Berwick. Much as Pennywhistle would have preferred to lead any pursuits, his proper place was in his office coordinating operations, more a manager than a warrior.

It might take weeks to detect any patterns in his enemies' movements, but he had an idea that might trick them into focusing their attentions in one area. It involved planting a rumor about the Flodden Treasure, a rumor that might sow dissension and misdirection.

There was a knock on his office door. "Come."

Maxwell entered. "My command is ready, sir. I look forward to the results of the next move of this chess match."

"I am not so sure it is chess, Mr. Maxwell. In chess every piece has a fixed value, only one can be moved at a time and only in certain ways, and the movement of each is confined to a small chequerboard. Whereas in the contest ahead, the playing pieces have shifting values, many pieces will be in play simultaneously, and movements will be unpredictable. I think what we are doing is akin to what the Americans call poker, which contains elements of bluff and guile. In poker, it is less about playing your hand than playing the man across from you. The trouble is that I know very little about my opponent, his tendencies and vulnerabilities, whereas he likely knows quite a bit about me and mine."

"True, but once we discover his name, we can began making inquiries. Such a man must have a past."

"Perhaps that ledger that Heatherington brought furnishes a clue about my opponent's name. Unlike the others, one man had a name for an entry, rather than initials. I think that may have been done to indicate his special importance. If we can figure out what tie his code name of "Waverley" has to his real one, we may be able to figure out his identity."

"*Waverley* is a novel by Walter Scott. While the book was published anonymously, it proved so popular that Scott's authorship became generally known. Now the fame of the book is widespread. I myself read it with keen enjoyment."

Pennywhistle started in inspiration. "It just struck me. This may be a case where the choice of disguise reveals much about the person behind it. Is it possible my opponent happens to have the same name as a famous author and so uses a code name derived from one of that author's most famous works? Since it must gall my opponent to hide in the shadows, this may be his inner mind's way of getting attention. "

"It's certainly worth looking into," agreed Maxwell.

***

"Mrs. Pennywhistle," cautioned Bill Masters, "I appreciate your enthusiasm, but you must remain at a discreet distance. There is always the possibility of violence in these raids, and I would not want to see you exposed to harm."

"I thank you for your consideration, Sergeant Major," huffed Sarah Pennywhistle, "but really, I am no babe in the woods. And I remind you that it was I who was able to discover the owner of The Magic Lantern when nobody else could. This wretched institution has plagued the city for far too long and I want to be there when it is shut down. I want to see the esteemed Mr. Thomas Soames get what is coming to him. It galls me no end that he was able to enjoy the admiration of the city in his capacity as an importer of silks and linens when most of his actual profit came from an opium den and a crooked gaming establishment."

"Please calm yourself, Mrs. Pennywhistle, I am on your side. I lost a brother to opium so my commitment to end this vile place is just as strong as yours. Now, please stand back and let my men do their jobs."

Masters had five men ready with swords and pistols because he always prepared for the worst. It was just after dawn, the time when Magic Lantern was at its lowest ebb. Many customers would be passed out, grossly intoxicated, or basking in an opium haze after a long night of gambling and would offer no resistance. Management would likely be tidying up and counting the money from their overnight haul. Masters was less interested in customers than the management. Customers would be sent packing, while Soames and any dealers who worked for him would be arrested. Soames would likely hang, while the rest would suffer transportation.

Masters was first through the door. The guard posted at the front entrance moved to shout an alarm but a right cross from Masters cut him down. His men fanned out in search of the dealers while he made for Soames office. Soames usually came in at this time every day; incognito and using a back entrance. His office was hidden behind a bookcase, but Sarah Pennywhistle's informant knew exactly where it was and how to open it.

Masters pressed a small latch on the right side of the bookcase, and it slowly swung open. Soames sat at a small desk counting a large pile of bank notes then looked up in shock and surprise as he found himself staring down the barrel of a pistol held by a grim looking man.

"You're under arrest!" barked Masters. "Now please do something stupid so that I have an excuse to shoot you."

Soames put up his hands and spoke with barely controlled panic. "Are you sure you want to do this? I can make it worth your while to call things off. The money before me is yours, if you will just go away. I have powerful friends who will also reward you. I—."

"Shut up! Your time is done! Your money won't buy your way out of this and the people who have bankrolled you are being arrested as we speak."

Masters saw Soames his hand reaching into a desk drawer and guessed it was for a pistol. Soames had just put his hand on the pistol's butt when Master's fired. His shot hit Soames between the eyes and he and his chair flew backwards.

Masters had never relished killing but this case was an exception. He saw his dead brother's face in his mind's eye, and it gratified him that the perfumed monster that lay at his feet would never ruin another's life.

Masters ignored the corpse and put the pile of money in a canvas sack that he had brought with him. The door to a small safe was ajar, so he opened it and took the cash within. As agreed with Sarah Pennywhistle, these ill-gotten gains would be used for good. She would see to it that they were donated to The Society for the Relief of Distressed Widows and Orphans.

Five dealers were arrested. Their hands were bound, and they were marched off to a holding cell by one of Masters men. The rest of his command rounded up two gentlemen and six others who were anything but gentlemen. Masters gave them a stern speech.

"I am letting you go and giving you a second chance at life. This is the end of the Magic Lantern, and I shall see to it that a replacement never happens. If you seek to destroy yourselves, you will have to do it in a place other than Berwick."

The men listened bleary- eyed and Masters was not sure how much of what he said was understood. Some stumbled off into the new day while others had to be prodded at the point of a bayonet. *Someone should keep on eye on those men,* thought Masters, *or they will suffer the same fate as my brother.*

He walked across the street to where Sarah Pennywhistle was standing, a pleased look on her face. He noticed that she had been joined by Lady Pennywhistle, who also wore a satisfied look.

"The job is done, Mrs. Pennywhistle, but are you sure about the rest?"

"I am! We need to send a message and that can best be done by wiping this place from the face of the earth."

"I agree," said Sammie Jo. "Light your torches. I shall enjoy watching this place burn."

"Very well," said Masters. His men did as he ordered, and the half-timbered structure was set ablaze. Since the wood was so old, it burned quickly.

Sarah and Sammie Jo watched until the place was reduced to ashes and rubble.

"Justice is finally done," said Sarah.

"Thanks to the power of women," replied Sammie Jo. "We would never have found out the owner's name and schedule but for your lady friend's careless mouths at our last high tea. It's amazing what men say during pillow talk."

"I am sorry that I doubted you about the power of a woman's network."

"Think nothing of it, Sarah. We're fighting the same war."

***

Three miles away, Angus and James Heatherington talked as they rode, reviewing Pennywhistle's instructions. Angus estimated they had an hour remaining until they reached the first line of Reiver sentinel posts.

"Now remember our story, James, you were captured, and I helped arrange a daring escape. Be sure to mention how brutally you were treated in captivity. That will add to your credibility. I will say that I had to disappear for a few days to help you."

"And I shall say that we were ambushed because of information being by a turncoat among the Reivers and that my colleagues died saving me. That will set a fox among the pigeons."

"Yes, the more they worry about who is the traitor among them, the less they will think about the truth of our stories."

"We need to wait a bit, before we mention the treasure. The more unsettled their emotions, the more likely that they will embrace a narrative that promises a reward beyond imagining."

"A betrayal, a miraculous escape, and a treasure within their grasp will give them a lot to think about," said Angus.

"I feel the two of us have been played for fools for far too long," said James." It will be good to return the favor."

"This will be the beginning of a whole new life for us, James. It will be a chance to set right some of the bad things we have done. "

"It would be a relief to live a life free of chaos and violence. I can think of nothing better than to wake up every morning and know exactly what the day ahead will bring."

Two riders emerged from the tree line ahead.

"Show's on," said Angus.

"Earlier than expected. They must be eager to see us."

"It's Mark Rowell and Daniel Dunne. Hard cases with hot swords and itchy trigger fingers. The powers that be are worried. Be careful, Angus."

Rowell and Dunne approached cautiously.

The Heatherington's pasted on false smiles, seeming to welcome friends eager to speed their safe return.

Rowell and Dunne stopped abruptly twenty feet away and Dunne spoke. "You two have been missed. We have been sent to escort you back to the usual spot. Our chief has questions for you both."

"Your tone sounds unfriendly, Dunne," said Angus. "We two have just had a harrowing escape. Congratulations are in order."

"Do tell," said Dunne sarcastically.

"We are eager to meet with the chief," said James. "We come bearing gifts. We possess a piece of information that can make all of us a great deal richer."

"Would you care to reveal to us what that is?" said Rowell.

"You and Dunne are underlings. This information is for the chief's ears alone. He will undoubtedly want to pass it on to those higher up on the Great Chain of Being."

"Are you saying you don't trust us to keep the secret?"

"I am only saying what our chief would say. You know that he likes to play things close to the chest. What he chooses to tell you, and the rest of our fellows, is up to him. Neither you nor I is empowered to decide how widely this information should be broadcast."

Rowell glowered. "I suppose you have a point. The chief has become suspicious of late because some vital information has leaked. He is searching high and low to find that source.

You will understand that your recent disappearance makes you suspects."

"We are good and loyal troopers, Rowell," responded Angus with asperity, "We have never failed the chief and if you will convey us to him as quickly as possible, some of the information we will provide may well help him identify the traitor."

"We plan to do just that, Heatherington," said Dunne. "Just make sure that your hands never go anywhere near your weapons."

"You don't trust us, Dunne?"

"You two may be telling the truth but since your brother is present and the four sent out with him are not, I have to wonder about their fates. At the very least, the kidnapping of the Pennywhistle girl failed, and the chief will want to know why."

"We were ambushed!" exclaimed James in feigned anger. "I was lucky to escape with my life. My mates and I were betrayed; probably by this same informer that the chief is so worried about. Ask yourself, why would I give information to the same men who would be likely to kill me? Isn't it far more likely that I am an injured party rather than a rat?"

"Again, it is possible that you are telling the truth. But as you say, I am just an underling, and it is only the chief who should make that determination."

"I assure you that we will cause you no trouble," said Angus. "We are eager to clear our names and reputations."

"You had better be telling the truth, Heatherington." said Dunne. "If either of you makes a move I don't like, we will not hesitate to shoot you both."

"We won't give you cause. Besides, why would you want to shoot two people who can make you a lot richer? You may think we are lying about that, but if you shoot us, you will never know. Come, escort us! We will ride in front, so you have clear shots at our backs if we give you any cause to doubt us."

Chapter 12

Net Gains

1st December 1816

Pennywhistle settled comfortably into his red leather office chair as he slowly sipped his second cup of coffee and read his copy of the *London Times* that had been delivered with the morning post. He scanned the headlines quickly and soon found the article that he sought and read it carefully. It was titled "Important Developments on The Scots Borders." No name was given to its author; *The Times* simply stated, "from our special correspondent."

That special correspondent was Deborah Dale, who was due to call upon his office momentarily.

Good press garnered support for his agenda from both from the locals and government officials in London. Most importantly, he was sure that his shadowy opponent read *The Times*. He wanted to give out just enough information to keep that opponent fearful of what might come next, but not enough to anticipate where he would strike.

Deborah Dale had a great sense of drama and specialized in writing compelling portraits of both the victims of crime and the nasty souls who had victimized them. People who normally kept silent were coming to him with valuable information because of her stories. She made it plain that Pennywhistle had put the city's criminals in a state of constant turmoil and had inaugurated programs to bring relief to those hurt and impoverished by their activities. She made it plain that cleaning up the city was part of a much wider campaign to make the entire Border area safe and secure: informing her readers that over the next several weeks she would tell them more of the details of that campaign and its first results. He was certain that the purpose of her upcoming visit was to find out how effective his new network had been.

Pennywhistle put down the paper and smiled wryly. The Pennywhistle in *The Times* was a wise and omniscient figure that bore little resemblance to himself, but she had at least avoided using the nickname that he disliked.

There was a knock on his office door.

"Come."

It was Bartleby, Sarah's butler. "Mrs. Dale is here for her appointment. Shall I show her in?"

"Please do."

Deborah entered with her notepad and pencil at the ready, dressed in a prim black dress that suggested she was a woman of quality about important business. He bowed and bade her sit in the chair opposite his desk.

"I can ring for tea and scones, but I presume you want to get directly to business as usual."

"Correct. I see no point in wasting time on fripperies, Sir Thomas. Let's get started."

"The men of my network have had innumerable small fights with Reiver bands. Many of our foes have been killed and the rest driven off in disarray. Several of my men have been wounded but none killed. The Reivers are becoming far more cautious, and reports of thieving, burglaries, assaults, murders, and acts of vandalism are down by 50%. Acts of extortion are becoming rarer with each passing day. My people roam widely and talk to many locals, both those of the better sorts and those of the middling and lesser sorts. All report they are feeling much safer. Even more importantly, since their level of fear is greatly reduced, they are more willing to report suspicious activities and so we have been able to stop many crimes in the planning stage."

"That's impressive."

"We still have a long way to go. In the end, the victory will be won by changing the hearts and minds of the people that we serve. People living in fear get little done, and that brings want and poverty. People living in safety get a great deal done because they look to the future with hope and seek new ways to improve their lot in life."

"Would you say your program is as much an economic one as it is one of public safety?"

"Yes, but I cannot wave a magic wand and fix the problems caused by the economic woes plaguing our country. What I can do is ensure that criminal elements will not add to those woes."

"Could you tell me a few examples of families who have been helped by your efforts? I fully understand if you want to change their names and locations."

"Three come to mind, Deborah. One family was losing twenty sheep per week due to raiding parties of ten or so. It was a family of only five, and so they were able to offer no defense when these brigands appeared in the dead of night. After we arrested a certain notorious local that everyone feared, the raids ceased. We would not have known his identity but for one man with the courage to come forward and tell one of my roving constables everything he knew."

"Sometimes one brave man can make a great deal of difference. You yourself are proof of that."

"A second family ran a local inn and refused to pay the protection money that was expected. The extortionist promised to return with a band of men and burn the place down. When he did, my men were waiting and captured the entire lot. The capture of that gang caused another one who had been extorting an inn several miles away to abandon their efforts."

"It's like knocking over the first piece in a row of dominoes, isn't it?

"True, but many more dominoes will have to fall before my job is done. The last example gives me the greatest hope. A Reiver raiding party of fifty was spotted around midnight by one of our hilltop watchers. He lit a warning beacon that was widely seen, and soon other watchers lit theirs. As the Reivers rode, they began to realize that their raid had lost the element of surprise and that they might be met by an armed reception party. Dissension broke out and soon the band split into small groups who returned whence they came. They would indeed have been confronted had they proceeded: the promise of fighting working just as well as real fighting. Reivers have always operated in secrecy and our network is taking away that advantage."

"Those people that you are going to put on trial, do you think any of them will inform upon their associates in return for clemency?"

"I am sure of it, and I am prepared to be merciful if I receive specific names and locations."

"I know you will not answer my next question, but I shall ask it anyway: do you have any idea who is behind all of this criminality?"

Pennywhistle thought carefully, understanding that what he said would swiftly become known to his principal enemy. Or as he now knew, twin enemies: Lord John Maxwell and Walter Scott. His guess about Scott had been a good one, and the man did indeed have a traceable past.

"I do not have a name, but I have a pattern. I assure you that I will have a name soon and when I do, that man will be hunted down ruthlessly. Think of it this way; we are systematically taking down a pack of criminal dogs. As the pack grows smaller the power of the pack leader diminishes; both to threaten and do harm. The members of the reduced pack will also come to see that their leader is losing his power and will be less amenable to any threats that he uses to keep them in line."

"So, you see Reivers as packs of wild dogs?"

"I do. Such dogs are scavengers and prey upon the vulnerable. The pack mentality that drives them can also be used against them. And it is well to remember that abandoned, domesticated dogs sometimes join wild packs. It is the same way with citizens who feel abandoned by an impoverished society. The more we reduce both poverty and the power of the wild packs, the more we prevent good people from crossing over to the wrong side of the law."

"Wild dogs are usually just shot, Sir Thomas."

"True, but domesticated dogs can sometimes be returned to their former lives if an effort is made. My goal is not only justice but a lasting peace. That can only be achieved if I work toward reconciliation and reconstruction rather than vengeance and punishment."

"It sounds like all you need is time."

"And patience. All things come to him who waits."

***

The cold, miserable sleet of December 1st matched the weather in Walter Scott's soul. Though he sat in a comfortable black leather chair in front of a roaring fire, sipping a glass of expensive claret, he felt the bleak winds of discontent blowing through his soul. This was the fourth time that he had read the story of Pennywhistle's latest exploits in *The Times,* and he drew the same conclusion as he compulsively reread the hated words: *Warden Pennywhistle is gaining the upper hand.*

Pennywhistle had begun a war of attrition that Scott knew he would lose, and that war increased in speed and power with each passing day. The articles from *The Times Special Correspondent* painted Pennywhistle as the kind of man who commanded not only respect but inspired those under his protection to try to be just like him. Scott envied the words written about his opponent and wished that they had been written about him. The trouble with living in the shadows and commanding hidden power was that you could receive no public recognition of how far you had risen above your modest origins, nor any acknowledgement of the *de facto* control that you exercised over a great many people.

Scott wondered when it would be time to cash out his chips and seek a *modus vivendi* with Pennywhistle. His opponent did not seem the sort of man who would settle for less than complete and unconditional surrender, but the government in London was another matter. Pennywhistle's operation had to be expensive and a serious drain on the finances of a notoriously frugal government.   Strange weather, bad harvests, food riots, labor unrest, and roving bands of destructive poor were causing the government an unending series of headaches. Scott reasoned that a quick end to the Border troubles would be welcome, if the only price the government had to pay was the issuance of a pardon, and the grant of a title. But for that to happen the misery level had to be ratcheted up to the highest degree.

Though he was dismayed that Pennywhistle's network had frustrated his small forays, he believed some larger ones might have a different result. He was pleased with the training the Frenchman Lefebvre had furnished his new model army and had decided to give them a combat test.

Two columns of one hundred men each had departed from their encampments just before dawn: each column contained fifty infantrymen and an equal number of cavalrymen. Scott wanted to hit Pennywhistle where he was vulnerable enough that his newly trained men would prove decisive.

He had chosen Kelso and Jedburgh, on the western edge of Pennywhistle's command, for his strike points. A dozen miles separated the two, within supporting distance of each other if you employed cavalry. His intention was to strike them both simultaneously. Pennywhistle's outposts were situated in the spectacular ruins of two large gothic abbeys; the heavy walls and buttresses would provide shelter to his men. He deemed that of no great importance since the garrisons at both places were small, consisting of a land sergeant, a few of the Yeomanry, and some half- trained local volunteers. It worried him that his columns were relying on scouting reports that were a week old, but Pennywhistle's resources were spread thin, and he doubted that much changed since the initial reports. The ungodly weather would also be an ally since most soldiers might well have relaxed their vigilance and would be seeking shelter. He checked his pocket watch and smiled as he noted that the twin attacks should begin in thirty minutes. It would be a pleasure to give the smugly confident Pennywhistle a bloody nose.

***

"We're in for trouble," said Sergeant Major Masters to Michael Griffin, the land sergeant in charge of Kelso. "A scout just galloped in and has reported the approach of a column of 100 men, two miles distant."

"I have no experience of combat," said Griffin to Masters, "so I will turn operational command over to you and follow your instructions. We have only twenty men, and five-to-one odds worry me. What do you propose?"

Masters explained his plan quickly and reassured Griffin that the two secret weapons he had brought would prove decisive. Pennywhistle had sent them, Masters continued, because he thought his opponent might strike at one of his more vulnerable outposts. Masters had asked to be put in charge of their delivery because of his experience in their use. Two duplicates of those weapons had also been sent to Jedburgh because of a similar vulnerability.

Masters made good use of the next twenty minutes. He posted ten men behind the walls next to one of the Abbey's flying buttresses and told them to lie low and stay quiet. The other ten were positioned just in front of the two nine-pound mountain howitzers. Those guns had been placed below the brow of a low hill to the west of the abbey walls. The lightweight guns had been reassembled two hours before, having been delivered on the backs of four mules. The second ten men would serve as artillerymen, though they had only been given a quick course of instruction by Masters an hour before. Masters had himself quickly cut the fuses for six rounds of spherical case shot, better known as shrapnel. Their position would enable them to remain hidden until the last moment. Howitzers were designed to fire in an arc rather than a straight line, so a hill presented no problems.

Masters watched the enemy deploy as they mounted the crest of a small hill a quarter mile away and was impressed despite himself. These men had been schooled by a drillmaster who really knew his business, yet the difference between battle and training was the difference between night and a nightcrawler. The infantry deployed in open skirmish order, three feet between each man, and slowly advanced with their bayonets leveled. The cavalry formed into two ranks, a hundred yards behind the infantry. Each rank was tasked with protecting the flank of the advancing infantry.

Masters was surprised at the lack of a proper reconnoiter, but the sleet had changed to a pounding rain and his opponents apparently thought that it would serve as an excellent cloak for their actions.

Masters bided his time and whispered to his infantry to hold their fire until he gave the command. They were nervous but eager, so he warned them to aim low. He let his opponent approach to within two hundred yards, before he ordered the twin howitzers to fire.

The two shells rose high in the air and burst directly over the heads of Scott's men. Masters was pleased that he had cut the fuses right. The exploding shells showered Scott's men with hundreds of shards of lead, with edges like sharpened obsidian spears. The center of the line disintegrated, as dozens of men fell. The rest milled about in confusion.

The horses to the rear neighed loudly in fear, telling Masters that they had never been under fire.

"Now boys, give 'em hell!" Masters line of musketeers rose to their feet and fired three volleys in the next two minutes. That was slow for experienced regulars, but good for men in their first fight. Since thirty yards was the optimal range for a volley of smoothbore muskets and the current one was almost seven times that, most of the balls missed. The driving rain and strong wind also contributed to the outcome, but what mattered most was not casualties but confusion. The troops left standing milled about in uncertainty, awaiting orders that never came. Masters guessed that one round had finished the NCO who led them.

But musketry was only a supporting player in this drama: the star was the artillery. The twin howitzers fired again, and this time their shells exploded a little farther to the rear, striking at least a dozen horses. Most of the remaining horses reared in terror, while six bolted from the field, despite the best efforts of their riders to control them. Horses were pack animals, and the remaining ones soon caught the infection of panic. The line of horses disintegrated.

Masters' men reloaded and fired another volley. That volley mostly went wild, but it proved to be the one thing too many for the infantrymen still standing. They threw down their arms and ran. Just before they fled out of range, the howitzers fired the last of their shells, killing only a few but ensuring that there would be no attempt at a rally.

Masters' men let out a ragged huzzah that was drowned out by the cold winds that had risen to thirty miles an hour. Though soaked and sweaty, his men had kept their powder dry and done their duty.

To his men's surprise, he ordered them to advance and search for the wounded.

"Do you want us to bayonet them?" asked one innocent looking twenty-year-old rookie.

"Of course not!" Retorted Masters. "We are soldiers not murderers, and the wounded deserve proper care. They are no threats to anyone, and I remind you that those now in distress are your countrymen. Misguided though they may be, they might yet see the light and return to the side of right if given the chance. Mercy is the hallmark of the good soldier!"

His men agreed, and over the next hour the wounded were brought to improvised dressing stations. Several of his men recognized relatives among the injured and talked with them quietly.

Jim and Bob Reid were typical. Jim had fought with Masters while his brother Bob had fought with the intruders, "You damn fool, Bob! I warned you about the Reivers. So did Mama! We both told you no good would ever come of joining bandits. Look at you. I ain't sure you will ever have the proper use of that right arm."

Despite his harsh words Jim held his brother tenderly.

"I am so sorry," whispered Bob through tears of pain. "I was just tired of being dirt poor."

"Mama is going to give you a tongue-lashing the like of which the world has never seen when I get you home." Jim's tone softened as tears formed in the corners of his eyes. "She might even send you to bed without your supper."

Bob smiled wanly. "Right now, the sight of my own bed sounds pretty damn good." Then he passed out.

Masters realized this strange little war was as much a family conflict as it was a military event. The key to winning would be in putting broken families back together. Victory would belong to men who were just as much healers as they were soldiers.

The fight at Jedburgh was also a victory for Pennywhistle's men, but the outcome was bloodier and crueler because Sergeant Major Pyestalker was vicious and vindictive. His tactics were much more aggressive than Masters and the choreography of his fight was very different.

Pyestalker used his guns in the way Napoleon did, as offensive rather than defensive weaponry. The muskets of his twenty-five men were used only to protect the gunners manning the howitzers and not as separate elements in the battle. The gunners manhandled their fieldpieces forward, ten paces after each round, driven hard by the flat of Pyestalker's sword. Considering how outnumbered he was, his actions would have been suicide if he had faced experienced soldiers. But he read his opponent well and they assumed that his placement of howitzers in plain sight meant that their commander must have many more supporting troops just to the rear.

The nerve of his opponent wavered after four salvos, and Pyestalker knew it would take only a small push to break them beyond repair. The easy solution would have been to fire one more salvo, but he was a dramatist and his blood was up. He ordered a bayonet charge. His men caught his fire and charged, despite the glaring disparity of numbers.

The enemy broke as expected, chased gleefully off into the rain by a quarter of their numbers. Pyestalker reined his men in with difficulty, then directed them to deal with the wounded, writhing on the field.

"I want them dead! Every last one of them. They are all traitors and blackguards. If I find even one wounded man drawing breath after five minutes, I shall punish the man standing nearest him with twenty lashes!"

His men saw the red glint in his eyes and knew that there was no arguing with a madman. They reluctantly did as they were ordered; twenty men died in the next few minutes.

Pyestalker formed his men up for an inspection after the grisly deeds were done. "You have done well. I will see to it that every man here receives two tots of rum in reward. Remember today for this is how these evil Reivers must be stamped out! With fire and brimstone! You are the Israelites of old and these are the apostates of Sodom and Gomorrah!"

William Marsden and Richard Polk were just starting their second tot of rum an hour later. They were sufficiently in the grip of an alcoholic haze that the worst parts of what they had just done had faded, but alert enough to know that their actions had gone beyond rough justice.

"We won," said Marsden. "Why does my stomach feel queasy and my heart sad?"

"It's because we did not win the right way. That's a lot better than losing, but it sure as hell isn't something that you can boast about." He sighed, "at least our training paid off."

"That it did, but I did not feel that I was using might for right. You remember on the first day of training, when Warden Pennywhistle told us that motto should be the model for our conduct?"

"I do."

"Seems to me, that old Pyestalker wasn't listening. Or maybe he just does not care. Something is wrong with that man!"

"You're right, everybody knows it, but no one is stupid enough to confront him. He would probably just shoot the man who disputes him."

"That ain't his style. I think he would choose a flogging; let the man die slowly by a thousand cuts."

"You know, I think I recognized one of the men that I bayoneted. I think it might have been Bill Withers, the butcher's boy. I only met him twice, but he looked a lot like his father. I saw a flash of recognition in his eyes just before he passed, so I am pretty sure that he knew me."

"I feel old right now, Bill, as if I have lived a dozen lifetimes in an hour."

"So do I, Dick. Like someone has wrung my soul through a washer and rather than cleaning it, has left it with more dirt."

"I read a few books about battle when I was a boy, and I can't never recall any soldiers feeling like we do now."

"Maybe all that fine stuff written about battle just ain't true."

"It could be that all those writers were drunk when they wrote, like we are now. Drunk enough to blank out the bad parts of war and silly enough to represent the rest as noble."

"When I joined up, I had this fantasy of someday telling a grandson of all the glorious deeds that I had done defending the Borders. The way I feel right now, I don't even feel worthy of having a grandson."

"Pyestalker says we should just leave those dead to be food for crows, but I think they deserve a decent burial."

"He would never permit that! I think he would strike down any man who suggested it."

"But I think most of our mates agree with me. We could do it at night, in secret."

"Even if all of our mates threw in with us, Pyestalker would grill everyone relentlessly to find out who the ringleader was, and someone would break."

"Probably true, but you know it's the right thing to do."

"I do, but I ain't drunk enough yet to consider doing it."

"Let's finish this second tot and see how we feel."

"Done!"

Hamish Morrison and Len Morrison, two of those broken by Pyestalker's men, did not stop running for two miles. When they reached a small stand of beech trees that gave shelter from the rain, they collapsed.

Hamish opened his canteen, took a long gulp, then handed it to Len. The water refreshed both but did nothing to quiet their nerves. Hamish produced a large flask from his right pocket and took a long sip. His face relaxed and he emitted a long sigh. He then handed the flask to Len, who took a long pull.

"Cheap stuff," said Len. "But it helps a lot. I think it's Whistlestop Whiskey."

"I have never felt so tired," replied Hamish. "I feel like I have been on a workhouse treadmill for a week."

"I still can't make sense of what happened, Hamish. One minute we were in a line and the next we were running," said Len.

"I heard two booms, then all of a sudden it was like we were caught in a hailstorm. I heard some men screaming and then I saw Sergeant Donald fall. Richardson started to run, you know they don't come any braver than he, and five others start to follow. I figured he knew something I didn't and that I should join the parade right quick."

"I followed you. I heard gunfire and more booms behind me, but I never stopped to look back."

"I never got a chance to fire a shot."

"Are you going back to our camp?"

"Hell no! I've had enough, Len. I count myself lucky that I got away with just a big scare. I don't want to go up against those folks again."

"Raiding is a lot different from soldiering and pays better too. Now that I have been in a real battle, I can't think why soldiers are willing to fight for so little money."

"Probably because they are men like us: out of work with nowhere else to go. You realize that if we quit, we will be back to where we started."

"Not quite. I've stashed away a lot of jewelry that I never reported to our leaders. I figure if I could find a good fence, I could get two or three hundred pounds. That would be enough to buy me a fresh start in London."

"I'd like to tag along. There is nothing for me here since my sister died."

A horsemen galloped up with a pistol in his hand. "You two! Up and follow me. We must proceed to the rally point. We can still retrieve the situation. You must not give up hope, you..."

Hamish reached under his coat and produced a pocket pistol, then shot the rider in the chest. "No one is going to tell me what to do anymore!"

"What do we do now?"

"Come with me to Greenlaw where I have hidden my stash of loot. We will work things out from there."

"We stick together, right?"

"You are my stepbrother, Len, and the closest thing I got to a real family. I'm never going to abandon you, no matter how bad things get. Besides, I need somebody to watch my back, and you need someone to watch yours too. With all these criminal sorts about, you can't be too careful."

Both men snickered at the irony. The sleet changed back to rain and came in driving sheets. Soaked and cold, both men trudged off in the direction of Greenlaw, chewing the last of their soggy bread as they moved. They saw no fugitives from the recent battle because they were headed in the opposite direction of their broken comrades; toward a coaching inn that was a popular watering hole for three well known fences.

***

James and Angus Heatherington had done some fast talking when they had returned to the Reiver band that they had earlier deserted. Although the Reivers sometimes gathered for large scale raids, they were divided into groups of fifty and the headquarters of the groups were dispersed throughout the Borderlands. Each group had been given the name of a knight of King Arthur's Round Table, because Scott liked to promote the idea that the Reivers were members of a New Round Table.

James and Angus belonged to The Lancelot Group, based near Morebattle. The leader of the group was a wily gamekeeper named James Mitford. Like James he worked on the Paxton estate of Lord Maxwell. Reiving was a part-time occupation for most of the men; many of them held some kind of job, though these typically paid but poor wages. Those jobs sometimes gave them access to information that was useful for directing future Reiver raids.

The hardcore Reivers remained chronically unemployed and tended to be the bitterest and most vicious of the lot.

"That story about treasure is hard to believe," said Mitford cynically to Angus. "You've convinced me about why the kidnapping went wrong, and I think your brother acted correctly. I know you went to Berwick because you'd heard rumors about the Flodden Treasure, but so many legends have circulated about that over the past three centuries that I think you may have been the victim of yet another tall tale. You would be far from the first man to be seduced by the lure of the Flodden riches."

"I can understand your skepticism, Mitford, which is why I have brought proof."

Mitford's eyebrows knitted in suspicion. "And what kind of proof would this be? Don't tell me it's a treasure map. Over the last three centuries dozens of forgeries have been circulated."

"It's not a treasure map, it's a piece of the treasure. Two pieces in fact."

"Let me guess, you will have to go on some considerable journey to produce them."

"No, I have them in a pouch that I have been carrying in my right armpit. And I can produce them directly."

"If what you say is true, our men will want to see this, so I will gather them round. I warn you that if you are playing me false by showing me worthless baubles, the men will not take kindly to it." The menace in his voice suggested a beating lay in store if Angus was lying.

The men gathered in a circle around Mitford and Angus, their faces mixtures of eagerness and skepticism.

Angus brought forth the leather pouch and poured its contents into his open palm. That palm held a large gold coin with the face of James IV emblazoned on it; valuable but not extraordinary, though it clearly dated from the time when the Flodden Treasure had been buried. The second took the men's breath away: it was a large, blood red ruby, exquisitely cut and polished. "That's the Ruby of Falkirk," said Angus with the air of a master showman. "The legend says that when it is secure in the possession of the King of Scotland his throne is safe, but when it is lost he will fall from power. I am sure you all recall that James IV died at Flodden."

Heads nodded and murmurs of wonderment coursed through the crowd. Even the cynical Mitford was awed.

The gem was valuable, but it was not the Ruby of Falkirk. It was a stone lent to Pennywhistle by the Earl of Westminster, who was willing to allow it to be used as a lure. Pennywhistle had given it to Angus, to establish his bona fides. Pennywhistle knew that every confidence game needed a shiny object to start, and one that had an existing, exotic storyline was best: those exposed to it had already been conditioned to believe in its truth.

"I am impressed, Heatherington, but where is the rest of the treasure?"

"All I know is that it resides somewhere on the Whistlestop estate. I believe some special receptacle has been built there to keep it secure."

"Why such an obscure location? Our last raid savaged the place."

"It is because you savaged it that the discoverer of the treasure chose it, guessing that it is the last place anyone would look for a treasure. I was given these two pieces by a dying man who was the discoverer's chief lieutenant."

"Who was the discoverer?"

"I do not know his name, just that he was one of three men who found the treasure. The other two are now dead; I suspect infighting among the trio. I believe the discoverer has gone into hiding, to consider his options, but the truth is we do not need him since we have a general idea where the treasure is."

"Do you think the Warden has any idea of what is hidden on his property?"

"I do not, else he would already have seized it."

"This is very important news," exclaimed Mitford. "The Big Man will want to hear this as soon as possible."

"But you do not even know who he is."

"True, but I know people who do. I am certain that he will want to speak to you personally."

"I am more than willing to tell him everything I know. I not only want to clear my name, I want to bring glory to it."

"I do not want to waste any time. I will give you an immediate escort of four men to take you to the Bastle of Liddesdale. The chief there will know how to get in touch with The Big Man."

Angus rode off a few minutes later, pleased that Pennywhistle's plan was working. He had two goals. The first was to confirm The Big Man's identity as Walter Scott. The second was to lure Pennywhistle's enemy to Whistlestop where he would be met with a well-prepared ambush.

James Heatherington remained behind with the rest of the Reivers. He too would be a messenger, but he would say nothing to the other Reivers. He planned to tell Lord Maxwell that he had been specifically told not to divulge the treasure information to him. That would sow dissension between Maxwell and his partner. The best way to unbalance the opposition was to get them to fight among themselves. His brother had been right: in the end, there could be only one criminal overlord.

***

"I am not sure that we have any business planning a winter ball quite so soon, Sammie Jo. I am still shaken by the attempt to kidnap Sally, so I think we should wait. We must make sure she is sufficiently well guarded before we expand her social horizons." Sarah Pennywhistle sighed as she surveyed the hundred-foot ballroom decorated in the beige and gold style of Louis XVI.

"I think you have it backwards, Sarah," argued Sammie Jo. "You need to show the world that you are not afraid, and you need to do it in a very public way. You need to demonstrate your contempt for the man who ordered your daughter's kidnapping. Remind him that he is not in charge of the way that you and your family will live their lives. We should invite all the pretty people in this town. In fact, since Sally is sixteen, we could make this her coming out ball; make her societal debut an event that no one will want to miss. In unsettled times, nothing calms people more than a grand dance."

"You have a point, Sammie Jo, but I don't want to take any risks with my daughter's safety."

"That's where you're wrong, Sarah. The way I see it, you can either empower the good or enable the bad. This Border mess is not going away unless we all pitch in. Now is not the time to play ostrich. I promise you that Tom will provide very heavy security for this ball, but it will be very discreet. He will make sure that Sally is never very far from someone who would willingly surrender his life to protect her."

Sarah looked dubious. "I don't know. I just don't know."

"Then why don't you ask Sally herself? From what Marco told me, she found the abduction attempt quite an adventure, where Marco had the chance to play Tristan to her Isolde. I think you may be projecting your own fears onto your daughter. The young are very resilient."

Sarah sighed in sadness. "You could be right. Ever since Peter died, I have treated my daughters as life preservers and have perhaps been too protective of them."

"That's understandable, Sarah, but ask yourself what Peter would have wanted for them. He was a brave man, and I do not think he would want his daughters living as prisoners of your fears."

"He would have wanted them to live full lives, of course." Sarah closed her eyes, deep in thought. When she opened them, she spoke in quiet resignation. "Yes, Peter would have wanted the ball to go forward. But Sammie Jo, if we do this, it will have to be very carefully orchestrated. I would want to be heavily involved in the planning and if I said no to a particular detail, I would want my word to be law."

"Nothing would happen, Sarah, that went against your instincts. I have been thinking of a certain governess who has made a name for herself in the wrong way. She comes from a good but impoverished family, but she has developed a reputation for defying authority, speaking frankly, and sometimes acting as if she just didn't give a rat's arse for what polite people thought." She smiled wryly. "In short, she is a lot like me."

"I am not sure that I understand."

"She could almost be a twin to your daughter Sally. Dressed in the right clothes, given some special makeup, and supplied with the right coaching, it would be hard to tell her from Sally. I think she could be persuaded to impersonate Sally to confuse any kidnappers. A double would give Sally the chance to be in two places at once and cut the odds by half that she might be abducted. Now mind you, I don't think Tom's enemies would be fool enough to try that, but this would give us a way to cover our bets."

"Could this girl be persuaded to do that?"

"Her name is Jane Bennett and yes, I do. She has a taste for adventure which is why she is doing badly as a governess. I need a new lady's maid, and it would be fun to have one who shared a similar attitude toward life. I can introduce her to you, and you can see for yourself."

"I dislike putting a stranger at risk, but I also would like to honor what I think would be Peter's wishes. How soon can you make the introduction?"

"Sarah is waiting just down the hall."

***

Pennywhistle arrived at Whistlestop just as Sammie Jo was finishing her conversation with Sarah. This time he was accompanied by four members of the Northumberland Yeomanry as well as Nico. In the time since he had he had sent the 500 guineas, a great deal had happened, judging by what he was seeing.

A man lit a fire on a distant hilltop at the approach of his party. Two men appeared at the top of the redoubts on either side of the road a hundred yards ahead and waved to him. It pleased him that his party had been spotted well in advance of Whistlestop's main entrance. The lunettes and redoubts were well sited and looked about 90% complete. They were solidly built and of a piece with the best work of Marshal Vauban. He had been right to take a chance on Strata Smith.

The estate itself bustled with activity, and he sensed a cheerfulness on the part of its inhabitants that had not been there on his last visit. Four men walked the fields, now clear of any debris. They halted and waved to him. The sun had made a rare appearance and melted the thin coating of snow from yesterday's storm; almost as if the Fates had wanted to ready things for his reappearance.

The sheds and outbuildings were being rebuilt and were nearly complete. Two men operating a saw over a saw pit stopped their work and waved to him. A stocky fellow who appeared to be their foreman touched his cap when he saw

Pennywhistle. Two young women carrying buckets of milk put down their burdens and curtsied.

A group of ten drilling in the courtyard stopped their evolutions and came to attention. He recognized Scoggins as the man in charge as the rifleman snapped a salute. Scoggins had taken over from the drillmaster that Pennywhistle had sent, because the drillmaster told him that Scoggins was a natural instructor.

The forecourt walls were now a full six feet and in good repair, instead of four feet and in bad repair. The brewhouse in the distance showed no signs of the last raid and he observed Maitland and two assistants loading whiskey barrels onto a wagon. The whiskey revenue stream was again active.

The main gate that he rode through looked almost new and the Pennywhistle coat of arms, three half lions rampant, three crosses, and a large chevron beneath a crest featuring a raven's head, was no longer obscured by centuries of dirt.

The signs of fire and strife on the main tower had been erased and two men were applying a coat of whitewash to its lowest section as he approached. They put down their brushes and grinned at him with a joy that was far different from the false cheer that subservient men displayed when an absentee landlord unexpectedly reappeared.

Two girls near the painters curtsied then dashed inside the tower's main door. Pennywhistle had just halted his horse when Strata Smith and Maude Dacre emerged from the main door. Just the people he wanted to see. Both looked glad to see him.

He turned to his four escorts. "I won't be needing you for some time. Why don't you visit with your four mates while I go about my business. I am sure they will be glad to see you and you will have many things to talk about. I shall be curious to hear their impressions of what has taken place here over the past month."

"Very good, Sir Thomas," said Keaton, the brashest of his escorts who always acted as their spokesman. The four saluted and trotted off toward the small barn that had been turned into an improvised barracks.

Pennywhistle dismounted and advanced to meet Dacre and Smith. Dacre seldom smiled, unsurprising considering the grief that she had recently endured, but a small upturn of her thin lips suggested that she was pleased to see him. "It is good to welcome you, Sir Thomas, but we could have prepared a proper reception if you had given us some warning."

"I far prefer a surprise visit where things are unburdened by any rehearsed artifice. I am impressed by what I see. This estate seems transported here from another universe compared to what I saw a month ago."

Maude's lips curved upward but stopped just short of a smile. "You must be tired and hungry after your journey, so why don't you come in and let me offer you some refreshment. Nothing fancy, I am sorry to say, just plain country faire; sausage, biscuits, and beer. I do, however, have an apple pie in the oven and it should be ready momentarily."

Pennywhistle smiled. "Just the news my growling stomach needs to hear."

"Do you mind if we take the meal in the kitchen? The dining hall is still undergoing repairs."

"Not at all. Some of the most important decisions in history have been taken in kitchens."

"I will give you a full report on our progress as we eat, and I think you will be pleased."

"Excellent." He turned to the silent geologist. "Please join us. I shall be eager to hear of your progress as well."

"Thank you, Sir Thomas. I do indeed have a lot to tell. Not only about my work, but about the many fascinating fossils that I have uncovered. This estate is a treasure trove of unusual specimens." Smith spoke with the excitement of a child describing his haul of Christmas gifts to a friend.

The meal proceeded slowly, as Maude and Pennywhistle conversed at length. The food proved delicious, but Pennywhistle thought that the beer was anemic and bland, though he was no great hand at judging beer since he seldom drank it. The wonderful pie more than made up for the beer and it made him think that it would have gone better with a glass of cold milk: an American custom that Sammie Jo had told him about.

When Pennywhistle finished his pie, Maude concluded her recounting of the estate's progress. "That's about the lot of it, I think. I can bring out the ledger books if you like. I have accounted for every shilling that you sent us."

"No need for that. You are everything that I thought you to be, and you have my complete trust. I would like a guided tour of the estate and like to hear first-hand the stories of some of its inhabitants. And Mr. Smith, when that tour concludes, I should like you to show me where you found those unusual fossils and tell me why they are so significant. I would also like to hear what can be done about the canal."

Smith smiled like a Cambridge student just told that he had been awarded double firsts. "It would give me the greatest pleasure, Sir Thomas."

The tour proved pleasurable because it confirmed what Pennywhistle had seen earlier. The estate was in better shape than it had been before the raid, the people were industrious and optimistic, and a sense of order and purpose overlay the place like a magic mantle left behind by Ceres, Goddess of the Harvest. He spent two hours after the tour listening to the stories of everyone from old folk to children and felt like the benevolent uncle who should be dispensing presents. It was a part that he wanted to play, but he had some news to deliver that would wipe away the smiles of the people surrounding him.

He stilled the wings of the butterflies in his stomach, stiffened his resolve, then cleared his throat and moistened his unnaturally dry lips with his tongue. He spoke as the benevolent uncle that he wished he was. "My friends, I am very pleased by what I have seen. You have all done well and this place looks better than it has in centuries."

The assembled crowd beamed with pleasure.

"But now I have some distressing news to deliver. A storm is coming!"

The crowd looked at each other in consternation, wondering if he was referring to the recent ungodly weather.

"I believe this place is going to be attacked. Probably sometime in the next two weeks."

A low chorus of "oh no, oh no, that cannot be, that cannot be," rose in response.

"I give you my promise that this time the result will be much different than the last. This time you will not fight alone. This time you will have my full support and that of the troops under my command. This time those attacking this place will feel the full force of our collective wrath. At least those who are still alive to feel anything at all."

He stopped, wanting to gauge the reaction of the crowd. He expected uncertainty, vacillation, or fear. What he got was angry resolve.

"We're with you, Sir Thomas! We're going to be victors, not victims," shouted Scoggins.

"We will give them a whipping that they will never forget," yelled Maude's daughter Minnie.

"We will pay them back tenfold for what they have done to us," shouted Mary Simmons.

Tad Simmons, the oldest man on the estate, looked down disdainfully at the crutches that held him erect and proclaimed, "I am so angry, that I don't even need these." He threw his crutches down and hobbled unsteadily forward. "I aim to fight too!"

"Me too!" proclaimed a child of five. "If my grampa can fight, so can I!"

"And I have plenty of whiskey to reward everyone once the battle is done," added an enthusiastic Maitland.

"I may be just a geologist," said Smith. "But I have put in a lot of time and effort into this place. I am not going to allow such a treasure trove of science to be despoiled by brigands. I will fight too!"

"I want vengeance," shouted May, Maude's other daughter. "Those Reivers killed my father and brother, and I want to make them to pay in blood."

"Time to settle accounts, once and for all," bellowed young Harvey Ross.

Pennywhistle was gratified by the confidence and loyalty that he had inspired. He meant it when he had called them friends. He had no doubt that they would prevail in the fight ahead, though he wondered how many of the faces before him would be lying six feet under three weeks from now.

Pennywhistle disliked making speeches, but the crowd expected some acknowledgement of their support. "My friends, we face a tough road, but at its end lies a better future for us all. Our opponents will find us just like the strange weather of late: unpredictable, overwhelming, and terrible. We will be a mighty tempest that will awe Mother Nature herself!"

The crowd cheered.

Nico joined them because he now understood a truth that had eluded him in the East Indies. Killing sometimes had to be done to preserve life, and refraining from it at certain times could be considered an immoral act. He had felt the pain and anguish of Whistlestop's people. The heartbreak in their stories cut him deeply and it struck him that there was no difference between pirates on a ship and those on horseback.

Pirates in the East had been abstractions, save for one bloody encounter. Even Marco's tale of his run in with the Reivers described victims that he had never met. The people of Whistlestop had made those abstractions chillingly real; his squeamishness about killing vanished and he realized that his resignation from the Sea Service had been a mistake. Fate was offering him a chance to correct his missteps. Pennywhistle had rescued him when his mother had died; helping to rescue the people of Whistlestop was a way to honor his adoptive father by emulating his action.

Lewis had been right. His compassion had been a mistake. "Pirates" and "compromise" were two words that did not belong in the same sentence. It was time to do some killing, and this time, he would be no Hamlet.

Chapter 13

Invitations

15th December 1815

"Scott is an idiot," snarled Lord John Maxwell to his younger brother Charles.

Maxwell was surprised to find his tongue growing belligerent in a place that he used for reflection. The book lined study was paneled in soothing chestnut colored oak and had marble busts of Descartes and Voltaire placed prominently on two small Pembroke tables. The compact room featured a marble fireplace adorned with pilasters and fertility symbols copied from ancient Rome, two Chippendale camel back settees upholstered in cream and gold satin, and a restful landscape of Weymouth Harbor at dawn by John Constable. Neither man availed himself of a sitting position but paced back and forth opposite each other; like two hostile ships who stopped only long enough to deliver an occasional broadside. Lord Maxwell was sober, but his brother showed the effects of a night of heavy drinking.

No candles illuminated the room, because Maxwell had just entered the study when he was ambushed by his brother. The only light came from the two tall windows in the French doors. Since the day was overcast and sundown was fast approaching, the light in the room was murky and uncertain.

"Scott's men completely bungled the kidnapping of Sally Pennywhistle," growled Lord Maxwell. "They have alerted Sir Thomas that his niece is a target, and he will take extraordinary measures to ensure her protection."

Their physical differences reflected their differing personalities. Lord Maxwell was tall, rapier-thin, with a hawk-like face that perpetually wore the expression of a raptor about to strike. His brother was short, squat, and had a heart-shaped face; his usual expression that of a friendly country parson about to impart an amusing story.

"Perhaps that explains the invitation you received to Sally's coming out ball," responded Charles. "The ball may be a way to publicly show that Sir Thomas is unshaken by the kidnapping attempt, and that he is so confident that Sally is safe that he is inviting all the important people of Berwick and the surrounding area. Since you are the greatest landowner in the area, it is natural that you should receive an invitation, though I doubt that he has any idea of..." Charles cleared his throat, "your other activities."

"I hope not," hissed Maxwell," but there have been several troubling leaks from Scott's people lately, as well as numerous desertions. His ability to keep them in line is slipping and his new model "army" fared poorly at Jedburgh and Kelso. Speaking of invitations, I received an invitation to dine with him at the Hermitage to discuss, as he put it, 'matters of mutual concern.'"

"Will you attend?"

"No, I fear it is a fatal invitation. I believe Scott wants to eliminate me, probably using the twin portcullis trick that he used on other enemies. Like many other things, he thinks the twin devices are a secret, but I have known about them for some time. I plan to tell him that it would not be convenient to meet with him immediately because of some shipping issues that require my complete attention. That will buy me time to make other plans."

"Do you believe what that Reiver told you about the Flodden Treasure?"

"I think he speaks the truth."

"Perhaps that is why Scott wishes to have dinner with you."

"I think so too, but not because he wants to formulate a joint plan for its capture. If Scott had wanted to share the information about the treasure, he would have sent his fastest rider to me upon his first receipt of the news. I think this treasure has pushed his greed to an insane level and that he has no plans to share the treasure with anyone."

"What do you propose to do?"

"I think Scott's organization may be ripe for new leadership. It is time I do to him what I believe he wants to do to me. It occurs to me that a way to prove myself to his people would be to successfully carry out something that he failed at."

Charles abruptly halted in mid-stride, then gasped as his face turned white. "You don't mean..."

"Yes, I do. I shall kidnap the Pennywhistle girl and bring her here."

"John, I do not like what has happened to you since you partnered with Scott. Every day, I have witnessed you throw more and more of your good qualities to the wind and invite dark traits to take their place. You have been a party to a laundry list of bad deeds and now you wish to add kidnapping to that list. The girl is only 16 and innocent. Surely, she can be left out of your plans."

"There are no innocents in the game that I am in, Charles. Merely players and pawns, those who act and those who are acted upon. Since I have been given an invitation to the ball, it will be the perfect way to arrange for my minions to kidnap the girl. No one would expect such a great lord like me to be connected with anything so sordid as a kidnapping."

Charles eyed his brother with a combination of pity and disgust. "That's just what it is, John, sordid -- and entirely unworthy of the noble lord that you still can be if you will just listen to your conscience and stop treating it as an annoying nuisance. I warned you about getting involved in this business in the first place, and I am ashamed of myself that I did not remonstrate with you more strongly. Scott has debased us both. There is still time to cut your losses and abandon Scott. From what you tell me, he is on a downward spiral. Rather than get sucked into that vortex, you should step back onto the high ground of morality."

"Really, Charles, for an intelligent man you sometimes demonstrate a naivete that is as remarkable as it is curious. I knew that when I embarked upon this path that there was no going back. I never deluded myself as you do. I know the darkness in my heart, and I have learned to embrace it rather than shun it. I have followed its lead, and it has taken me to where we are now."

"But it has cost you a wife and a son! And your real heart is paying a price. I know that you have been suffering chest pains frequently over these past few months, as if your body is exacting its revenge for your refusal to pay any attention to your conscience. Even now, your complexion looks pallid and unhealthy, and you no longer move with the energy of the athlete that you once were."

"Don't lecture me on what it has cost! What's done cannot be undone and I refuse to dwell on the past."

"Come now, John, you still have a chance to make amends with Maximillian. From what I hear, he has turned his life around and has become a close confidant of Pennywhistle. He is not the wastrel boy that you sent off to the army. He will probably be at the ball. You should use the ball as an occasion for reconciliation, not as an opportunity to commit another crime."

"People do not change their basic natures; they only learn to disguise them. Maximillian has caused me no end of troubles. I gave him everything and he threw my gifts back in my face. I bailed him out of so many scrapes that I lost count. He was a lost cause from the start."

"I'm weary of your wallowing in a cesspool of anger and hatred. If you won't reach out to Maximillian, then I will. I would like to get to know my nephew. I will grant him a second chance, even if you will not."

"Your tongue has always been careless, Charles. How do I know that when you meet him, you might not tell him certain things that I want to remain secret?"

"I would never do that."

"I know you, Charles. You might want to help your nephew's career by giving him a few tidbits that you deem harmless but would in fact be damaging to me. You are a creature of impulse and often do not think things through. I can picture you burbling along with a drink in hand, wanting to mend broken fences, and letting you heart overwhelm your common sense." Maxwell began edging closer to the old leather colored mahogany desk that contained his darkest secrets. Its ball and claw feet were supposed to represent a dragon's talons seizing pearls of wisdom, but he liked to think of them as representing his grip on the world of the Borders.

"You would find the world a better place if you listened to your heart."

"The heart pumps blood, no more, no less. I care nothing for what the poets say about its mystical qualities. I have indulged your weak nature for a long time Charles, and I am at the end of my patience. I want your promise that you will have no contact with Maximillian."

Two lightning bolts flashed in the sky: throwing the combative expressions of the two speakers into bold relief. The eye- searing flashes were followed by deep growls of thunder. Waves of rain smashed the large windows in the study's French doors, and one of the two threatened to burst open. As Maxwell stepped forward and locked it, a crow was hurled into it by the powerful wind. He started but wondered if the crow's violent death was a warning about what lay ahead.

Charles's face flushed in anger. "No, not this time! I have played the spineless brother for far too long. The biggest mistake of my life has been allowing you to dominate me. You have turned me into your lickspittle, and I won't stand for it any longer! I want to reclaim our proud family name. You have done nothing but dishonor it! I would have given anything to have a wife like you had; kind, gentle, and loving. She was far too good for you, John. I think you simply could not stand her overwhelming decency and that's why you pushed her down the stairs."

Maxwell blinked as if hit by a lightning bolt but slowly moved to a position half a foot from the top drawer of his desk.

"Oh yes, John. I never told you, but I saw what you did." His hands tightened on the top of the second settee as he steeled himself to speak the secret that had been slowly rotting his soul. "I was at the other end of the hall, in the shadows, and you never knew I was there. All these years I have kept the truth to myself and tried to drown it in drink. I went along with 'the accidental fall' story that you told everyone else because I let you bully me. I am done with that! Push me too hard and I might just have to speak to the authorities. There is no statute of limitations on murder."

"How dare you, you little pipsqueak! After all I have done for you! I must have your promise that you will never say anything to anyone about Carol's death. Give it now... or else."

Charles laughed derisively. "Is the great lord of all he surveys finally afraid? Good! It's about time you felt some of the fear that you have put into the rest of us. Maybe deep down you are the kind of man who can dish it out but can't take it. I like seeing you reduced to human dimensions."

Maxwell sighed. "I had hoped it would never come to this, but you leave me no choice." Maxwell reached into the top drawer of his desk and produced a small pocket pistol. He pointed it at Charles' heart.

"I keep this for emergencies, and our situation certainly qualifies."

"Wait, John, be reasonable, you really don't want to—"

Bang!

The shot hit Charles in the left pectoral, and he staggered back in shock. He put his hand to his chest and endeavored to speak but no words came out. He swayed back and forth for a few seconds then collapsed. Maxwell stood over his corpse. "You damn fool! You never did know when to shut up."

He went to the side table and poured himself two fingers of Glen Livet. He pondered how to explain Charles' death, then decided he did not have to. Charles was a heavy drinker and known for making impromptu journeys. He would put it about that Charles had decided to embark on The Grand Tour and would be gone for quite some time. He and his man Bradford would bury the body after dark in some pine barrens at the edge of the estate. Bradford could be trusted to keep his mouth shut.

He thought about what his brother had said. He admitted to himself that he was curious about his son. A reconciliation was not possible because they were too much alike, but it would please him to know that his son had become something more than a drunken buffoon. The kidnapping of Sally Pennywhistle under his son's nose would be quite a coup.

He walked over to the chair behind his desk and sat down. He slowly sipped the whiskey as he began planning the abduction. It gave him something to take his thoughts away from what he had done to Charles. The ball was in one week. Plenty of time to come up with a plan. Obtaining the Flodden Treasure would require more complex planning.

A thought hit him, and he smiled at its perfect timing. Possession of the Flodden Treasure would allow him to quit the crime business once and for all. If Scott could be publicly blamed for all the Border Troubles, it would end any speculations by the authorities as to his involvement in them. If Scott's murder could be explained as the righteous slaying of a bad man, then he himself might be seen as a hero. He knew the government was tired of the money that it was spending to repair the Borders, and they would be predisposed to believe that a lord with one of the oldest titles in Scotland had been justified in taking extraordinary measures to end it. Pennywhistle would be an obstacle to that, but the kidnapping of his niece might cause him to reorder his thinking. It was a crude plan needing a lot of refinement, but it could be made to work.

***

"I thought you should hear the news directly from your chief accountant, so I have brought him and his books to you," said Perry to Walter Scott.

Scott sipped his coffee in his favored spot for deep thinking: in a chaise lounge chair on the rooftop terrace on Hermitage Castle. The splendid view of rolling hills, narrow valleys, and fast running streams always buoyed his spirits. He had just finished an excellent meal of poached salmon and rice, but his stomach was making hostile noises, and his after-dinner coffee was failing to exert its usual calming effect. His operation was in trouble and his carefully laid plans were falling apart. "Very well, Perry, I need the specifics of what I expect will be bad news."

Peter Postle did not look the part of a studious accountant. He was tall, lean, and fit, and his manner was direct and assertive. He was only 25 but had been well known as a mathematical wizard since childhood.

Postle sat down in the lounge chair next to Scott and opened a large ledger book so that both men could see the entries clearly. "Thank you for seeing me, Mr. Scott. You told me when you hired me that I should keep you closely informed of the state of your finances, and that if anything untoward arose that I would be granted an immediate audience."

"I did, Mr. Postle, and you have used it wisely; never bothering me with a problem unless it was a truly vexatious one that required an important decision on my part. What is it this time?"

"Our overall revenues are down 50% over the past month. I have been over the figures many times to be sure. I have made charts to track the revenues of our key enterprises, and they all show a disturbing downward spiral. If this trend continues, we will be reduced to 20% of our expected revenues by New Year. We need a large influx of cash, and very soon, to maintain our present operations. Allow me to take you through the various accounts and you will see what I mean."

"Good! I will need details if this problem is to be fixed."

Scott spent the next two hours examining the books with Postle and his stomach roiled more and more as each page was turned. Almost all the of the protection rackets had been shut down in Berwick, and the few that remained were generating a fraction of their usual revenues. Not only that, but Postle told him that most of the ringleaders of those rackets were in jail awaiting trial and a few had already been hanged. The people of Berwick were fighting back, and no replacements for his jailed and executed lieutenants were willing to step forward. Most of the criminal support network of these lieutenants had either fled the city or gone into hiding. Berwick was now an extremely safe place to walk at night.

"I hate to say this, Mr. Scott, but we are looking at a full-scale collapse of the rackets by February if something is not done."

The situation in the countryside was a little better but not by much. Many estates were refusing their monthly tribute, and those who did pay had sent much less than the expected amounts. Reprisal parties sent to exact retribution had been spotted well in advance of their destination by Pennywhistle's early warning network. Beacons had been lit and targets alerted. Pennywhistle's auxiliaries had fought several successful actions against enforcement parties, and such was the auxiliary's reputation that now even the mere threat that they had been alerted was enough to cause enforcement parties to turn back.

The same held true for thieving raids. The Reivers had grown cautious and would only carry out an excursion if they could be sure they would meet no armed opposition. Desertions had risen to an alarming rate and new recruitment had ceased entirely. People were beginning to embrace the peaceful alternatives offered by Pennywhistle's policies.

His new model army was suffering from supply problems, both of arms and victuals. It was an expensive proposition at the best of times, and in bad ones was a severe drain on his resources. The men were discontented, and desertions were increasing. The defeats at Kelso and Jedburgh had worsened things and rumors of a general mutiny had begun to circulate.

The charities that he funded had ceased operation altogether, and now the only charities that were functioning were those sponsored by Pennywhistle.

Most distressing of all, over the past two weeks, he had received no funds at all from the fencing and shipping operations under Lord Maxwell's control. Maxwell had apparently made a deliberate choice to sever his operations from Scott's. He had refused his invitation to a parley and now seemed to be embarking on an independent course. Scott had considered having Maxwell killed, but such was the prestige of his title and heritage that his death would likely raise questions that he did not want asked. He wondered if Maxwell saw himself as Scott's replacement. It was a definite possibility. Maxwell's sense of self- importance, arrogance, and magisterial confidence had swelled to cosmic proportions, and he likely felt that he could take over Scott's operations with ease. Scott wondered if he should expect an assassination attempt.

"That's the lot of it, Mr. Scott," said Postle as he finished. "I wish I could add a few rays of sunshine, but you pay me to be honest and the future looks bleak."

"I would not have you tell anything less than the full truth, Mr. Postle. Let me ask you this: if nothing is done to remedy this dire situation, how long would it be before all my operations grind to a complete halt?"

Postle closed his eyes for a few moments and Scott knew that his mathematical mind was swiftly calculating a bewildering torrent of numbers and their applications.

Postle's face looked old and weary when he spoke. "Probably March, April at the very latest. Something drastic will have to be done, and very soon if that outcome is to be prevented."

"I feared as much. Thank you for your honesty. Do not lose heart, Mr. Postle, I have some ideas that will extricate us from our present problems. I know many depend upon me, and I promise you that I will not let them down."

"I have faith in you, Mr. Scott."

"Thank you, Mr. Postle. I know our funds our low, but I am confident that you can find a way to pay yourself a 10% bonus for your efforts today."

"Are you sure, Mr. Scott? Frugality seems to be in order."

"Nonsense! My key assistants shall never want for a proper reward." Scott reached inside his pocket, then tossed a half crown to Postle. "Treat yourself to a good dinner at the Rose and Crown. You have earned it. Now be off with you!"

Postle grinned and departed. Scott frowned and sank back into his chair. "Mr. Perry, would you please get Sergeant

Lefebvre here as fast as possible? I need to speak with him on a matter of urgency. "

"Certainly, Sir." Perry heard something unexpected in his master's voice, barely suppressed panic.

Scott finished his coffee in one gulp then reclined his chaise chair as far back as possible. He closed his eyes and began to think. Perhaps it was time to cut a deal with Pennywhistle, but he could not do that from a position of weakness. He needed to convince Pennywhistle that he was stronger than he was, and he had to offer him something compelling: something that his superiors in London would accept as a final solution. The answer was the Flodden Treasure. If it was as great as it was rumored to be, it would probably be worth at least 200,000 pounds at today's market value. The trouble was, he had only a general idea where it was. Rumor had it that the chests were stored in a barn somewhere on the Whistlestop estate, hidden under a haystack. It puzzled him that Pennywhistle did not yet know about the treasure, but his source said the finder was uncertain about how much he would get to keep if he informed authorities.

It would take a full-scale search to find it. Before that could happen, the inhabitants of the estate would have to be subdued and rendered talkative, in case the treasure's location had changed. They had proven troublesome before and so he would have to hit them with overwhelming force. It had to be done at a time when he could be sure that Pennywhistle would not be present, since reports had him visiting the estate with some frequency. He had also installed a small garrison of ten soldiers, who would have to be dealt with. Some fortifications were nearing completion and that worried him.

He had received word that a grand ball was planned two nights hence, to celebrate the social debut of Pennywhistle's niece. It was a certainty that Pennywhistle would attend and would be the perfect time to strike at Whistlestop. The question was could his new model army be ready on such short notice?

Perry escorted the man who could provide the answer into his presence: Sergeant Lefebvre, who had trained them and knew their capabilities better than anyone else.

He explained what he had in mind to Lefebvre. "Can it be done? Yes, or no?"

Lefebvre gave a gallic shrug. "You ask for the impossible, Monsieur: to give a definite answer to a question that it would take a seer to answer. I can only give you my best guess. It would be difficult given the time involved, but if your men were pushed to their limits, it is possible. The trouble, Monsieur Scott, is that the men's morale is poor, and they have a defeatist attitude. They are slipping into the mentality of barracks soldiers rather than active campaigners. The prospect of a long march in winter weather will be most unwelcome. Soldiers that have no tradition of victory are very hard to motivate. It is possible that the call to such an action could even provoke a general mutiny. If the soldiers were promised some extraordinary reward for their efforts, it would help a great deal."

Scott saw the doubt in Lefebvre's eyes and debated inwardly whether his men should be told the general object of the expedition. He had only planned to tell them that they were searching for four chests that contained, "objects of importance." Operational secrecy was important but sometimes too much of it worked against you. Greed was a powerful motivator, particularly to soldiers who were underpaid. Asking them to fight for the capture of an estate that they could not care less about was far different from asking them to fight for gold, silver, and jewels. Giving each man a tiny fraction of the treasure would only slightly diminish its value.

"What if I told you, Sergeant, that I can promise your men enough money to guarantee them a life of comfort and ease?"

Lefebvre's eyebrows arched in skepticism. "I do not see how that is possible. It is evident to us that you are hurting for money since the soldiers have received no pay this week."

"That is about to change, Lefebvre. You see, there is a treasure hidden on the estate. The Flodden Treasure."

Lefebvre gasped. "The Flodden Treasure? I have heard of it and so have my men, but surely it is just a legend."

"It is not a legend. I have two pieces of it in my possession. I can show them to you as proof."

Lefebvre started. "That is incredible! I should welcome the chance to see them. My men would wish to see them too. It is one thing to talk about treasure, but quite another to display pieces of it. An extraordinary prize can summon extraordinary efforts." Lefebvre stroked his chin in thought. "If everything you say is true, I will revise my earlier evaluation. The thing can definitely be done. You might even want to accompany me, to be present at the moment when the treasure is found."

"Good! Come with me, Lefebvre, and prepare to be amazed."

***

James Heatherington was back at work as the assistant ghillie on the Paxton Estate, but he was now acting as Pennywhistle's spy. Maxwell had asked him a lot of questions about his time in captivity and about Pennywhistle, and he had told him exactly what Pennywhistle wanted him to say. When he had brought news of the Treasure, his stock with Maxwell soared.

Pennywhistle had told him to watch for anything out of the ordinary or untoward on the estate, and one thing stood out. He had seen nothing of Lord Maxwell's brother for the past week. Unlike Maxwell, who was aloof and haughty to those below his station, Charles liked to talk with the servants on the estate and frequently asked them about their jobs, their families, and what they wanted out of life. Charles was a philosophic chap, and every so often retired to a quiet wooded spot on the estate to write his thoughts in what Heatherington guessed was a diary. That spot was part of Heatherington's bailiwick and so the two had had occasion to talk frequently.

Since Charles had disappeared, Lord Maxwell's behavior had changed. While he had never been a ray of sunshine like his brother Charles, he had grown increasingly quarrelsome and suspicious. He sometimes stopped, grumbled to himself, and grimaced, rubbing his chest vigorously, as if to mitigate pain. Unlike his brother, he had never been much of a drinker, but Heatherington had smelled whiskey in his breath during their last three encounters. He sensed something was eating at the man that could only be quieted by large doses of alcohol.

Maxwell's relationship with his brother had frequently been contentious, and Heatherington did not buy Maxwell's story that Charles had suddenly departed on the Grand Tour. Charles liked to travel but he had never embarked upon a journey that took more than a fortnight: the Grand Tour of Europe's chief cities and sights usually required at least a year, even at a breakneck pace. Moreover, Charles liked to travel in style with the best food and wine. He had checked with Charles' usual suppliers of culinary exotica, and they had recorded no orders beyond the usual. He had talked to most of the servants on the estate and no one had been involved in any special preparations for his departure. Most tellingly, the spare carriage that Charles used when he traveled the countryside had never left the carriage house.

Lord Maxwell possessed a bad temper and cruel nature which caused Heatherington to wonder if he had finally had enough of Charles and had taken the ultimate step to silence him. He was close to his own brother and found the idea of fratricide shocking.

If Charles had been murdered, it was important that Pennywhistle be told.

Heatherington waited until midnight to make his move. He wanted to be certain that no one was about in the Paxton Mansion. There were guard dogs patrolling the house and grounds, but they knew him and a few treats would keep them quiet.

Heatherington did not even have to break into Charles' quarters. The tall French doors that opened onto a piazza opposite his bedroom were usually unlocked, since he was a light sleeper and frequently went outside to gaze at the stars. James opened them and tiptoed into the bedroom. Satisfied that he would remain undetected, he lit a small candle.

The maids had been busy and so the bedroom looked well-ordered and spotless, unlike the way it usually looked when Charles had been in residence. He checked the closets and Charles' wardrobe was intact and undisturbed. Very peculiar for a man supposedly going on an extended journey.

It occurred to him that Charles's diary might tell him a great deal. He guessed that it was probably hidden in a locked bureau at the far end of the bedroom. The lock was easily opened with the small pick and tension wrench that he had brought. The interior of the desk was honeycombed with storage slots that were crammed with papers. He spent the next half hour looking through the papers, but they contained nothing of interest. He was about to give up when he noticed a small nub at the end of the only slot that was not filled with papers.

On impulse he pressed it, and a large hidden drawer slid open. He recognized the diary that Charles wrote in but there were many others as well. Each diary had a year marked on it. There were 15 in all. He stuffed them into the haversack that he carried, then closed the desk and relocked it.

He took the diaries to his quarters, prepared a large pot of tea, and began reading. The hours until dawn ground slowly by as he discovered the deepest secrets of the Maxwell family; Charles had committed every outrage perpetrated by his brother to paper. Most shocking was that Lord Maxwell had killed his own wife in a fit of temper. He was also deeply involved in ongoing criminal activity. The diaries only alluded to most operations, but five especially notorious ones were described in detail. It was clear that Charles had frequently tried to dissuade him from those endeavors, but to no avail. There was enough evidence in the diaries to hang Maxwell; strong enough so that his title and lineage would not give him a way to evade justice. He wondered how he could get the diaries to Pennywhistle. The answer came at 9 am the following morning courtesy of Maxwell himself.

Maxwell's man, Bradford, presented himself at the door of his cottage. "Lord Maxwell needs you for special duty this evening, Heatherington. He is attending a ball in Berwick and wants an armed escort of four for his carriage. He has heard rumors of highwaymen planning to ambush people on their way to the ball, and he wants to take no chances. He likes you and knows that you are a stout fighting man. He also thinks that because of your recent... uh...experience in the city that you have a good read on the mood of Berwick. Consider yourself among the favored few, Heatherington."

"I shall be happy to accept the duty. It is an honor to serve such a great man as Lord Maxwell."

"She can't be dead. She can't. I spoke to her two days ago and my sister was in the best of health." Tears of disbelief coursed through Peter Postle's quivering voice. He took his cup of tea and threw it against the grey wall of his small office.

"It was a raid gone wrong, Peter, the Reivers were drunk and targeted the wrong cottage." Mark Dayton was a neighbor and close friend of the Postle family. "I think they raped Jane several times before they cut her throat."

Postle's tears stopped. He clutched his stomach, bent over, and retched. When he recovered, he spoke with anger mixed with sadness. "Those men who did this must be found and made to pay!"

"It may take some time to find them. I expect that they have gone into hiding because they fear Scott's wrath."

"Damn it! Scott is responsible! He sent them! And I know just where to find him. By God, I will strangle the man with my own hands."

Dayton put his hands on Postle's shoulders. "Calm down, Peter! You are talking like a resident of Bedlam. Scott is too well protected. What you contemplate would be suicide!"

"But he has promised to see me whenever I request an audience."

"Your face would give you away an instant! Jane would never want you to throw your life away trying to avenge her memory. There has to be another way to hurt Scott."

Postle bowed his head in thought and said nothing for what seemed an eternity to Dayton. When Postle's head rose, his tears had ceased, and his eyes were hard. He spoke with the icy calm of a professional accountant telling a client that his business had failed. "There is, Mark. It's about killing with information. Not only can I bring him down but the Reivers in hiding as well."

Dayton's eyes widened in understanding as he grasped what Postle contemplated. "Of course! You keep his accounts, and he trusts you with his deepest secrets. If that information found its way into the wrong hands you could wipe his legacy from the face of the earth. He is a prideful man and that would sting him mightily. Probably be the last thing he will think about before the long drop at the end of a rope."

"I need to have a very extensive talk with Warden Pennywhistle. I know exactly where he will be tomorrow evening, at his niece's debut ball. Scott left early this morning to inspect his...new model army." Postle spoke the last three words with contempt. "Something big is in the works. If I can get this information to the Warden in time, he may be able to stop it."

"Let me help, Peter. Anything at all."

"I know that as an ostler you have access to some very fast mounts. I trust you could whistle up two of the best."

"Consider it done."

"You can also serve as a lookout. Scott has roving guards in the castle and me carrying out piles of books might arouse suspicion."

"I am in this with you to the end. Jane was very dear to me as well. You are not the only one who wants revenge."

"It's more than just revenge, Peter. I realize how wrong I have been, turning a blind eye to all of Scott's misdeeds and the pain that he has inflicted. I was seduced by the pay, the chance to use my gifts fully, and the power that comes with being a keeper of secrets. I am ashamed of what I have done, but now I think I have a chance to put things right."

"You are being too hard on yourself. You are human like the rest of us and succumbed to temptation."

"Perhaps, but now I need to be stronger than ever have been. Come, Mark. Let us be moving. I want to be in Berwick before nightfall."

***

Pennywhistle valued his solitude, but since becoming Warden of the English East March he'd had had precious little of it. His position compelled him to receive a constant stream of visitors with all manner of requests, complaints, suggestions, and confidential information. He had become an ombudsman extraordinaire, forever dealing with emergencies; putting out various metaphorical fires, and, like the Dutch Boy of legend, sticking his finger into miscellaneous holes to hold back floods caused by ruptured dikes.

He always travelled with two bodyguards at Maxwell's and Sammie Jo's insistence, but he found the unwanted surveillance annoying. His bodyguards were both good men but far too talkative for his taste. He had finally had enough and managed to slip away from his headquarters unnoticed. He needed a quiet dawn stroll to clear his head and review the final preparations for Sally's ball. He liked seeing the city awaken and pulsate with the promise of a new day. He reveled in the optimistic mood which pervaded the city, far different from the dark atmosphere present when he had arrived.

He had just rounded the corner marking the intersection of Pudding Lane and Northumberland Street, when two large hands struck his neck and back from behind, propelling him into a wall. The blows knocked the wind out of him, and he was dazed for a moment. Unable to draw his sword, he lashed out with an elbow, catching his assailant in the diaphragm. He swiveled sideways and struck out with a backfist to the face of his attacker. The attacker staggered backward but recovered quickly, adopting a fighting stance that suggested he had had training in some Far Eastern martial art. His opponent was a big man, and the shape of his eyes argued that he had some oriental ancestry. Pennywhistle stepped back as well and placed himself in the fighting posture associated with savate, the French art of street fighting.

His opponent advanced in a flash then kicked at his shin, which Pennywhistle blocked with a kick of his own. Next came a punch toward his face, which Pennywhistle deflected with his left forearm. His enemy launched a palm-heel strike with his other arm, which Pennywhistle knocked aside. Pennywhistle riposted with two palm-heel strikes of his own, which his attacker deflected. Both men chopped at each other's necks four times but none of the strikes connected because both men were equally quick at blocks.

Pennywhistle aimed a punch at his attacker's head, but his assailant sidestepped, grabbed Pennywhistle's elbow, and threw him into the wall. Pennywhistle crouched low and jumped to the side. He ducked the next blow and shot his own arm over the man's shoulder, pulling him close. He used his left knee to strike him three times in the stomach. The man broke Pennywhistle's grip and shoved him back, but not before

Pennywhistle's fist landed a blow to the base of his neck. Pennywhistle danced away from two punches, then darted forward and struck the man solidly in the chin with a right cross. The man staggered back, then launched a wheel kick, which Pennywhistle ducked. He punched the man in the groin and his opponent howled.

The man staggered but refused to fall. He kicked at Pennywhistle's knee and missed, but his right hook connected with Pennywhistle's chin and sent him reeling. Pennywhistle recovered quickly and backpedaled to get more fighting room. His attacker charged, but Pennywhistle went down on one knee and extended his other leg, causing the man to trip and fall.

The man righted himself and came at him again. Pennywhistle stopped a punch to the head with an x-block, then launched his own punch to his attacker's stomach, which connected solidly. His opponent folded and his hand reached beneath the cuff of his trousers, trying to extract a knife from a scabbard strapped to his shin.

Pennywhistle kicked his hand away, then grabbed his other arm and shoved him into the wall. Pennywhistle pinned him and kicked his groin from behind. The man lashed out with an elbow that broke Pennywhistle's grip and shoved him back. The man swiveled to face Pennywhistle and kicked at his groin.

Pennywhistle sidestepped then focused all his attention on the center of the man's sternum. He launched a short, straight-line punch at it, putting all his determination and every ounce of his hip and calf muscles into it. The impact froze his assailant as his heart abruptly stopped. He blinked as if the life switch in his brain had been turned off, then collapsed without a sound.

Pennywhistle shook his head several times, as he sucked in lungfuls of air. He concentrated on slowing his breathing and focusing his thoughts. At that instant his two bodyguards rounded the corner on the run. They raced up to him with looks of embarrassment on their faces.

"Are you alright, sir?"

"I'll live."

"Why did you sneak off without us, Sir? You know we have sworn our lives to protect you."

"Because I so badly needed time to myself that I did something stupid and violated my own rule of never venturing out alone. You have my apologies, gentlemen: it won't happen again."

Pennywhistle and his men looked down at the body.

"Looks like a rough customer," remarked one bodyguard. "Who do you think sent him, Sir Thomas?"

Pennywhistle pointed to the corpse's left forearm.

"The tattoo is a tong sign: the green dragon of Ghangzhou. The Green Dragons are the most notorious of Chinese gangs. I think that he is a recently arrived sailor from the *Wenhou*, a ship from Canton that docked yesterday. Since he was a newcomer, I think this attack was a hastily organized commission arranged by some low- level malcontents whom I have ousted from their rackets."

Pennywhistle stretched his arms and flexed his shoulder muscles to fight off the usual post battle torpor. "And now gentlemen, I have had my daily exercise as well as my dose of solitude. My appetite is roused. I am guessing that you two have not yet eaten, so let's' return to headquarters for a hearty breakfast."

"Amen to that," chorused his bodyguards."

***

"We still have time to call off this ball, Sammie Jo. As the hours close on its approach, I grow increasingly anxious. I know this will be the social event of the season, and I realize that Sally is excited, but can your husband absolutely guarantee her safety?"

"Not unless she hides in her bedroom, Sarah, locks the door, and stations a squad of soldiers outside." Sammie Jo took the book she had been consulting on ballroom etiquette and placed it back on its shelf in the large library. "But you and I both know that's not in her nature, and deep down, it is not in yours either."

Sammie Jo knew that her husband had taken every reasonable precaution. Soldiers would be posted at all the entrances and exits, and invitations would be carefully checked. Two incognito soldiers would circulate among the party guests. All the catering help had been thoroughly vetted, as had the people hired to decorate the ballroom. The musicians in the orchestra had been personally interviewed by Pennywhistle since he loved music.

Sarah sighed in resignation. "Very well, let's continue the preparations. What about this girl who has agreed to serve as Sally's double. Jane Bennett, wasn't it? Is she still agreeable to her part?"

"More than agreeable; Jane relishes the part that she will play. You have been so busy preparing for the ball that you have failed to notice that she has been following Sally around for the past two days. The girls have struck up quite a friendship. Sally has been helping Jane to mimic her movements, manners, and speech, and she has proved an apt pupil. Seeing the two stand side by side, I would swear that they were twins. When they speak and I close my eyes, I cannot tell their voices apart."

"But Sally has friends who will notice the difference. What about them?"

"She has told her friends that she has arranged a great party game whose rules and outcome can only be gradually revealed during the party. She has told them to trust her and play along with things that may seem odd or unexpected. Being teenaged girls, they love the idea that they are privy to a secret that is hidden from adults and relish the thought of having a laugh at their expense. My guess is that the adults who know Sally will be confused and uncertain, but too polite to say anything. Those who do not, will not detect the imposture."

Sarah smiled gently. "I have to admit I was wrong about you, Sammie Jo. I was suspicious when we first met and thought you a cynical opportunist."

"I get that sometimes but most just say it with their eyes. I'm an acquired taste, and I have made a fair number of enemies among snooty society ladies, but I have acquired many more friends. You have given me the benefit of the doubt and have taken the time to get to know me. Back where I come from, I would give you a great big bear hug and call you sister. But that isn't the way things are done here, so I will hold myself back and abide by local custom."

Sarah smiled. "I think I could bend the rules a bit, just this once, as long as no one will report me to the local society tattletales." She stepped forward and embraced Sammie Jo.

The embrace was uncertain but in Sammie Jo's estimation, the gesture represented a big step for Sarah. She might not quite have a loving sister-in-law, but she had gained an ally with whom she could work effectively.

Her newfound pleasure stopped when her peripheral vision spotted her husband slinking by in the hall, followed by his two bodyguards. Her husband looked like he had been in a hard fight, while his bodyguards appeared to be in pristine order. She instantly connected the disparate appearances and scowled. She shoved the half open door fully open. "Stop right there, you damned renegade knight, Thomas Pennywhistle," she snarled. "You've got a lot of explaining to do! And you ain't leaving my sight until you fess up."

Pennywhistle cringed; he was in for a verbal pummeling far more severe than the physical one that he had just endured. His wife was his best ally, but sometimes only the best ally could tell a man his worst shortcomings. He braced himself as the torrent of harsh words began.

***

Nico Ruzzini and Strata Smith stood atop the parapet of the large earthen redoubt just outside Whistlestop's main gate. "You've been a lot of help, Nico," said Strata Smith. "Your military background has been a big asset. My books have been helpful in laying out these fortifications, but some details were left out because the author assumed a military man would be reading his work, and he did not want to waste time belaboring the obvious."

"It's been an education for me as well. I have learned a great deal about rocks, soils, and drainage. I have come to like this place a great deal, and I think I could use my knowledge to make this estate the wonderful place that Sir Thomas thinks it

357

can become. In fact, I am going to ask Sir Thomas if I might take up residence."

"That Collins girl wouldn't have anything to do with it, would it?" said Smith with sly amusement.

"Is it that obvious?"

"Every time you two are together your faces glow like twin suns. People passing by can almost feel the heat you two generate."

"If things keep going as they are, I would eventually like to make her my wife."

"Hold on there, Nico, you are only 14. Are you the kind of sailor who has a girl in every port? I thought you had taken a shine to Sybil Pennywhistle, or is she just yesterday's news?"

"Sybil was just a flash in the pan, but my heart tells me that Rosalind is the one."

"Well neither of you will have a future if this place falls to the Reivers."

"I think we have done everything we can, Mr. Smith. I can't think of anything else. Are you certain they will come?"

As if in answer, a uniformed rider trotted up to the pair. "Just the people I want to see. Well, Maude Dacre too. Sir Thomas has an important message that he said I was to deliver verbally to you three and no one else."

"I will fetch Maude," said Smith, who dashed toward the door. He knew Pennywhistle would not have sent a messenger if he did not think he had obtained some critical information.

"I was impressed by the fortifications on the way in," remarked the rider to Nico. "Oh, forgive me, I forgot to introduce myself. John Rennie, esquire, at your service. Oops, make that Private Rennie. I am still getting used to being an active member of the Northumberland Yeomanry."

"It's a pleasure to meet you, Private Rennie."

Smith and Maude walked quickly up to the two. Both looked worried.

Rennie spoke calmly, "Sir Thomas told me that he had received a reliable report from one of his scouts at dawn this morning. Groups of armed men have been observed on the roads over the past two days. Two scouts shadowed them and found that the various groups converged at a large camp outside of Duns, on the Scottish side of the border. The camp is filled with around 1200 men and is bustling with training activity. The scouts believe that some movement of the troops is contemplated, probably in the next few days. Sir Thomas believes the object of that movement will be Whistlestop since the camp is only 15 miles from here; a day's march. He wants everyone here on high alert."

"They will find us ready for them!" growled Maude with an angry resolve. "Everyone, and I mean everyone, has been practicing their drills daily. Those blackguards are going to find that they have stuck their heads into a lion's den. I presume Sir Thomas is sending reinforcements."

"Yes," said Rennie. "That's the second part of my message. 160 infantry are marching here as we speak and should arrive in the next few hours. Sir Thomas is keeping his cavalry and 100 infantry men in reserve at Berwick because he believes that there may be some diversionary assault made on the city while Whistlestop is attacked. Once he is satisfied Berwick is safe, he will come to your relief as swiftly as possible."

"I don't like it at all," objected Smith. "It means we will be on our own when the attack comes."

"But Mr. Smith," said Nico, "160 trained soldiers added to the ten already here will give us plenty of punch to hit back at the Reivers when they come. And the rest of us are no mean fighters either. Remember what you told me when we started: 'One man behind fortifications is equivalent to ten in the field.'"

"I did say that. It's just that I never thought I would have to put it to the test."

"Let me calm your nerves, Mr. Smith," added Rennie. "The distance from Berwick to Whistlestop is short. At a fast trot, the cavalry could be here in just over an hour."

"I have a theory," said Nico. "It's just a hunch mind you, but I think that we at Whistlestop are just one element in a much larger plan."

"Could you explain, Nico?" said Maude.

"Sir Thomas never does anything by half measures. He wants to wipe the Reivers off the board and end their threat to the Borders once and for all. I think he will use his favorite formula: stall and the hook. Whistlestop is the stall, to fix the enemy in place. His cavalry is the hook, to sweep around their rear and take them by surprise."

"Very interesting," replied Rennie. "Sir Thomas told my commander to be ready for some very active duty in the next few days."

"I wonder exactly when the Reivers will come?" said Maude.

"Sir Thomas once told me that the best time to attack was either at dawn or just after the worst weather imaginable. Those are the times when men's reflexes are at their lowest ebb," said Nico.

"That reminds me, Mr. Ruzzini, Sir Thomas wants you in command."

"Me?" blurted a startled Ruzzini. "It's a great honor, but I have so little experience and I..."

"Fear not, Mr. Ruzzini. Sir Thomas is sending his two most senior sergeants as your 'advisors.' He trusts that you will follow their 'suggestions' to the letter. Both have had a great deal of combat experience, and Sergeant Major Masters once defended an outpost in Spain like Whistlestop."

"That's a relief!" said Nico. "It will be a lot like *Dispatch*. I was in command of men much older than myself, but I always listened to the suggestions of the senior petty officer."

"I think we should call everyone one on the estate together; have what the Americans call a town meeting," said Maude.

"An excellent idea, Maude," responded Nico. "Sir Thomas says that many battle plans are ruined due to excessive secrecy. The trouble is if a plan goes wrong and the troops executing it have no idea of its general design, their ability to correctly improvise is greatly limited. Sir Thomas believes 'the need-to-know' criterion for sharing information should be interpreted in the broadest fashion."

"The left hand should always know what the right hand is doing?"

"A fine way to put it, Maude."

"You three seem to have things well in hand, "observed Rennie. "Now if you will forgive me, I must depart. Sir Thomas will want to know that you have been put in the picture." Rennie touched his helmet in a salute, pivoted his mount, and trotted off.

"I am going to ring the alarm bell," said Maude. "It may frighten some but it's the fastest way to get everyone together. In fact, if it does frighten a few that may be a good thing. We all have a big test ahead of us."

"I have no doubt we will all give a good account of ourselves," said Nico. "I have a suggestion."

"What's that?" asked Maude.

"Tell everyone to watch the skies. Everything depends on the weather."

*****

Pennywhistle slowly sipped his coffee as he watched the dawn break on December 16, the day of Sally's Ball. The sky was clear for the moment, but he spotted cumulonimbus clouds in the far distance. The temperature was just above freezing, and the air was still. He hoped the weather would hold until the ball was done, but there was an old saying in the Borders: "when clouds look like towers the earth will be refreshed by showers." The ones he was seeing fitted that description and Berwick was prone to sudden storms that blew in off the North Sea.

He leaned back in his leather office chair and closed his eyes. Events had reached a critical juncture, and he was sure that his chief opponent would strike Whistlestop in the next 24 hours. He had learned quite a bit about Walter Scott, but the important thing was that Scott was not a military man, and everything he had done was more in line with a criminal's mentality rather than that of a soldier. His probing of Pennywhistle's outposts was amateurish, and his forces displayed imperfect training and leadership. Success as a London criminal master player did not guarantee success as a military overlord, though Scott's ego was probably so large that he would be unable to grasp that truth. He gathered Scott's chief motive was to rise above his modest beginnings, and so he was more interested in money and prestige than in exercising actual governance over the Borders.

He had to know that his efforts were unsustainable. Pennywhistle had shut down all his rackets and what had been a torrent of thieving raids had dwindled to a trickle. Pennywhistle shifted in his chair, opened his eyes, and drank the last of his coffee. He asked himself what was the one thing that all criminals craved. The answer was an easy one: respectability. Every successful criminal wanted to have legitimacy conferred on him by a lawfully constituted government. Rather than being an enemy of the ruling elite, a prosperous criminal wanted to join their ranks.

He wondered if Scott was preparing to cut his losses and flee the country. No, Scott was a social climber and would want to stay in Britain, if for no other reason than to show one and all how far he had come from his modest origins. It was possible Scott might seek a bargain to allow him to keep his ill-gotten gains and retire into the quiet life of an English country gentleman.   There was a precedent for this dating from Elizabethan times. That pragmatic sovereign had been more interested in maintaining order than serving justice.

Pennywhistle would never bargain with a scoundrel, but he could not be sure that the government in London would not consider a certain type of accommodation. Sidmouth had made it clear that he simply wanted the Border problems to go away. Pennywhistle understood his command was costing the government a lot of money, and Sidmouth wanted that hemorrhaging of cash stopped at the earliest moment. It was up to him to make sure that Scott's fate rested in his hands, not Sidmouth's.

There was a knock on the door of his office. "Come."

Maxwell walked in, a look of worry on his face.

"Pour yourself a cup of coffee and take a seat."

"Thank you, Sir Thomas, I shall do just that."

"Do you really think my father will come tonight?"

"He responded to the invitation affirmatively, and I have no doubt that he will attend. He does not know that we know that he is Scott's partner in crime. What better way to dispel any unwanted speculation than by attending a very public event, and probably presenting a handsome present to its honoree?"

"My father always did relish the parties and soirees of the social season. He has never been the quiet type."

"My guess is that his principal reason for attending is that he is curious about you." Pennywhistle paused and his face darkened. "Your father has wronged you cruelly and your resentment of him is understandable. But I think you would be the first one to admit that you and he both have tempers that can quickly become ungovernable. I will ask you directly. If you and he meet, can I trust you to behave civilly?"

Maxwell stared at his feet and his face assumed a hard expression. "I want to say that I will be the perfect gentleman, but deep down, I am just not sure."

"Then I think that you should stay away from the party entirely. There will be plenty of time to speak with your father when we accumulate enough legally actionable information to formally arrest him. You realize at the end of all this, he faces the gallows."

A wave of conflicting expressions crossed Maxwell's face. "I do, and you are right that he should die because of the long arm of the law and not by the swift justice that I should very much like to administer. I will abide by your suggestion and not attend the ball, however, I need to face him directly at some point, if for no other reason than to show how wrong he was about me."

"Remember our primary object tonight is to protect Sally and the city. You should stay with the Northumberland Yeomanry for the entire night."

"So, you have deduced that an attempt will be made to abduct Sally?"

"Yes, it would be a bold stroke designed to make me amenable to bargaining. I think my opponent is getting ready to cash out his chips, and he knows that my intention is to pursue him until he dangles from the end of a hangman's rope."

"But he must know that you will have her under close surveillance."

"True, but I still think the attempt will be made because I sense a growing desperation on his part. You have just come from inspecting the Northumberland Yeomanry. Do you think they are ready for battle?"

"I do; we have 200 blades eager to taste blood. The men are hot to try out the skills they have been practicing so zealously for the past weeks. I think a few words of inspiration from you might be in order, Sir Thomas; they look up to you. I know you dislike speech making, but they see you as a hero of the greatest battle of the age and your approval would be a great boost to their already high morale."

"Very well, once we finish here, I will carry out a short inspection, though I already know what the results will be. I should also tell you that I received word last night that the men I sent to Whistlestop have arrived at their destination. Masters' note said he has already scouted the best locations for their placement. The two howitzers I sent have been fixed in the redoubts in front of Whistlestop's main entrance."

"How soon do you think you will be ready to move, Sir Thomas?"

"I realize that it would be stupid to attack Berwick's fortifications, but desperate men do strange things, and I want to make sure the walls are secure before I depart. I would guess that the ball will finish in the wee hours, so I anticipate moving our forces just after first light."

"We won't exactly be facing another Waterloo, will we, Sir Thomas?"

"True, but then we won't be going up against Bonaparte either."

There was a knock on the door. "Come."

The door opened and Sammie Jo and Sarah walked in. "Hope I ain't bustin' up your gentlemen's gab fest but I thought you should know we are all set for the party. Sarah and I just got done going through the final checklist. This party should be a real showstopper. Ain't that right, Sarah?"

Sarah looked dubious. "It should be, but I still worry about Sally's safety."

"Whatever worries you have Sarah, place them in my hands and let me deal with them. You and Sammie Jo should focus on making this party the most joyous occasion possible."

"Thank you, Tom, the more protection Sally has the easier I can breathe. I want Sybil and Sally to grow up in a society that they can be proud of, and that can never happen until the fear plaguing this land is banished once and for all. It's times like this I miss Peter's support." Tears filled her eyes, and her voice choked. "He would be so proud of Sally! It is so unfair that his life was snuffed out. When I think of the bad men that still walk free, it makes me angry! There is no justice in the universe!"

She began to sob, and Sammie Jo put her arm around her. "Go ahead, let all your pain out, Sarah. You bottle stuff up just like Tom and it's tearing you up inside. You have kept a stiff upper lip since Peter passed and stuffed your feelings: I don't think you ever truly acknowledged your grief. A good long cry is a way to start. I am with you all the way. I want to help you pick up the pieces of your life and put them back together."

"Thank you," whispered Sarah between sobs. "I really need a friend right now."

"I ain't leaving your side."

Sarah threw her arms wholeheartedly around Sammie Jo, who understood she had finally acquired a real sister-in-law.

CHAPTER 14

A Ball and a Trojan Horse

16th December 1816

Lord John Maxwell was enjoying his carriage ride to the Pennywhistle Ball. Four armed riders accompanied the carriage, and a special wheeled construction followed behind, ostensibly a large gift for Miss Pennywhistle's coming out. The wooden construction was fascinating to behold, but its real purpose was hidden. He planned to donate it anonymously, intending to spark a mystery about who had sent it.

As the carriage rumbled through the snow just starting to fall, he read with satisfaction a letter that he had received in the morning post. It was a response to a long letter that he had sent the week before. It was from the Duke of Bedford, a good friend who had the ear of many of Lord Liverpool's most influential cabinet members, including Lord Sidmouth. Bedford had been impressed by his revelation that he had identified the man behind the Border troubles, and was interested in his claim that he could use his personal resources to bring the man to justice. Bedford suggested that he coordinate his efforts with Pennywhistle. He added that though the government had been impressed with

Pennywhistle's efforts, many members of the opposition were screaming loudly about their cost and were threatening to cut the Warden's funding.

He put the letter down and took a sip of hot green tea to warm himself. He smiled both at the taste of the tea as well as the set of events that his planned actions would trigger.

Bedford hinted that the government would be very grateful for the help of the greatest lord in the area. Maxwell interpreted "grateful" to mean a variety of benefices directed his way. Those would likely include the end of any efforts to look too closely into his personal affairs. He might even be advanced a step in the peerage. Viscount Maxwell had a good ring to it.

He had been careful not to name Scott in the letter to Bedford. That secret was worth its weight in gold. He wondered if Pennywhistle suspected Scott, but decided that speculation was pointless because he would find out soon enough. He was willing to work with Pennywhistle but only if he had leverage that he could use against him. That leverage was his niece, Sally.

He had gotten word from a spy he had placed among Scott's men that he was planning an attack on Whistlestop. He guessed that was where the Flodden Treasure resided. He decided that he would let Scott absorb the human costs of capturing the treasure before he made any efforts against him. A rider pulled alongside Maxwell's carriage. "My Lord, could we stop for a minute? The uh... construction seems to be having a problem with its wheels. We may have to tighten the pegs holding them to the axles."

Maxwell frowned. "Oh, very well, but be quick about it. Be careful with the wheels. Handle them as if they were made of the finest porcelain. The last thing I want is one of them falling off."

"Understood, my Lord. We will treat them as if they are the crown jewels."

James Heatherington bristled at the delay. He carried all of Charles' diaries in his saddlebags and intended to turn them over to Maxwell's son when the group reached Berwick. He was not sure how he would manage that, but he thought it likely that Maximilian would be present at the Ball, and he believed that where there was a will there was a way. He trusted Maximilian to the same degree that he distrusted his father.

***

Twenty miles away, his brother Angus stomped his boots and rubbed his hands together as he struggled to ward off the effects of the cold night air. Ten other men did the same thing, circled around a large bonfire. One named George Gregson spoke to Angus. "The snow is growing thicker. I think that means we are in for a blizzard. I think we will be given the order to stand down and return to our tents very soon. This will be a night to shelter in place since it will likely be the worst kind for marching. What do you think, Angus?"

"I am not sure, but I do think Mr. Scott is very eager and I am certain that our comfort is not the first thing that comes to his mind. I remember reading about the American General Washington who used a blizzard to cloak a successful surprise attack on the Hessians at Trenton, and I know Mr. Scott is a great admirer of Washington."

"Marching in a blizzard would be insane, Angus."

"Perhaps, but it would also be unexpected. I confess that I am surprised that Mr. Scott plans to accompany us. I expected he would leave the details to Sergeant Lefebvre. Correction, Colonel Lefebvre."

Gregson smiled. "His recent promotion surprised me too, but I suppose it makes a certain amount of sense. After everything that went wrong at Kelso and Jedburgh, Mr. Scott probably decided his men should be led by someone with real combat experience, even if he was neither a Scot nor an Englishman."

"It is strange to be led by a Frenchman," said Angus. "I know many of the men do not quite trust a man who fought for Bonaparte, but I would rather be led by a former member of the Imperial Guard instead of an amateur who learned all his soldiering from books."

Three hundred yards away atop a small hill, Scott and Lefebvre talked. Both had wrapped their cloaks tightly around their bodies to ward off the cold.

"We must move tonight, Lefebvre. We can't wait any longer. We have 1,000 men full of fighting spirit that is eager to be unleashed."

"Perhaps you are looking at a different army than the one I am seeing. With all due respect, I would call their morale...uncertain at best. I would advise against an attack, Mr. Scott. A snow filled night march is difficult even with well-trained troops, and I regret to say that your men stop well short of that. Now if I had two more months to further train these men the odds for success would be greatly improved."

"I have paid you very well, Lefebvre, and I expect results," snarled Scott. "You implied that you could work miracles when I hired you, and tonight I expect to see proof of that."

"I think you are bewitched by this treasure, Mr. Scott. I recognize the symptoms of gold fever. That strange malady often causes men to take unwise chances. Surely, we can wait a day or two until the weather improves. You said you would tell the men about the treasure. Why have you not yet done so?"

"Because I have not found the right moment. I wanted it to be a surprise, delivered when they needed it most. From what you just said about their morale, this may be the perfect moment. We must march tonight!"

Lefebvre gave a Gallic shrug. "I can get the men moving but I cannot promise success in the battle ahead. A fight on a snowy night makes it impossible to tell friends from foes and our men are just as likely to shoot each other as the enemy. Let me suggest a compromise. Delay the march until midnight. Give the men some extra time to eat, drink, and rest. If we arrive just after dawn, we will still have the element of surprise, but at least we will be able to see what we are doing."

Scott thought for a minute. "How long will it take to cover the distance to Whistlestop?"

"The normal marching speed of infantry is two miles an hour, so it would take five hours under normal conditions," replied Lefebvre. "In a snowstorm, it would likely take ten. Ten hours in a snowstorm will be hellish, and the men will be greatly fatigued when they arrive on the scene. They would also need one or two stops to refresh themselves with food and drink so that would add at least another two hours. That would put us into position to launch an attack around 10 am tomorrow. As a young soldier, I fought at Eylau. That battle was conducted in a driving snowstorm and because of that, *l'Empereur* could achieve only a draw. Though I am good at my profession, I do not think I can accomplish what the greatest soldier in history failed to do. I know it is not what you want to hear, but I counsel caution."

"The word caution is hateful to my ears, Lefebvre. The men trust me, they will heed my words."

"They fear you more than they trust you, Sir."

"That works just as well. Now assemble the men while I think of exactly what I shall say."

"Very well, Mr. Scott, but I hope that you understand that if no treasure is found, the men will be very angry. It is even possible they might turn on you."

"You worry too much, Lefebvre."

"That is why I am still alive, Mr. Scott." He gave one final gallic shrug. "I will assemble the men as ordered, but don't say I did not warn you."

Ten minutes later, Scott addressed a long line of surly soldiers, their mood dark after Lefebvre had given them their arduous marching orders. They brightened visibly at the prospect of treasure, and their changed countenances encouraged Scott to let his tongue become expansive and make promises that he was not sure that he could keep. He felt his gambit had worked. The question was, for how long?

Heatherington listened carefully. He had received exactly the information that he needed. The prospect of a snowy night march would give him the perfect opportunity to slip away from the column, and he knew where he could quickly lay his hands on a fast horse, courtesy of man that he considered a good friend and who had become equally disenchanted with the Reivers. Heatherington could reach Berwick long before the column arrived at Whistlestop because he was a good rider.

The soldier's reactions to Scott's words varied.

"These orders stink."

"I need a lot more sleep than four hours."

"My shoes have holes in them. How do they expect me to make a long march?

"My stomach is growling. Where are those extra rations?"

"Gold is exciting. I have never been more awake than I am now."

"I am going to need an extra tot of rum to get through this cold night."

"Amen. Rum, give me rum!"

"Let's just finish this damn business. I want to go home."

The conflicted reactions of his comrades became a blur of noise in Heatherington's ears, but the emotions behind them were clear. His comrades did not want to fight but would do so if it meant they could end their military careers with gold and jewels.

He hoped that his brother James would be waiting to meet him in Berwick. He and James were warriors who resented playing the roles of mere informers. It was time to draw their swords.

***

Sally Pennywhistle was angry. The ball had been underway for an hour, and she was still restricted to her quarters. She liked her impersonator, Jane Bennett, but had not anticipated how much she would resent her *doppelganger* stealing her thunder as the belle of the ball, even for ninety minutes. The lovely melodies of the orchestra three floors below her were loud enough that she heard them clearly: she pictured in her mind the wonderful dancing going on and cursed the fact that she was not whirling and twirling in front of her friends. The weather angered her too. A small storm that looked to be on the verge of becoming a big one had slowed the arrival of carriages bearing important people. She watched a parade of coaches, each arriving fashionably late, from her third-floor bow window.

Then she started as a spectacular sight came rolling up. It was a wooden replica of the Trojan Horse on wheels. At ten feet high and twenty feet long, it was only a fraction of the size of the legendary original, but it was still impressive. It was pulled by four large Clydesdales and guided by two men who rode atop the horses at the front of the yoke. Two other men rode in front carrying torches, as if to add special illumination to a remarkable sight.

Phileda Cameron, a friend of Sally's who had been watching the arrivals of partygoers gasped in awe, then raced inside to tell Jane, aka Sally. Jane, accompanied by her two bodyguards and five other girls quickly gathered beneath the arrival portico to watch. A chorus of "Oooh"s and "Aaah"s erupted. One of the torch bearers rode up to the edge of the stairs that Jane was standing on and beckoned her to come forward. When she had approached within arm's length, he handed her a large envelope. "For you, Miss Pennywhistle." She opened it and pulled out a colorful card decorated with lots of heraldic symbols. She read its message aloud. "From a secret admirer who wishes to know you better. May this small token revivify your interest in *The Illiad*."

Sally heard and wondered who her secret admirer might be. Not many knew of her interest in *The Illiad*. She had told her mother's French teacher, but he did not have the kind of money to fund such an expensive gift.

Then the torchbearer threw his torch at one of Jane's bodyguards, setting him afire. He immediately produced a shillelagh, spurred his horse forward, and clubbed her second bodyguard in the head. The girls screamed in terror.

A trap door opened in the horse's belly and two men jumped down. They grabbed Jane and clamped a cloth over her face. They hoisted her unconscious form upwards into the horse's belly and then followed themselves, pulling the door shut after them. A second later, the mounted men applied their spurs, and the horses began to move.

The girl's screams attracted two guards who quickly found a blanket with which to smother the fire burning on their comrades back. They fired shots at the fast-disappearing intruders, but the distance was too great for their rounds to have any effect.

Amidst all the confusion, Lord Maxwell's carriage came rolling up. He stepped out and looked puzzled, but what had happened was all part of a carefully orchestrated plan. "What is going on here?" he asked.

He was quickly informed of the situation. "That is monstrous!" He motioned to his four-armed retainers. "Go after them! Stop them and bring the girl back! Unharmed!"

The riders expected the order. They nodded to him and rode off. They were not pursuers but escorts, tasked with making sure the Trojan Horse got safely out of the city.

The Trojan Horse had been built for a New Year's Party fifty years before: it had been intended to shelter three men who would pop out at midnight, dressed as living incarnations of the New Year. Maxwell remembered it from a story told to him by his father after his spy had informed him of Sarah's interest in the *Illiad*. He had found it stored in a shed and decided that it could be the centerpiece of a clever plan.

The remaining girls had fled inside and soon the entire ballroom knew of the abduction. Pennywhistle and Maxwell were in the Warden's office when they were informed. "Mr.

Maxwell, rouse a troop of Yeomanry and give chase. We must stop them before they leave the city!"

"But we are only two blocks from the main gate. No Yeomen can move that fast."

"Damn it, you're right! Follow them with all possible speed."

"I assume you're coming."

"No, confound it, I must stay and see if any ransom note turns up, but my guess is whoever arranged this wants something other than money."

"Do you think my father or Scott is behind it?"

"Quite possible, but I have no shortage of enemies. The sailor who attacked me this morning had no connection with either your father or Scott, and this could possibly be linked to the efforts of his sponsors to disrupt my plans."

Maxwell dashed down the stairs and into the courtyard where he had stabled his horse. He spotted his father's carriage and cursed that he would not be able to confront him. He jumped into the saddle, put the spurs to his stallion, and arrived at the Yeomanry's quarters five minutes later. The Yeomanry were horrified at the news of the abduction and moved quickly. Twenty men were armed, mounted, and ready to ride in ten minutes.

The abductors were already a mile into the countryside. The guards at the city's main gate were confused: they had been told to allow easy access to the city to all party guests and believed that the horse had already served whatever purpose it had been designed for. Once outside the city wall's, the abductors abandoned the Trojan Horse and transferred the girl's inert form to the back of a horse.

The abduction group was short one man. James Heatherington had dropped behind just before the group had passed through the city's main gate. He headed directly to Pennywhistle's headquarters, distressed to find that Maxwell, the man with whom he had worked, was gone.

Upon his urgent representations to the four soldiers that now guarded the mansion's front entrance, he was immediately shown to Pennywhistle's presence.

"Heatherington? What on Earth are you doing here? You are the last person I expected to see."

"I am doing the job you gave me, Sir Thomas, to spy on Lord Maxwell. I wish I could have made it here before the abduction, but joining Maxwell's escort was the only way I could leave the estate without arousing suspicion."

"So, Lord Maxwell is behind the abduction!" thundered Pennywhistle.

"Yes, he is, and I know exactly where he is taking Sally. It's a groundskeeper's cottage, at the far northern edge of the Paxton Estate."

"Excellent! Mr. Maxwell is leading the pursuit. As an assistant Ghillie, do you know of any small path that might provide a faster route to the cottage than the main road? One that might allow Mr. Maxwell to arrive before the abductors?"

"Yes!"

"Good! I want you to mount up immediately and ride after Mr. Maxwell. I want him and his men waiting in ambush when the abductors arrive."

"I shall be happy to, but before I depart, I want to give you this." He handed Pennywhistle a large bag.

Pennywhistle opened the bag and noted that it was full of small notebooks.

"What are these?"

"The diaries of Lord Maxwell's brother, Charles. I believe Maxwell had him murdered but I cannot prove it. If you look through the diaries carefully, you will find enough evidence to formally charge Lord Maxwell with a variety of crimes. Charles states in the diary for the year 1801 that Lord Maxwell murdered his wife. He was standing in the shadows and witnessed the whole thing."

"His son has suspected that for many years. Finally, he will have proof." Pennywhistle looked Heatherington in the eye. "If these diaries contain what you say, they are an answer to my prayers. When this Border business is wrapped up, I shall see that you are handsomely rewarded. Now, be off!"

"Right, Sir Thomas!" Heatherington touched his hat in salute and was gone.

Pennywhistle opened the diary of 1801 and quickly found the entry that described the murder of Lady Maxwell. It was exactly as Heatherington had said, making it likely that what he had stated about the diaries containing evidence of other crimes was true as well. He would have liked nothing better than spending the next several hours examining the diaries in detail, but he had to act before Maxwell left the party. He relished the idea of arresting Maxwell and doing it at a party would add to his embarrassment. It was also a way to show the guests that no man was above the law, no matter how distinguished his pedigree.

Sammie Jo and Sarah hailed Pennywhistle as he left his office.

"Thank God, Sally is safe!" exclaimed Sarah. "But she is sobbing her heart out. She says you must get her friend Jane back."

"Have no fear, Mr. Maxwell is chasing Jane's abductors as we speak. I anticipate that she will be back in this house by tomorrow morning."

"Thank God!"

"I also know who arranged the kidnapping."

"Let me guess," replied Sammie Jo. "Lord Maxwell."

"Exactly. I finally have enough proof to arrest him. I have the written equivalent of a deathbed confession."

"Where did you get it?"

"One of my informers. From the documents he brought me, I believe Maxwell is guilty of two murders, his wife and his brother."

"Murdering his own kinfolk!" exclaimed Sammie Jo, "A man can't get any lower than that."

"I would welcome the chance to watch his execution," said Sarah contemptuously. "My husband never liked him and frequently said he belonged at the end of a hangman's rope."

"It's time that we stop talking and start handing out justice. C'mon, Tom. Let's go make an arrest!"

***

The two Heatheringtons rode like madmen but in opposite directions: Angus rode toward Berwick while James rode away from it. The strange weather that had been plaguing Britain was on full display; the burnt orange snowfall had gone from flurries to severe snow in a matter of hours. It had turned from powdery flakes into wet, heavy stuff and the wind had kicked up. The result stopped just short of whiteout conditions, but visibility was still only a few yards.

Because of the weather, Angus could only manage a slow trot. He estimated he could make Berwick just after 11.

Angus's last memory of the column was an ill ordered formation of angry men, grumbling loudly as they marched. The snow that was slowing his horse, would also slow marching men, giving the defenders of Whistlestop more time to prepare. He wanted a hot meal and a bed badly, to fight off the hunger and fatigue that grew with each passing moment. But each time those thoughts intruded, he reminded himself of the innocents at Whistlestop and thrust those hopes aside.

James Heatherington rode for twenty minutes before he located Maxwell's men. They were frustrated that they had located The Trojan Horse but had found no sign of any abductors. Heatherington told them where the abductors were headed, and Maxwell formed his men into a long line that followed Heatherington's lead. The paths that he led them on were narrow and winding; they would have been hard to find in good weather and nearly impossible in bad.

A half hour's ride brought them to the cottage, a modest structure of stone with a thatched roof. Maxwell had his men dismount and position themselves in the woods just south of the cottage. They tethered their horses to trees twenty yards to the rear. The heavy snow might be a problem because moisture was the enemy of gunpowder, so Maxwell told his men to keep their pistols holstered and warned them they might have to rely on their swords.

"Before you do anything, let me talk to these men, Mr. Maxwell," pleaded Heatherington. "I know them. They are not bad souls. They were all coerced into this. Give them a chance to surrender peacefully."

"Very well, Heatherington. You have shown yourself to be reliable and have good instincts. The Warden we both serve seeks reconciliation, and our primary objective is to rescue the girl and that requires special care. But at the first sign of trouble, I will not hesitate to unleash the fury of my men. Is that understood?"

"Perfectly, Mr. Maxwell."

***

Peter Postle reached the gates of Berwick while Maxwell's men settled in for what they hoped would be a short wait. Postle had debated whether to wait until the following day to deliver his information, but every time he thought of his sister's rape and murder the awful weather became nothing more than a trifling annoyance.

When he reached the Pennywhistle mansion and dismounted, he was immediately confronted by four soldiers who treated him with the greatest suspicion. They grilled him relentlessly, which puzzled him until one explained what had just happened. It took fifteen minutes of heated expostulation to convince the soldiers to let him see the Warden, but even then, they told him he would have to wait outside, until the Warden said he was ready to receive him.

While he was waiting, a breathless Angus Harrington arrived. He was treated with equal suspicion and explained the importance of his mission with equal fervor. A soldier conveyed his message to Pennywhistle and returned five minutes later. "The Warden will see you both in ten minutes."

Pennywhistle strode into a ballroom full of men and women whose mood was anxious and confused, in contrast to the gaiety, color, and extravagance of their attire. All eyes turned toward him. Since he was accompanied by two stern-faced soldiers with pistols drawn, the crowd quickly grasped that this was not a social call. Sammie Jo and Sarah walked briskly behind the guards.

The crowd parted in front of him and watched with surprise as he strode straight toward Lord Maxwell. Maxwell's face reflected surprise as well.

Maxwell summoned a fake smile, extended his hand, and spoke in a voice that sounded like warm butter. "Warden Pennywhistle, it is a great pleasure to meet you. I have heard so much about you. I am so sorry for what has happened to your niece."

Pennywhistle declined the hand and spoke his response with the firm tones of the lawman doing his duty. "The pleasure is most assuredly not mutual, my lord. I have heard a great deal about you as well, most of it negative. This evening, I received information that confirmed my worst suspicions. I am placing you under arrest for the murder of your wife, Lady Carol Maxwell. I believe you are also guilty of the murder of your brother Charles Maxwell, and I intend to have your Paxton estate searched for his body."

Maxwell started in shock and clutched his chest hard.

Pennywhistle produced a newfangled invention, handcuffs. He jerked Maxwell's arms down and out, then slapped the twin bands around Maxwell's wrists.

The crowd gasped.

Maxwell looked at his imprisoned wrists with disbelief. "This is insane, Warden. I have done nothing wrong. Whatever the information you have, I assure you that it is false. Let us go someplace private and settle this unpleasantness like gentlemen." His voice came out a mixture of a rasp and a wheeze.

"The only place you are going this evening, my Lord, is a holding cell. I will speak to you at my convenience, when I will present a formal bill of indictment. I will send a copy of that bill to your solicitor, and he can do with it as he wishes. I hope he knows a good barrister to argue your cause in court because the case against you is airtight."

"This is outrageous, ridiculous!" sputtered Maxwell. "I have many friends in London, and when they hear of this travesty, they will demand my immediate release." Maxwell glared at Pennywhistle. "I guarantee you, Sir, that I will make you regret this event to the end of your days."

Pennywhistle's voice turned icy. "I too have many friends in London, but with a difference. Mine will stand by my actions whilst yours will likely abandon you when they understand the gravity and extent of your crimes. Be advised that the murder I am charging you with is only the first of many felonies that I intend to hang around your neck. I believe that you are also responsible for the kidnapping of... Sally Pennywhistle. I am sure it will surprise you that your men kidnapped the wrong girl. A rescue is underway as we speak, and I have no doubt that it will be successful."

Maxwell's face looked stunned as well as guilty. "You can't do this! You can't!" Maxwell's voice had changed from defiant to pleading.

"I can and I will. This conversation grows tiresome, and I have more pressing matters that need my attention." Pennywhistle turned to the soldiers. "Take him away. The head turnkey at the Berwick Jail will know exactly what to do with him."

The two soldiers grabbed Maxwell by the arms. He struggled briefly but stopped when one of the soldiers slapped him hard in the face. The soldiers frog marched the dazed prisoner from the ballroom amidst the looks of stunned disbelief from the crowd.

Pennywhistle turned to the partygoers, his heart in his stomach because he had failed to prevent an abduction that he had long anticipated. He pushed his despondency aside and spoke as confidently as he could. "I am sorry for all the unpleasantness tonight, and I will make every effort and to ensure that the kidnapped girl will be back in this house before dawn, safe and sound. There is plenty of food and drink and you are all welcome to stay until she is returned. I will have the orchestra play to soothe jangled nerves. I have alerted the coachmen outside that some of you might wish to depart directly."

The crowd looked at each other in shock and uncertainty. Shock that a man they completely trusted had let them down, and uncertainty about whether to stay or go. A host of whispered conversations arose as couples debated what to do.

At that moment, Sally Pennywhistle appeared by her uncle's side. It was clear that she had been crying, but she summoned a look of steely resolve and spoke to the partygoers in a voice that was mature beyond her years. "Please, please, everyone, stay. I see fear and doubt in your eyes, but I have every confidence that my uncle will bring my friend back unharmed. I would like to talk to every one of you. I know we can't have a proper coming out ball, but that does not mean that you cannot get to know me."

Pennywhistle realized that the party could now furnish the chance for a coming out of a different kind; one that would showcase Sally's character rather than her social status.

The orchestra leader chose that moment to commence playing Mozart's *Solemn Vespers*; the pure divinity of the work enfolding the crowd in a comforting embrace and exuding a calming influence.

Sammie Jo and Sarah joined Pennywhistle and Sally. "Leave this to the women, Tom," whispered Sammie Jo. "We three will calm things down while you go about your business."

"Are you sure?" responded Pennywhistle. "I have failed these people miserably and I feel I have to do something to put things right."

"Positive. We three will circulate and explain that you had to leave because there may be other threats to the city and that you need to attend to them. We will make it clear that the safest course for them is to stay right where they are. Now go!"

Pennywhistle looked dubious.

"Trust us," said Sally.

"The crowd will come round," offered Sarah.

The three did not wait for Pennywhistle's response but moved confidently into the crowd, beginning the process of greeting and reassuring. Pennywhistle had seldom felt so low but realized he was out of his depth and accepted that they could do what he could not. He quietly exited the room and walked briskly to his office.

"Gentlemen," Pennywhistle said, addressing Postle and Heatherington, "come inside, but understand that my time is limited because events are moving quickly. I will give each of you ten minutes to explain yourselves. Choose your words wisely and waste not a second of my time. Is that understood?"

"Yes," said Postle.

"Perfectly." said Heatherington.

The two men glared at each other.

Pennywhistle asked Heatherington to speak first because he knew him, while he had had never met Postle, though his manner suggested that he was reliable. The next twenty minutes flew by, and Pennywhistle was amazed by what he heard. Heatherington's information demanded that he move quickly, but Postle's meant that if he won the battle ahead, Scott could be formally charged and eventually be lawfully executed. That was assuming that Scott would be present of course, which was not guaranteed. He seemed a man content to leave his dirty work to others, while he sat safe in some unknown sanctuary.

"I am grateful for the information, gentlemen. Mr. Postle, you may remain here. My men will find you food and quarters. Mr. Heatherington, you look like you need a hot meal and plenty of rest, and I will be happy to provide it."

"True, Warden, but I would still like to come with you. A quick meal and a fast catnap will do the trick. I believe I can be of help. Scott's men will listen to me. I think many of them do not really want to fight."

"If some of Scott's men might be willing to defect, that would indeed reduce the butcher's bill. But are you sure you are up to it?"

"Sir Thomas, the prospect of ending this Border misery once and for all is a powerful tonic for fatigue. I promise I will not let you down."

"I will give you one hour to get ready. I need that time to review some maps, assemble my kit, and issue the proper orders. If you cannot make that deadline, I will not think the less of you."

Pennywhistle did not wait for an acknowledgement. His blood was up, and his mind was awash with plans and possibilities. He quickly exited the office and proceeded to issue an order to William Smithers, the most intelligent of his household soldiers. "Listen carefully, I want you to commit this to memory and then take the fastest mount in the stables and convey this message to Yeoman Thornton at his quarters. He is the fastest rider among the Yeomanry with the best chance of getting through this abominable weather. I told him a week ago to hold himself in readiness for the errand on which I shall now dispatch him. Are you ready?"

"Willing and eager, Sir."

"Proceed with all possible speed to Whistlestop. Warn Sergeant Major Masters, Maude Dacre, and Nico Ruzzini that they can expect an attack sometime in the next twelve hours. Tell them to rouse every inhabitant, ready every defense, and raise their state of alert to its highest level. I shall depart Berwick with a relief force within the next two hours. I will assume command upon my arrival, but until then Sergeant Major Masters and Mr. Ruzzini will be in charge, and they are free to use their discretion to handle all emergencies that may arise. Have you got all that?"

Smithers repeated the message word for word.

Pennywhistle walked briskly to the map room, wanting to make sure that he had not missed some mostly unused paths that might give him a way to spring an ambush. Fifteen minutes later, he had devised a complete plan of attack.

"Man proposes but God disposes." The old aphorism seemed appropriate because the weather was the wild card in his plans. He debated whether to wait a few hours to see if the weather would moderate, then decided that the greed of his opponent would cause him to push on, regardless of how bad things were. He could do no less. His men were better trained than Scott's and their superior discipline would enable them to better endure the foul weather.

He made some calculations. It was eight miles to Whistlestop. The normal rate of advance for cavalry was six miles an hour, and the rate for infantry was two miles an hour.

The weather would likely cut that in half. He checked his watch; two minutes after midnight. If he could get his force ready to move by 1 am, his cavalry could be at Whistlestop by 4, and his infantry by 9. It would be a punishing ordeal and would reduce their efficiency once battle was joined. Then he reminded himself that the same would be true for Scott's men, but their efficiency would be reduced far more drastically.

It was time to roll the dice.

***

Maxwell's men waited only twenty minutes before Jane's abductors showed up. The snow was falling fast and hard, and it was difficult to see much of anything. Maxwell saw moving shapes rather than people. Maxwell waited until he could discern the men unloading a bundle that he thought was the girl. "Stop right there. You are all under arrest!" He yelled it with the full force of his lungs, but the wind made his demand hard to hear.

The men carrying the girl stopped in surprise and looked in his direction. Maxwell shouted his demand a second time, and this time the men set the girl down and put their hands up. Maxwell advanced on them with his sword drawn, Heatherington at his side. Maxwell's men took their cue from their leader and advanced as well. They were angry and menacing: the Galahad in each roused by the specter of an innocent girl brutalized by brigands.

Heatherington shouted, "You know me! Do just what he says, and you might live."

The abductors recognized Heatherington's voice, and their faces showed that they believed him.

Maxwell stopped a foot from the hostage- takers. "If any harm has come to that girl, you will all hang."

The abductors quivered in fear. "We haven't hurt her at all. She is fine, just groggy from the drug we used," sniveled one man who appeared to be their leader.

"Heatherington," said Maxwell, "take a look at the girl and tell me if this man is speaking the truth."

Heatherington did as he was ordered. He examined the girl and found no marks or bruises. He cradled her in his arms. "Where am I?" She whispered, half awake.

"You are safe now," said Heatherington tenderly. "We will get you back to Berwick faster than you can imagine, and you will soon be sleeping in a warm bed."

"That sounds goo..." The girl fell back to sleep.

Maxwell spoke harshly. "It would be far more efficient if I just executed you miscreants and saved myself the trouble of escorting you back to Berwick for trial. But Heatherington says you were forced into it and has pleaded for your lives."

"We were forced into this! I was told my son would be killed if I did not cooperate."

"I was against this from the start, but my daughter was threatened."

The other two abductors bobbed their heads vigorously in agreement with their mates.

"I will stake my life that they are telling the truth," Vowed Heatherington.

Maxwell had no intention of executing these men, but he had wanted to test their sincerity.

"Very well, I will spare your lives, with the proviso that you will testify in court against the man who put you up to this."

"Yes, yes, yes!" chorused the men.

"Consider my mercy an early Christmas present. Now let's get the girl inside the cottage. I presume there is food and drink within; enough to revive her for the journey back to Berwick."

"Oh yes," said one of the men. "The cottage has provisions for two weeks. I can cook up enough vittles right quick to feed you and your men as well. I make a damn good stew."

"Then do so at once. It is imperative that we get back to Berwick as quickly as possible. Heatherington, see to the girl."

"With pleasure, Mr. Maxwell."

Maxwell wondered where Pennywhistle was just now. He was annoyed that his mission prevented him from being at the side of the man who had done so much to save his soul. He hoped that situation could be remedied in the next few hours.

***

Maude Dacre received Pennywhistle's message just after 2 am. Considering the weather, the rider had made exceptionally good time. Before taking acting on his message, she fed the man a bowl of stew from the cauldron that she always kept warm, and a cup of coffee from a pot that she heated in the embers of last night's fire. She sent word to Nico and Masters to come to the kitchen forthwith, then asked messenger for clarification of the situation in Berwick. He gave her an honest appraisal and most of what she heard was not unexpected.

Maude was not caught off guard because she, Nico, and Masters had been planning for an attack for a week. All the inhabitants of Whistlestop, as well as its garrison, knew the details and had been sleeping with one eye open for that same period. It was as if a stage had been prepared and all the actors had learned their parts. Two dress rehearsals had been performed the previous week and today would be opening night. But unlike a play, if the actors did well there would be no demand for a second performance.

Maude sped up the steps to the tower's roof and rang the alarm bell vigorously. That done, she raced down the stairs and met with Nico and Masters who had just arrived on her doorstep. She told them what the rider had said and the three went over a few last-minute details.

The response to the alarm was only slightly inferior to the speedy one of the Minutemen of Massachusetts, and soon the entire population of the estate had assembled in the courtyard. Maude mounted a small stage, along with Nico and Sergeant Masters. Three large bonfires that had been built the previous week were lit to provide illumination and warmth. Since Maude represented both the soul and voice of the estate, all eyes fixed on her.

"A large force of Reivers is on their way here as we speak. Sir Thomas will be departing from Berwick shortly with reinforcements. After today, we will be able to live in peace and will no longer have to behave as slaves to fear!"

A loud cheer went up, then everyone quietly went to work. All the ingredients and stores necessary were in place and ready to go.

Maude's daughters and two of their friends soon brought four cauldrons filled with stew to the boil, as well as an additional one containing coffee. Maude trusted that she had a few hours before the enemy arrived and wanted everyone to have a hot meal and a stimulating beverage before venturing into the cold winter's night. The inhabitants formed a line leading into the kitchen, each person armed with a trencher plate, spoon, and tin cup. Maude dished out the stew, while her friend Mary Loxley poured the coffee. Maude and Mary both offered words of encouragement as they performed their jobs. It took thirty minutes to feed everybody, but from the satisfied looks that her friends gave her, Maude considered it time well spent. When each person departed, he or she was issued a stout wool blanket that could be used for additional protection against the cold.

The soldiers collected their weapons, loaded their cartridge boxes with sixty rounds, and proceeded to their positions. Forty soldiers manned each of the two lunettes, while forty more manned each of the twin redoubts. The remaining ten crewed the two howitzers that had been posted on a small rise of ground, just to the rear of the redoubts. The rise was slightly higher than the terrain on which the lunettes and redoubts had been built so the guns could freely sweep the approach road to Whistlestop.

Most of the soldiers who manned the fortifications had never seen action, but the men commanding them had endured plenty of it. Sergeant Major Masters commanded Lunette One, Sergeant Grant Lunette Two, and Sergeant Meadows Redoubt One. All three were veterans of the Peninsula as was Sergeant Mason, who would command Redoubt Two. The two howitzers were under the control of Corporal Carstairs who years before had served as a member of the Royal Artillery.

Nico spoke to Masters once all the soldiers were in position. "I think we can hold them. What about you?"

"I agree completely. This is where our training pays off. This fight will be as it should be, with my men bearing the brunt of the battle, and the citizen soldiers acting as a reserve. If Sir Thomas arrives in time, we can wipe these scoundrels off the face of the Earth. Now comes the hardest part."

"What's that?"

"The waiting."

Ruzzini nodded in agreement, thinking back to his experience with pirates on Sumbawa. He had felt doubts then about the part he had to play but this time he felt none.

Mary Simmons had been placed in charge of issuing cartridges to the civilians, along with her soon-to-be husband Toby Scoggins. Scoggins had proposed to her the week before and she had accepted on the condition that the wedding not take place until Whistlestop was safe. The people of the estate liked Scoggins and given his military experience, they were happy that Masters had chosen him to advise Mr. Ruzzini on the command of the civilians.

All people capable of wielding a weapon had been issued a musket. Those too old, too young, or too infirm to fight would act as messengers, powder monkeys, or gun loaders.

Masters had divided the civilians into three divisions. The first would man the upper floors of the tower, the second the outbuildings in front of the tower, the third would line the curtain wall around the courtyard. He knew them to be good people, but he also knew their limitations. They did not have to fight well, they merely had to fight.

Harvey Ross and Ronald Peters, the two teenagers judged to have the best eyesight of anyone on the estate, would man the lookout peak. They had each been issued a Congreve Rocket; to be lit the moment they sighted any intruders.

Joan and Claire Johnstone manned the far-left section of the curtain wall. Their sister had been murdered by the Reivers and their father had been cruelly used by them. Their father had been too badly injured to fight but would reload their muskets and pass them ammunition.

"I am looking forward to this. I want my pound of flesh, I want my revenge," said Joan.

"I do too," said Claire. "We'll show 'em that girls can fight just as well as boys."

"If anything happens to me, I want you to..."

"Shut up Joan, you are going to come through this just fine. We all are!"

The Thornton boys posted next to them heard the exchange. "Hey Claire, I bet we two will kill twice as many of the Reivers as you two," said Giles Thornton in a cheerful boast.

"Five pounds says you are wrong," answered Claire. "Are you man enough to accept the wager?"

"You're on!" replied his brother Oliver.

Private Marsden spoke to his friend Private Morgan as both took up their positions on the fire step of Redoubt One. "This should be where we get to see just how well our marksmanship training works, but I can hardly see anything."

"I am not sure it will matter today," replied Morgan. "The road narrows twenty yards ahead. If we shoot fast and low, we should be able to do our jobs just fine. And the enemy will be even worse off. With all the snow and earth in front of us, we will be very difficult to spot. We are 12 feet above the road so it's likely that when they elevate their pieces, they will fire too high. I think we are nearly as safe here as the barracks in Berwick."

His friend cast a cynical glance at him.

"Well, almost as safe."

Alan Maitland and Strata Smith both possessed considerable mechanical skills and had cooperated to create two curious infernal devices. They were barrels of powder with flintlock mechanisms attached. Those mechanisms were attached to a tripwire. When the tripwire was touched, the flintlock would fire, and the barrels would detonate. Smith had gotten the idea from a story that he had heard about Sir Thomas' brush with death. His horse had stepped on a similar one in America, and he had been blown sky high. By some miracle he had survived the experience. Smith did not believe the victims of his devices would enjoy a similar divine protection.

Smith and Maitland placed the barrels in the center of the approach road but did not have to worry about burying them, since the fast-falling snow could cover them completely in a very short time. The two stretched their trip wires across the road and attached them to the base of two tree stumps.

"This should give the Reivers a nasty slap in the face," said Maitland.

"Better than that, these should stop them cold. Their screams will provide the men in the redoubts with targets, even if they cannot see what they are shooting at."

"If we are lucky, we might remove a dozen or so Reivers at a single stroke."

"Even if it's just five or six, we will completely wreck their marching order."

Tad Simmons, a man of ancient body but combative temperament, had been placed in charge of the improvised powder magazine that was housed in a newly reconstructed barn. He knew he would not have much to do since no one thought the fight would be a long one requiring the issuance of more powder. Mostly his job was to see that the powder stayed dry. That did not require any work since the new roof showed no signs of leaks. He took out his knife and began to whittle. If only he had been twenty years younger, he knew he would have killed more Reivers than any man on the estate.

The most pitiable person on the estate was a girl of 13 named Judy Siddons. She had completely abandoned her assigned task and had hidden herself in the far corner of a barn. She sobbed and shook, hoping that the world would go away. Her small spaniel tried to offer her comfort by licking her hand in sympathy, but she barely felt his tongue.

Even the children had parts to play. Daniel Richardson and his cousin Polly were both only seven years old, but they had been placed in charge of keeping the tower's barnyard livestock calm: the cows, chickens, and pigs had been herded into a large corral at the rear of the courtyard. All were mooing, clucking, and oinking.

"They're scared, just like I am," said Polly.

"I am, also," replied Daniel. "But have no fear; I shall protect you."

"That makes me feel better, but who is going to protect them?" said Polly pointing to the cows.

"I don't know, but maybe that passage we learned in Sunday School will cover it."

Polly gave him a puzzled look.

Daniel smiled gently. "The part of the Good Book where it says that God gives special blessings to the beasts and the children."

CHAPTER 15

Accounts not Quite Settled.

17th December 1816

Scott's advance toward Whistlestop ground to a halt at 8 am.

"The men must have a few hours rest, Mr. Scott," pleaded Lefebvre. "Between straggling and desertions, we have lost one third of our force, and it will only get worse if we do not rest. Since it's stopped snowing, the men should be able to clear a few spots for camp fires. A hot meal would do wonders for them."

"But the weather is finally clearing, Lefebvre," scolded Scott. "Sunrise is only half an hour away and we will have fair weather for battle. We only have four miles to go."

"For men exhausted to the point of collapse it might as well be four hundred! I will settle for an hour's rest for my men, without camp fires."

"Very well, but one hour and no more. I do, however, want you to send out scouts to conduct a reconnoiter of our objective."

"I shall do that immediately, Mr. Scott."

***

Pennywhistle reached Whistlestop as the top of the sun peaked above the horizon. Unlike Scott, he had halted his men for two hours during the worst of the storm. A grove of trees that shielded them from the weather's worst effects and validated his last-minute decision not to split the infantry and cavalry.

His arrival was greeted with cheers and a collective sigh of relief. The soldiers stayed in their fortifications, but most of the civilians raced toward his horse, greeting him like he was the second coming. He welcomed their enthusiasm because it was evidence of high morale. He made a few obligatory remarks of praise and hope, then told the crowd to return to their posts. Maude, Nico, and Masters appeared and suggested they convene an informal counsel of war in Maude's kitchen. He agreed but first gave orders to his troops.

Angus Heatherington was glad that no one recognized him from his previous visit. He was grateful for the chance to make amends for his bad behavior. The never say die spirit that he felt from the people who thronged around Pennywhistle impressed him, and it confirmed his wisdom in wanting to be part of their fight.

Pennywhistle ordered his cavalry to a position at the rear of the tower's curtain wall; the small pasture was just large enough to accommodate their horses. He told the men they would receive their final orders shortly, and that they should use the time to feed and water their horses and grab a quick bite to eat from the contents of their haversacks. Sally's party had generated a lot of leftovers, and the choicest morsels had been donated to his men. He had his infantry fall out and commence eating.

He dispatched four Yeoman trained as scouts to examine the main road leading to Whistlestop for any signs of the enemy.

"I am pleased with your dispositions; you have made good use of the forces at your disposal," said Pennywhistle as he examined the map prepared by his council of war.

"Thank you, Sir Thomas, I think the three of us make a very efficient team," responded Nico.

"I have to confess that I am surprised we have not been attacked," said Masters.

"It is just possible that our opponent has done the sensible thing and ordered his men to stand down because of the weather. But...I think that is unlikely. His gold fever will eventually get the better of him. Now that the sky has cleared, I would estimate that he will arrive sometime before nightfall. But before we make any further plans, we will need to hear what the cavalry scouts have discovered."

"I think everything is shipshape and Bristol fashion, Sir Thomas. With your men, mine, and the civilians, we will have close to 500 men," said Masters. He pointed to the map. "There is a road that a child named Polly showed me that has interesting possibilities. Well, it's more of a cow path, but I think our men could adapt."

Pennywhistle rubbed his chin in thought. "I see what you mean. Perfect for a flanking movement. I have an informant who has told me that my opponent has roughly 1,000 men, so we will be outnumbered 2-to-1. My informant also told me that the men we will face are not fully trained and that their morale is indifferent. And we will have the advantage of position as well as artillery. When Scott attacks, he will metaphorically thrust his head into a sack. All we must do is choke off the sack at its base."

"Speaking of heads," said Maude. "I should like to see Scott's put on a pike outside the entrance to this estate. I think everyone else here feels the same. It would show the world what happens when you trifle with the people of Whistlestop."

"I should prefer to take Scott alive."

Pennywhistle was met with looks of surprise and shock. "Whatever for?" asked Nico.

"Only at a public trial will the full evidence of his crimes become known. The trial will also reduce him from a great criminal lord to an ordinary scoundrel who is nothing special. After all the chaos in this region, the public needs to know that the rule of law has been firmly reestablished, and that vigilante justice will no longer be tolerated. In a way it will be a suitable final chapter in the story of the Reivers that harks back to the 1300s. Like a good novel, the ending will be unexpected yet plausible and satisfying. Rather than the story ending with a bang, it will end with a whimper."

"A novel? Hmm. I had never thought that we have been living fodder for fiction these past few months," observed Maude.

"I think you all may become better known throughout the kingdom than you ever expected. The Correspondent for *The Times* wants to write a book about what has happened here and the people who brought it about. She wanted to accompany me, but I ordered her to stay back in Berwick until it was safe to come here. Her last book about Waterloo was a best seller, and I expect that one full of the human drama of this place will do nearly as well."

"Would that be Deborah Dale?" exclaimed Maude.

Pennywhistle nodded.

"Oh my god! I read her Waterloo book!"

There was a knock at the kitchen door. Maude walked over and opened it, confronting a soldier with an unsettled look on his face. "I have a message for Sir Thomas."

Pennywhistle rose and faced the soldier, "Well, what is it? I did not expect to be disturbed."

"Your wife just rode into the courtyard, Sir Thomas. She has that lady correspondent with her.

"Damn and blast! I told them both to stay in Berwick."

"Looks like I am going to get to meet Mrs. Dale a lot sooner than expected," said Maude.

Pennywhistle turned back to the soldier. "Tell both that I want to see them here. Immediately!"

"Very good, Sir Thomas," replied the soldier, who quickly disappeared.

"Head strong women," snapped Pennywhistle, "you can't live with them, and you can't shoot 'em!"

"I know a little something about headstrong women," retorted Maude. "I've been one these past fifty-two years and I think I've done a lot more good than harm."

"I'm not saying that strong women don't do a lot of good, I'm just saying that they are poor at following orders and worse at being predictable. Just when you think you have them all figured out, they prove that you haven't a clue about what makes them tick."

"Forgive me, Sir Thomas," said Nico, "but I think that you may be mistaken. People look up to your wife and want to be like her. The fact that she is willing to endanger her life for the sake of the folks on the estate will make her an inspiration. I think she will have the same effect on them that Good Queen Bess did when she spoke to her men at Tilbury, just before the arrival of the Spanish Armada."

Sammie Jo walked through the door just as Nico finished. "Good Queen Bess. I love the comparison!" laughed Sammie Jo, who turned to face Pennywhistle. "Oh, stuff that anger, Tom, and don't be an old sourpuss. You're stuck with me, and you'll just have to make the best of it."

"But you promised to stay safe, Sammie Jo."

"I know, but Deborah was determined to come, and I couldn't let her go without an escort."

"That's a lame excuse."

"Maybe, but deep down, aren't you glad to have me at your side?"

"Maybe just a little," admitted Pennywhistle grudgingly.

A trooper came running up to the open door, almost out of breath. Pennywhistle recognized him as one of the scouts. "Corporal Craig reporting, Sir. We found Scott's men Sir Thomas! They are on the move and only three miles distant."

"I need a full report," exclaimed Pennywhistle with excitement. "And make it quick!"

Craig's summation of his scout confirmed most of Heatherington's information, but Pennywhistle's guess about the weather reducing Scott's forces was correct. Craig estimated the enemy at around seven hundred. His men had also captured all of Scott's scouts, who confirmed his estimate. As Pennywhistle finished digesting the report, a second soldier appeared in the doorway. "I just spotted two Congreves, Sir Thomas. The hilltop lookouts can see the enemy."

That meant the enemy was now two miles away. "Masters, it's time for you to assume command of the lunettes and redoubts. Nico, you will command the civilians, but I trust you will heed the advice of Scoggins because he has seen a lot of combat and knows the people here better than you."

"Of course, Sir Thomas," replied Nico. "We have a good, shared- command arrangement."

"I will take charge of the reserve and unleash it when the enemy is ripe for a counterstroke. Maude, I think my men will not have much need of your nursing skills, but our enemies will. Now, I must depart and tell Sarn't Major Pyestalker the role for his cavalry."

"Wait; you want me to nurse enemy wounded?" huffed a puzzled Maude.

"Yes! We are not barbarians. It is our obligation to assist them according to the laws of war. Our opponents may disdain those laws, but we are nevertheless bound to obey them. If the Borders are to be made whole again, mercy must play a large role. I think some among those that we will face are lost souls who took a wrong turn and can be rehabilitated with the right combination of understanding and guidance."

"I wish the lot of them would fry in hell," hissed Maude.

"Sorry Maude, but the devil will have to wait until I am done with them. We can continue this discussion after the battle, but for now I need everyone to man their posts."

The three nodded at Pennywhistle, just before he dashed out the door.

He opened the map that Masters had given him when he issued his orders to Pyestalker.

"It's a good plan, Sir Thomas, but that path is narrow, and my men will have to go single file," replied Pyestalker. "It will take at least twenty minutes to negotiate the path and then deploy into a line. I can promise you no aid for that interval."

"That is more than sufficient time to give Scott's men a thorough thrashing. Your primary job is to block Scott's retreat. From what the map indicates, your men should debouch from the woods half a mile to the rear of where Scott's men are presently. Fleeing men who have just received a harsh drubbing will often surrender without a fight when faced by a line of cavalry."

"Forgive me, Sir Thomas, but these scoundrels should be wiped out to a man. If they are unable to resist, so much the better."

Pennywhistle did not like the bloodthirsty gleam in Pyestalker's eye. "This is battle, not butchery, Sarn't M'jr. I want a victory, not a massacre. Any man willing to surrender must be treated as a prisoner of war, not a target for swordsmanship. I want your word that you will follow the laws of war."

"You have it, Sir." Pyestalker's voice and face hinted that he did not really mean what he had just said.

Under other circumstances, Pennywhistle would have relieved him on the spot, but there was no time to spare and Pyestalker was a skilled cavalry commander. "Very well, Sarn't M'jr. Form your men up and begin your advance. Good luck!"

"Thank you, Sir, but my men have skill, so we don't need luck." He saluted Pennywhistle crisply and Pennywhistle returned the courtesy with equal exactitude.

Pennywhistle mounted his horse and rode up to the entrance to Lunette One. He took up a position next to Masters and unfurled his glass. Scott's men were a mile and a half down the road, marching in two columns with four-man fronts. The infantry marched creditably but short of expertly.

No skirmishers or cavalry vedettes preceded the column which he found strange, but he put it down an amateur commander's overconfidence.

Two mounted men led each column, and none of the four matched Scott's description. Pennywhistle guessed that he was at least a mile behind his men, just out of sight; not daring to show himself until the battle was decided. He probably had only left his lair because of the bewitching spell cast by what Pennywhistle knew to be chimaeral gold and gems.

Behind the plodding infantry, followed 75 horsemen at the slow walk. It surprised him that the Reivers, who were famous for their mounted mobility, had so few horses. So much the better for him. Hobblers were small horses while his cavalry had full size mounts that were thoroughbreds: giving his Yeomanry a distinct advantage in a close quarter fight.

"I plan to open fire in twenty minutes, Sir Thomas," said Masters. "Does that meet with your approval?"

"It does. I trust your judgement and ask you to exercise it freely in the fight ahead."

Pennywhistle knew it was important that his presence be seen by all, so he rode slowly toward his next port of call, Redoubt Number One. He spoke briefly with Meadows who perfectly understood his role. It pleased him that Meadow's men looked eager to fight.

He next proceeded to the two howitzers. "How soon do you think you can bring those men on the road under fire, Corporal?"

"Fifteen minutes," said Carstairs. "I have a clear line of sight from here and I have been watching them through my spyglass. At this range, spherical case shot will work best." Spherical Case Shot was better known as shrapnel, named after its inventor Lieutenant General Henry Shrapnel.

"My men have cut the fuses expertly. The shells should detonate fifteen seconds after leaving the barrels. The arc of the shells should send a torrent of lead rain down on the Reivers' heads."

Pennywhistle continued to the courtyard, where he spoke to Nico and Toby Scoggins, after briefly talking with the Johnstone family and the Thornton brothers. "We're ready, Sir." said Nico. "Morale is high, and a lot of the people here are itching to dish out revenge. The only fear some have is that the soldiers will fight so well that they won't have a chance to join in."

"I would second that, Sir Thomas," crowed Scoggins proudly. "My fiancée had her sister murdered and won't rest easy until the road ahead is slick with Reiver blood." His face brightened and a smile creased his lips. "I have a very personal reason for wanting to win. My fiancée won't marry me until the Reivers are finished once and for all."

Though Pennywhistle was glad of the civilian's fighting spirit, he sensed a dangerous undercurrent of smoldering rage that troubled him. It was an all- consuming desire to wipe out those who had repeatedly committed murder and rapine, and it allowed for neither quarter nor mercy, reminding him of demonic possession. While he sympathized to a point, that desire could swiftly spin out of control and could turn victims into replicas of their victimizers. Endless blood vendettas had prevented the unification of Italy, and he wanted to ensure that no Celtic copies ever took root in the Borders. In a way, he was dealing with abused children wanting to violently lash out, and he would have to play the part of the responsible adult.

He paid his final call on the reserve infantry. He formed them up into a single column to facilitate quick movement. He told the hundred men that they would be used to plug any breech, or more likely, exploit any opening presented by the enemy. He spoke a few expected words of encouragement and said he knew he could rely on their professionalism. The men liked being seen as the equal of regulars, since most had been private citizens until recently.

"Three cheers for Sir Thomas," shouted one man who had been a tinsmith two months before. "Hip, hip, huzzah! Hip, hip, huzzah! Hip, hip, huzzah!"

He welcomed the chorus of approval because it showed confidence in his ability, but as usual the men under his command were crediting him with a God like omniscience that he could never in a million years possess.

Boom! Boom! The men marching at the heads of the enemy columns triggered Smith's two landmines. Twenty men fell and the columns stopped in confusion.

Boom! Boom! The howitzers fired. Carstairs judgment about distance, barrel elevation, and fuse length proved excellent. The twin shells exploded fifty feet above the heads of the two columns, killing six and badly wounding a dozen. One of the men killed was Lefebvre, his skull split in half by a shard the size of a man's palm. The men of the columns looked at each other in shock, unable to credit the death of the man who had trained them. Their will wavered dangerously until one sergeant began shouting, "Gold and treasure, gold and treasure!" Greed restored their resolve, but it was strictly a short-term expedient.

After an interval of muddle, a second NCO hectored them back into a semblance of order and the columns resumed their advance, though more slowly than before.

Boom! Boom! Two more shrapnel shells exploded, dowsing the columns with more hot lead. Six men were killed outright and a dozen more lay mewling and puking on the ground.

The columns halted 150 yards from Lunette One. Scott's senior NCOs had determined that the frustrated men had to be given an opportunity to do something, anything, or they would give into an instinct that was strengthening with each passing second: to run like deer pursued by hunters. Their sergeants began transitioning into the men into two lines, in preparation for delivering a volley possibly followed by a bayonet attack. Their movements were slow, halting, and clumsy.

Though the distance was poor for a volley, Masters knew that men were most vulnerable when they were shifting from column to line: neither fish nor fowl. "Fire!" bellowed Masters, and 40 muskets crashed out. His men reloaded quickly and discharged another volley 20 seconds later. A third volley followed 30 seconds later. Half aimed low as instructed, but the rest succumbed to the excitement of first combat and fired too high. Probably one third of their balls found a mark: a high percentage considering the range and the fact that their Brown Besses were smoothbores with only bayonet nubs for sights. Nevertheless, the net effect of the three volleys was to rip several large gaps in the two partly formed lines.

A chorus of groans and ululations rose from the columns. Men looked at each other in disbelief as they realized that they had been lied to about the kind of opposition that they would face. As it dawned on them that their exiguous training was wholly inadequate to the task ahead, a score of them muttered the exact same words. "I didn't sign up for this."

A second after Masters' men had finished, the forty men in Lunette Two fired three volleys of their own, striking the two lines in different places and adding to the carnage. The six volleys had killed and wounded 160 men, and those left untouched milled about in misery and confusion. The wounded rolled and moaned in agony, further disheartening the survivors. The sergeants again chanted, "Gold and treasure, gold and treasure," but its restorative effect was much weaker this time. Two NCOs restored enough order for their squads to discharge ragged volleys, but the remaining men were too bewildered to follow their example.

Two more shrapnel shells burst above the heads of Scott's men and ten more men collapsed. The lines were wavering, barely retaining a semblance of order. Masters knew the warning signs of an impending collapse and sent his fastest runner to Pennywhistle with a suggestion.

Pennywhistle concurred with its conclusions and ordered the men of the two Redoubts forward, to reinforce the efforts of the men in the luncttes. Meadows and Mason moved their men to take up flanking positions at oblique angles to the two lunettes so they could pour in deadly enfilade fire into the flanks and rear of the lines. Three volleys crashed out in just under a minute. Their three hundred bullets felled ninety more men.

Two more shells burst, and thirty more men collapsed. Masters watched through his spyglass and saw that several small groups of men had broken away from the lines and were running in the opposite direction.

Pennywhistle had shifted his position to the high ground just astern of the howitzers. He unshipped his spyglass and drew the same conclusion as Masters. He ordered the reserve column forward.

The musket men fired twice more and Carstairs men lobbed an additional two shells at Scott's men. The enemy lines had fragmented into small knots: a few men stood frozen, while some walked, and some ran towards the rear. One sergeant who attempted to spark a rally by yelling, "gold and treasure, gold and treasure," was bayoneted for his trouble.

Pennywhistle knew this was the decisive moment. He formed the reserve column into a line and ordered a general advance. "Charge bayonets and forward at the quick step!" he shouted as he waved his sword.

His men advanced in a brisk but orderly fashion; bayonets leveled. Masters was an old hand at executing complicated maneuvers quickly and so formed the infantry in his vicinity into two lines which took up positions behind Pennywhistle's advancing reserve.

Pennywhistle galloped to the front of the three lines and again shouted, "forward my heroes, at the quick step!" The men moved smartly; not exactly The Coldstream Guards but good for men who two months ago hardly knew one end of a Brown Bess from another.

The infantry's advance was quick and deadly; a red juggernaut wielding unimaginable power. The remaining fragments of the two lines gaped fearfully at what was coming, and the last vestige of order vanished: Scott's men became a rabble frantically racing to any place but where they were. Many threw down their arms to speed their escape. Pennywhistle expected to round up the rabble in short order and compel their surrender.

The furious actions of enraged civilians destroyed Pennywhistle's plans. Ignoring Ruzzini and Scoggins commands to hold in place, the people of Whistlestop grabbed their weapons and raced forward to join the fast-moving redcoats. It was a mad rush, with every civilian acting as his own general. Even the children joined in, not understanding but caught up in the fevered excitement. The civilians had no bayonets for their muskets, but many had grabbed scythes, picks, and pitchforks as substitutes, and were brandishing them wildly as they ran. They screamed and shouted as they surged forward, a collective insanity transforming even youngsters into homicidal maniacs.

The estate mob soon reached the rear of the redcoat lines. By now, all of Scott's men were running in retreat, their backsides presenting juicy targets for the predatory instincts of people lusting for revenge. The mob's insanity was infectious. Urged on by the shouts, curses, and cheers of the crowd, the redcoats abandoned their measured advance and broke into a run. While the redcoats had no special animus toward the Reivers, the mass hysteria overwhelmed their discipline and made them one with the enraged civilians.

The combined mob quickly caught up with the enemy and began a mad orgy of stabbing, thrusting, slashing, and gutting.

Pennywhistle shouted for everyone to stand down, but his men and the civilians were so bewitched by bloodlust that he might as well have been shouting into a hurricane. He witnessed Mary Simmons club a man four times with a musket butt, a feral smile blossoming when she had reduced his face to a bloody pulp that looked only vaguely human. The Thornton brothers beheaded two men with their scythes. The Johnstone girls pitchforked two men in the back, and eighty-year-old Tad Simmons swung an ancient cudgel that crushed the back of a Reiver's skull. Two children stomped their feet violently on the heads of Reivers writhing on the ground.

Two wounded Reivers, on their knees and begging for mercy, had their mouths slashed by May Dacre's long dagger. Her sister Minnie, close behind, clubbed a Reiver into unconsciousness with a stout rolling pin. Their nephew, ten-year-old Wee Willy Robertson, followed in confusion; not understanding why his normally kind aunts had become raging tartars.

The mob's mood was gleeful not grim, and Pennywhistle realized that their uncontrolled butchery represented a collective catharsis of Whistlestop's damaged soul. The redcoats had no such excuse, but madness had its own agenda.

Angus Heatherington watched in horror. He knew many of the men being slaughtered, but realized that if he made any effort to arrest the butchery, the crowd would see him as just another brigand to be slain.

Pennywhistle had served under Wellington and now faced a situation close to what the Iron Duke had faced after the bloody capture of Badajoz on April 6, 1812. His well-disciplined army had degenerated into a mass of mindless marauders and had written one of the darkest chapters in the history of the British Army over the next three days. An orgy of burning, looting, raping, and killing had followed, and it was not until exhaustion seized control that they again heeded Wellington's orders. Pennywhistle's situation was worse in a way because the ringleaders of his mob had never had any military discipline in the first place.

Some of the Reivers fought back hard; determined to take as many of their attackers with them as they could before they gave up the ghost.

Pyestalker spotted the islands of resistance and ordered his men to charge. They began cutting and slashing in the confused melee with a glee that was encouraged by Pyestalker, his eyes ablaze with the fervor of a Spanish Inquisitor reveling in the burning of heretics.

Pennywhistle continued shouting for sanity, but no one paid any attention. His efforts to play the stern lawgiver were being overwhelmed by a tide of raw emotion that was as uncontrollable as the sea itself. He had never felt more impotent and knew he was looking at the start of a massacre. It was at that moment that Maxwell and twenty horsemen galloped up: men who had not been possessed by the insanity. Maxwell had drawn the same conclusion as Pennywhistle. "This must be stopped!"

"Agreed, I want you and your men to follow me in and shout as loudly as they can, 'stand down, stand down, Warden's orders.' Tell your men to use the flats of their swords to force attention and threaten violence to anyone who does not listen."

Sammie Jo galloped up.

"What the blazes are you doing here? I have enough to worry about!"

"I saw what was happening, and I thought I could help. I remembered what that soldier had said about good Queen Bess, and I might just be able play that role now. Sometimes people will listen to a righteous woman even as they ignore a good man. C'mon, Tom, you need all the help you can get."

"I don't have time to argue. Follow me!" exclaimed Pennywhistle. He moved slowly into the swirling melee, slapping people on their backs with the flat of his sword and yelling for them to heed his words. Maxwell and his people waded in next, spreading themselves throughout the crowd. Sammie Jo rode behind, her compelling physical presence and steady voice proving more effective than either Pennywhistle's or Maxwell's efforts. But it was still not enough. The killing slackened but was far from stopping.

Pennywhistle's desperation increased with each passing second. Noticing that Pyestalker was not heeding his commands, he angrily rode up to him. "What's the matter with you? You heard my order, now obey it!"

Pyestalker looked him straight in the eye. "I am the right arm of the Lord and must deliver his vengeance! His will be done!"

Pennywhistle beheld the crazed face of a religious fanatic and knew Pyestalker was beyond reason. He drew his pistol and shot Pyestalker in the forehead. He toppled from the saddle and the crowd paused for a moment.

May Dacre was about to dispatch another Reiver, when her nephew grabbed her wrist, "No, Auntie, no! That's Cousin James! Don't you recognize him?"

May started, realizing that under all the powder grime lay a face she knew. It suddenly hit her that some of the other wounded men could also have relatives among the residents of Whistlestop.

Wee Willie bent down and unstopped his canteen, then pressed it to the wounded man's lips. The wounded man drank desperately. "Never you fear. We're going to help you, Cousin James," whispered the boy. The wounded man stroked the boys head in gratitude and then died. Willie began to sob.

The simple act of kindness made May and Minnie realize the insanity of what they had been doing. The crowd noticed as well. May bent down and took the body of Cousin James tenderly in her arms. She began humming the haunting, melancholy "MacCrimmon's Lament."

A moment later, Minnie began to sing its words in a clear, contralto voice that carried far.

Doon Coolin's face the night is sailing,
The banshee croons her note of wailing;
My blue eyen wi' sorrow are streaming,
For I noo will never return, MacCrimmon

No more, no more, no more, MacCrimmon;
In war nor in peace shall return, MacCrimmon;
Till dawns the sad day of doom and burning,
MacCrimmon is home no more returning
.

Several other women joined Minnie in song as the crowd's mood began to gentle.

The breeze on the bray is mournfully moaning;
The brook in the hallow is plaintively mourning;
But my blue eyen with sorrow are streaming,
For I noo will never return MacCrimmon.

A host of men joined the women, and the rest of the crowd stopped to listen.

No more, no more, no more, MacCrimmon;
In war nor in peace shall return, MacCrimmon;
Till dawns that great day of doom and burning,
MacCrimmon is home no more returning.

Most of the crowd now joined the chorus as the verses were sung a second time: tears of remorse crept into many of the voices. Maude Dacre's soprano voice soared above the rest. Since she was the linchpin of Whistlestop and the greatest fire eater among them, her change of heart had a great impact on the crowd.

The singing broke the killing spell: music truly did have "the power to charm savage breasts, soften rocks, and bend oak." When it stopped, the crowd had resumed at least part of its humanity. Pennywhistle noticed looks of sadness, chagrin, and disgust appearing on many faces, as the mob began to realize what they had done. Some wore looks of confusion and befuddlement, as if terrible spirits had borrowed their bodies and used them to commit awful deeds. Others wore looks of sympathy as they recognized distant family members among people that they had earlier regarded as monstrous brutes. Mary Simmons and the Johnstone girls began to weep. The Thornton brothers threw down their scythes in revulsion, and Simmons vomited. Most of the redcoats looked at their feet in shame, appalled at how completely they had forgotten their training.

Several members of the crowd imitated Wee Willie's actions and gave water and food to wounded relatives and estranged friends. The remainder of the mob did not follow their example, but their mood was beginning to soften.

Sammie Jo trotted over to Pennywhistle. "Do you think the worst is past?"

"I do. The mob is still unsettled and dangerous, but I think that now they can be reasoned with as individuals rather than automatons. A woman's gentle touch is called for: they are far more likely to listen to you and Maude than to me. They will need to see the survivors as people again; fellow countrymen of the Borders gone astray but not beyond hope. That's a lot to ask but I am persuaded that you two can convince them to help the wounded back to Whistlestop where they can be sorted out and cared for. Once that is done, we have some hope of returning this place to normal."

Sammie Jo looked dubious. "That's a tall order, but I can manage it. Now aren't you glad I came?"

"For once, I am glad that you did not listen to me. You truly are my better half."

Maxwell trotted up. "I think that we are out of the woods, but we still have Scott to worry about. I haven't seen or heard of anyone who matches his description."

"Nor have I. My guess is that he is on a very fast horse, heading back toward his lair to grab some money and valuables before fleeing the country. With his army smashed and the information I received from Postle, he is finished."

"Who is Postle?"

Pennywhistle realized Maxwell had no way of knowing about Postle and explained the damning information that he had delivered.

"Then you have more than enough evidence to hang Scott."

"I do."

Deborah came riding up, a troubled look on her face. "This is not the story that I intended to tell. My editors may not want to print the unvarnished truth and might wish me to sugar coat the rougher parts."

"No," said Pennywhistle bitterly. "Tell the story accurately and do not leave out the ugly parts. I would remind you that the story is not yet done. The villain behind all of this remains at large, and the last act of the drama just past has yet to be played out. Whistlestop is about to be turned into a giant hospital, and I think you will see a return of the better natures of its inhabitants once they have a chance to nurse the survivors of their actions."

"You look depressed, Sir Thomas, but none of this was your fault."

"No, a commander must be held accountable for the actions of his men, no matter how far they may stray from what he intended."

A thought hit him, and he blinked and shook his head hard. He cursed himself for being an idiot because he might already have the information needed to pinpoint Scott's whereabouts. His brows knitted, his lips pursed, and his eyes grew dreamy and far away.

Sammie Jo knew what the look of intense concentration portended, and put her fingers to her lips, warning her companions to keep silent until his cogitations were finished.

When he had departed Berwick, he had taken one of the ledger books that Postle had provided, intending to look it over carefully once that battle was done. It covered the financial transactions of Scott's nefarious empire for the past month. He drew it from his saddlebag with mounting excitement, intending to look for any financial transactions that seemed unusual. The problem was he had no idea what was usual, but he had noticed earlier that Postle used three kinds of ink, each denoting a different type of financial activity. Red signified monies owed, black signified monies paid, and blue signified new enterprises. He opened the ledger and began leafing through it, noting that over the past month the amount of red ink greatly outnumbered the amount of black; clear evidence of how much damage Pennywhistle had done to Scott's operation. Entries in blue were few, but one word kept cropping up: Dunbar.

Dunbar was a small port of no great importance on the North Sea, thirty miles North of Berwick. Its harbor was slowly silting up, yet it could still accommodate ships the size of frigates. He began to examine the entries related to Dunbar, and noticed most of the expenditures were for provisions and victuals of the kind you would buy if you were going on a long sea voyage. Then he saw one entry for 8,000 pounds. It had a single word next to it: *Seahorse*. He put the clues together and they pointed to one conclusion, Scott had bought himself a ship and crew. *Seahorse* was his vehicle to flee the country if everything went wrong. Dunbar must be where Scott was headed now.

"I know that Eureka look, Tom," exclaimed Sammie Jo. "You look like you have just discovered how to build a perpetual motion machine."

"I have him, I have him!" shouted Pennywhistle in triumph. "I know where Scott is going! If I move fast, I might just be able to catch him." Pennywhistle quickly explained his deductions to his three companions.

"Hot damn!" bellowed Sammie Jo. "I do believe that you're right. Why don't you let me, Maude, and Maxwell handle things here. I know you don't want anyone else to shoot your fox."

"But I don't want to shoot the fox, I want to hang him. Now I need to round up a posse. I hereby anoint you Good Queen Bess for a day."

"Be careful, Tom. Very careful."

"Since when have I not?"

Sammie Jo laughed. "Pretty much every time you face danger."

He leaned over in his saddle and kissed Sammie Jo. "I promise I shall return unharmed."

"Good luck, Sir Thomas!" shouted Maxwell.

Pennywhistle quickly rounded up his posse, consisting of the five best riders of Pyestalker's command as well as Angus Heatherington. Heatherington knew the roads in the area intimately, and his hatred of Scott was great enough that it overpowered his need for sleep.

The distance from Whistlestop to Dunbar was thirty miles. If Scott used multiple horses and pushed them hard, he could cover the distance in a little over three hours. Pennywhistle and his posse would need multiple horses as well. He explained his problem to Heatherington who knew all the stables in the area.

"There are three stables where you can find good horses. As a Warden, you have the power to commandeer them, since this posse will be engaged in a lawful hot trod."

"I shall be happy to pay for them with chits," responded Pennywhistle. "I don't want any to feel resentful."

Heatherington explained that there were two roads to Dunbar. One was a macadamized turnpike, while the second was little better than a cow path. The second was shorter than the first but would be harder to navigate. Despite his indifferent horsemanship, Pennywhistle chose the second.

The temperature rose as the posse rode, and the snow began to melt. Doubt assailed Pennywhistle as he rode. If he was wrong, Scott might well escape justice entirely.

The hours flew by quickly. Pennywhistle's men knew they had been granted a singular honor and it increased their determination. They did not like changing mounts twice, since each time they received horses that were far from the thoroughbreds that they had started with, but they accepted the necessity of the process.

The posse reached a hilltop above Dunbar just after 1 o'clock. Pennywhistle unfurled his spyglass and spotted a docked ship that was larger than all the others in the harbor. Provisions were being loaded aboard it and there was a high level of activity among the crew: just what you would expect of a ship momentarily intending to set sail. It had to be the *Seahorse.*

He panned his glass along the main road leading into the town and spotted three horsemen galloping hard. Very, very hard, exactly like desperate men fleeing a terrible fate. Pennywhistle spoke to his posse as he pointed to an intersection a block from the docks. "No shooting unless his guards resist; they will be useful witnesses at Scott's trial. Leave Scott to me. Now follow me down, and let's end this damn business once and for all."

The posse moved at a quick trot and reached the intersection a minute before Scott and his men. Pennywhistle split his men into two groups: the first to stop Scott and the second to emerge from the rear, to prevent him from reversing course and put him in an inescapable box.

Pennywhistle waited until Scott was fifty yards away to spring his trap. It all happened so fast that Scott was caught completely off guard. Scott's guards saw the looks on the faces of Pennywhistle's men and made no attempt to reach for their pistols. Pennywhistle trotted up to a white-faced Scott. "I have looked forward to this meeting for a long time, Scott. We are going to get to know each other a lot better in the coming weeks. The public is going to get a chance to get to know you a lot better as well. You will finally get a title and fame, of a sort. *Felon Par Excellance* shall be your title, and you will be known far and wide as the greatest criminal in the land."

Scott sagged in his saddle like a deflated balloon.

"I have all your financial records, and they will be damning evidence in court."

Scott scowled. "That damn stinking Postle. After all I did for him!"

"Murdering a man's sister is hardly a way to make friends."

"I would offer you a bribe Pennywhistle, one beyond your wildest dreams, but from what I have heard you are too stubborn to do the smart thing."

"You seem to think everyone is like you Scott, motivated solely by greed. It must puzzle you that principle is far more important to me than money. And from what I saw of your books, you are hurting badly for money. No wonder you fell for the Flodden Treasure hoax."

"Hoax? Hoax? Whatever do you mean?"

Pennywhistle laughed. "For a clever man you are astonishingly gullible. You fell for one of the oldest confidence tricks in the book: the prospect of buried treasure. Those two objects that you believe came from the treasure, were planted by me."

Scott's jaw dropped and his eyebrows flew skyward. He hyperventilated for half a minute before calming himself sufficiently to speak. "Are you going to permit me a barrister for my trial, or will the whole thing be a sham proceeding?"

"Your trial will be honest, fair, and above board. I will permit you any attorney that you wish, and I will even pay for his services. I want one and all to see that even with the best lawyer, the case against you is so airtight that no amount of legal legerdemain can save you from the hangman's noose. The public must have no doubt that you are guilty of a myriad of crimes. You wanted fame, so take heart. Your trial will likely be the trial of the century. But I am tired of talking. We need to get moving. I am taking you back to Whistlestop before sending you to jail. I want the men that you abandoned to see just how far you have fallen."

Sammie Jo proved a capable queen for a day and worked well with Maude. Whistlestop became a giant hospital, and the wounded received good care. The earlier hatred of the Reivers gradually faded as one and all on the estate pitched in to help with nursing duties: the wounded Reivers slowly changed from hideous monsters to ordinary men. There were two hundred wounded in all, but the majority were so badly hurt that Maude guessed that no more than a third could be saved. Added to the three hundred killed in the battle, the butcher's bill would come to 500.

The two hundred unwounded prisoners were subdued and remorseful. Most felt betrayed by Scott. Maxwell spent the time after the battle speaking with them: the conversations were much more interviews than interrogations because the captives needed little encouragement to tell all they knew, and many freely confessed to crimes. It would take days to interview the lot of them, but from the pattern emerging, it seemed to Maxwell that 80% would be pardoned, 15% transported, and 5% executed.

At three in the afternoon all activity stopped as a joyous event occurred.

"Do you, Tobias Scoggins, take this woman, Mary Simmons, to be your lawful wedded wife?"

"I do."

"And do you, Mary Simmons, take Tobias Scoggins to be your lawful wedded husband?"

"I do."

"Then I pronounce you man and wife." Private Thomas Kane was an ordained Anglican minister who had enlisted in Pennywhistle's forces two months before because he felt that his words from the pulpit were doing nothing to stop the criminality plaguing Berwick. It pleased him greatly that he was performing the happiest of duties, and he hoped that the union would shortly bring new life to an estate that had been cruelly used.

The Johnstone girls produced a flute and a violin and began playing a lively air that demanded dancing. The newlyweds and three other couples responded to the invitation and danced with a lovely madness that made everyone forget what had happened that morning, at least for twenty minutes.

"I feel a lot different right now than I did after *Dispatches'* fight on Sumbawa," remarked Ruzzini.

"How so?" queried Masters.

"On Sumbawa, I felt like what we did was only writing an end to one small chapter in a disagreeable book, but today I feel that we have closed the book on Reiver raiding entirely."

"I think you are right, but I also think it will be a while before the Borders return to the good order that the rest of Britain enjoys. Deep wounds do not heal overnight."

"I agree, but what matters most is we have stopped the bleeding once and for all and can now apply the sutures." Nico looked upwards at the sky, just beginning to cloud over. "I do believe that the strange weather that I encountered in the Indies may have followed me home."

"Do you honestly think that a volcano thousands of miles away could be affecting our present weather?"

"I do."

Just before sundown, Pennywhistle and his posse arrived. The prisoner Scott was met with boos and jeers. Many of his former followers threw rocks at him. Their guards had to flourish their bayonets to keep the prisoners from literally tearing Scott limb from limb. The look of abject humiliation in Scott's eyes pleased Pennywhistle, though he found it ironic that he was saving a villain from a fate that he deserved. He knew that if Maxwell had been in charge he would have turned a blind eye and let rough justice prevail.

It took until midnight for Pennywhistle to settle the thousand and one details that occurred as the result of the fight, and he knew that he would face a thousand and one more on the morrow. He also knew he was looking at a myriad of trials. When he sank into Sammie Jo's arms in the bed that Maude had given over to his use, he felt like he was a thousand years old.

"I'm proud of you, Sugar Plum. You handled things like a master magician, always seeming to have just the right trick up your sleeve."

"That's funny, because I feel like a man given a 100 pounds of bricks to stuff into a 50-pound bag."

"Sounds like you could use a little love to lighten your burden," cooed Sammie Jo as she placed Pennywhistle's hand on her breast.

"That is a splendid idea, Sammie Jo, but right now," his eyelids fluttered, "I am just too damned tired." He put his head on Sammie Jo's shoulder and passed into a deep sleep filled with pleasant dreams.

***

23rd December 1816

The day dawned bright and clear, and the weather had moderated. The mercury stood at forty degrees and most of the snow from the storm four days before had melted, leaving only traces behind. It was a good day to escape the drab routines of the city and do some pleasant exploring in the country. Sally and Marco were determined to do just that, but their exploring had a purpose, seeking the Treasure of

Flodden. They had started searching three weeks before and had gone to Flodden six times, but had found nothing except a lot of mud, rocks, and pieces of broken swords. Most treasure hunters would have gone the way of their innumerable predecessors and given up, but the enthusiasm and optimism of youth was strong in both, and they determined to give themselves until New Year's before they ceased their quest.

Sally might be a fully-fledged debutante now, but she remained a tomboy at heart and her taste for adventure was as lively as ever, while Marco imagined himself as Walter Raleigh reborn and saw Sally as his Queen Elizabeth. Like Raleigh, Marco treated his Queen with gallantry and was honored to assist her in the search for her personal Holy Grail. Both thought his stepfather was wrong in consigning the treasure to the realm of myth.

Both had dressed and equipped themselves sensibly for their adventure. They wore sturdy trousers of heavy grey moleskin, woolen vests replete with pockets, and long aprons of thick leather. Broad brimmed brown hats covered their heads, while stout leather gloves and Wellington boots did the same for their hands and feet. Each carried a small spade and pickaxe, attached to metal hooks that hung from their rucksacks. Passersby would never have suspected that they belonged to the better classes, though today the field of Flodden was completely deserted.

Today was different in one respect from their previous outings. The arrest of Scott meant that they no longer had to be accompanied by armed guards.

Marco and Sally had been systematic in their previous digging, having agreed to divide Flodden into four quadrants. Since the first three had yielded nothing, today's target would be the southwest corner of the fourth quadrant. After tying their horses to a tree, both dismounted.

"I think that spot over yonder is a good place to start digging today, just behind those two boulders," said Marco, pointing his finger.

"Why there?"

"Just a feeling, Sally."

"I think that a spot nearer the small brook to its right would be better."

"Tell you what. Why don't we both play our hunches and see what happens. That doubles our chances of finding something."

"That makes sense. We can make it a friendly competition: my hunch against yours. I think today is the day, Marco. I can feel it in my bones."

"Women's intuition versus man's instincts. How very droll! Then let's be about our work!"

Both smiled at each other, tipped their hats, and began walking toward their preferred digging sites. They had ventured only a hundred yards, when Sally suddenly vanished, as if by a magician's wand.

Marco blinked in astonishment: it was as though the earth had just swallowed her. He rushed forward and discovered that a large sinkhole had replaced the ground that Sally had walked on. He looked into it and saw Sally lying dazed at its bottom, six feet down.

"Are you hurt?" He shouted in fear.

She shook her head twice and looked up. "I do not think so. I don't believe anything is broken."

"I'll be right down and help you out of there."

Sally pulled herself to a sitting position and assessed her surroundings. Her mouth fell open and her heart skipped a beat. "Marco, I see the entrance to a chamber twenty yards to my right. I don't think its natural because I can see marks made by picks."

"You don't think..."

"It could be. Get down here right now!"

Marco leaped down then helped Sally to her feet. They were inside a tunnel that was man made. It was twenty feet long and had five and a half feet of headroom; enough to accommodate the short statured men of 1513. There was a metal door at the end with a padlock, but the little sunlight that penetrated made it hard to see things clearly.

"We're going to need torches."

"And you thought I was silly to include them in our inventory."

"Looks like women's intuition has won our little contest."

They clamored out of the tunnel and raced toward their horses. Each drew a small torch from a saddle bag and lit it with a flint and striker. Its head was covered in pine pitch and burned brightly. They proceeded back to the sinkhole, climbed down, and bent low.

They advanced slowly, their hearts racing, wondering if their quest was at an end. The padlock yielded to one blow from Marco's pick. Sally shoved open the door, and crawled through the narrow entrance, her torch held in front. Four large chests lay in front of her. Their design was centuries old, but they were in good repair. Each had a brass unicorn affixed to its front, a traditional symbol of a Scottish king. They all had rusted padlocks that looked to have remained untouched since they were first put there.

Sally crawled back to Marco, hugged him with one arm, and planted a quick kiss on his lips. "We found them! We've found them!" Her voice rippled with joy and excitement. "But they look very heavy and will be hard to move."

"We can figure that out later."

"I think we owe all of this to the strange weather of the last six months," said Nico. "The tremendous rains have saturated and loosened the soil to the point where sinkholes are possible. I think the storm of four days ago provided the final preparation for this one. All that was needed was the weight of one person to trigger a collapse."

"This is the first time that I have been grateful for awful weather," responded Sally. "Now will you do the honors?"

"With pleasure, Sally."

Marco brought his axe down hard on the lock of one chest and it shattered. Sally and Marco smiled at each other, and both held their breath. Marco pushed the top of the chest open, and his and Sally's eyes were met with a sea of gold coins. Sally picked one up and carefully examined it. It was coin called a groat, worth five pounds in 1513 but a great deal more at present market value. It featured the head of King James on one side, surrounded by the word JACOBUS, Latin for James. The reverse featured a unicorn.

Sally handed the coin to Marco who also examined it. "That unicorn means it was made at the Edinburgh mint. There can be no doubt that these coins are real."

Both laughed loudly in joy, then thrust their hands into the chest trying to get an idea of how many coins it contained.

"I'd say four hundred," remarked Sally.

"I'd say the number is closer to five."

"We can count it all later. Let's open the other chests."

Sally and Marco did so over the next half hour. Chest number two was also filled with groats. Chest number three was as well, but these groats were of silver and so would have a smaller value.

Chest number four proved the most dazzling. It was filled with jewels rather than coins. Most were placed in signet rings, necklaces, stickpins, and broaches heavy with gold and silver inlays. Sally picked up a silver necklace inset with three large rubies and fastened it around her neck. "What do you think, Marco?"

"I think it is a necklace befitting a queen. But this one," Marco reached into the chest and produced a gold necklace with a single large diamond at its center. "Suits you a great deal better. Try it on."

Sally did so and Marco gasped in awe. "That diamond is so bright, that it is nearly blinding."

"It's unfair that I should be the only one with jewels." She reached into the case and grasped a gold signet ring with a large green emerald at its center. "Try it on."

Marco placed the ring on his ring finger, and it was a perfect fit.

"You'd make a great king, but a king should also have this." She reached into the chest and pulled out a gold stick pin in the shape of a unicorn, two small rubies providing the fire to its nostrils. She pinned it to the collar of his shirt and smiled. "It's wonderful, but there is still something missing." She found a large silver broach in the shape of a starburst with a ruby at its center and looked at it closely. "Yes, this is just the thing." She pinned it to the front of his leather apron. "Perfect."

"It's impressive but it doesn't really go with this apron. It's like trying to make a pauper look like a prince."

The two spent the next hour trying on pieces of jewelry, giggling and laughing as they did so. They were living a fairy tale and revealing in a regal version of playing house, but finally common sense prevailed. "How do we get this stuff back to Berwick, Marco? And who should we tell?"

Marco thought for a moment. "I have no idea how to transport it, but I know someone who will: your uncle, my stepfather. He absolutely needs to know. I have an idea. I will stay here and stand guard over the treasure. You will mount up and head back to Berwick. If you push your horse, you can be in Berwick very quickly. It's still early, so I think you can have Sir Thomas back here before nightfall."

"Yes, Marco, that makes perfect sense." She kissed him quickly. "It looks like Christmas has come early this year!" She climbed out of the hole, raced to her horse, and galloped off like a woman possessed.

She made it to Berwick in ninety minutes. Once inside the Pennywhistle mansion she marched to her uncle's office where she was stopped by his military secretary. "Sorry, Miss Sally, but Sir Thomas is busy right now. He is in the process of deciding who is entitled to pardons and left strict instructions that he is not to be disturbed. Perhaps at the end of the day he will be able to grant you a short audience."

"I quite understand." She curtsied politely than made a motion as if she meant to walk away. The secretary nodded then went back to his paperwork. Sally put her head down and ran past his desk. When she reached Pennywhistle's door, she did not bother to knock but shoved it open and plunged through. Pennywhistle looked up in surprise when she appeared in front of his desk like a strangely attired will- o- the wisp.

He put down his pen and looked at her with amusement rather than anger. "Let me guess. You've been treasure-hunting again and wish to beg me for a few soldiers to assist in future expeditions."

"No, uncle! Marco and I found the Treasure. We found it! We found it!" She capered in glee.

Pennywhistle blinked half in astonishment and half in skepticism. "Are you certain? I love you, but you are sometimes prone to exaggeration. Calm down and please tell me exactly what you have discovered."

Sally took a deep breath, reached into her pocket, and took out a pair of silver earrings that featured green emeralds suspended from short chains of gold. She placed them on Pennywhistle's desk. "These are just a sample of the stuff we discovered. We found four chests, and they contained lots and lots of coins and jewels. It's the most fantastic thing that has ever happened to me. You need to drop everything and come with me, so you can see for yourself!"

Pennywhistle realized that he had been so keen on using the myth of the treasure that he had never considered for a moment that the treasure could be real.

"Have you told anyone else of this discovery?"

"No, uncle, I came straight here."

"Good, the fewer people who know about this, the better. We need to keep it that way, but we can let my wife and Mr. Maxwell in on the secret. He rose from his desk abruptly.

"Follow me!"

Pennywhistle proceeded directly to his secretary and told him to cancel all appointments for the remainder of the day. Since he had a full schedule of people demanding his attention, there would probably be many upset with him. He quickly shared the news with his wife and Maxwell who were as stunned as he to find out that a legend had become fact.

The four arrived at the entrance to the sinkhole just after three, as the sun was beginning to sink below the horizon. They had each lit a torch so when they reached the bottom there would be plenty of illumination.

"Am I glad to see you!" said Marco to Pennywhistle. "Now, prepare to be amazed." Marco opened the top of the first chest and Sammie Jo's eyes bulged in astonishment. Maxwell's look became that of a studious banker as he began to calculate the value of what he was seeing. Pennywhistle wore a faraway look as he started to contemplate how the treasure could best be used.

Sally grabbed Sammie Jo's arm. "All those coins are a sight but let me show you something a lot better." She brought Sammie Jo to the front of the fourth chest and opened it. Sammie Jo gasped in awed delight. "I haven't seen anything this grand since Vienna. Even the Countess Esterhazy would be envious." Esterhazy had been one of the richest women at the Congress of Vienna and had earned herself fashion immorality by wearing a dress that was covered entirely in diamonds.

"Go ahead, try a few items on. I think that diamond tiara would look good on you."

Sammie Jo placed the tiara on her head. "It feels right, how does it look?"

"Glorious; like it was made for you."

Sammie Jo and Sally tried on jewelry while Pennywhistle and Maxwell began counting coins. Maxwell brought a halt to the process after an hour. "I've seen enough to know that we are looking at coins worth at least 200,000 pounds. I would guess that the jewels will fetch an additional 100,000 pounds.

I suggest that we get this lot to Berwick where we can conduct a detailed accounting in more civilized surroundings."

"I can send a wagon tomorrow morning, but I fear you and I will have to drive it and load the treasure. I don't want this secret to leak."

Sammie Jo heard the conversation and offered her opinion. "That's going to raise some eyebrows, Tom. A warden driving a cargo wagon will stick out like a blackbird in a flock of bluejays. His chief lieutenant riding by his side will seem strange as well. Why don't you let Sarah and I drive the wagon? Sarah will have to be told anyway. Marco and Sally can help. I noticed that there are two iron brackets on either side of each chest. I gather they were put there so wooden yokes could be run through them so that four people could lift each chest. If we could attach ropes to the handholds on the yokes, and outfit a wagon with a hand winch and pulleys, the four of us could handle the job. I know how to use a winch and pulleys since I once helped my father pull up tree stumps from a ravine that he wanted to turn into a pasture."

"An excellent suggestion, my dear, and one that should work. However, we face a greater problem: what is to become of the treasure once it is inventoried and catalogued."

"Wait! "Said Sally suspiciously, "Don't we get to keep it?"

"I hate to rain on your parade but technically the treasure is *Droits du la Courenne*. That translates as rights of the crown. Since the Treasure belonged to James IV, the direct ancestor of our present sovereign, the treasure should legally become the property of George III. As his chief lieutenant in these parts, I am obliged to return it."

"I am afraid he is right," agreed Maxwell.

"That isn't fair!" objected Marco.

"It should be finders keepers!" Sally whined in sadness.

"I agree," huffed Sammie Jo. "It don't seem right that the government in London should suck up everything and leave the two who found the treasure no richer than when they started."

"They would probably receive a finder's fee of two hundred pounds if I pressed the government hard."

"C'mon, Tom. That's like somebody recovering a herd of runaway thoroughbreds and being given a lame pony as a reward."

Pennywhistle rubbed his chin in thought. "I agree with your objections. There may be a way around this dilemma, but it would involve me breaking the letter of the law to be true to its spirit. The money would be better spent if it were spread evenly around here rather than given over to Liverpool's Government. The Borders need a great deal of fixing." A sly smile crossed Pennywhistle's face. "I could skim a third of the top before sending the rest to London. The portion we retained could be turned into stocks and government shares that would guarantee a steady income to fund the city's various charities. Since Maxwell is a banker, he will know how to discreetly invest the money without drawing any attention to its source."

"I can guarantee that those investments would raise no red flags if they were shielded from direct scrutiny by a layer of shell trading companies," said Maxwell. "That would take some work to accomplish, but I would be happy to perform it in the service of such a good cause. The jewels would be harder to dispose of but since they have been gone for three hundred years, they could be explained away as having an obscure foreign source. Many aristocratic friends of my father would be delighted to add them to their collections and would probably not care overmuch if they had an uncertain provenance. I also think that since Marco and Sally found the treasure, they should each be permitted one souvenir of jewelry, at least so long as it is not too large and conspicuous."

"I know just what they should be!" proclaimed Marco. "A ring for each of us to signify our engagement!"

"Oh, Marco!" gushed Sally. "Yes, yes!"

"I have no objections to your marriage, but you two need time to get to know each other." said Pennywhistle. "I have always believed in long engagements; two years is a good term and 18 is a far better age for marriage than 16."

"I don't mind a long engagement," replied Sally.

"I can live with that," agreed Marco.

"Of course, your mother would have to give her consent, Sally, but I doubt she would oppose your wishes."

"Why Thomas Pennywhistle, you old hypocrite!" chuckled Sammie Jo. "You and I had known each other for less than a month when we got married."

"Yes, but that was in a theatre of war. It was either marry you or lose you forever."

"What astonishes me even more," continued Sammie Jo, "is that you are talking about money laundering even though you are the chief upholder of the law."

"You are right, in a technical sense, but when I accepted this commission, I understood that my job was to stop the violence and put the Borders back together. It was my hope to make them even better than they were before this terrible business started. Using part of the treasure to do that seems in keeping with the spirit of the Christmas Season."

"What about us?" chorused Marco and Sally.

"I think I could employ a tried-and-true Royal Navy formula here. When a prize ship is taken, the sailors involved are entitled to one eighth of its value when it is sold at auction. One eighth of one third of this treasure could be quite a bit of money. You and Sally could divide it between yourselves as you see fit, though I am sure Sally's mother will want a say in the matter."

"I think that very fair," said Marco.

"But before we do any of this, I want to play Father Christmas."

"What do you mean?" asked Sammie Jo.

"I want to see that every person in the Poor House gets a golden guinea on Christmas morning." He turned to Maxwell. "Do you think you could use your contacts at Baring Brothers to exchange a few of these old coins for their value in present day money?"

"Child's play."

"Excellent! I will simply say to the Poor House Warden that a pouch of coins was dropped off on my doorstep by an anonymous benefactor, and that I am merely carrying out his request to see that everyone in the Poor House gets a share; that includes even the wizened little boy with the crutches, Jim Little. I can think of no better Christmas present than observing the surprise and joy on their faces."

"But then you won't get any credit, Tom."

"I was raised to believe that the finest charity is always anonymous."

"Why Thomas Pennywhistle, underneath that rational exterior you are nothing but a wide-eyed sentimentalist. Next thing I know you will be wanting to put up a Christmas tree just like folks do in Vienna."

"What a wonderful idea! We could invite the townspeople to help decorate it on Christmas Eve. It could become a symbol of peace and reconciliation."

"What's a Christmas Tree?" asked Sally.

"It's a tall tree decorated with candles, glass ornaments, and all manner of colorful, shiny baubles. I think it could eventually become a tradition in this country," replied Sammie Jo. "People might even want to put small ones in their homes."

"There is a grove of Scots Pines not far from Berwick that could supply a suitably tall candidate," said Sally.

"I would be happy to chop one down," added Maxwell.

"Maybe two," added Pennywhistle. "One for the city and one for Whistlestop."

"You know," observed Sammie Jo, "Christmas isn't just a season but a feeling. And right now, I feel pretty good."

CHAPTER 16

Justice

27 December 1816

"Justice delayed is justice denied," Pennywhistle had explained to Deborah Dale ten days before. "It is important that the chief author of the Border miseries be brought to justice as swiftly as possible, so that people can see that no man is above the law, no matter how much power, wealth, or connections he possesses. Walter Scott is guilty of many capital crimes but prosecuting him for every single one would take months. I had originally wanted the full extent of his villainy to be known but over the past few days I came to realize it was far better to focus on a single felony. I have therefore decided to charge him with only one crime: the murder of Matthew Dacres. Getting a jury to understand many deaths is much harder than getting them to understand one. Putting a single face on a larger tragedy can make that face a stand in for others who have died. Matthew Dacres was a well-beloved figure at Whistlestop, and many witnesses will testify to that. The jury will want to see his murderer punished."

"So, you believe that Matthew Dacre's name will be more powerful after death than before?" asked Deborah.

440

"Yes, I do," responded Pennywhistle. "And I know how you think, Deborah, as well as other members of The Fourth Estate. You like heroes and villains, whites and blacks, light and darkness. Nuance and subtlety confuse your readers. Your readers like someone they can cheer and someone they can revile. Matthew Dacre is dead, but your readers will be happy to cheer on the prosecutor who seeks justice in his name. Walter Scott will shortly become a name spoken with the greatest disgust and revulsion. You can make Scott a *cause celebre* and turn him into the modern-day equivalent of one of the scoundrels who murdered Thomas Becket in Canterbury Cathedral. I will be giving you exactly what you want: all you must do is report it accurately.

"So, you are using me to serve your own ends?"

"Yes, but you are using me as well to get a good story. We have always had a relationship where each needs the other. But am I wrong in thinking that real justice is as important to you as it is to me?"

"No, you are not wrong. Justice is why I entered this profession. I wanted to give a public voice to people who had none."

"And that is what you will be doing when you write the story of Scott's trial. While testifying about Matthew Dacre, the witnesses from Whistlestop will certainly allude to Scott's other crimes and other victims. You can interview those witnesses when the trial is done. You can deepen and expand their stories: you can take the skeletons of testimony and turn them into creatures with flesh and blood. You told me you wished to write a book about the Border troubles. While the book might not have a happy ending, it certainly could have a satisfying one."

Deborah thought for a moment. "Very well, I will agree to a clandestine partnership. But don't expect me to ignore any facts that may emerge which might put you in an unfavorable light."

"Just report the truth, warts and all."

As Deborah took her seat and prepared to hear the closing arguments for the final day of Scott's trial, she realized that Pennywhistle had been as good as his word. Pennywhistle had appointed a prosecutor two days after Scott's capture, and that prosecutor had assembled a case within twenty-four hours. The case was presented to a grand jury the next day and they had returned a true bill by the day's end.

Jury selection had taken a full day, Pennywhistle instructing the judge to do his utmost to find people who had no opinion about Walter Scott. That proved exceedingly difficult as gossip about his crimes had spread like wildfire in the days following his arrest. The jurors finally chosen were all men who owned property valued at fifty pounds or more. Most were tradesmen: two thirds had served on juries before and were familiar with how the legal process worked. Juries were notoriously fickle and exercised great powers of discretion. Despite instructions from the judge about only weighing the evidence formally presented, juries were sometimes unwilling to condemn a man for a capital crime unless the case was airtight: nearly 40% of those indicted for capital crimes were acquitted.

The judge of the case had agreed to Pennywhistle's request to sequester the jury for the course of the trial. The unusual request was granted because the judge understood that the townspeople would likely make great efforts to influence the jury's verdict.

The barrister that Pennywhistle had chosen to argue the prosecution's case was Thomas Blackstone, a shirttail relative of the famous legal scholar. He had a bulldog's tenacity, a Shakespearean actor's voice, and the easy-going manner of a pub owner. He was a fine legal craftsman but spoke the language of the common man and was able to frame complex legal arguments in ways that made them simple to grasp. Most importantly, the juries liked him.

His opponent was William Wallace, who claimed to be a direct descendant of the 13th century fighter for Scottish independence. Pennywhistle had hired him for Scott's defense simply because he was the only man willing to undertake it. Wallace was a quixotic soul who liked lost causes, and he had become good at defending them. He was formal in manner, but what he lacked in approachability he made up for in the earnestness with which he argued his cases.

The trial took place in the dining hall of the Berwick Guildhall, a venue that could accommodate 1,000 people. It was packed with spectators, and a crowd of 1,500 waited outside. The spectators came from every class and most represented people who had been victimized by Scott's rackets. They were rowdy and eager for blood. Judge Hardcastle Holmes, the justice of the peace presiding over the case, had to frequently stop the proceedings to threaten them with ejection if they would not cease their noise.

Pennywhistle chose not to attend as he feared his presence might prejudice the jury to return a guilty verdict.

This would be the fourth and final day of Scott's trial: English murder trials generally lasted only two days: Scott's was an exception because his villainy was exceptional. Deborah had dutifully recorded every detail in her notebooks.

Blackstone presented more than thirty witnesses, while Wallace could produce none for the defense. The most damaging was Peter Postle. With Blackstone's guidance, he carefully showed how the evidence in his accounting books proved a direct connection between Scott and Matthew Dacre's death. Wallace's only rebuttal was that Postle had falsified the entries because of a personal animus against Scott.

Maude Dacres testimony provoked the greatest emotional reaction. Her iron character broke down on the stand and she gave way to tears. Three members of the jury felt their eyes grow wet and sobbing was heard among many in the spectator's gallery.

Wallace fought hard for his client and did his best to discredit Blackstone's witnesses during cross examination, but it quickly became clear that he had no case at all.

Scott betrayed no emotion throughout the proceedings. Deborah wondered if he was so astonished at being finally brought to justice that he had literally been struck dumb.

Blackstone began his closing arguments with a summation of the testimony of his thirty witnesses. He highlighted the most moving moments of their stories. Two of the most damning were Scott's bodyguards. They had been pardoned by Pennywhistle in return for their testimony and provided direct evidence of this master's motives and intentions. He then explained how the law defined murder and told the jury how those moments exactly met the specifications for murder in the first degree. He concluded his fifteen minutes with, "and so, gentlemen of the jury, there can be but one outcome to all that you have heard. If you have any regard for justice, any concern for those harmed by Matthew's Dacre's death, and any compassion for his widow, you must find Walter Scott guilty of murder in the first degree. I have every confidence that your consciences and hearts are sound and that you will do the right thing."

Wallace's closing arguments lasted five minutes. His chief contentions were that Blackstone had not proven his case beyond a reasonable doubt. He cited several inconsistencies among the witnesses and maintained that Scott had never issued an order that had explicitly stated, "kill Matthew Dacre." Wallace put on an impressive show of emotion since he could not argue the facts, but it was clear from the jury's faces that they found his arguments unconvincing. He concluded his arguments with "Gentlemen of the jury, if the facts do not exactly fit, then you must acquit." He sat down despondently and whispered something to his client that caused Scott to shake his head.

The judge gave brief instructions to the jury then directed them to retire to reach a verdict.

The spectator's gallery buzzed with speculation. Their faces were filled with a variety of expressions ranging from expectancy to anger, but Deborah sensed that they had confidence that the jury would return the correct verdict.

The jury returned after one hour. The two attorneys and Walter Scott rose as the 12 men filed into the jury box.

"Mr. Foreman, have you reached a verdict?" queried Holmes.

"We have, my Lord. We find the defendant, Walter Scott, guilty of murder in the first degree."

The crowd began cheering as Walter Scott sank back into his chair and began to sob quietly.

The judge banged his gavel angrily and barked "silence, silence!"

The crowd reluctantly complied, mostly because they wanted to hear the sentence pronounced.

"Walter Scott," said Holmes in funeral tones, "it is the judgement of this court that as punishment for your crime that you shall be taken to a place of execution and be hanged by the neck until dead. The sentence is to be carried out in 48 hours. May God have mercy on your soul. Bailiff, do your duty."

The bailiff nodded, placed handcuffs on Scott, and frog marched him from the room. The bailiff had to support him, as Scott's legs shook and seemed likely to give out at any moment.

The crowd went wild with cheers, and this time Holmes gave up trying to silence them. Deborah realized the shouts represented a collective sigh of relief for the city of Berwick. Justice had finally prevailed, and a great evil would shortly depart this world. Many more trials would follow, but they would be short ones that would function as simple mopping up operations. The monster's head had been cut off: it would just be a matter of burying the body.

Deborah followed the people of the spectator's gallery into the streets where a carnival-like atmosphere swiftly took control. People laughed, danced, and slapped each other on their backs, giving plenty of opportunities for small time pick pockets to ply their trade. The street vendors selling pies, sausages, sweets, and beer experienced a great surge in business. Several beggars appeared out of nowhere, hoping to take advantage of the generosity that the happy verdict might engender. One man had anticipated the verdict and began shooting off fireworks. The crowd cheered as they burst in the crystal-clear sky. Once the show ended, many made their next destinations the nearest public houses.

Deborah stopped people at random to get their reactions to the verdict. By the time she finished two hours later, she had plenty of material for her dispatch to London and the foundation for a bestselling book. Five people who represented crowd archetypes summed up what she had heard.

"That scoundrel Scott is getting just what he deserved!" offered one old woman.

"Now the city can begin to live again," offered one middle-aged man.

"It will take years to recover from the damage Scott caused, but today is a good beginning," said a foppishly attired young man.

"A curse has been lifted," remarked an older cleric.

"Business is going to boom now that the man behind the rackets is gone forever," said a haberdasher's apprentice.

Such was the rejoicing that the Warden of the city's Poor House released the inhabitants from any work to join in the celebration. Jim Little hobbled slowly on his crutches, but his face brightened as he passed a secondhand clothing store. Jim spotted a suit of clothes in the window that would be a wonderful replacement for the rags that he wore. The gift of a golden guinea that he had received as a surprise Christmas gift would be more than enough to buy it, and he would still have money left over to buy many weeks of dinners at the inn across the street from the Poor House.

Pennywhistle received the verdict in his office, delivered by Mayor Flanders himself. His reaction surprised the mayor who expected jubilation. "It is the right outcome but handing out a sentence of death, no matter how well deserved, is never something one should rejoice about. The gallows for Scott's execution were finished this morning. After reviewing hundreds of cases and searching for any reason to grant a pardon, at least thirty men will have to be bound over for trial. They will swing from the same gallows as Scott."

***

Maxwell had avoided Scott's trial because as the Warden's chief lieutenant, his presence might place undue pressure on the jury to return a guilty verdict. He was pleased when word reached him of Scott's conviction but began to wonder how his own father's trial would unfold. Despite enormous temptation, he had listened to Pennywhistle's advice and had postponed speaking to his father until he could act like a civilized gentleman rather than an abused son. He needed to check on the lesser prisoners still awaiting trial, and thought his emotions under sufficient control that he could manage a short visit with his father after he did so.

Maxwell received a shock to the soul when he reached the Berwick Jail. Chief Turnkey Brewer rushed out to meet him, a look confusion on his face. "Your father has escaped! I don't know how. I check his cell every two hours, and he was sound asleep at noon. But when I checked just now his cell was empty! I trust my men; I don't see who among them could have betrayed me. I have already called out the guard."

Maxwell scowled and his self-control vanished. The old poisonous anger returned, making it difficult to think clearly. The thought of his father slipping the noose of justice caused his stomach to burn and his jaw to unhinge. He felt an overwhelming need for a drink, but an even more powerful one to smash his father into a pulp. "It's not your fault, Brewer. My father is a rich, clever cad and can always find the one man willing to sell his soul for the right amount of coin."

"My men are loyal and have worked with me for years," responded a puzzled Brewer. "You have my deepest apologies, Mr. Maxwell, and I promise that your father will not remain at liberty for long."

"My father believes that loyalty is always for sale and sadly, he is not often wrong." His jaw hardened and a ball of emotion clogged his throat. "His heart is weak." Acid rose in his throat as he noted the irony in his words. "And so, I do not believe that he can have ventured far." He put himself in his father's shoes and tried to think where he would go; it would likely be a place he was familiar with, one that would accord him enough safety so he would have the time devise a way to get out of the city.

Then Maxwell remembered something from childhood: a heated quarrel his father and mother had had about his father housing a mistress in the city of Berwick. He had kept that mistress in a flat that was part of a block of apartments that he owned. As far as Maxwell knew, his father had never sold those buildings. The more he thought about it, the more certain he became that his father had chosen that flat as his temporary bolt hole. That flat lay only three blocks from Maxwell's present location.

"I will handle this alone," he told the astonished Brewer.

"Are you sure, Mr. Maxwell? My men would be glad to assist you."

"Quite sure." Maxwell did not wait for his response and spurred his horse to a brisk canter. Celebrants clogging the streets jumped out of his way and a few shook their fists at him. He checked the twin pistols in the holsters on either side of his saddle, but realized he only needed one shot to accomplish his purpose. Nevertheless, he would bring two in case one misfired. He had to be sure that his father never harmed anyone again. A small voice warned him that what he had intended was a complete contravention of Pennywhistle's policies, but the anger bewitching his heart and rattling his bones ensured that it went unheeded.

Maxwell dismounted when he reached his destination, then hitched his horse to a post and drew the pistols from their holders. He walked into an unremarkable three-story building of white stucco with a grey slate roof built around a central courtyard. He advanced slowly down the long, dark hall but heard no noises from any of the flats; the building must have been deserted for some time. He stopped when he came to the door of the flat that he sought. The lock on the door looked to have been recently pried open. He kicked the door hard, and it flew wide open.

He beheld his father sitting in an old leather chair sipping what he guessed was a glass of champagne. His father turned toward him and wheezed, "oh, it's you." His voice was a mixture of boredom and irritation.

Maxwell walked over to his father and pointed his pistol at his forehead. He full- cocked the hammer, then noticed his father's face was grey and that he was sweating profusely. He was taken aback by how pathetic a man he used to fear now looked.

Sensing his son's hesitation, the elder Maxwell looked up, then barked a laugh followed by two deep coughs.

"You never had the will to do what was necessary. You've always been weak, always a disappointment."

Maxwell junior lowered the pistol. "What's wrong with you?"

"I'm dying, you idiot! The old ticker wants to cheat the hangman. I thought I had at least a year left, but I realized I had only a few hours. I wanted to die a free man, alone and unbowed, and now you've come to spoil my last exit. I am surprised that you found me. Perhaps you are not as stupid as I thought. When I sent you away, I thought you would be dead within a year."

"It gives me the greatest pleasure to prove you wrong."

"You have two pistols: you want to be sure that I am not left only wounded."

"True, but now I see you as a little man growing smaller by the minute."

"I'm not done yet," hissed his father angrily. "I have plenty of fight left, and it would give me great pleasure to settle accounts with you before I cross over the River Styx. I can think of another use for your pistols. I propose a duel. Consider it a test of courage and character."

"A strange request from a dying man since most seek absolution. But then, you have always taken perverse joy from defying convention."

"I can live with my sins! I require no forgiveness from you!" His slate grey eyes turned cruel and crafty. "Come with me to the courtyard. We start with our backs to each other, count ten paces out loud, and then turn and fire." He saw doubt in his son's eyes and his own confronted them with a sadistic certitude. "Be honest, wouldn't it be more satisfying to shoot me rather than watch me slowly expire?"

Maxwell's eyes blazed angrily. "Yes, it would be. I can see how stupid I have been to believe that you might someday grow a conscience."

"I have always had a stronger will than yours and I am curious to see if anything has changed. I certainly have the will to shoot you, but I wonder if the defect of mercy will not cause you to hesitate at the last second."

"I always feared that I would turn into you because I worried that we shared the same basic nature. Warden Pennywhistle showed me how wrong I was." Maxwell's blood boiled. "Since you are incapable of any decent human emotion, I accept your challenge. You're nothing more than a damned old rat that needs extermination."

Maxwell Senior smiled evilly. "Even at half strength, I am a better shot than you will ever be! I welcome the chance to introduce you to Beelzebub."

Maxwell junior glared at him. "You murdered my mother, you bastard! I think of her every time I gaze into your rotten eyes!"

"Marrying that bitch was the worst mistake of my life. You're just like her: a spineless milksop."

The two proceeded to the central courtyard, slowly, Lord Maxwell taking halting steps as his lungs struggled to ingest air. The sky had clouded, the temperature had dropped, and a light snow had begun to fall. The younger Maxwell handed the second pistol to his father. They looked at each other with hatred, but each knew the other would stay true to the code of dueling. They put their backs to each other, and both began to count as they walked.

"One, two, three, four..." knowing that his father had killed six men in duels made each second an eternity to the younger Maxwell, "five, six seven, ..." Maxwell's mouth turned dry as dust and his palm felt greasy. The falling snow felt cold on his cheek, and he wondered if it presaged the coldness of death. "eight, ..." His thudding heart missed a beat as he heard a gasp, faltering steps, and an "oh, shit." He turned quickly to face his father. The elder Maxwell clutched his chest and dropped his pistol. He shuddered violently, grimaced, and then collapsed.

The younger Maxwell darted over to his fallen father and cradled him in his arms. His father looked into his eyes with angry defiance. "The worst day of my life was the day you were born. I deserved better than you." His breathing stopped abruptly, and his eyes closed forever. Maxwell touched his fingers to his father's carotid artery and felt no pulse.

Tears welled up in Maxwell's eyes for no reason that he could comprehend. He hated the man that he held yet felt no glee at his father's passing. In the last seconds of his life, his father had proved himself unable to rise above his hateful nature and for that he pitied him. He realized he could show himself better than his father by uttering three simple words. "I forgive you." He looked into his father's lifeless eyes as he spoke, and felt a great burden being lifted from his soul. He realized that by forgiving his father, he had forgiven himself as well.

He was Lord Maxwell now and determined to restore the honor of that ancient title. He felt pangs of sorrow, but they were outweighed by feelings of relief. He could close the nightmare book of his childhood and complete his personal redemption. By conquering himself, he could finally move on to the life that his mother had wished for him. He said a silent prayer for her soul then left the building with a far lighter step than when he had entered it.

30 December 1816

Pennywhistle hated public executions but sometimes they were cruel necessities. They brought out the worst in human nature because they attracted large crowds: the brutal instincts of the mob banished the humane sensitivities of the individual. Rather than feeling pity for the person being executed, crowds enjoyed watching the person die. The executions of celebrity criminals were particularly popular: some in London attracted more than 20,000 spectators. If the hanging was done right, the long drop broke the felon's neck, and he died instantly, disappointing the crowd. If it was done poorly, as was often the case in local venues, the drop did not kill and the person would thrash violently for several minutes: jerking and twisting, while passing gas and expelling feces and semen. The more violent the struggles, the more the crowds loved them. Pickpockets found the crowds easy prey, showing the questionable value of public executions as deterrents to crime.

Pennywhistle wanted his executions carried out all at once and done before New Year's. He disliked the idea of one or two executions each day because it dragged out the process of closing the city's war with the Reivers. He needed people to know that the worst of the Reivers were gone once and for all. The trials of those accused of lesser crimes, the ones likely to result in transportation to Australia, would be held after New Year's, giving him plenty of time to review their verdicts for extenuating circumstances that might allow him to mitigate their sentences. He had so far granted three hundred pardons; all those chosen giving their solemn word that they would engage in no unlawful activities and signing an indenture obligating them to seven years of community service. Most of the men captured at Whistlestop had been sent home and only five were among the men who would die today.

A gallows platform had been erected on a hill outside the walls of Berwick, and he had made sure the platform was fitted with proper trap doors so that all deaths would be instantaneous. 30 men were scheduled to die today, and five nooses meant five men could be executed simultaneously: all carried out in a little over an hour. Those to be dispatched would be hooded and gagged. Scott would not receive a celebrity death; he would die unrecognized alongside four others. Pennywhistle refused to allow the men any last words to humanize their crimes.

A crowd of 3,000 had gathered. The day had turned grey and cold: snow flurries flecked cheeks as the wind rose. Maxwell and Sammie Jo watched as Pennywhistle took his place in front of the platform. His discomfiture with his role was clear from the look of distaste on his face, which mirrored their own. He spoke loudly to the crowd.

"I am here today to see justice done. I will refrain from reading the sentences of these men because their names deserve no recognition. There will be no more executions after today because I want this wound cauterized all at once. This is a solemn occasion, so I ask you to refrain from boos, cheers, or any other kind of outburst. Since these men will soon face a justice greater than that of earthly courts, consider yourselves in a church of a kind where a vow of silence should be observed."

The crowd said nothing, having caught the gravity of Pennywhistle's words. Pennywhistle allowed an Anglican Priest to give a short blessing to the condemned men, then spoke the words that mattered most. "Hangmen, do your duty."

The first five felons were brought up to their places. Hemp nooses were placed around their necks, then tightened. The five assistant executioners signaled to the chief one that their charges were ready. The chief executioner pulled a short master lever, and all the trap doors abruptly dropped open.

The crowd gasped but made no exclamations.

The nooses were swiftly removed from the dead men and their bodies were allowed to drop into a pit below. Pennywhistle said anyone who wished to retrieve a body for burial would be allowed to do so after the executions were done. Any unclaimed bodies would be buried in pauper's graves or given over for dissection. Since he had long ago studied to be a doctor, Pennywhistle favored anything that advanced medical knowledge.

A second group of men was marched up for execution and the deed was swiftly done.

This time the crowd merely murmured.

By the time the last batch of men died, the crowd had turned completely silent. But though they uttered no words, their faces spoke loudly. Their expressions were ones of astonishment, relief, and satisfaction. Astonishment that, for once, powerful brigands had not escaped justice, relief that their lives would no longer have to be lived in fear, and satisfaction that the final chapter in a centuries old book had finally been written.

James Jackson shivered as he watched the executions. But for a pardon, he would have been among those executed. He had participated in numerous strong-arming episodes and had badly injured several people. Pennywhistle had pardoned him because he had risked his life to stop his fellow enforcers from raping and a woman and her daughter.

Peter Postle watched the proceedings with satisfaction: proud that his evidence had done the most to convict Scott and relieved that the ghost of his murdered sister could finally rest easy. He looked forward to his new career as Warden

Pennywhistle's chief accountant; finally able to employ his remarkable talents in the service of a good man rather than a bad one.

Angus Heatherington hugged his brother James after the last man died. "Finally, the worst of the Whistlestop monsters are greeting their new cloven-hoofed landlord! I never thought that I would see the day! We can both start life anew," said Angus with optimistic conviction. "The new Lord Maxwell promises to be a wonderful change from his father. Though I wonder what he was thinking when he appointed you chief ghillie of Paxton," joked Angus.

"He felt he owed me," responded James with unexpected seriousness. "I found the body of his beloved Uncle Charles and enabled him to give it a decent burial."

Pennywhistle felt he had aged a dozen years by the time the executions had ceased. The crowd gradually dispersed as a few came forward to claim bodies for burial. Sammie Jo walked up to him and threw her arms around him in sympathy. "You did the right thing, Sugar Plum. Every man deserved his fate. A lesser man would have condemned hundreds, you settled for a 30. Now let's head home. I know you ain't much of a drinker, but I think a good stiff shot of whiskey would do you a power of good right now."

Pennywhistle sighed in fatigue and resignation. "It would take all the whiskey in creation to banish what I feel, but a jolt or two might help just a little. I can't help thinking that if I had been smarter or cleverer that I might have found a better solution than the one just carried out."

Maxwell stepped forward and placed his left hand firmly on Pennywhistle's right shoulder; something he had never done before. Both he and Maxwell were wary of touching, but now it felt good and natural to Pennywhistle. He suspected that it had to do with an inner peace conferred upon Maxwell by coming to terms with his father's death.

"Don't try and second guess yourself, Sir Thomas. No perfect solutions have ever existed for the problems that you have faced. You came up with the best that were humanly possible. Concentrate on what you have accomplished. Scott and my father are dead, the worst Reiver miscreants are gone, and the lesser ones will soon depart these shores for a distant land. The least harmful offenders have returned to their homes and will likely never step outside the law again. Business in the city is undergoing a Renaissance and people walk the streets and fields of this land with hope rather than fear. I believe a great wave of prosperity lies just beyond the horizon. Now, if you could only solve the problem of this ungodly weather, I might just recommend you to the Vatican for canonization."

Both men smiled wryly, and Pennywhistle's mood lightened.

A woman wearing a servant's attire walked tentatively up to Pennywhistle, holding an infant in her arms; uncertain whether such an important man would grant a humble washerwoman a brief audience. "Pardon me, Sir Thomas, I hope I am not bothering you, but I wanted to thank you."

Pennywhistle smiled gently. "Please draw near and speak freely. Exactly what do you want to thank me for?"

"My husband was falsely identified as a man in the August raid on Whistlestop who murdered a man when he was in fact at home with me on that terrible night. You suspected the sole witness was lying because he coveted me and wanted to separate me from my spouse. You inquired into his background and found him a serial perjurer. Not a man in a million would have done so. It is only because of you that the awful man who sought to steal my life departed his own just now."

Pennywhistle expelled a deep breath, thanked her, then thrust a silver half-crown into her palm. Her eyes widened in gratitude as she curtsied and departed. A wronged woman speaking her heart-felt truth struck just the right note to release the accumulated tensions of the past week. He suddenly felt exhausted and barely able to stand. He looked Sammie Jo straight in the eye. "I think I am going to need a little nap."

Sammie Jo noted that her husband's eyes were struggling to focus and looked about to flutter. "I think you might need to rest a tad longer."

Pennywhistle dropped asleep on his feet. Sammie Jo and Maxwell gripped his shoulders firmly, rousing him sufficiently so that they could guide his uncertain footsteps toward the nearest bed. He shuffled forward, half awake: his fading consciousness focused only on a soft pillow.

Even saviors need sleep, thought Maxwell.

Epilogue
An End and a Beginning
6th January 1817

Many would have found it strange to put up a Christmas tree on Twelfth Night, but it had taken Pennywhistle longer than expected to conclude his duties as Warden, and January 6 was the first day that he had the time to return to Whistlestop. He wanted the tree to symbolize much more than the Christmas holidays: he wanted it to fulfill its ancient pagan role as a symbol of rebirth. And with the end of the Reiver madness, Whistlestop could finally undergo a full rebirth.

The tree was a twelve-foot-tall Scotch Pine and had been erected in the central courtyard of Whistlestop, opposite the main tower. The entire population of the estate had turned out to decorate it. Each person had fashioned his own ornament to be placed on the tree, and a small line of estate people had begun forming to do so. It was a good day for decorating: the sky was a bright blue, and the temperature stood at 35 degrees on the Fahrenheit Scale. Pennywhistle found the Centigrade Scale of the Metric System more efficient, but his efforts to introduce it into the Borders had been met with profound indifference.

He and Sammie Jo headed back to the courtyard after having walked the estate with his architect's plans in hand. He had explained to her what the estate would look like in two years' time, and she had been impressed. "I like your vision, Tom, and I think I will be right at home with all the trees and streams, but I confess that I am going to miss London."

"I thought you found it dirty, noisy, and confining."

"It is all that, but it's fascinating too and I owe the city a lot."

"How so?"

"Those musical gatherings that I hosted brought me real joy, and I learned a heap about what wonderful melodies can be created by good instruments in the right hands."

"They were glorious, and I remember them fondly."

"I had an ulterior purpose."

"Which was...?"

"Music reawakened something magic in you that completely bypassed your pain and wounds. I brought in street performers whose silly routines made you laugh, despite yourself. Music and laughter saved you, though I believe that my vigorous efforts in the bedroom added a lot of energy to their efforts."

"Are you saying they were a course of...treatment?"

" Yup! Those expensive, so-called *experts* of Harley Street prescribed a never-ending round of purges, emetics, and odd pills that I knew from experience were as useless as trying to close the shutters on a house caught in a tornado."

Pennywhistle laughed at the analogy and realized that humor did indeed work miracles.

"When you kept getting worse, I finally gave those learned quacks the sharp end of my tongue and the pointed toe of my boot and sent them packing. I figured that in a city as large as London, that I might be able to find an Indian like the man who saved my life many years ago."

"A stranger in a strange land looking for a miracle cure. You were a brave woman indeed!"

"I used your network of friends to point me in the right direction, and my quest took me to parts of the city that I bet even you have never seen. It's amazing how much deference is shown to a woman with a title, an expensive dress, good manners, and a speaking voice that is flavored with plenty of snobbish Mayfair vowels. I had to advance my title a few steps, to make it more impressive."

"My God," gasped Pennywhistle. "You impersonated my Godmother!"

Sammie Jo laughed. "Margaret worked with me to help me copy her speech and her mannerisms. She had gained wide public attention for helping Waterloo veterans and knew her reputation for humanity would open a lot of doors."

"And you eventually found your medicine man."

"And damned lucky I was too! Your savior was a Dakota Indian named was *Tetonkaminnesota—Buffalo rider from the land of sky-blue waters*"—intoned Sammie Jo solemnly. "He prepared a lot of special herbs and vegetables that he and I spoon fed you. You don't remember because you were barely conscious."

"Are you saying that an untutored aboriginal produced a more effective treatment than those of Britain's best physicians?"

"Damn right, that's exactly what I am saying! If I had trusted those perfumed quacks from Harley Street, we would not be having this conversation because you would be dead."

"You really have come a long way from the lil' ole country girl that I married!"

"That frontier waif still lives inside me, but I realize that I have changed a lot. When I landed in England, I was just a backwoods sprite, little better than a child in the ways of the big world. I have only fully grown up in the old world, though I come from the new. My present horizons have expanded beyond my wildest dreams."

"At least you will have someone you know living not far away. Since Mr. Maxwell is now Lord Maxwell, he has decided to bring his family north and make the Paxton mansion his chief residence. Oh, and I meant to tell you, his money laundering efforts are well underway; he believes that he has found three buyers for the Treasure's gems and jewels. Berwick's charities will shortly be funded for many years to come, and Marco and Sally should each receive a very tidy sum."

"I am amazed by how much Maxwell has changed, thanks to you. When I first met Maximillian, I found him as arrogant as he was obnoxious. I thought he would die by either a gambler's bullet or from the sword of some outraged husband. Now he is someone that I trust utterly."

"People need second chances. So do estates."

Pennywhistle and Sammie Jo had just reached the edge of the courtyard, when Mary Simmons, now Mary Scoggins, placed the first ornament on the tree: a starburst made of tin with a red center fashioned from sandstone. The crowd clapped and cheered in approval. Maude stepped up next and placed a white ornament shaped like a manger on the tree. The crowd clapped again. Nico advanced and placed his ornament on the tree: a camel with one of the Three Wisemen atop its back.

"Nico wants to stay on at the estate," whispered Pennywhistle to Sammie Jo. "He says working with Smith has caused him to become fascinated with geology since it relates to vulcanism. He wants to help supervise the construction of the new mansion, and I shall be glad to have his assistance."

Sammie Jo turned her head to reply when her peripheral vision spied a well-dressed rider headed toward the estate's main gate. She tapped her husband on the shoulder and pointed toward the rider. "Were you expecting any special guests?"

"No, and I did not invite any. This ceremony was intended to be purely for the people on the estate. That rider looks official. My guess is that he is some kind of government messenger. Deborah's articles in *The Times* may have something to do with his arrival."

Sammie Jo pulled a face. "I don't like the sound of that. It's time you were done with government service."

The rider made directly for Pennywhistle, stopping just in front of him and dismounting.

The messenger smiled and spoke with a voice suffused with optimism and good cheer. "Good day, Sir Thomas, my name is Miles Fairbrother. I have been sent by Prime Minister Lord Liverpool to give you an important message." He handed an oversized letter to Pennywhistle. "I think that you will find that it contains the best of news. The Prime Minister would like you to decide about the appointment mentioned within in the next 48 hours. I will be staying at the Red Lion Inn for that period, and I shall be delighted to convey your answer to London. However, an immediate response would speed your confirmation to the post."

Fairbrother waited patiently while Pennywhistle tore open the red wax seal, and read the letter's contents out loud, so Sammie Jo could hear them. "Know all men by these presents that His Majesty King George III is greatly pleased with the actions of his well-beloved and trusty servant, Thomas Pennywhistle. It is His Majesty's pleasure that he be elevated to the rank of baron in the peerage of the United Kingdom of Great Britain and Ireland, with the title *Baron Pennywhistle of Whistlestop*. It is also Our Pleasure that he be appointed to the post of His Britannic Majesty's Envoy and Plenipotentiary to the United States of America."

"Well bust my behind with a lemon rind! The fancy title is damn fine but the new job kind of blows up our plans for Whistlestop."

"There is no reason that work on the mansion cannot continue while we are in Washington. The new job would give you a chance to find out what happened to your brothers, while it would give me an opportunity to wrap up some of the issues that I discussed with John Quincy Adams. My guess is that his good wishes had something to do with this appointment."

"I suppose there is nothing I can say that would talk you out of accepting."

"If you absolutely want me to decline the appointment, I will accede to your wishes."

"You'd be impossible to live with if you turned this down, so I will stow my objections and try to make the best of things. Trying to separate you from your duty is like trying to separate a cat from a mouse. I hope you realize that our boys may end up sounding more like me than you."

Pennywhistle kissed her softly. "Thank you for putting up with my addiction to duty. I see this new appointment as a chance to clear up a lot of long-standing problems between Britain and the United States and bring two English speaking nations closer together."

"You always said that the job just finished was about reconciliation, and it looks like the new one will be more of the same."

"If the one word associated with me on my deathbed was 'reconciliation', then I would die a happy man. He started, then smiled. "Wait, Sammie Jo, you said our *boys*, not Nicholas. Are you..."

"Yes, I am. You are going to be a father for a second time." Sammie Jo grinned as her dancing eyes held his as warmly as an embrace.

"Congratulations, Sir Thomas!" exclaimed Fairbrother with joy, narrowly restraining himself from clapping Pennywhistle on the back.

"Thank you. You may tell His Majesty that I have been, and always shall be, his faithful servant, and that I am honored to accept this appointment."

THE END

Author's Notes for The Wraiths of Whistlestop

The Wraiths of Whistlestop is a work of fiction, but parts are based on events that really happened and people who once lived. The world in which the book takes place has been accurately rendered.

The chaotic environment of the Scots/English Borders described in *Wraiths* did exist, just not in the nineteenth century. This novel represents speculation on what a return to the Reiver madness would have looked like in the Regency Period.

The real Reivers carried out their depredations from roughly 1300 to 1600 and behaved in the manner expressed in this novel, using the weapons and tactics detailed by this writer. The Reiver Wars were based on ties of blood and family akin to those ingrained in the modern *La Cosa Nostra*. Reiver criminal enterprises presaged those of current New York mobsters.

The violent and lawless no man's land of the Borders emerged because the aggressive English King, Edward I, saw an opportunity to gain hegemony over Scotland. The untimely death of Scotland's King Alexander II in 1286 left an infant female as his heir. Edward inserted his own man, Edward Balliol, as her regent. Balliol proved unexpectedly independent, and a frustrated King Edward launched a series of raids to bring him back into line. These incursions eventually escalated to full blown war, bringing forth such figures as William Wallace and Robert the Bruce on behalf of Scotland. Bruce eventually defeated Edward's son Edward II at Bannockburn in 1314, giving Scotland her independence.

In fact, Bruce lacked sufficient power and wealth to exercise anything more than nominal control over the Scottish Lowlands, ensuring that the frontier between England and Scotland would be run less by representatives of two crowns than by warlords, brigands, and criminals. The worst part of the Reiver plague occurred between 1513 and 1603, ending when James VI of Scotland became James I of England and stopped the Reivers from playing the two crowns off against each other.

The practice of gavelkind, where each son inherited an equal portion of his father's estate, gradually reduced the marginal farms of the Borders to small plots that could no longer support the young men to whom they were granted. Those hard-pressed youths were willing to do anything to supplement their meager incomes, and so they formed an unending source of recruits for Reiver bands.

The position that Pennywhistle holds in the book, Warden of the East English March, was a real one and its representatives truly did wield the power of petty sovereigns. A few used that power wisely, but many more used it corruptly; often seeking personal gain as they carried out vendettas against their enemies. The Elizabethan Sir John Forester was the most offensive of the wardens: a cynical opportunist who eventually got title to lands that he stole and was put in charge of policing the same people with whom he had once ridden side-by-side. The approach that Pennywhistle uses to quell the Border unrest is borrowed from the one used by one of the more successful Wardens, Sir Robert Carey.

While there was no actual Treasure of Flodden, James IV did bring a quarter of his household monies to the Battle of Flodden, and they disappeared after his death on that field.

The funds were never found, though it is likely that they were clandestinely split between the English victors and the Scots who had abandoned their king.

The hideout of Walter Scott, Hermitage Castle, is a splendidly menacing place in Roxburghshire, Scotland. Though it does contain dual portcullises, it does not have any caverns beneath.

The inspiration for Whistlestop was Neidpath Castle near Peebles, Scotland. It is popular today as a wedding venue.

Paxton House, the home of the fictional Lord Maxwell, was erected between 1758 and 1766 and is located six miles from Berwick- on -Tweed. It is considered the finest example of Palladian architecture in Scotland.

The topography of the Border Lands and its fortresses, towns, and cities is described factually.

The severe shrinkage of the British economy caused by the end of the Napoleonic Wars is presented accurately. The transition from a wartime economy to a peacetime one resulted in widespread unemployment, labor unrest, and a glut of goods lacking markets: poor harvests increased those effects exponentially. Things became so bad that there was a near insurrection in one isolated section of the Scottish Lowlands in April of 1820.

The reactionary government of Lord Liverpool had a great fear of revolution and tended to see hints of it in any event that involved large public gatherings of people. The Home Secretary, Lord Sidmouth, responded ruthlessly to labor unrest and was indirectly responsible for the notorious "Peterloo Massacre" of 1819 in Manchester. 60,000 peaceful protestors seeking expanded representation in Parliament were charged by a mass of cavalrymen, resulting in 15 deaths and 800 injuries.

The Year 1816 was called "The Year Without a Summer," because of the severe climate change caused by the eruption of Mt. Tambora in 1815. Its explosion was the most violent in recorded history:1,600,000 times more powerful than the nuclear bomb dropped on Hiroshima. The Volcanic Explosivity Index (VEI), vulcanism's counterpart to the Richter Scale, ranks eruptions on a scale from 1-8. Tambora is ranked a 7, while the much more famous eruption of Krakatoa in 1883, rates a 6. The eruption of Mt. Vesuvius in 79 CE, rates a 5, while the Icelandic volcano Eyjafjallajökull, which greatly disrupted European air travel in 2010, is given a 4. The explosion of Mt. St. Helens in 1980 rates a mere 3.

Each step on the VEI scale represents an explosivity increase of 10X. A VEI 5 explosion is ten times more powerful than a VEI 4 and 100 times more powerful than a VEI 3. The VEI 8 explosion of Mount Toba on Java, 74,000 years ago, was thus 1,000,000 times more powerful than the current eruption of Italy's Mt. Etna which rates as VEI 2. Toba's explosion was so catastrophic that it may have reduced humanity to only 10,000 breeding pairs.

The description of Tambora's eruption and its effects, as seen by Nico Ruzzini, is based on eyewitness accounts. The closest British ship to the explosion was the East India Company brig, *Benares*, which was 500 miles away, while the real *HMS Dispatch* was 800 miles distant. Piracy and slavery, as also witnessed by Nico, were both serious problems in the archipelago surrounding Tambora's home island of Sumbawa. Tambora's explosion halted much of the East Indies slave trade for several years.

Tambora's eruption spewed enough debris into the atmosphere to form a stratospheric aerosol layer of fine particulates that reduced and deflected sunlight, resulting in a three degrees Fahrenheit drop in the average temperature in the Northern Hemisphere. The altered weather played havoc with temperatures worldwide for a full three years, causing floods, droughts, agricultural disruptions, local famines, and food riots. England had the wettest and coldest summer in its recorded history in 1816. Snow falls of orange, red, and brown became regular features when the chill of late autumn set in, and blood red sunsets told even simpletons that something was wrong in the skies above.

The weather in Switzerland turned so continuously rainy that it caused dangerous flooding. Mary Shelley, who was visiting with a circle of literary friends, was stunned by the cold and the violent electrical storms that accompanied the downpours. She later stated that the bizarre weather helped inspire her to write *Frankenstein.*

In America, snow fell in Albany, New York on June 6, ice crystals coated plants on Long Island on June 7, and dark ice slicked a turnpike outside of Salem, Massachusetts on June 9th. The city of Savannah, Georgia, notoriously hot in summer, recorded its highest temperature for the month of July 1816 as 46 degrees Fahrenheit. A July freeze in Maine killed an entire crop of beans, squash, and cucumbers.

No reasonable man in 1816 would have connected the odd weather to Tambora, although a few gifted minds did speculate that the volcano's eruption could have caused some unexpected side effects. The best scientific thinkers of the day attributed the strange weather to an increase in sunspots. Benjamin Franklin was the first man to posit a connection between vulcanism and climate change, linking the eruption of the Icelandic volcano Laki in 1783 to a poor European harvest the next year, but most thought his theory too outlandish to be taken seriously. It was not until 1913 that a scientist first suggested that Tambora might have caused the Year Without a Summer; definitive proof had to wait until 1982.

The gang initiation sequence, racketeering activities, and enforcement tactics described are based on eyewitness testimony from members of New York's "Big Five" mob families. Like the people in the book who try to control Berwick's garbage industry, New York mobsters found control of the city's trash hauling to be tremendously profitable.

The infantry evolutions performed by soldiers in the book are based on those in the Dundas Drill Manual of 1795.

MacCrimmon's Lament is a haunting air that can be experienced on *Youtube:* its words and melody must be heard to absorb its full emotional impact.

The bastles mentioned in the book were fortified farmhouses. Bastle comes from the French word for fortress, "bastille." They generally had stone walls 3 feet thick and possessed two floors. The ground floor was for sheltering livestock and the second for sheltering the family. A barrel vault separated the two floors and access to the second floor was by a ladder that could be pulled up in times of danger.

William Smith, better known as "Strata Smith," did create the map described and is considered one of the fathers of modern geology. Because of the agricultural depression following the end of the Napoleonic Wars, Smith found it hard to find work after 1816. He was also victimized by a man who stole credit for his achievements and sold cheap unauthorized copies of his 1815 map. His London properties were seized for debt in 1819, and he spent several years without a permanent home. Finally settling in Yorkshire, he worked for years in menial jobs. Late in life he was rescued from obscurity by Sir

John Johnstone who brought his work to the attention of the government. He was granted a generous pension by King William IV and awarded the first Wollaston Prize in Geology; the geology equivalent of an Academy Award. In 1835, he received an honorary Doctor of Laws from Trinity College in Dublin.

The description of John Quincy Adams reflects his personality correctly and he did suffer from eye problems and a palsied hand. The issues that Pennywhistle discussed with him were real and important. Both British and American negotiators agreed to pretend that the War of 1812 never happened and worked quickly to restore the prosperous trading arrangements previously enjoyed by the two nations. All captured American sailors from the War of 1812 were repatriated to the United States by 1817 and no reparations were ever paid by Britain for the liberation of American slaves. Adams did become President James Monroe's Secretary of State and was largely responsible for writing the Monroe Doctrine, albeit with Britain's tacit approval. The Great Lakes Boundary between the US and Canada was finalized in 1818 by the Rush-Bagot Treaty and became a model for an unfortified border that was eventually extended to the Pacific Coast. The United States government never intervened directly on behalf of South American rebels against Spain and Florida was purchased from that country in 1819. The United States government never intervened directly on behalf of the South American rebels against Spain and Florida was purchased from that country in 1819.

The fur posts of the Northwest Company, which had merged with the Hudson's Bay Company in 1821, were mostly gone in the area east of the Rocky Mountains by 1830, though the Hudson's Bay Company maintained posts in the disputed Oregon Country until the Oregon Treaty of 1846.

Britain abolished slavery in its empire in 1833, but clandestine visits of slave ships to the United States continued to be a problem, despite extensive anti- slave patrols conducted by Royal Navy vessels.

This writer has worked hard to ensure accuracy in constructing the world that his invented characters inhabit but cautions the reader that this work is fiction designed to entertain, not history intended to inform. Historical novels can be great springboards into history, but they are not history itself. Speculative fiction can be compelling, but it should never be allowed to impersonate truth.

Suggestions for Further Reading

1. *A Time Traveler's Guide to Regency Britain 1789-1830* by Ian Mortimer. An easy–to-understand popular history of the period with emphasis on what day-to-day life was like for everyone from a peasant to an aristocrat.

2. *Tambora: The Eruption that Changed the World* by Gillien D'Arcy Wood. A dramatic, comprehensive recounting of Tambora's eruption and its effects on climate and people.

3. *Global Crisis: War, Climate Change, and Catastrophe in the Seventeenth Century* by Geoffrey Parker. A giant book of 1700 pages that is not for the faint of heart. While scholarly and systematic in its approach, Professor Parker is an outstanding writer with a globalist outlook who incorporates not just the perspectives of historians into his work, but those from a variety of scientific disciplines. This book is invaluable if you seek to understand just how much even minor fluctuations in climate can disrupt the course of human events.

4. *The Steel Bonnets; The Story of Anglo-Scottish Border Reivers* by George MacDonald Fraser. The best single account of border raiding, written with great wit and verve by the author of "The Flashman Series."

5. *Border Reiver 1513-1603* by Keith Durham. A short book that is part of the Osprey Men-at-arms series. It gives a good workmanlike account of its subjects and its many color plates arc outstanding.

6. *Five Families: The Rise, Decline, and Resurgence of America's Most Powerful Mafia Empires* by Selwyn Raab. A fascinating and frightening piece of investigative journalism that is essential to understanding how many of the criminal activities of the Reivers operated.

7. *The Map that Changed the World: William Smith and the Birth of Modern Geology* by Simon Winchester. The riveting story of a humble canal builder who did more than anyone to give geology a solid scientific basis and supplied extensive fossil proof that the Earth was millions of years old rather than mere thousands.

John Danielski

beowulf2100@gmail.com

John Danielski worked his way through university as a living history interpreter at historic Fort Snelling, the birthplace of Minnesota. For four summers, he played a US soldier of 1827; he wore the uniform, performed the drills, demonstrated the volley fire with other interpreters, and even ate the food. A heavy blue wool tailcoat and black shako look smart and snappy, but are pure torture to wear on a boiling summer day.

He has a practical, rather than theoretical, perspective on the weapons of the time. He has fired either replicas or originals of all of the weapons mentioned in his works with live rounds, six-and twelve-pound cannon included. The effect of a 12-pound cannonball on an old Chevy four door must be seen to be believed.

He has a number of marginally useful University degrees, including a *magna cum laude* degree in history from the

University of Minnesota. He is a Phi Beta Kappa and holds a black belt in Tae-Kwon-do. He has taught history at both the secondary and university levels and also worked as a newspaper editor.

BELLERAPHON'S CHAMPION

BY

JOHN DANIELSKI

Deep within each man, lies the secret knowledge of whether he is a stalwart or a coward. Three years an unblooded Royal Marine, 1st Lieutenant Thomas Pennywhistle will finally "meet the lion," protecting HMS *Bellerophon* at the Battle of Trafalgar.

Not only will Pennywhistle be responsible for the lives of 72 marines aboard *Bellerophon* but their direction will fall entirely on his shoulders since his fellow Marine officers consist of a boy, a card shark, and a dying consumptive. If he has what it takes to command, it will take everything he's got.

In the course of battle, he will encounter marvels and terrors; from valiant foes to women performing miracles, from the skill of acrobats to the luck of the ship's cat, from a dead man still full of fight to a coward who has none. He and his marines will meet enemy élan will with trained volleys and disciplined bayonets. Most of all, he will meet himself; discovering just how dark his true nature really is.

Europe will be changed forever by Trafalgar, and so will Pennywhistle.

PENMORE PRESS
www.penmorepress.com

ACTIVE'S MEASURE

BY

JOHN DANIELSKI

It's 1810 and Royal Marine Thomas Captain Pennywhistle has been assigned to command the marines on HMS Active; a frigate that is part of a small squadron tasked with wresting control of the Adriatic from the French. It's a sideshow theatre until Napoleon's new plan for European dominance suddenly makes it critically important. Pennywhistle faces a dangerous opponent who could be his twin: equally smart, resourceful, and relentless. Sparks fly when their paths cross, and the destiny of an entire region hangs in the balance. Another kind of sparks fly when Pennywhistle meets the beautiful Carlotta: a fiery Italian whose beauty masks an iron will and an independent way of thinking. Pennywhistle will face sword fights, gun battles, and a fortress- clearing that will require him to use a secret weapon. Outnumbered and outgunned, he will have to defend an entire island against a surprise attack. A showdown at sea lies ahead, one in which Active will take his measure. She will demand all of Pennywhistle's talents if he is to prove himself worthy of her respect.

PENMORE PRESS
www.penmorepress.com

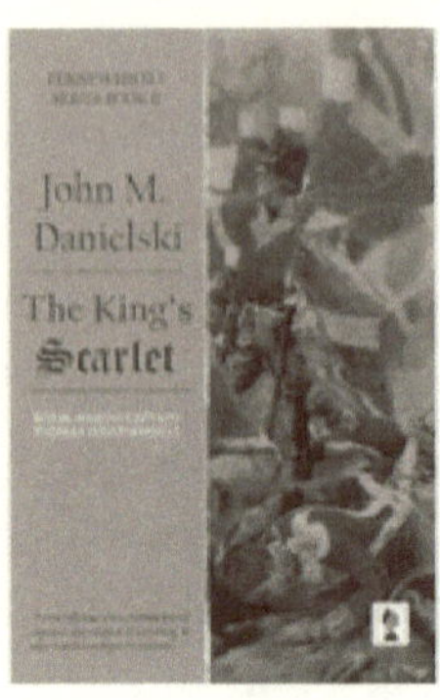

The King's Scarlet
by
John Danielski

Chivalry comes naturally to Royal Marine captain Thomas Pennywhistle, but in the savage Peninsular War, it's a luxury he can ill afford. Trapped behind enemy lines with vital dispatches for Lord Wellington, Pennywhistle violates orders when he saves a beautiful stranger, setting off a sequence of events that jeopardize his mission. The French launch a massive manhunt to capture him. His Spanish allies prove less than reliable. The woman he rescued has an agenda of her own that might help him along, if it doesn't get them all killed.A time will come when, outmaneuvered, captured, and stripped of everything, he must stand alone before his enemies. But Pennywhistle is a hard man to kill and too bloody obstinate to concede

BLUE WATER SCARLET TIDE

BY

JOHN DANIELSKI

It's the summer of 1814, and Captain Thomas Pennywhistle of the Royal Marines is fighting in a New World war that should never have started, a war where the old rules of engagement do not apply. Here, runaway slaves are your best source of intelligence, treachery is commonplace, and rough justice is the best one can hope to meet—or mete out. The Americans are fiercely determined to defend their new nation and the Great Experiment of the Republic; British Admiral George Cockburn is resolved to exact revenge for the burning of York, and so the war drags on. Thanks to Pennywhistle's ingenuity, observant mind, and military discipline, a British strike force penetrates the critically strategic region of the Chesapeake Bay. But this fight isn't just being waged by soldiers, and the collateral damage to innocents tears at Pennywhistle's heart.

As his past catches up with him, Pennywhistle must decide what is worth fighting for, and what is worth refusing to kill for —especially when he meets his opposite number on the wrong side of a pistol.

PENMORE PRESS
www.penmorepress.com